ALSO BY B. CELESTE

Underneath the Sycamore Tree

Lindon U
Dare You to Hate Me
Beg You to Trust Me
Lose You to Find Me

LOSE YOU TO FIND ME

B. CELESTE

Bloom books

Published by Bloom Books, an imprint of Sourcebooks
P.O. Box 4410, Naperville, Illinois 60567-4410
(630) 961-3900
sourcebooks.com

Cataloging-in-Publication data is on file with the Library of Congress.

Printed and bound in the United States of America.
VP 10 9 8 7 6 5 4 3 2 1

For my friends, who listen to me talk about the books I'm either reading or writing twenty-four-seven because I have no other life

PLAYLIST

"Lose You to Love Me"—Selena Gomez

"Wish You'd Miss Me"—Chase Wright

"Flowers"—Lauren Spencer-Smith

"Better Off Without Me"—Kyle Hume

"Afterglow"—Taylor Swift

"Breath"—Breaking Benjamin

"Take Back Home Girl"—Chris Lane ft. Tori Kelly

"Hold Me While You Wait"—Lewis Capaldi

"Marry Me"—Thomas Rhett

"From the Ground Up"—Dan + Shay

Prologue

RAINE

THE UNIVERSITY FOOTBALL FIELD looks different set up for the graduation ceremony. Instead of the bleachers being full of fans sporting Lindon's bright red team colors, it's a crowd of people in formal wear supporting their loved ones, spread in rows of folding chairs across the turf.

A pressure builds in the pit of my stomach when I hear *Raine Joanna Copelin* announced through the microphone. On wobbly legs, I look to the crowd and see a blur of faces cheering me on. Mom and Dad are there beside each other with big smiles on their faces despite the divorce drama they've been going through for the past few months, and Mom's sister, Aunt Tiffany, is perched on her other side, holding up her phone to take a billion pictures that she'll undoubtedly tag me in later.

Skin tightening as I shake the long line of hands before accepting my diploma, I turn to face the front of the stage and roll my shoulders back to stand taller. There's a warm buzz creeping along my skin as I hear one voice in particular cheering me on louder than anybody.

From the corner of my eye, I see Caleb Anders clapping the loudest, along with half the school's football team cheering right alongside him.

Normally, the former running back whistling at me is the one everybody has their eyes on when he's standing on this field. There isn't one game of his that I missed during the season. I'd sit beside every other fan watching the Dragons take on their opponents, feeling the anxiety of every chase, tackle, and touchdown that came with the intense game.

I keep reminding myself that this very moment has been one I've been dreaming of for years. The start of something new—a big future with *Dr. Copelin* printed on an office door in bold lettering to a practice that is solely mine.

But I know the future is murky when it comes to other people's plans for me.

Namely, Caleb's.

My ears ring when the ceremony ends and everybody tosses their caps into the air. I barely register callused hands pulling me to the side when our class disperses with a newfound freedom tied to four years of steep debt.

Caleb wraps me in a big hug, which I instantly return despite the *thump, thump, thump* of my pounding heart. Can he feel it drumming against his chest? When he pulls back, there's a glossy look to his eyes that sets off alarm bells.

Because I know that the future Caleb wants is about to be thrown into my face in front of all these people.

A future I can't give him.

My stomach drops at the same moment as he does onto one knee. I hear a collective gasp come from the people around us as they watch the scene unfold.

The panic seeps in as he looks up at me with those warm

chocolate eyes that have always made me feel so loved and taken care of.

When he pulls out a small black velvet box, I know exactly what's resting inside before he even opens it to reveal the beautiful white-gold ring sitting in the holder. The sun hits the small diamond, making it shimmer like the hope on Caleb's face as he asks me those four words.

"Will you marry me?"

The ringing in my ears intensifies, drowning out the crowd waiting for my response. My eyes lift to graze the eager bystanders and lock with Mom's and Tiffany's stricken faces, then Dad's blank one as he stares at the ring my boyfriend of seven years is holding.

Thump, thump, thump, thump.

When I finally look back down at the twenty-two-year-old with a boyish smile, I know without a single doubt in my mind that I love him. I've loved him for a long time— long before he gave me that little stuffed polar bear holding a heart that had *I love you* stitched into it.

It was our thing. *His* thing. When the verbal words were too much, he'd gift them to me, and I'd felt them all the same.

I love you.

Be mine.

Happily ever after.

I'd fallen in love with his wit and how much he cared for his family. The boy kneeling in front of me with wavering lips as he awaits my answer is a family man to his core. He's going to take over the hardware store in Lindon, a legacy his father has built for many generations to come.

Which is the problem.

Legacies like that will leave a mark on the world along with huge expectations that I can't live up to.

But Caleb can't know about the reason why.

Because then he'd know the truth about what happened that summer back in 2015.

Inhaling deeply, I let out an unstable breath and slowly start shaking my head. "I'm sorry. I'm so sorry, Caleb."

No matter what, I'm going to break his heart. Whether it's now or ten years into the future.

With a glassy gaze that I fight, I stare down at the gorgeous ring that I want so badly to be wearing on my finger right now.

Despite the crack that becomes bigger and bigger in my own heart, I whisper, "I can't."

Chapter One

CALEB

LINGERING EYES WATCH ME as I walk down the narrow hallway dimly lit by fluorescent lights. One of the rectangular fixtures flickers, making my eye twitch until I force it still and ease my tense facial features. I'm exhausted though. Tired of saving face and trying to act like my world isn't about to collapse around me.

It's day four in the new unit.

Same group of overworked nurses.

Same grumpy, elderly oncologist.

Same distraught, teary-eyed mother.

Consoling her has been nearly impossible, but it doesn't stop me from trying. If there's anybody who deserves to be bitter with the world right now, it's Denise Anders. After thirty-six years of marriage, she's going to have to say goodbye to the man she's considered her soulmate from the day they met.

I can't even pretend I understand what it feels like to lose the love of your life, because I'm not sure the girl I thought was mine ever was. Not after how easily she gave us up.

I'm so sorry, Caleb. I can't.

Three months later, and those words still haunt me. You'd think after nearly a decade together I would have known what to expect from Raine. Specifically, the three-letter word to the question I'd been wanting to ask her for a long-ass time. *Y-E-S.*

Turns out I didn't know shit about the freckle-faced redhead.

"They know," Mom says under her breath, peeling me away from my pitiful thoughts. She muffles her soft sniffle with the tissue I passed her when we entered through the sliding doors of the hospital. Her eyes go to the staff as we pass by them. Sad, sympathetic smiles flash in our direction, only adding to the anger festering inside me.

I want to rip those smiles off their faces. Every single one. "They don't know anything," I tell her as she blots her reddened, puffy eyes. They're the same color brown as mine, but the tears have made them darker than the bags resting under them. "Miracles have happened before."

Do I believe it'll happen here? No. Dad's brain cancer was diagnosed too late and spread too quickly. A week and a half ago, we were told by the oncologist that all they could do is make him as comfortable as possible at this point.

The door is ajar when we approach it, and I see the same pretty nurse, Emma, on morning rotation taking his vitals. He's awake and talking to her, a tired smile on his face that somehow still manages to meet his eyes, especially when he turns to see Mom and me enter the room.

"You're here," he greets in a hoarse voice. He coughs into the fist that isn't hooked up to tubes and wires, shooting an apologetic look to the petite raven-haired girl documenting his vital signs on the computer.

Mom instantly walks over, pecking Dad's temple before brushing her hand through the stubble of hair growing back from where they needed to shave his head for surgery. It came back whiter than ever. Dad said that if he grows out a beard, he could play Santa in the town's next Christmas parade.

What none of us bothered to say was that we aren't sure he'll make it that long. I think he knows that too, but that's Dad. Always making plans. Always optimistic.

"Hey, old man." I walk over and clasp his hand, not squeezing nearly as hard as I want to. He returns the gesture, his strength not even a third of what it used to be. The man who would always amaze me as a child for being able to loosen rusty bolts, rebuild car engines, and spend hours in the hot sun helping Great-Uncle Joe with hay season on his farm now amazes me for something completely different.

For simply *being here* and fighting.

That's all he's done since they found the tumor on his head scan.

Dad looks between Mom and me. "Did you eat something before you came? The food here is awful, but sometimes Emma"—he shoots his nurse a playful wink—"sneaks in snacks and leftovers from the break room."

My eyes go to the girl in question, but she won't meet my eyes. Instead, Emma focuses on finishing up what she came here to do before rolling the computer into the corner. "You're all set, Mr. Anders. I'll check in on you later."

Mom doesn't notice the small wave she offers them, but I do. I look at my parents for a moment, who are already lost in murmured conversation, before I slip out the door after her.

"Wait up," I call out, jogging over to where Emma has stopped. She's fidgeting with the badge clipped to the breast

7

pocket of her pink hospital scrubs. "Hey," I say, rubbing the back of my neck. "Look, I'm sorry about the other night. I got pretty swamped at the store, and by the time I closed, I was exhausted."

Her gray eyes go behind her to the nurse's station, where a few girls around our age are standing and watching us. They start whispering, causing Emma to turn back to me, looking a little nervous. She lifts her shoulders nonchalantly, but I can tell I must have hurt her feelings for not texting her. "It's okay, Caleb."

I bend down and press a kiss against one cheek, watching both of them color subtly like they always do. "We both know it's not." She's too nice for her own good sometimes. It makes me feel like a giant dick when I have to back out on our plans. "Thank you for sneaking snacks in for Dad. He's always been picky about food, but it's so much worse now that his options are limited to what the hospital serves. Mom and I think he's losing weight faster than he should be."

She shifts on her feet, crossing her arms over her chest and tucking her hands into her armpits. "It could be his body's way of fighting. It takes a lot of energy to battle all the infected cells his body is producing. The medicine is only part of the healing process."

It's the same spiel I'm sure she's given other families who have loved ones fighting for their lives. He's doing his best considering how advanced things have gotten. We should be grateful he's fighting at all.

Not wanting to think about it any longer, I ask, "Do you want to reschedule dinner?"

Once again, her eyes go behind her. This time, a finger goes up from her shift supervisor, gesturing for her to come over. "I don't know, Caleb..."

I step toward her, lowering my voice. "I know why you're hesitant, but I promise not to bail this time, and I won't ask anything about Dad."

There's nothing that says she can't date a patient's family member as long as she's not sharing important information that violates HIPAA. I checked into it before I even asked her out a few weeks ago.

Her eyes soften. "When you didn't text me back last night, I thought that was a sign that we should reconsider this. You've got a lot going on right now between your dad, the store, school. And I'd understand if you're not ready for anything right now after what happened with your last relationship."

Emma knows I got out of a long-term relationship, but I never went into the details of how serious it was. Like how I'd planned on marrying Raine before being brutally rejected on one knee. I'd decided my pride could only take so many hits.

The fewer people who know, the better.

With a heavy sigh, I swipe at my tired eyes. "I really am sorry about not getting back to you. It didn't have anything to do with you—us. Every time I started to reply, Mom needed something. It got so late that I ended up passing out. Things haven't been going as smoothly as I'd hoped they would."

I've been managing the best I can on my own for the past couple of months without dumping my issues onto anyone, no matter how much I've wanted to. The number of times I've nearly broken down, wondering how the fuck I got here, without the woman I still love, watching my father die, and trying to move on as if that could somehow help it hurt less, is too many to count.

I don't want to unload that on the one girl who could be an escape from that part of my life.

So I stand a little taller. "I'd still like to take you out again. I can pick you up at seven tonight if that sounds good. You mentioned how badly you've been wanting a burger, and there's this really good brewery over in Woodland that serves some of the best I've ever had." When hesitation floods her eyes, I add, "I could honestly use a break from life. I'm looking forward to a date."

It's unfair of me to ask her for anything, but it feels good to be selfish when all I do is offer myself to everybody else.

Rubbing her arm, she lets out a tiny breath and smiles faintly. "Okay." Moving back on her heels, she reaches out and brushes my hand. "I'm looking forward to it. I'll see you later. Okay? *Text* me."

I watch her walk off and find myself frowning at the emptiness still hollowing my chest even after the plans are made.

I *do* need a break. From summer classes. From the store. From *this*. As horrible as it makes me sound, I need Emma to give me a distraction, even for an hour or two. I need to feel like there's someone out there who can offer me even an ounce of the peace I'd once had.

She'll never replace Raine, but she might replace *something* that'll fill the hole Raine left behind after I begged her to tell me what was wrong.

"I'm confused," Raine tells me, tears welling in her eyes as she paces around my old bedroom at the football house. "It's always been us, Caleb. How isn't that terrifying to you? What if there are things I can't give you someday? What if there's something out there we don't know about? Other people we could be missing out on?"

I stop her. "Where is this coming from? It's always been us against the world. What could you possibly not give me that would make you question if we're good enough to make it? I love you. Isn't that enough?"

Her lips quiver as she swipes at her cheeks and shakes her head. "I don't know if love can be enough this time. Not forever."

Those words still hurt like hell.

She was worried there was something else out there—something *better*. It was a punch to the gut to think she was looking for somebody who could be everything I wasn't. Since when was love not enough? When was *I* not enough for her?

"I can't do this." That's what she told me when she walked toward the bedroom door that day, avoiding my touch. *"I'm sorry, Caleb. I can't do this."*

It was the world's biggest non-breakup. She didn't tell me it was over, didn't tell me she was through. Didn't tell me she didn't love me. In between the lines, and evidently the tears, was the truth.

She was over it. Over me. Over us. Because she didn't think our love was enough for us to last.

"Caleb?" Mom calls out, breaking my train of thought. Her voice is too cheery for something bad to have happened, so I force myself to walk back into the room, where I catch my father's eyes.

In that frail, all-knowing voice, he says, "She's a nice girl, son."

I don't recognize my own voice when I murmur a robotic "Yeah. I know she is."

Mom says, "Make sure you're ready, baby boy. You'll only hurt yourself more if you try to force something. And it's not fair to Emma or anybody else if you're not fully healed from Raine yet. The heart needs time to recover."

11

This time, I don't say anything.

Because I don't want to bullshit them with false promises like they've been getting from doctors this whole damn time.

~

I was fifteen when I went to my first house party that a classmate was throwing while his parents were out of town. A few of my friends on the high school football team decided to go together, but it didn't take long before we all disbanded to drink and try picking up girls.

That night was full of other firsts too.

First time I asked a girl to dance with me. First time I played seven minutes in heaven. And the first time I *almost* kissed a girl.

All firsts I shared with Raine Copelin.

I'd seen the girl with dark red hair plenty of times before at school. Her head was almost always buried in a thick book in the library, with a pen in her mouth that she tended to chew the end of as she read. She'd sneak in her favorite snack, Milk Duds, until the librarian caught her and lectured her about how there was no food or drinks allowed in the library.

We'd interacted a few times before the party, but mostly in passing. Like when the pen she'd been chewing on leaked and she had blue ink all over her face. Or when her shoelace was untied in gym, and I was afraid she'd trip doing our mandatory two laps before every gym class began.

That party changed everything.

"We don't have to do anything," I promise her, readjusting in the dark closet we were shoved into after the bottle pointed at each of us. I was surprised she was even at the party, much less

participating. She never seemed like the type who was interested in being around a lot of people.

Her squirming gets worse as she looks toward the door, then back at me. "Won't they figure it out?"

I shake my head. "Most of them are drunk. They don't even know left from right. I think we're safe."

A small smile appears on her face. "What do we do for the next"—her eyes go to her phone screen—"five minutes?"

I said the one thing that jump-started the next seven years. "Tell me about you."

So she told me about how she was an only child, her mother worked as a tailor, her dad was in real estate, she had been trying to get a dog for the past year to no avail, and she was planning on going to college to become a psychologist or counselor.

The rest came after.

I stare at the yellow Milk Duds box on the counter display beside the register at Anders Hardware and grumble to myself before closing my textbook and pushing up from the counter.

"Finding everything all right, Phil?" I call out to the elderly man who's in here at least once a week for some new project he's doing. Ever since he retired, he's been restless. If it's not his house he's working on, it's one of his neighbors' or kids' places. It seems to make him happy to keep busy and his wife even happier to have the man with cabin fever out of her hair for a while.

Phil walks out of the plumbing aisle holding a new valve kit. "Found it on my own this time, kid," he tells me, dropping it onto the counter in front of me. "Don't suppose I can get one of those loyal customer discounts, do you?"

My lips quirk up at the corners as I ring him up and apply

the employee discount for ten percent off. "I got you, Phil. Who's this for? Last week, you were replacing the leaking garden hose for Mrs. DeMarcus over on Third Street."

He passes me a fifty-dollar bill, which I make change for as he tells me all about how his son-in-law doesn't know anything about being handy. "I'm telling you, son, my Maise could have done so much better than that city slicker. But she loves him, so what's a father to do?"

Love is a pain in the ass like that. It hits you hard and keeps a firm grip on you even when you wish it didn't.

Phil puts some of the spare change in the glass tip jar that's got a few pennies and quarters in the bottom. "Tell your dad I said hi. The missus and I have missed seeing him around. We're wishing him the best."

Adam's apple bobbing, I nod. "I will. Good luck on the new project. Let me know if you need anything else."

After he leaves, I drop back into the seat and stare at the candy display again. Despite all the assignments I'm behind on, I decide to reorganize a few things in the store instead.

After an hour, all the candy is off to the side and out of my line of sight, Milk Duds included. If Dad ever sees it, I'm sure he'll have a thing or two to say, but I'd rather have my peace of mind since I'm the one out of my family who spends the most time here.

I pull out my phone and send a quick text to a few friends and one to Emma.

Me: Looking forward to mini golf tomorrow

She's working, so I don't expect a response anytime soon. After our dinner date, I drove her home and kissed her goodbye. She wore bright red lipstick that was inviting as hell, but it still felt nothing like the soft pair of pink lips that hardly ever saw makeup at all. I wish she'd invited me in, but it was probably better that she didn't.

Sometime later, Emma replies with three red hearts and nothing else.

All I can think is…Raine hated emojis.

Chapter Two

RAINE

LIGHTNING CRACKS ALONG THE sky, accompanied by another rumble of thunder that rattles the porch windows behind me, but the rain never comes. It's hot and humid, and the wind whipping the trees is causing the branches to make unruly noises against the glass that have the tiny dog in my lap whining as we watch the storm unravel around us.

Fingers grooming the fur of my aunt's mixed mutt, I whisper, "It's okay, Buddy. Your mom will be home soon to curl under the blankets with."

Walking, feeding, and cuddling the cutie curled up on me only makes me want a dog ten times more than before. Especially now that I'm on my own. They say dogs make the best companions anyway.

When Aunt Tiffany heard I'd be in Virginia for the summer, she wanted to stay with me at the family cabin so I wouldn't be completely by myself like the pathetic, broken-hearted college graduate that I am. Usually, my parents and Caleb would show up for a week or two around the Fourth of July, but not this year. Mom and Dad are in the middle of their divorce, and Caleb is probably casting a spell to curse me for breaking his heart, so that leaves my mother's cynical sister who likes to make comments about how love is for fools anyway.

Though Tiffany hasn't exactly been around lately because she likes to sneak off to the local community center under the guise of volunteering. I'm not completely naive to the inner workings of Radcliff. The community center doesn't typically take volunteers, not even when they host senior bingo.

She doesn't think anybody knows about Casey, the attractive bohemian man who works behind the counter at the building. The women in my family like to act like they're better off alone after every single one of them wound up divorced, starting with my great-grandmother Claudette, followed by my grandmother Maud, Aunt Tiffany, and now my mother.

Apparently, my aunt wants to keep her newest man under wraps as if that'll somehow break the curse we all seem to think we're stuck with. It's sort of cute watching her sneak around like a teenager. Pointless but cute.

I find myself smiling at the feisty woman who looks just like me and my mother. From our porcelain-doll skin to our lean statures to our dark brown eyes with speckles of gold in them, we all look nearly identical, with the exception of our various shades of red hair. Mom and Tiffany both look like reincarnations of Susan Hayward—Dad's favorite classic movie actress. But because of his chocolate-brown hair, mine is a dark shade of burgundy with brown and red highlights that's pretty in its own way but nothing like either of my parents. And maybe that's a good thing.

I learned to be independent to a fault because of the women in my family who had to do so much on their own when their relationships fell apart. I spent years looking up to Tiffany and Grandma Maud, wanting to be just like them because I could see the strength in their motivation to build something beautiful for their futures. They were both dealt shitty hands with the men in their lives but managed to get out before it was too late. I didn't know my grandmother very well before she died, but I was told plenty of stories that always made me cautious about how I'd mold my future.

I swore to myself that I'd never wind up in the same situation as any of them, miserable from my choices.

Well, congratulations, that bitter little voice inside my head taunts. *Now you're alone too, all because of one secret. Happy now?*

The next crack of thunder scares me out of my quickly declining thoughts. My startled jump makes Buddy tumble off my lap and bolt through his doggy door into the house.

Despite this cabin being full of fun memories with the people I love, there are some bad ones too, with people I hardly even knew.

Summer was always the season full of mistakes.

The crushing feeling in my chest reminds me that those mistakes are what got me here in the first place.

I think of the boy with brown eyes that I'd fall asleep to dream of almost every night. His eyes were always soft, warm, and full of love whenever they were directed at me.

But those beautiful eyes instantly changed when I opened my mouth at graduation, and to this day I still think about those two words I told him.

I can't.

I can't.

I can't.

Now I'm in a different state, getting eaten alive by tiny bugs as the humid air frizzes my hair. All because of one night after s'mores, one too many beers, and a cute blond boy who flashed me a smile.

It isn't even that night I regret. I was young and dumb, but I didn't owe anybody anything. It's everything that happened afterward that haunts me.

Tiffany told me I should just stay in Virginia instead of going back to New York for grad school, but I think it's only because she wants more family here. Ever since Maud passed away, she hasn't had many people in the area unless we visited for the summer. All she has is a small apartment in northern Virginia, the cabin here, which is in Mom's name, and the man she pretends she's not half in love with because she doesn't want to believe in that sort of thing.

Aunt Tiffany never minced her words whenever I'd visit during the summer. "Don't put all your eggs in one basket," she'd tell me whenever I'd bring up my high school sweetheart. It isn't as if my family ever disliked him. A man like Caleb is impossible *not* to like, and even my cynical aunt admitted as much. Still, her comments over the years fed into the anxiety I felt when he dropped to his knee in front of the crowd of people at graduation and asked me to spend the rest of my life with him.

In spite of my family watching and expecting me to say yes, I couldn't force it out. I love Caleb. But are we capable of loving each other forever if we can't give each other everything we want out of life?

Swallowing, I pull my legs up to my chest and grab my notebook from the tiny table that my grandfather carved from a log. The end of the blue pen is chewed up from all the mindless gnawing I do when I should be reading a new case study to keep up on the psychology assignments bound to drown me when grad school starts in the fall. The only benefit to being surrounded by failed relationships my whole life is figuring out how badly I'd love to fix them for others. That's why I want to become a counselor.

Clicking the pen to release its tip, I open to the page I left off on, already marked up with little comments in the margins of the pages.

More lighting flashes across the sky.

More thunder shakes the ground.

Nibbling my bottom lip, I rest my head against the back of the chair and stare up at the sky, trying to sort out my thoughts.

I hear car tires make their way up the gravel driveway and know it's my aunt's friend bringing her back. I take a deep breath of the muggy air before setting my feet back down and watching as Tiffany carefully exits the passenger seat of the car parked several feet away.

I force a smile when I hear my aunt's friend call out, "She's a pretty one, Tiff." I think her name is Jodi. She always covers for my aunt whenever they're out because heaven forbid anybody knows she's dating someone.

Tiffany closes the door and looks at the woman behind the wheel. "She's a smart one too. Learned a lesson we certainly didn't at her age. Look at her, being able to travel and have alone time whenever she wants. I'm a little jealous I didn't leave sooner to have that experience for myself."

Smart would have been following my heart no matter how many times I was warned by the woman walking up the steps that the heart would get me nowhere in life.

"Think with your brain, Raine."

The human brain is our most complex organ, and unlike our hearts, it gives up far too easily.

When Tiffany sees the skeptical look I'm giving her, she wiggles her finger at me. "I don't want any comments from you. I seem to recall a time not that long ago when you were sneaking back in after that surfer wannabe was dropping you off from the party you went to."

Heart hammering at the reminder, I lower my pen and stand with a frown. "Don't bring him up. It was a long time ago."

My aunt rolls her eyes. "Nobody is a saint, Raine. Not even you."

As if she has to remind me.

~

The second my toes dip into the cool pool water a few days later, I'm instantly brought back to my sixteenth birthday. Since my birthday is in July, I always spent it poolside with my family barbecuing. They'd invite the neighbors because most of them had kids around my age, and we'd make it a neighborhood party.

That summer, I met Cody. Considering the blond-haired, blue-eyed seventeen-year-old changed my entire perspective on life after one hookup, I never even knew his last name. His family was only visiting friends for a few days. The invite he'd gotten to the party was a fluke. Looking back now, I should have never entertained him when I had Caleb, even if we hadn't had the exclusivity talk yet.

But I knew the second he flashed his charming smile that made me blush I was done for. Had I known that I'd agree to sneak off later that night after the bonfire? No. But

I definitely wasn't drunk enough to blame alcohol for my decision to sleep with him.

Dunking my head underwater, I come up for air and comb my wet hair out of my face with my fingers.

"I'm heading out," Tiffany calls to me from the back door. "Your mom left a message on the landline. She said you weren't picking up your phone."

Frowning, I wade over to the edge of the pool and lean against it. "I thought you said you were going to hang out here with me. Are we still ordering pizza later? I finally found the takeout menu buried in the kitchen drawer."

If Aunt Tiffany remembers it's my twenty-third birthday, she doesn't say so. I didn't hear her say it when I walked into the kitchen earlier, and she's made no mention of it in the hours since.

She looks at her watch. "I made plans already, but I'll let you know if I'm back in time. Buddy has already been out and is sleeping in the guest room, so he'll be fine until tonight. Enjoy the sunshine!"

Watching her leave, I push up from the tile and grab my towel from the lounger. When I find my cell, I see some missed texts from Mom and a couple of missed calls from former sorority sisters. After returning a few people's birthday wishes, I see Mom's number pop up on the screen again.

Swiping to accept, I put my cell to my ear and say, "You said you'd call last night."

Mom sighs. "I'm sorry, sweetie. Your father called to finalize some things for our appointment. I swear, that man can't even be decisive about our divorce. One second he wants it, the next he doesn't."

The last thing I want to hear about is my parents' divorce for the millionth time, so I work on wrapping my towel around my body and sit on the edge of the lounge chair. "Did Tiffany call you? She said she was going to check in with you about coming down here before I head back to New York, but she was tired after dinner, so I don't know if she brought it up. She didn't even want to watch *Real Housewives*."

Mom makes an amused noise. "I think your aunt is finally realizing that she can't keep at it like she used to. She texted me at two in the morning the other night. *Two!* She's going to be forty soon. It's ridiculous how she acts like a preteen sometimes. We spoke earlier today about me coming down at some point, but I don't know, Raine. I may not be able to swing it this year. Things with the divorce have been dragging on longer than I expected, and I don't want to keep delaying it being finalized. But enough about that. I won't bore you with the details."

My whole life I've had to hear them bicker about something. Dad left a few dirty dishes in the sink. Mom didn't set the code for the garage door. It never failed.

Dad has always loved me, but I don't know if he's always loved her. He's never cheated, at least to my knowledge, but it was obvious that he wasn't all that invested in making things work. Which, sadly, is probably for the best in the end. The only thing I truly care about is if they're happy, even if it means them living two separate lives.

"I'm sad you're not here," I tell her quietly, playing with a loose thread on the towel. "The neighbors put a new pool in, so I got to spend the Fourth there while they grilled. It was fun. The whole neighborhood basically got together. You would have loved it."

Mom loves being social. It was one of the reasons I liked her being here. She took the lead when people talked us up, and that way I didn't have to answer a million questions about my life.

"I wish I was there too. I'll do my best to find time before you're back here for school. Which reminds me—"

I groan, knowing what's coming next.

"Are you sure that you want to go back to Lindon? You have other and frankly better options for getting your master's and certification. I googled it and saw at least three other universities that would be a better fit for your academic level. You'd have a better reputation with degrees from one of those."

We both know it isn't the school's reputation that she's trying to save me from. "I already told you that I'm going to be fine, Mom. It's not the end of the world. Lindon is my home, and nothing will change that."

When she's quiet, I know it's because she's trying to find any excuse to convince me otherwise. But she knows I'm right. Lindon is where I was born and raised. All my memories are there. The good and the bad.

Caleb is a mix I can't avoid forever.

"I just worry," she finally admits softly.

"I know."

"I want you to be happy."

"I know."

"Maybe if your father stops trying to take half of everything, we can get you into a better program elsewhere once you finish your first semester. Or you could talk to him about it. You've always had him wrapped around that little finger of yours."

Eye twitching at the undertone in her voice, I rub my clammy palm down the side of my thigh. "I'll think about it."

I won't.

I've made up my mind already.

Hoping to turn the conversation around, I change gears with a hopeful tone to my voice. "Since today is my—"

"Baby, I've got to go. Your father is calling me *again*."

Blowing out an agitated breath, I say, "Okay. Well, can you call me—"

The call ends before I can finish my sentence, leaving me staring at the background picture of me and Caleb from last year. I changed it shortly after graduation, but my chest tightened whenever I looked at the pretty garden picture I replaced it with. It was too much change too quickly.

With the reluctant truth that the people closest to me forgot my birthday, I spend the rest of the day watching sappy eighties movies and sulking in my room.

Just before I go to bed, a text comes through from the last person I expect.

Caleb: Happy birthday

Chapter Three

CALEB

I'M GRABBING MY RATTY notebook off the desk and sliding my pen into the pocket of my jeans when the professor says, "I expect the first draft of your business proposals to be in my inbox by midnight tomorrow. All late assignments will have two points deducted for every hour it hasn't been submitted. I'm not allowing any excuses because it's summer. I don't care if you're going on a beach vacation. Send your work in before you hit the surf or whatever the hell you kids do for fun."

Squeezing my eyes closed at the newest addition to my growing to-do list, I swear silently to myself and push up from the desk. Even if I approach Professor Neilson, the likelihood of him giving me an extension isn't as strong as from my other teachers.

In fact, this assignment *should* be easy considering I've been working at Dad's store basically my whole life. I learned to count by helping with inventory, learned addition and subtraction while helping with the books, and learned manners and common courtesy by watching my old man deal with customers.

I owe Richard Anders a lot and want nothing more than to make him proud by taking over Anders Hardware. Football might have been a pastime I loved to share with my buddies from the day I joined the youth team to the day I signed on as Lindon U's running back, but the family business was always going to be the endgame. Which means anything I can learn now to be successful will be helpful before…

Throat tightening at the inevitable news we're bound to get about Dad, I clear it before walking up to the older man wearing his usual tweed attire. "Professor?"

Neilson looks up. "I'm looking forward to your proposal, Caleb. I assume you'll write one based on the hardware store."

I hold back the slight flinch. "Yeah, I was thinking about it. But I was wondering if—"

"Trust me, you don't want to reinvent the wheel. If there's something in place at Anders, tweak it to fit your vision for the business. It'll make your life a lot easier."

The knowing look he gives me has me backing down from asking for an extra day or two. I'm supposed to go in to the store after my last class, then head over to the hospital before visiting hours end. It doesn't provide a ton of time for me to focus on homework, but I'm not about to say that to Neilson.

Dad's declining health isn't a secret, especially not in a small area like Lindon. I've rarely used it as a reason to get out of anything, and when I have, it's because I couldn't physically do whatever I was supposed to. I've gotten a few bad marks on class projects that I'd normally ace. My professors would comment on the obvious decline of my classwork and offer certain extensions or extra credit work for me to up my overall GPA once I opened up about the reason, but I never liked it. I was better than using my Dad's circumstances to get a helping hand. Even if I needed it.

People like Professor Neilson don't seem like the type to offer sympathy. Mostly because he isn't keen on giving athletes an extra helping hand like some of the faculty tend to. He said during my very first class with him that he wasn't going to set a bad example by giving anyone a free pass just because they can catch a ball and score a touchdown. I received the message loud and clear then, and it hasn't changed now, even if the circumstances have.

Shoulders dropping a fraction at the late night ahead of me, I murmur, "Good idea, sir. I'll see you on Monday."

He gathers his things without so much as giving me a second look. "Have a good weekend. Tell your father I said hi. I've been hoping for the best."

I'm glad he doesn't look at me, or else he would have seen what I hate anybody witnessing on my face.

Weakness.

Scrubbing my face with my hand as I walk through the quad, I try to mentally prioritize everything going on today. Mom is with Dad right now, which means he'll have company until I can close down the store. Maybe if it's slow enough, I'll be able to start on my assignment and see if Dad can help later since he always likes getting involved in my business courses. It brings back some normalcy.

As though he's not dying.

I think we both like playing pretend.

I head toward my beat-up Ford that Dad gave me when I first got my license. If I were smart, I'd pool together some of the money I've been saving and find a new one that doesn't nickel-and-dime me at every corner. But this truck, though coated with rust and whining from old age, holds a lot of valuable memories with the people I love that I'm not ready to give up.

Not yet.

Maybe not ever.

Cranking up the AC that only works half the time, I head toward Main Street to grab the largest cup of coffee that Bea's Bakery has before going to my shift. Once Raine quit at the hardware store after my botched proposal, we had a spot open that we couldn't afford not to fill. Business always boomed at the beginning of summer, right when Dad got too sick to help run it and life got too messy to handle an entire store on my own. Even if it feels like I'm doing ninety percent of the work anyway, it's nice having Ronny, my part-timer, there when I go to class.

"There's my boy." Bea, the owner of Bea's Bakery, greets me when I walk up to the counter. The older woman gives me a once-over with a *tsk*. "It looks like you could use some caffeine. Have you not been sleeping?"

"You have no idea," I reply tiredly, knowing there are dark bags under my eyes that age me a few years beyond my twenty-two. "Can I get a large of my regular? And maybe one of those blueberry scones if you have any left. I could use a pick-me-up."

"Working today?"

"Yes, ma'am." *When am I not?*

"And how is school going?"

"Busy."

"You know," she remarks, starting to prepare my order, "you don't need to get a master's degree to run a business.

Your father has taught you plenty already. Hands-on experience will teach you the rest."

Pressing my lips together, I remain quiet. I've heard that before—from Dad. But there's a lot I still don't know and things Dad won't have time to teach me. The last thing I want to do is fuck this up and ruin everything he worked so hard to build.

When Bea places a to-go cup and pastry bag in front of me, she adds, "All I'm saying is that it won't do you any good to run yourself ragged, boy. Neither of your parents wants to see that happen to you, least of all now."

Swallowing, I give her a solemn nod and try passing her some money.

She swats my hand away. "On the house. I think you need it. Now go before you're late. And think about what I said. Food for thought."

I pick up the items, trying to smile half-heartedly. "Giving away free things isn't exactly smart business, Bea. I may not know a lot, but college has taught me that much."

Her smile grows. "One day, you'll see that paying it forward when somebody needs it most will get you a lot further in life than holding out a hand in expectation."

Taking that into consideration, I walk out and head down the street to where my truck is parked outside the hardware store.

I'm almost relieved when I see nobody besides Ronny inside. It'll give me time to work on homework before going through receipts, monthly bills, and inventory. That's something Mom usually does, but she spends most of her time at the hospital these days, and I don't feel right bringing anything to her while she's there. When she offers, I always tell her I've got it under control.

"Slow day?" I ask, voice hopeful as I drop my things behind the counter.

Ronny shrugs. He's thirty with a baby on the way. The second one. He says this job on top of the full-time gig he has at the post office will help them bring in extra income, which is a big reason why Mom agreed to add him to the payroll. She's a softy, especially when babies are involved. "Been quiet most of the day, but you know that can change at any time."

When he's gathering his things and clocking out at the computer by the register, I say, "I hope that's not the case."

He slaps my shoulder and squeezes once. "I do too, man. I talked to your mom about adding on another couple of shifts to help a little more. I'll see you tomorrow, and we can talk about the schedule."

I nod. "Thanks, Ron. Tell Ana I said hi."

When I'm by myself, I take out my notebooks and personal laptop to begin working on assignments I'm behind on for school. If I don't submit a few of the assignments loading on my screen, my GPA will drop significantly. Again.

Not even five minutes into the paper I've pulled up, the bell to the front door rings and three older men, including Phil the fixer-upper, walk in, asking for help picking out the proper supplies for their plumbing project.

Underneath the counter, my hands squeeze together before unclenching. I have to take a long, deep breath and an even longer sip of coffee before standing up and offering the smile Dad told me to form even on the bad days.

"Follow me," I tell them.

~

"You look like hell, son" is how Dad greets me a few days later, his voice raspy but his dark eyes glinting with humor.

My lips kick up as I close the door. "I'm pretty sure that's supposed to be my line," I tell him, pulling a chair up to his bedside and looking at the tray of food in front of him. "You've barely eaten. Did Mom get you anything from the deli like you wanted? I can call and see—"

He waves me off. "We both know Gretchen's closed for the night. I'm not hungry, anyway. The new medicine has made it hard to eat. Everything tastes metallic still." That was one of the symptoms of the old medicine he was on. Apparently, it hasn't gone away like it was supposed to. "If I'm going to get good food, I want to actually enjoy it."

My eyes go to the door for a moment before glancing back at the food he barely picked at. There's applesauce, a favorite of his, and a sad-looking sandwich that I can't blame him for not touching. "Mom is going to ask for a report as soon as I get back," I remind him, picking up the little container of applesauce and passing it to him after opening it. "And I'd rather not lie to her. I was raised better than that, remember?"

Those frail, chapped lips lift at the corners for a brief moment. "You're a pain in my ass, you know that?"

A lump forms in my throat as I watch him wrap his skinny fingers around the plastic container and pick up the spoon resting on the tray. "I know I am. Speaking of, would you mind going over some homework with me if you're up for it?"

That perks him up. "Which class?"

I'm in two courses this summer until the fall semester starts in a couple of weeks. I only get a week and a half off before diving back into a full semester of coursework.

"Business Ethics. Neilson had us submit a business proposal a few days ago and gave us some feedback when we got them back today. He said he'll give us extra points toward our next exam grade if we tweak the proposals based on his suggestions and resubmit. I could use your advice on a few different ideas I had that could go well with his comments."

I don't tell him that I really need the extra points. I'd like him to think I'm still prospering so he isn't worrying about more than he needs to. Dad may not agree with my choice to go to school for my master's in business administration, but he supports me regardless.

He watches me carefully before focusing on the food in his shaky hands. "I don't think much needs to change at the store. If it's not broke, don't fix it."

I figured he'd say as much, but that doesn't mean there aren't certain upgrades that could benefit the business that this project could be a good outline for. "I'm not planning on doing anything extravagant. Just a few—"

"I'm not even dead yet, and you're already trying to change everything," he says, cutting me off in a sharp, uncharacteristic tone.

We both fall to silence. I feel my heart drop into the bottom of my rib cage while he heaves a long sigh and shakes his head.

"I'm sorry," he mumbles, closing his eyes and setting his applesauce down. One of his fingers scratches his temple. "I don't know why I said that."

The doctor said this could happen.

I've noticed little changes in him ever since the tumor was found. His temper is shorter, and his mood swings happen in the blink of an eye. The six-foot-five man who's nothing more than skin and bones lying in front of me used to be a giant teddy bear. He rarely raised his voice unless it was justified and nearly never lost his temper.

Rubbing the back of my neck, I readjust in the chair and look at the TV, which is playing a golf game. Dad hates golf. "Don't worry about it. Want me to see if there's something else on the television?"

He blinks, slowly looking up as if he didn't even know there was anything on. "I don't mind this. Why else would I go to all your games and watch you play it?"

I blink. "I didn't play golf."

For a moment, he looks perplexed by that. It takes him a few seconds before he slowly nods in realization. "Right, right. Football. Damn good player too. I remember when that coach of yours back in high school talked to your mom and me about convincing you to talk to the recruiters."

"He wanted me to consider somewhere other than Lindon. I didn't know he talked to you guys about it."

Dad hums. "Many times. Said Notre Dame was watching you. A shame."

A shame? He never seemed interested in me pursuing that career path.

For the rest of the night, he watches the television screen as if he's always been a huge fan of the boring sport playing. I remember all the times he'd rant about how slow the game was and how nothing exciting ever happened unless a gator popped up from whatever green they were on down south. When Mom bought him a polo shirt, Dad said he'd wear it when they went out to a nice dinner and then lied about it suffering a washing machine accident.

The quiet gives me time to do some homework at least, with Dad asking questions every so often. I don't bring up any changes to the store again or his diminished memory, and he doesn't ask about them.

It's a little bittersweet, but I let it go.

When visiting hours get close to ending, I readjust my feet where they're propped on the end of the bed and ask, "How are you really feeling? No bullshitting me. I know you try saving Mom's feelings from getting hurt, but I want to know the truth."

His eyes trail to mine with hesitation, the glassy, dark orbs showing just how unwell he really is without him having to confirm it. "It's not that I'm trying to preserve anybody's feelings, Caleb."

I watch as my old man's throat works with a thick emotion that I can't even begin to imagine. He's never been very vulnerable with his feelings, at least not to me. So whatever is clouding his eyes, making them glaze over with fresh tears that he fights to hold back, tells me that he's got more going on internally than he allows any of us to know.

His Adam's apple bobs again. "I'm tired, son. So damn tired. And I'd be lying if I said I wasn't a little scared too, but I think I'm starting to accept things. So don't think I'm trying to downplay anything for you and your mother. We all have to make peace with the life we're given, and I think it's my turn to do that. No more fighting the inevitable. Sometimes you simply have to accept it."

There's nothing for me to say after that.

He pats my arm, as if he understands the turmoil going on in my head.

Not even I do, though.

35

Chapter Four

RAINE

A BEAD OF SWEAT trickles down the side of my temple as I pull my hair back into a tight updo and perch on the edge of the pool while dipping my feet into the water. I release a sigh of relief and lean back, closing my eyes and listening to kids laughing, adults gossiping, and dogs barking in the distance.

My ears perk up to the sound of somebody dropping down beside me. Christopher Hayes, one of my summertime buddies who comes to town for a few weeks during the season, shoots me the same goofy smile that's usually on his face.

"I was wondering when you were going to show up," I tease, nudging his shoulder with mine.

It's hard to imagine that the boy sitting next to me used to be the shortest one in our friend group since he's well over six feet now. He's also paler than me, which is evident in the way his Irish skin all but glows in the glaring sunlight.

"Did you put on sunblock?" I ask, a little worried about

him going shirtless. I don't blame him since it's ninety-four today, but I remember a few years ago when he got sun poisoning and was sick for weeks.

Chris rolls his eyes, sliding his legs into the pool that our elderly neighbors always leave open for people to enjoy. "You're such a mom," he muses.

A twinge of pain settles into my stomach at the teasing jab.

In exasperation, he adds, "My mom wouldn't let me leave the house until she watched me put it on."

My eyes do a scan of the lawn to see if Mrs. Hayes is out here with her adorable French bulldog. "I haven't seen her much this summer. I haven't had a chance to stop and fuss over Pumpkin when they're out walking."

The face he makes has me smiling. "She heard about all the bear sightings and has been terrified to walk her usual trail. One of my cousins showed her TikTok videos of bears going after tiny dogs, so now she's petrified of bringing Pumpkin anywhere people have reported seeing the cubs. I'll tell her you said hi. I'm not sure she's coming today."

I frown. "That makes two moms then."

His brows dart up. "Janet isn't here?"

My mother's name only deepens the frown as I kick my feet in the water and watch the little ripples move outward. "Nope. My parents are finally going through with the divorce that they've been threatening each other with all these years."

It's a little embarrassing to admit, but most of the people who've lived near my family's cabin have heard at least one fight from my parents whenever they were here. Almost every time they get heated, it leads to one of them saying they're going to file for divorce. Even though I've accepted this is the best route for them, thinking too deeply on it isn't something I like doing.

Chris doesn't say he's sorry like everybody else does, which makes me even more grateful for his friendship. But what he says is almost worse. "No Caleb either, or...?"

My body stiffens at the innocent inquiry. It was only a matter of time before one of my friends here asked about him, considering I've managed to avoid it so far. I assumed Tiffany told people not to bring him up, but she never confirmed or denied doing that whenever I'd mention how the local gossip hadn't said anything about Caleb's absence.

People are accustomed to seeing him around for a few weeks, especially the small group of friends we used to hang out with. It's the same people who congregate in Radcliff every summer, with a few additions here and there. Cousins, friends of friends, newcomers in town for the summer, or whoever one of us is dating at the time. We've all had our fair share of extras who we've invited along and people we've tended to keep as a summer secret for however long they last.

My mind goes to Cody again, causing my lips to twitch downward.

Voice hoarse, I say, "Caleb and I sort of broke up."

Chris straightens, eyes widening as he turns his body toward me. "No shit. I can't believe he broke up with you. What an assho—"

"Stop," I plead, giving him a pained look that has him pursing his lips. Confusion pinches his brows when he sees the hurt on my face. What he obviously doesn't understand is that it's the self-inflicted kind of pain brought on by my own conflicted feelings. "It's not like that. I...it's really complicated, and I'd rather not talk about it because I'm trying not to think about it. Nothing bad happened though. There's no reason to call him anything. He's still…Caleb. He's still a good person."

His cheeks pinken as he relaxes his body and stares down at the way I twist my hands nervously in my lap. "Sorry. I just wasn't expecting that. We all thought he was going to propose. Mom even asked if I thought you'd show up this summer with a ring." When he sees me wince, he cringes. "I think I'm going to shut up now. Sorry. Again."

Chris's awkwardness is sort of endearing, so I manage to push past all the heaviness weighing down my shoulders and change the subject. "Are you going to see the fireworks at Howie's? I saw him earlier and he mentioned the huge bonfire they were doing beforehand to celebrate the end of the summer."

The smile I'm greeted with makes me feel a little better, even though I'm sad I'll be leaving soon. Chris asks, "Want to go together? I think Amanda and her newest boy toy are going to be there. Collin too. I don't know if he's still seeing that girl. Stephanie? April?"

I roll my eyes at the botched names. "Her name was Penelope, and I don't think they're together anymore. He's been posting about some girl named Mika lately."

Chris pops his lips. "What's with people not being able to stick to one person? It's—" When he sees the twisted face I make, he groans. "Shit. My bad. I just meant that Amanda and Collin go through people like crazy. Sometimes I think that they should just be together. They'd be perfect for each other."

I tip my head back and close my eyes again, letting the sun soak into my skin. "Trust me," I tell him in a murmured voice, "there's no such thing as a perfect couple. Everybody has flaws. It's about how you embrace those flaws that makes or breaks people."

We don't talk much after that even though it's obvious Chris wants to ask questions. He'll have to get in line though.

~

I'm swatting away another bug and regretting not bringing repellant spray to Howie's like my aunt told me to when Chris walks over to the empty lawn chair beside mine.

"You look sad," he notes, bumping his knee against mine. "I know your mom called when we first got here. Is everything okay? I know you're upset she couldn't make it down here."

I'm not sure "okay" is the best way to describe anything involving my mother. Janet Copelin, soon to be Snyder again, has always been on edge about everything, especially when it comes to her relationship with my father. I never know what she's going to say when I see her name on my phone.

But it never stops me from picking up when she calls, because I know the only reason they stuck it out so long is because of me. And while I appreciate the effort, I wonder what would have been different if they had just called it quits a long time ago.

There'd be fewer fights.

Less inconsistency.

We would have all been *happier*.

I hate thinking about all the times I was angry at them for putting me through the tense fights at home, especially when there was nothing I could do.

Stretching my legs out, I watch the bright orange flames

of the bonfire crackle and pop. "Yeah, everything is fine. I wish she had come. The divorce has been…" I think about it before shaking my head. "Not ugly, but not pretty either. It's like neither of them wants to be the bad guy, you know?"

My father texts me almost every day to check in on me. Sometimes, when he's talkative, he'll call, but neither of us likes talking on the phone that often. It's after we get talking about school, job applications, and life that he'll ask about Mom. I never want to turn the conversation over to her because it leads to the same thing every time.

Frustration.

I'm tired of being the person in the middle, hearing it from both sides. I keep telling myself it's practice for when I'm certified. After all, isn't helping struggling couples like them what I want to do?

Chris nudges me again, amusement coating the friendly smile spread across his lips. "You keep doing that. Spacing out. Want to talk about it?"

My answer is an instant "No."

His chuckle is quiet as we both watch the other people gathering around the fire and surrounding yard. Howie has a big place, and it's a known hangout during the summertime that usually leads to too much beer, pot, and a lot more that I never participate in. It reminds me of Alden Field back in Lindon, where I shared plenty of experiences with Caleb.

Crossing my arms over my chest, I blow out a breath and look to Chris to try pulling myself away from those lingering memories. "Do you want to take a walk?" I'm feeling too antsy to be sitting around watching Amanda dance like she's auditioning for a new version of *Dirty Dancing* or a joint be passed around by Collin and his pretty new friend.

Chris instantly jumps up, offering me his hand to help

me stand. It's sweet, but I shake my head and tuck my hands into the pocket of the hoodie I stole years ago from Caleb. It used to have our old high school mascot on it, but it's so faded from all the times I've worn and washed it that it's a basic blue sweatshirt now that's shrunk enough to fit me halfway decently.

This sweatshirt is the first one Caleb let me borrow when I came to see one of his football games. He asked me during lunch one day if I was planning on going, which I laughed nervously at. We'd barely talked besides a few passing things in the hallways, so I wasn't sure why he was asking. I couldn't even name all the positions on the field, much less how the game worked. But I went anyway. When he saw me on the bleachers, he jogged over during halftime with the sweatshirt in his hand and told me I looked cold. Then he introduced me to his parents, who I'd seen around town but didn't really know, and they told me to sit next to them.

It was the beginning of something beautiful. His parents both explained the game whenever I had a question, and we'd all cheer Caleb on while sitting at the edges of our seats.

Fiddling with my hands in the pocket of the hoodie, I walk alongside Chris in a peaceful silence. As we're rounding the fishing pond that Howie installed on his property a few years ago, I can't help but ask, "Why don't you ever bring anybody here during the summers? I know you must have a ton of admirers back home."

We stop at a footbridge in the middle of the pond and lean on the rails. I smile to myself when I look into the water, hoping to see something. I've never been a huge fan of fishing, but I used to go with Dad and Cal—

No, I scold myself. Thinking about him always makes everything hurt worse.

Throat tightening, I turn to Chris to see him looking at me with a funny expression. "What? Do I have chocolate on my face from the s'mores?"

He keeps staring quietly.

"Should I not have asked about the girl thing? It's none of my business. I was just curious. You're a good guy. You deserve somebody who makes you happy."

The last thing I expect my friend to do is step toward me and press his lips against mine in a rushed movement that instantly startles me. My hands dart out with panic and push on his shoulders a little harder than I mean to, making him lose his balance and go over the edge of the railing and into the water.

My hands grip my mouth as tears prick my eyes, blurring them as I quickly look over the edge and yell, "Are you okay?"

Chris resurfaces past the ripples and moves his short hair back. People start running over, pointing, laughing, some yelling and asking if he's all right.

My fingertips brush the lips he touched, the ones only two other boys have before, making the tears build quicker.

From fear. From hurt. From a mix of emotions that I can't quite grasp as they take over and tighten my lungs.

I don't want to think about either of those boys or else I'll think of all the horrible things that have happened that led me here.

Choices made.

Regrets that haunt me.

It's too much.

I wait long enough to hear Chris say he's okay before running off, elbowing my way through the crowd of familiar faces and feeling déjà vu all over again.

Because all I ever do is run from men.

Chapter Five

CALEB

THERE HAS ALWAYS BEEN a rush when I'm on the field that starts the moment my cleats dig into the turf. Nothing compares to the freeing feeling of the air whipping through my helmet as soon as I take off, running each yard with the ball cradled in the crook of my arm until the stadium explodes with noise as the touchdown is made.

Football was the mindless escape I took for granted practically my whole life. It was nothing more than a pastime—a hobby I'm damn good at to this day.

I've never regretted choosing Lindon over the University of Tennessee, Notre Dame, or any other college that offered me full rides and big opportunities for the future. As far as I was concerned, my future was rooted right here in my hometown where I'd mold something big for myself one day.

Anyone who knew me knew I saw Raine Copelin as the person I'd do that with.

Like Coach Crowe, my old high school football coach,

who would sidle up beside me after games whenever I looked into the crowd searching for her and my parents. He'd say the same thing every time, as if he was hoping one day my answer would change. "Something tells me you're not looking for the scouts here to watch you play, are you?"

And the instant I laid eyes on the girl who sat by Mom and Dad every single game since the first one she attended our sophomore year of high school, I'd wave with the dorkiest grin on my face and say, "No, Coach."

He'd smack my back and tell me I was making a mistake by not seriously considering other colleges, but I would never let him convince me otherwise. Because the future other people saw for me was full of seven-figure contracts and Super Bowl rings.

Whenever I saw Raine wave back at me or point at the borrowed jersey with my number on it, I knew without a doubt in my mind I was looking at the lifetime of happiness I'd get without all the materialistic things attached.

During one of the last games I had with Coach Crowe, I told him my life was in Lindon and smiled when he asked, "You'd give up a free ride to college and a successful football career all for one girl?"

The amount of confidence I had when I replied that night was the same amount I had the day of graduation with the ring box sitting heavy in the pocket of my gown.

I'd been so sure when I told Coach Crowe, "Nah, not for one girl. All for *the* girl."

Because that girl was going to say yes.

I wonder what I would have done if I knew how wrong I was back then. Would I have attended a different school? Traveled and played football somewhere else for a while before coming home to work at the store? I don't know.

I never will.

"Dude, watch it!" DJ—Daniel Bridges Junior—calls out, cringing when the football we've been tossing back and forth nearly collides with my face. The golden-haired boy with major golden retriever energy used to be my teammate on Lindon U's football team in undergrad. Unlike me, the wide receiver currently jogging over to me wanted to go pro. If it hadn't been for a shoulder injury, he might have tried. "You good? One second you were here, the next you were spaced. What's up?"

I pick up the ball and tuck it under my arm, shaking my head. "Just tired."

"Bull," he counters, stealing the ball and spinning it on his finger. "I saw you chug two huge cups of coffee from Bea's, and we both know she makes it strong. There's no way you're still tired after that."

All right, so I did caffeinate pretty hard this morning when I met DJ and Matthew Clearwater, another former teammate, at Bea's Bakery. I couldn't stay long, but I downed way more coffee than my heart can probably handle in less than an hour and then went to the hospital to see Dad before I took my shift at the hardware store.

"Dad had an episode this morning," I murmur, blowing out a long breath and gripping the back of my neck. "He started talking about how he didn't want to miss any of my games. I guess he forgot I graduated already. It got me thinking about how things should have been. At the beginning of the year, I had a healthy dad and an amazing girlfriend who I bought a ring for. Everything was good. Now..."

DJ is one of my best friends, but I feel weird talking about Raine when I know he and his girlfriend, Skylar, still talk to her. It isn't like I have anything bad to say. I would never make them pick sides, knowing she doesn't have a lot of friends outside the circle we'd formed together.

He sighs, gripping the ball in his hands and nodding once with a sad expression molded across his face. "I get it, man. Shit hasn't been easy for you lately, but dwelling on that stuff isn't going to help you now."

Just because that's the truth doesn't mean it's any easier to accomplish. When I told Dad I wasn't on the football team anymore, he started threatening to call the coach thinking I'd been kicked off. "You're the best that goddamn team has. Give me his number."

It took twenty minutes for him to remember that I graduated. That I *chose* to leave that life behind.

Mom tried to hide the glassiness in her eyes as she watched the scene unfold, but I saw it long before she left to get coffee from the cafeteria, as if she actually likes the overpriced sludge they serve.

Swiping a palm over my jaw, I shake my head and glance at the apartment building that gives me some semblance of peace when I'm not buried at the store, hospital, or school.

The red house was converted into four different apartments that Stanley Yager—the owner, contractor, and landlord—used Anders Hardware's supplies for. I helped him order everything he needed and would occasionally even go over to help on smaller projects in between all my other responsibilities. When the building was finished, Stan offered me a good price on one of the units. He even lowered the monthly rent as long as I shovel in the winter and mow the lawn in the summer.

The apartment isn't much, but it's the one space not riddled with a ton of memories that suffocate me. I've been able to make new ones here since I moved from the football house after graduation.

47

"Have you heard from her?" DJ asks, bringing my attention back to him. When I don't answer right away, he asks, "Have you heard from Raine?"

Lips twitching, I shake my head. "Not since I wished her a happy birthday."

I may have looked her up online a few times, but she rarely posts. Neither of us are big on social media, but we get tagged a lot by people who are. Which is how I know she's been staying with her aunt Tiffany at their cabin in Radcliff and going to bonfires a few times a week with the group we used to hang out with all the time. Does she see the way Chris looks at her in those photos? Did she do anything about it now that we're not together?

I'd torture myself with every photo, reading through the comments about how good she looks—how *happy* she looks—but I seem to be the only person who sees that her smile doesn't actually meet her eyes. I don't know if I should be happy about that or not. It isn't that I want her to be miserable, much less be the reason for it, but it means that we feel the same.

Neither of us are okay, or we wouldn't be here. Misery loves company after all.

Clearing my throat, I brush it off. Brush *her* off the way I need to. "Like you said, I can't dwell on that shit. I've got a date with Emma tonight anyway. We're checking out that new brewery that opened. They're doing half-priced drinks."

There's a slight change in DJ's face that has my head cocking. He doesn't say anything before he tries looking neutral again, but he's never been the best at hiding what's on his mind.

"What?" I press knowingly. "Just say it."

A sheepish smile curves his lips. "I guess I'm wondering how things are going with Emma. It's obvious that you're not over Raine. How could you be after all these years together? I want you to be happy, bro, but I don't know if this is the best idea. There's nothing wrong with taking a little break from the dating scene."

Maybe I shouldn't have asked. "Emma is a good person."

"I don't doubt it. Anybody you give your attention to must be," he answers easily. "But even if somebody is a good person doesn't mean they're good for *you*. It hasn't been that long. Jumping into something might not be the best idea."

I nod. "You're right, but I like her. It isn't like I'm going to get serious with anybody right away. She makes things easier. That's all that matters for now."

I can tell DJ doesn't agree with me, but he doesn't say so.

"Thank you," I tell him, despite our opposite stances on this. "For being my friend."

His smile eases. "You don't have to thank me for that. You've got a lot of people on your side, Caleb. We've got your back."

That's the thing about breakups. There are always sides people choose, but I don't want that for either of us. I'd like to think there's a reality where we can coexist with the same people, especially since she'll be back soon for graduate school.

Easier said than done though.

~

Emma hasn't stopped squirming since we were seated thirty minutes ago by the beady-eyed host, nor did she eat her food when it was delivered. My fingers have grazed my burger to assemble it, but her distance has my appetite waning.

"What's wrong?" I finally ask, knee bouncing under the table. My mind goes to Dad.

We've agreed not to talk about him and his diagnosis when we're out, but if she knows something about him, I want to know now and figure out how to tell Mom later.

Her eyes are timid as they peek up to meet mine through the thick lashes she's coated with makeup. She always wears some at the hospital, but nothing like tonight. I would have had to be blind to see what kind of a heartbreaker she is in the red shade of lipstick that makes her lips look fuller and the dark liner that emphasizes her moonlike eyes.

Ethereal is how Dad once described her.

She carefully sets down the fry that she's been playing with for the past few minutes and leans back in her chair. "I think maybe we should call it."

My brows pinch as I examine her plate to see if there's something wrong with the food. "Is the burger not cooked right? I can ask them to bring you a new—"

"I don't mean dinner, Caleb," Emma tells me, lips quivering. "I mean us. Or whatever it is we're trying to be. What I'm trying to say is that I think you and I should call it quits."

I sit back in my chair and feel my shoulders tense at the suggestion she's brought up before. I haven't exactly been model boyfriend material, but I haven't left her on read or bailed on plans since the last time. I've been open with her. Honest about mostly everything. I told her about Raine and me breaking up after graduation. I told her about Raine's uncertainty. I wanted her to know that it wasn't me, because I spent weeks on end wondering if it had been. But I saw the skepticism in her eyes that day.

Maybe it matched mine.

In hindsight, how could anyone get over someone they

50

claimed was the love of their life so quickly? I'd like Raine to answer that question for me so I stop staying up at night trying to figure it out.

After a few seconds of staring at the burger in front of me, I lift my eyes to hers and say, "I'm sorry if I did something."

It doesn't feel like enough, but there's nothing else I could say to make her feel any better for not trying harder. I'd like to think if things with Dad weren't the way they are, maybe I would put more effort in.

Then again, I never would have met Emma if he hadn't gotten sick. I think I'd take that trade.

"I'm an ass," I admit, scratching the column of my neck. "I know there's probably a guy out there who can give you a lot more attention than I can right now."

She quickly shakes her head. "You're not an ass. Honestly, Caleb, you've got so much going on that the last thing you need is to add time with me into your schedule. You should focus on your father and your classes. And…other things. I have work that keeps me busy anyway. It's fine."

I don't believe that. "Is it?"

She closes her mouth and evades my eyes, staring down at her plate. "It sort of has to be, doesn't it? We're on two different paths right now. We need to focus on ourselves, I think."

Why does that pack a punch? "I see where you're coming from, but I don't want this to end. I enjoy spending time with you. You're a great person, Em. And—"

Her palm lifts, facing me as a sad smile takes over her trembling lips. "Please don't. I've heard it before. The 'it's not you, it's me' angle. Guys always feel the need to tell me I'm an amazing person or that I'm pretty or funny to soften the blow for when they tell me they can't give me the long

51

term even before I've asked for it. I don't need to be complimented. Look, I think you need to figure some things out. Prioritize your family and yourself. That's what I'd do if I were in your shoes."

Her tone is delicate, and I know she means every word she says. I've always appreciated how blunt she is when it comes to what she wants. Which makes me feel like a bigger jackass for not figuring out what it is I can bring to the table. "When guys say those things to women, they're not just feeding you lines. They just know you're too good for what they can offer."

Scraping my hand through my hair, I shake my head when she stares down at her food. I had Mom chop off the long strands last month before the August heat got to be too much. When Dad's hair slowly started growing back, we went back to looking a lot alike.

Except Dad's face is different than it used to be. Long gone is the square jaw that I got from him, and in its place is a narrow, sickly bone structure that shows how unwell he really is. His cheeks and eyes are all sunken in; his collarbones and ribs show. He's always been lean, like me, but never like this.

Dropping my hand onto my lap, I debate what I can say or do.

"Can we just...spend time together? Go to dinners, a movie, maybe Putt-Putt again. Do things that are mindless fun. We can call it whatever we want. It doesn't have to be anything more than friendship, although I'd like it to be if we're being honest."

Her tongue dips out and wets her bottom lip as contemplation masks her face. "You make it really hard to say no. It isn't that I don't like you or want to try this. It's that I'm worried I'll get attached if we continue when you can't truly meet me halfway."

Who says I can't? "Like you said, I need time. Once I figure out how to compartmentalize some things, it'll be easier for me. For us."

Her eyes stay on her food. "Maybe."

Does that mean she's going to give this a shot? I wouldn't blame her if she says no, but my gut tightens at the thought of her rejecting me.

"I know it's not a lot, but I'm willing to try," I say quietly.

She peeks up at me, bottom lip in her mouth with a contemplative expression on her face. Eventually, she nods. "Okay."

Okay. We fall to silence for a moment or two before I finally break it. "Are we okay then?"

I've never liked hurting anybody's feelings, and despite us not knowing each other well enough, I like Emma. The last thing I want is hard feelings between us if this doesn't work out in our favor, especially since we'll be seeing each other quite a bit at the hospital.

Hopefully.

That sour feeling is back.

Reality.

It's heavy, holding me down.

Emma picks up another fry and puts on a smile, but it doesn't reach her eyes like it does when she jokes with her coworkers or talks with her patients or tells me about something she learned over the course of her shift.

Do I do that to women?

Maybe I should let her walk away.

Because if we give each other another chance, I could taint her—compare her to the girl who walked away.

I don't want Emma to leave.

But do I really want her to stay?

Chapter Six

RAINE

ONE THING THAT FOUR years of psychology classes have taught me is how to be logical, but another helpful lesson I got from all those stressful courses is that logic doesn't get you very far when it comes to personal matters.

I read somewhere that the heart has reasons for the choices we make that not even rationality can understand.

No amount of college classes can make sense of why we do what we do. That doesn't stop us from trying to make an excuse to justify our decisions.

Which is why I'm staring at the house that started it all, wondering why I thought coming to Radcliff would help me process anything. It suffocates me to be surrounded by all the things the younger, dumber version of me did here.

All I can think about while looking at the cute little cabin is the music that was blasting that night. Country, until somebody complained and switched it to hip-hop. There was a lot of loud laughter shared among friends as we drank. Flirty touches as someone passed a joint around the bonfire.

I remember the instant Cody's hand touched mine, I felt butterflies.

I know now that those were warning signals fluttering in my stomach—anxiety telling me he was trouble. To run far, far away from the temptation that led me to follow him inside.

You'd think being an A student means you're smart enough to make the right choices, but clearly being book smart doesn't translate well to anything else.

"You're not her anymore," I remind myself. Flattening my hand on my stomach, I feel a swarm of emotion that has my nostrils flaring.

I've made a lot of choices here that I can't go back and change, so I can only move forward in life the best way I know how. If that means being the bad guy in somebody else's story, at least they'll get a happily ever after with someone else.

Giving one last look to the house, I turn on my heel and walk down the street to where Chris is staying with his parents. I'd asked if he wanted to take a walk with me, but he never got back. I knew he was avoiding me because he always returned texts within minutes.

I'm not sure he'll answer the door when the first few knocks go unanswered, but then it cracks open and his familiar face appears. He stands there with arched brows as I rub my arm awkwardly.

"I want to apologize about the other night before I leave," I tell him.

He leans against the doorjamb of his family's rental house with his arms crossed. It's obvious that he isn't over me running from him because he usually invites me in by now. I'd get to pet his mom's adorable Frenchie and maybe even get some snacks she made. Her chocolate chip cookies are some of the best I've ever had.

Nibbling on the inside of my cheek, I add, "I figured it was better to apologize face-to-face. I didn't mean to embarrass you or anything at Howie's. You took me by surprise is all. I didn't think you were going to kiss me."

The subtle scoff he gives me has my lips curling into a frown. "It shouldn't have been that surprising. I've always had a crush on you, Raine. Everybody seemed to know but you. Even Caleb."

Hearing that name makes my heart hurt, and I doubt it's even true since he never said anything to me about it. "You and I are great friends. I wouldn't want to ruin it. Plus, I was with Caleb for so long…"

"But you're not now," he points out, voice rattled with irritation. He stands straighter and looks down at me. "What? You've got a thing for guys with C names except me?"

I know he's not referring to just Caleb. "I know you're upset with me, but you're not being fair right now."

"Why? Because you don't like bringing up *Cody* or what you did with him? I don't get why you'd go after a stranger when you could have just opened your eyes and seen me."

Why does he have to bring that up now? It's been a long time since that summer. "Caleb and I had just started seeing each other. It wasn't serious. Neither was what Cody and I did."

Chris rolls his eyes, stepping back and grabbing the door. "Cheating is cheating no matter how you want to justify it. Like you said, Caleb is a good guy. I hardly doubt he deserved that unless you had some sort of agreement saying the summers are fair game. I wonder what he's doing this summer. Or *who*."

My nostrils flare as anger boils under my skin from his

insinuation. "This side of you isn't flattering. You can be angry, but you have no right being a dick."

The thought of Caleb with another girl makes me want to vomit, but I know it's none of my business. I ended things so he could get the future he wants. If that can't be with me, it'll be with somebody more deserving.

Eventually, I'll accept that.

Hopefully.

Having come here for one thing only, I start backing toward the walkway. "Like I said, I'm sorry for what happened. If I led you on, I didn't mean to. I didn't have any idea how you felt, Chris. And that summer with Cody is hardly an indication of who I am or who Caleb and I were as a couple. Everybody makes mistakes. We all have to live with them. You don't need to make them any harder to remember than they already are."

Nobody understands what that singular decision did to me—how it changed me. And because I'm determined to bury it, nobody ever will.

For a second, remorse weakens his terse expression. If he feels bad for what he said, he chooses not to address it. Instead, he says, "I'll tell Mom you said bye."

I'd be lying if I said I wasn't hurt by his dismissal considering we've been friends for a long time. I guess I get it. Rejection never feels good, no matter who you're getting it from.

"Raine?" Chris calls out, stopping me before I get into my car, which is parked by the curb of his parents' house. When I turn, I see the person I know that he is under the masked anger. "Safe trip back."

I smile at him, hoping he won't be mad at me forever. "Keep in touch? I want to hear about how med school goes."

He stands at the doorway for a few seconds in silence before nodding. "Yeah. Sure."

The short reply hits me, and I have a feeling this is the last time I'll hear from him about anything.

That's what happens when you cross lines with friends. You can't go back to fix it when it goes wrong.

~

Lindon's Main Street always smells like a mixture of the businesses it offers. The pretty roadway is lined with historic brick buildings, donated benches, and greenery carefully planted and maintained by the town's garden society that consists of ten older women with nothing better to do. Today I smell pressed coffee, fresh roses, and something fried that makes my stomach growl.

One Saturday every month, which happens to land on today, the entire street shuts down traffic and invites vendors to come in and sell to the community. The sidewalks are always full of tables from the diners and cafés on the main drag where people sit and talk while people watching. A farmers' market is set up in the square where people can sell their homegrown goods, and there are always local bands playing on a makeshift stage in the middle of the street for everybody stopping by to buy local.

Lindon has always been a small community with a big heart. One of the many reasons I love it so much here, no matter the mixture of memories it holds. There are places to go and people to see who are supportive no matter what gossip is spreading. I didn't realize how much I'd miss it until getting back this morning.

Looking back at my time in Virginia, I spent way too

much time alone because I thought that was what I needed. I'd always been around Caleb and his friends, so solitude and time to think was what this summer *should have* been about. In reality, I used it as a time to avoid every ugly emotion that came at me. Turns out it takes a lot of energy to pretend like you can move on from the life you always thought you'd have with someone.

"I'm sorry," I'd told Caleb when he opened the ring box. It was a beautiful piece of jewelry. Maybe the prettiest I've ever seen. Plain yet elegant, which is perfect for me. Nothing showy or flashy or overdone. He'd chosen right.

Ever since I saw the white-gold band with the cushion-cut diamond placement, I've had dreams of it on my finger. One night, when I woke up in bed all alone, I had tears in my eyes knowing that he wasn't around anymore. There wouldn't be any more nighttime drives with the radio playing our favorite country songs while holding hands or pit stops at the creamery for Milk Duds blizzards in the summer or winters spent sledding down the high school's steepest hill until we nearly crashed into the bleachers by the football field.

When Tiffany saw my bloodshot eyes the morning after those memories hit me like a freight train, I knew I couldn't tell her that I thought I'd made a mistake. She would have told me that I needed to stay strong. *Women like us are better off alone*, she'd told me countless times.

But what even were "women like us"? Miserable ones? Lonely ones? Too stubborn for our own good because of our trust issues? I'd like to think I'm not as cynical as them, that all their years of talking about the curse make me wonder if I've internalized my own reflections on love and relationships. It'd make sense.

Waving at a few locals who are working their respective booths, I make my way toward the little bakery that has always been my second home thanks to the woman who owns it.

Bea squeezes me in a tight hug as soon as I walk in, the yummy sugar and spice scents lingering in the air and making me feel at peace. "It's good to see you, girly," the older woman tells me, pulling back to give me a once-over, clucking her tongue. "You've gotten a tan and lost some weight. I'll have to send you on your way with some of those molasses cookies you love so much. I made Elena help me with a fresh batch this morning before she went to school."

"How is Lena doing?" I ask of her teenage granddaughter. She's always a ball of energy whenever I'm here, and it's hard not to be amused when she gets stars in her eyes when some of the university's athletes come in for food and coffee. She had a huge crush on Caleb for a while that I thought was cute, especially when it would make him blush whenever I'd tease him about it. How could I blame the girl? He's a six-foot-two, all-American boy. He loves his family, football, and…well, me. His passion alone makes him attractive, but his looks are an easy bonus.

Bea moves around the counter and grabs a Styrofoam to-go cup from the stack and then grips one of the coffeepots closest to her. "I didn't think it was possible, but I swear that child got even sassier since she turned seventeen. It's obvious she was sent into my life as karma for all the things I did when I was younger."

I crack a smile. "That bad, huh?"

"She's boy crazy" is all the woman says as she pours coffee into the cup, then the creamer and six sugars I always include. I don't know how she remembers everybody's orders around here.

"She's young," I reply, shrugging. I can't say I was ever boy crazy, but that's because my teenage years were spent with one boy. Mostly.

Bea waves me off. "I finally spoke to Artie about that space above the lounge. I know it's not ideal for your first office, but it'd be a great start for you getting on your feet. And if you think about it, you'd be above the perfect clientele. Those girls probably need a little counseling."

The Novelty Lounge, a small strip club that was meant to draw in horned-up college students, caused a huge stir when it first went in. The town tried petitioning it from officially opening because people were afraid it'd taint Lindon's reputation. They're not fooling anyone though. Some of the same people who started the uproar are seen walking in and out of the glass doors which feature silhouettes of naked women on them.

"I haven't even started the term yet," I remind her, watching as she deposits my favorite sweets into a white paper bag. "I've got a year of regular classes, a six-week term in the summer, *and* clinical hours to get my certification before I can even entertain where to lay down roots."

"Lay down roots," she mocks, setting the coffee and bag down in front of me. "As if it's not going to be here. Why else would you be back? Plus, Artie knows all that already. He's willing to hold the space just for you. He's been complaining that nobody wants to rent it because of the noise. I bet you could convince him to do some soundproofing. He could get a discount for materials at—" She visibly stops herself before she says the hardware store.

My ex's family business was the only source of income

I'd had since I was fifteen years old. "I don't even have a job anymore to help me afford anything. Not an apartment and definitely not an office space, Bea."

We're quiet for a moment or two before she looks around the mostly empty café. "I'm looking for some help around here if you're interested. You know I'll work around your school schedule. That way you won't be overwhelmed with too much."

"I could use some money," I admit, nudging the floor with the end of my flip-flop. My eyes lock on the colorful pedicure I got with Tiffany right before I left. During the appointment, she told me to choose the red because it was sultry and would get men's attention. I chose green. The same shade Caleb always said made my eyes pop. "I'm back at home with Mom for right now until I figure something else out."

It's not an ideal situation considering I've spent a lot of time out of my parents' home. I found peace in the chaos of the sorority house I lived in during undergrad because at least I didn't have to deal with my parents' constant bickering. The most I had to listen to was some of my sisters crying over men who didn't deserve them or catty arguments over stupid things like groceries, clothes, or what charity the car wash funds went toward.

"If you see Artie before I do, can you tell him I appreciate the offer but that he shouldn't hold that space for me? It's going to be a long time before I'm ready to start my own practice, and there's bound to be somebody willing to pay him rent for the space before I ever can. I heard the town is doing a revitalization project and got a big grant for it, so that'll pull in business owners who are willing to deal with just about anything for the right price tag."

Bea's eyes give me a thorough study before nodding. "I'll pass it along, but I wouldn't be so sure. You know that man has always had a soft spot for you and what you want to do."

Artie Fisher is a sweet older man who owns a few different buildings on Main Street. Some were converted into student housing and others are office spaces. I know a big reason he's fond of what I want to do is because he lost his daughter to mental illness a long time ago. He's told me there needs to be more access to help and resources here. Help I'd love to offer to anybody who needs it.

Swallowing, I say, "It's hard to think about the next big step when I can't seem to handle the little ones right now."

She offers me a comforting smile. "I have no doubt that you'll figure it out. You're in a rough place, but it's bound to get better so long as you put the effort in."

Pulling out a five-dollar bill and stuffing it into the tip jar, I say, "You're right. I'll send you my class schedule so we can work around it. I might only be able to work about three days a week because I've packed on a lot of grad classes, but…"

"Don't worry about it. Elena is trying to save up for her own car, so she's been taking on as many shifts as she can when she's out of school. We'll figure it out."

"Thanks, Bea," I tell her, grabbing the items she refuses to let me pay for and heading toward the door.

I start to push it open when I hear, "He misses you. I wouldn't assume anything just yet. It may be hard for the two of you but not impossible."

Not sure what to say, I let the door slowly close again until I'm staring at the speckled water stains on the glass.

She adds, "Go easy on him. That boy has been through it lately, and I'm not sure how much more he can handle.

Everybody breaks eventually, no matter how strong they pretend to be for everybody else."

I pause, feeling my stomach drop as I turn to face her. "What do you mean? What happened?"

She frowns at the question before slowly shaking her head. I can't read the expression on her face when she replies with a somber, "Oh, girly. You really have no idea, do you?"

Chapter Seven

RAINE

THE HARDWARE STORE LOOKS so much bigger now that I'm standing in front of it. I've been debating for five minutes on whether I have the guts to actually go in, knowing who's in there. I saw the profile of his face as he helped an older woman grab a light bulb from the top shelf of aisle eight.

How could I *not* go in though? Caleb's family was like a second one to me basically my whole adolescent life. They took me in as their own and accepted me even before I started dating their son. His mom would send me home with leftovers, and his dad taught me how to change a tire and check the oil in my car.

His dad.

My stomach dips at the thought of the terrible news Bea shared, pushing me forward until I'm opening the door and listening to the familiar chime of the bell announcing a new customer's arrival.

I freeze when I walk far enough in to be met by the deep brown eyes of the boy behind the counter. They're not as warm as usual but tired. I've only ever seen them look this dull when he tried pulling two all-nighters in a row to help me study for my finals while also trying to prepare for his. He got sick, almost slept through his first exam, but managed to get through it with one of the highest grades in his class.

My throat tightens with emotion as I slowly walk forward, feet dragging out each step until I'm mere inches away from the counter where Caleb is standing stone-still.

"I had no idea," I whisper.

No "Hi."

No "How are you?"

That's a trivial question, and there's no way he'd answer me honestly. *Fine* is the word I'm sure I'd hear escape those full lips of his that I used to map out with my fingertip whenever we were lying together.

I fiddle with my hands, unsure of what to say or do. Breakup be damned, I want to walk around the counter and give him a tight hug—the tightest I've ever given. It's what he's always done whenever something happened with my family.

But I can't get myself to move.

Not forward.

Not back.

Caleb asks, "When did you get back into town?"

Civil conversation.

It's…awkward. Thick.

"This morning."

He simply nods.

"Caleb—"

"I can't do this right now, Raine" is what he tells me, staring at the laptop on the counter. He's never cut me off before, but I get it. I do. It only makes me want to hug him more.

I tuck my hands into the pockets of my jeans, looking

66

around the store. It's just us. No other customers or workers. I bet his mom is at the hospital with his dad.

"I'm sorry."

We both know the apology is for more than just his father's health. It's for everything. All the years. All the hurt. Everything I threw away. For the past, the present, and whatever the future holds.

Caleb, for once, says nothing to me.

It's bittersweet.

Emotion crams into my throat, choking me. I can't swallow. Can barely breathe. My eyes water as I make a single decision. "I had so much to think about this summer and none of it helped like I thought it would. It was lonelier than I thought it'd be."

Once again, he's silent.

"I want you to know how sorry I am for walking away. I don't know what I'm doing or where I'm going in life anymore. I'm just…" He doesn't need this pointless rambling when the last thing I should do is to make this about me. "I'm just sorry. You've gone through a lot, and you don't deserve it."

His dark eyes glaze before his lips press into a solid line. If he wants to say anything, he's not allowing himself to. Not that I blame him. I threw away a lot of years together.

The only thing I can think to do is walk around the counter, stop right in front of him, and hesitate for only a second before wrapping my arms around his tense torso.

He's also lost weight. He was lean before thanks to his position on the football team, but now I can feel bones that used to have a little more muscle on them that are no longer padded.

Two broken people.

I don't expect him to do anything.

Not hug me back.

Not say a word.

I only want him to know I care, no matter in what capacity. Because I do, and I always will, no matter how conflicted I am about how or why things ended.

So when he looks down at me, the few inches of difference between us making his gaze feel that much harder on my face as we stare at each other, I don't expect him to bend down and kiss me. Or to back me into the counter. And I definitely don't expect him to pull me in to him so close our bodies are melded together, until I feel everything.

Everything.

I gasp into his mouth when he picks me up by my hips and sets me onto the countertop. On top of the paperwork, receipts, and scribbled-on inventory sheets he's obviously been working on for a while.

We kiss for what feels like hours when it's more like seconds. His hands are on me, mine on him, and I realize this may be what he needs.

I don't stop him when he walks away.

Don't say a word when he locks the front door and flips the OPEN sign to CLOSED.

Don't voice my concerns when he walks back over to me, spreads my legs, and moves between them with an obvious intention.

He needs this.

So I'll give it to him.

Anything for Caleb.

It's me who kisses him again.

It's me who tugs on his shirt.

But it's him who groans, popping the button on my pants and sliding down the zipper before reminding me exactly how good he is with his hands.

Not a single word is uttered as we shed the bottom layers of our clothing, devour each other's mouths, and prepare each other for what's about to happen.

I bite my bottom lip when he guides himself to my entrance, not hesitating once before pushing in until he's fully seated.

And it feels like no time has passed at all.

The only noise that fills the empty hardware store is the sound of our heavy panting and the noises coming from me every single time he pumps into me.

There's no praise.

No gentle coaxing.

No dirty talk.

Just sex.

It's never been just sex with us.

And when he's close, I pull him into me and hold him there, hugging my arms tightly around his neck until he makes a distressed noise and jerks inside me until he's coming.

We stay like that.

For one second.

Two.

Five.

After about thirty, he pulls out, leans his forehead against mine, and shakes his head. I don't know what to say when he offers me a paper towel to clean up with or what to do when he walks into the back room after fastening his jeans and clenching the back of his neck without so much as a second look in my direction.

So I do the only thing I know how to.

I gather what little is left of my pride, readjust my clothing, and walk away.

Chapter Eight

CALEB

I TOSS THE FOOTBALL back to DJ, who's grinning at me after I spilled my guts to him. "I don't see what the big deal is," he tells me.

My mood, which hasn't been stable in months anyway, hasn't been quite right ever since Raine showed back up in town. It's been hard not to stalk her social media pages every day to see where she is, what she's up to, or if she's seeing somebody else. I've told myself the only reason that she ended things was because she wasn't sure she wanted to spend the rest of her life with me. She must have been confused since there was nothing to compare our relationship to. What else could she have been confused about?

It doesn't make it easier, but at least it's a reason I can let myself accept because it wasn't me or something I did.

As shitty as it is, Dad's condition has helped distract me from investing too much time in my ex-girlfriend and her whereabouts or how good it felt to be inside her again.

"We broke up" is how I reply, voice monotone at the

obvious reminder. I catch the ball he throws at me, gripping the sides and staring a little too hard at it. DJ told me I was always calmer whenever we played, which is why I'm out here when I have better places to be, but this doesn't seem to be helping any. "I shouldn't have had sex with her, especially not like that. It was…"

I slept like shit last night thinking about what I did, replaying how I hid in the back office like a fucking coward until I heard Raine leave. I don't know if it was what she said that led me to making a move or if it was my emotions getting the better of me. I was pissed off because of life, because of Dad, because of how hard I'm struggling with school, and not even her apology made me feel better. If anything, it made me angrier—more confused. Because I don't know if I can believe it.

Hearing her say she's sorry doesn't really mean anything if it doesn't change anything. Yet I still made a move so I could feel something other than bitterness.

All it did was remind me that I'm still not over her, which makes me feel even shittier for trying so hard to convince Emma to give me a shot. The second Raine touched me, I couldn't think of anybody else. Only her.

DJ's laugh causes me to lift my gaze and glare in his direction. "Dude, you hooked up with an ex. We've literally all been there. Be real with yourself. It's only been a few months, and you were together for years. Addicts always go back to their fixes at least once before they finally sober up. Hell, I'd say you're doing pretty good."

My nostrils twitch as I throw the ball at him with more force than necessary. "Don't compare those situations. She's not my drug. She's…" *What the hell is she?*

When it's obvious I'm in no mood for messing around,

71

DJ sighs half-heartedly. "Look, man. You know I like Raine. I like you too. It's hard trying to figure out the right things to say because I know you're hurting, and I suck at the heart-to-heart shit. But don't beat yourself up over this. It happened. The only thing you can do now is move forward. You have to focus on you at some point. Not Raine. Not Emma. You've got bigger fish to fry right now."

Knowing he's right, I shake my head and roll my shoulders. "When did you become so wise? It's a little freaky, dude."

He grins. "It's all these books Sky is having me read. Speaking of freaky, you should seriously read some of these. Romance novels are off the fucking charts, man. Best sex of my life after she reads those fuckers because they give her ideas."

The last thing I want to think about right now is sex. Or somebody else's relationship given the raw status of mine. Or lack thereof.

Plus, I like Skylar Allen—DJ's girlfriend. They went through a lot to be together, and I'm happy he found somebody who makes him smile so damn much. Even if it's a little grating sometimes when that lovey-dovey look lights up his face whenever he talks about her.

But I've been there before.

"Come on," I tell him, sighing and nodding toward my apartment. "The game is going to start soon, and I want to get a couple of things done beforehand."

He follows me inside the renovated two-bedroom apartment. "As long as we're not cheering on those fucking pussies at Penn State. I'm sick of seeing them all over the damn news when there are players who should be highlighted for their skills and not for the bullshit their teammates were part of."

DJ has been extra testy ever since one of the Penn State coaches admitted to throwing away some concerning complaints filed against their best players. I don't blame the guy. Coaches tend to do a little more than they should when their winning streaks are at stake, something Lindon University saw firsthand with our former coach, Coach Pearce. DJ spearheaded his removal last semester, which left the school scrambling to rebuild their coaching staff before the new season started.

"Alabama is playing against them," I say. We've always rooted for Crimson Tide anyway, but I know it's going to be an intense game thanks to the comments DJ is bound to make against Penn. "Anyway, are you ready for the semester?" I ask, knowing we have a lot of shared classes this year since we're both studying business for our MBAs. I walk over to the fridge and grab a couple of beers for us, setting one down in front of him. "Because I'm not, that's for damn sure."

"Are any of us?" he comments, lifting a shoulder in dismissal. "Doing the internship for Sky's dad this summer made me realize how much help I still need. I signed up for Alexander's marketing class this semester, hoping it'll be an easy A after all the marketing promotions I worked on."

I pull out my phone and frown when I see a new email from my adviser saying one of the classes I need is full. Grumbling to myself, I glance at the list of available courses she attached and pinch the bridge of my nose. "This is the third fucking class I can't get into. One of them is only offered every two years."

DJ's eyebrows arch up at my hostile tone. "Are you on the waiting list? I managed to get into one of my undergrad courses when people dropped during the first couple of weeks."

I shake my head in answer.

"Well, even if you don't get in, you'll have the chance to when it's offered next. You may not even need to wait two years. Professors pick up classes all the time."

Knee bouncing as I sit at the breakfast nook, I go through the rest of my emails before checking my final grades from my summer courses and cringe at the borderline passing marks. There goes my 3.0 GPA.

"I don't know what's going to happen in two years, DJ. I don't even know what's going to happen tomorrow. I worked my ass off to double up and get my MBA sooner, but then the shit with Dad…"

He comes up beside me, pulling out the only other stool I have, and sits down. "You don't give yourself enough credit. You know what you need to do, Cal. Running the store is in your blood. Give yourself some breathing room instead of burning yourself out. It isn't like there's a rush to get your degree, anyway."

I'm quiet as I crack the top open on the beer and take a swig. "I just wish things were back to normal."

That's when he asks a question I've never really thought about before. "What even is normal?"

And the more I think about it, the more I have no fucking idea.

~

Mom opens the door of their house for me with a huge smile on her face—one I haven't seen in a long time. It's odd that the first thing I feel is concerned, since her happiness is typically a sign that something good has happened for once. It's the way her eyes gleam as she ushers me in that has me cautious at best.

Before I can even ask, Mom claps her hands together once and says, "The boys came by to see your father today, and they told him they saw Raine leaving the hardware store."

She stares at me expectantly, as if I'm supposed to confirm or deny their claim.

The boys are a few guys who work at the town barn. When they're not out plowing in the winters or working on whatever overpriced project Lindon got approved for in the summer, they're in everybody's business. It's rare you can do anything without one of them ratting you out. Once, I got a speeding ticket and one of the town boys saw me and tattled to my dad. He called me not even two hours later asking how fast I was going and then lectured me on respecting the speed limits, especially near the elementary school where I was pulled over.

Walking over to the armchair where my parents' elderly basset hound, Frank, is curled up, I fuss over the graying mutt before turning to my mother. "There's nothing to tell," I inform her, watching her shoulders drop a fraction. "She didn't know about Dad, so she came to apologize."

I'm not quite sure *how* she could have been in the dark about Dad for this long. People were talking about how sick he looked long before the summertime. He'd brushed them and our suggestion to go to the doctor off until it was too late. By the time he was diagnosed in May, not even two weeks after my graduation, it was a whirlwind of bad news. He hadn't even done chemo before the specialists saw that the cancer was spreading.

Raine might not have been around this summer, but her family was. There was no way they didn't know.

I've never been one to share personal details about my

75

relationship with either of my parents, so I'm not about to start now. Mom doesn't need to know what happened between us at the store to get her hopes up that there will be a reunion anytime soon. That's something I plan on taking to the grave with me, especially because I know the woman who's watching me with sad eyes would scold me if she found out how I basically used Raine to distract myself from feeling something other than sadness.

What I'll never understand is why the only woman I've ever loved *let* me. Raine always wants to make everybody happy, but she shouldn't have had to go to those lengths that day. Did she want to because she knew I needed it? Or because she missed me too?

And why am I so focused on an answer when I should just let it go? I've got Emma. I shouldn't have had sex with Raine for a lot of reasons, but especially because of the nurse I'm supposed to see tomorrow night for a movie. What's worse, I don't want to tell her about my indiscretion.

"What's wrong, Caleb?" Mom asks, walking over and brushing my arm. "Did you two talk? Did you fight? Did you discuss—"

"It's not important," I tell her, walking past Dad's favorite recliner that hasn't been used since he was hospitalized. Sitting on the end of the couch, I blow out a heavy breath. "I know you've always been team Raine, but too much has happened, Mom. Yes, she stopped by. Yes, we spoke. She... said some shit that I'm still processing. But that's it. Please don't go making up anything in your head about us getting back together. That's the last thing I can focus on right now."

Her frown deepens as she stoops, petting between Frank's big, floppy ears. Mom knows even less than I do about why my relationship ended. How could she? It was hard to explain the reason Raine told me no when I don't truly understand myself. "I will *always* be team Caleb. Do I like Raine? Yes. I loved her like a daughter and am still fond of her because she's a good person. I will never understand how things went down the way they did between you two because you're one of a kind, baby boy. Any girl would be lucky to have such a sweet, kindhearted man in her life. But I also know that Raine's choice must not have been an easy one for her to make because it was always clear that you two loved each other very much."

This conversation isn't making me feel any better, which was why I came here—to be around one of the people who has always been in my corner. My parents have been my ride-or-die my whole life, and even just sitting around doing nothing with them brings me the kind of peace I need. Now more than ever.

Mom doesn't stop there. She walks over and sits down beside me, taking my hand. "She's always been a logical girl, but sometimes reason gets in the way of what the heart wants. Not that you asked, but just because things didn't go well doesn't mean they still can't. But if that's not what you want, I'll support you. I'll be on your side no matter what, as long as you're happy in the end. Okay?"

Raine has always analyzed everything in life, including us. I never really thought twice about it because she's studying to become a psychologist. It makes sense that she wants to dissect how people act and think.

But maybe logic is actually the downfall in relationships. If you can't dive off the deep end because you trust someone fully, then what the hell is the point? This whole time, I thought Raine and I trusted each other enough to make it official, to make it to the end, yet here we are.

Apparently, I was fucking wrong.

Staring at the floor, I murmur, "Okay."

Mom pats my hand before reaching for the TV remote. "By the way, your father told me to pass along that the security cameras in the store need some updating. It seems they only work half of the time, and he told me you'll need to check them out because of some strange footage on them."

My body locks up at what must have been recorded there recently.

Jesus Christ.

My voice is raspy when I force out a strangled "Got it."

Chapter Nine

RAINE

THE BAKERY FEELS DIFFERENT from the other side of the counter. More intimidating. "It's not that hard," Elena, Bea's granddaughter, tells me. She shows me how to make the next latte with a slick grin on her face. "You'll mess up a bunch at first, but I'm sure people won't care too much since most of the town likes you."

Great. A seventeen-year-old is reassuring me that I'll get pity votes if nothing else at my new job. "I never thought about what all went into each drink," I admit sheepishly, already tired from my first full week of classes.

The past five days have been filled with paranoia walking around the familiar campus, all because I'm doing it on my own for the first time without Caleb or the people I hung out with by my side. The girls I lived with at the sorority house have all gone their separate ways, not that I was particularly close with any of them. One thing I've been dreading all summer is what it would be like coming back knowing most of the people in my social circle were people Caleb was friends with: guys from the team and their girlfriends or people he made friends with from his classes. I didn't intend to rely so heavily on his extroverted nature to meet people, but I did.

Now, I have no idea who's in my corner. I don't even know if he is, despite our spontaneous hookup.

Sighing, I refocus on the cheat sheet by the counter to help guide me on how to make each drink that the bakery offers, which I have a feeling I'll need to study if I'm going to get this right. I'm usually not irritated so easily at myself for getting something wrong, but my emotions have been everywhere lately thanks to the stress of school, living back at home, and trying to figure out a new routine for myself. A routine *without* the boy I haven't been able to stop thinking about since I walked out of the hardware store with my dignity dragging on the sidewalk behind me.

I'm not sure if regret is what I've been feeling about our slipup, because I've never regretted a single moment with Caleb before. But there's an emptiness nestled into my chest where my heart should be. That black hole is the only thing I can focus on, and if nothing else, I hope that what we did took away from whatever darkness has been surrounding him.

Elena snickers. "Maybe we'll just have you get the food orders ready. All they take is either heating them up or shoving them into a bag. Easy. When Ivy first started working here, she almost killed somebody who had a tree nut allergy by accidently adding a hazelnut creamer to their coffee. So as long as you avoid that, you'll be fine."

Ivy Underwood is dating the new Giants tight end, Aiden Griffith. They both went to Lindon before he dropped out to start his professional career with the NFL and she followed. I sort of miss the snarky girl whose spot I'm basically filling.

It was funny to watch her banter with people and keep a no-fucks-given attitude with anybody who tried giving her flak. She was one of the few people who could make the broody football player smile, even when she pretended she was annoyed with him.

Bea walks out from the back holding a tray of freshly made peanut butter cookies with peanut butter cups baked into them. It makes my mouth water as I watch her set the tray down on the counter and open the display case. "Stop trying to psych out our trainee," she scolds the younger girl beside me. Then Bea glances at me from over her shoulder. "Help me put these away. And don't listen to Elena. Ivy wasn't *that* bad. She caught on fast, just like I know you'll do. Not that she ever admitted it, but she took a picture of our cheat sheet and took it home with her to study. Within two days, she'd memorized everything there was to make around here without needing to be told twice."

I smile at that. "Do you hear from her or Aiden at all?"

Bea nods as we empty the tray and make sure the baked goods are lined up in the glass case. "They visit whenever they're in town, and Ivy sends me postcards with pictures every so often. The last one I got is hanging right over there." Her finger points toward the corkboard where pictures, letters, and other papers are hanging by tacks. "Damn cute couple, those two. Ain't never seen Aiden smile so wide until he was around her."

So I'm not the only one who noticed. I'm smacked with nostalgia thinking about what it was like being around those two back when everything seemed so much less complicated.

"Let him in, Elena," I hear Bea say as I stare absently at the cookies, brownies, and muffins ready for the day. "He always gets his coffee early before heading to the store."

My stomach dips as I look up, finding Caleb walking through the front door. We haven't seen each other or talked since that day at the store. As if he knows I'm staring, his eyes move from Elena to me, stalling at the entrance of the café. *Is he going to walk out?*

The intrusive thought buries its claws in my mind as I see him hesitate before finally snapping out of whatever thought he was having and walking toward the counter. My chest tightens the closer he gets, and suddenly I remember every single sensation he brought alive on that store counter we used to do homework on once upon a time.

My new boss happily says, "I trust you can handle this customer? His order hasn't changed, so you'll be fine."

Fine. Why does it feel like I'm going to have a heart attack then?

Caleb stops in front of the cash register that I'm frozen at. "You work here now?"

He sounds as off as I feel. Fidgeting with the little apron that Elena helped me tie around my waist, I nod. "Bea offered me a job the day I got back to town."

The day I saw you at the hardware store.

Clearing his throat, he dips his chin and grabs his brown leather wallet, an old one of his father's, from his back pocket. "That was nice of her to do."

Nice seems so clinical. I'm not sure what to say right away, so the awkwardness between us grows. "Yeah..." Watching him pull out a ten-dollar bill, I manage to ask, "Same coffee? Regular with eight milks and no sugar?"

He peeks up at me through his lashes before giving me another nod. "Yes." There's a pause before a mumbled "Please."

We stand there exchanging money and change before I handle the order. I can feel his eyes on my back as I grab a cup and the coffeepot before counting out the milk shots. He never liked his coffee too dark and hates sugar in it because he's never had much of a sweet tooth, unlike me who's always kept a stash of Milk Duds and other sweets in the glove compartment of my car and inside each of my bags to pull out whenever I want them.

Once I set the cup down on the counter and tighten the to-go lid on the top, I ask, "How is your dad doing?"

Anybody would want to know, I reason. It's not out of line for me to ask about somebody I saw as family. I still do, even if I have no right.

Caleb shifts on his feet, wrapping those long, tan fingers around the Styrofoam cup before pulling it toward him. "He's...Dad. Too stubborn to act like anything's wrong."

We fall back into silence, save whatever Bea is doing in the kitchen. Pots rattle, and a curse sounds as something loud bangs against the floor. Then water runs and a heavy sigh comes from the older woman giving me a little too much time with her customer.

I wait for Caleb to say something, watching as his lips part and then close, but nothing but tension fills the space between us.

"Hey," I say quickly. "About the other day—"

"Raine, I can't. I just can't." He picks up the coffee, lifts it toward Elena, and then leaves before I can try bringing anything up.

The teenager behind me says, "Damn. That was awkward."

Then I hear a smack, a high-pitched whine, and a grumble as the blunt teen is yanked into the kitchen by her grandmother while I stand defeatedly at the register with a heaviness in my heart.

The kitchen of my childhood home smells like burnt sugar and something else that makes my nose scrunch, causing me to open a window near the sink and examine the mess covering the countertops.

"Mom?" I call out cautiously, picking up one of the pans on the stove that has something burnt and black caked on the bottom. "Did somebody break in and try cooking?"

Setting my backpack down on the table off to the side, I walk into the living room and listen for any sign of life. It isn't like Mom to experiment in the kitchen. That was Dad's thing.

"Mom?" When I hear rustling coming from her tiny craft room off the den, I poke my head in to see her at her sewing machine. "Hey. What happened in the kitchen? It looks like a tornado went off in there."

She lifts her head up, removing a pin from where she was holding it with her mouth and placing it into the fabric she's working on. "I didn't even hear you come home. I was going to clean up before you got back."

My eyebrows go up. "Last time you tried cooking, the fire department came and you blamed me for it because you figured they wouldn't judge a twelve-year-old for learning how to make her own food."

Mom laughs. "I forgot about that. It's a wonder you're becoming a therapist instead of searching for one." She pushes back from the desk and removes her tape measure from where it's draped across her neck. "I was trying to make caramel kettle corn. I saw a recipe online that looked easy enough to recreate. But then the caramel started burning and the smoke detectors started going off and everything was smoky. I'm surprised Mr. Applebee next door didn't call the fire department on me."

I'm ninety-nine percent sure he doesn't have his hearing aids turned on most of the time. It must be nice to drown things out without a care in the world. "You should probably soak the pan. That way, it's easier to clean."

She frowns. "Maybe we should just get new pans. I mean, we don't cook that much anyway, unless eggs count."

We do eat a lot of eggs. "Or maybe," I propose, following her into the kitchen, "we should learn how to cook so we're not spending our paychecks on takeout. We relied on Dad way too much."

If it wasn't Dad cooking all our meals, it was Caleb who was making things for me. I got so used to it, I never thought much about the obvious skill set that I should have started learning years ago.

Mom scoffs as she picks up the pan and sighs, walking over to the sink and running water over it. "We never relied on your father for anything. We've survived fine on our own."

Yeah, thanks to the pizza place and Simply Thai. Not wanting to go there, I nod reluctantly. "Yeah, you're right. Hey, speaking of Dad, did he mention that we are doing lunch tomorrow? I know you saw him yesterday when you met with the lawyers."

She hums, turning the water off and staring into the sink basin. "Yes, he told me you are meeting at the diner." Shoulders dropping, she turns to me. "I'm glad you two are still spending time together despite all this."

There's no reason why I wouldn't. Dad has never treated me badly. It was the exact opposite, actually. He'd take me on father-daughter dates every so often growing up. Mostly mini golfing or out to whatever movie was playing that I wanted to see. We'd always wind up at the diner after.

I miss having him around the house, especially because he'd always share late-night snacks with me when neither of us could sleep. Mom would scold us for eating after midnight, so we'd get sneaky. In the long run, I understand they're better off where they are now. In different houses, living different lives.

Instead of asking about how things are going between the two of them and getting forced to hear about God knows what, I gesture toward the other pots and pans scattered everywhere. "I think I saw a cooking class being offered at that new test kitchen in town. Maybe we can sign up and have a mother-daughter day. It could be fun."

Based on the flinch, I'd say she doesn't agree. "I can think of better ways to spend our day, and it's not listening to a pretentious chef tell me how to flip a pancake or season a chicken breast."

She clearly still has trauma from the time I spit out the pancake she made me for breakfast one day before school. I was six. I think I started crying about how rubbery it tasted.

Defeated, I grab my bag and haul it over my shoulder. "It was just a thought since we haven't spent much time together lately."

Mom had briefly apologized for missing my birthday by ordering my dinner the night I got home. Then she got a call from a client and had to get back to work, so we barely saw each other for my make-up celebration. Maybe it would have upset me more if Bea hadn't made my favorite dessert for my first shift, even putting the number twenty-three in icing on the cookie.

I start walking toward my room when Mom stops me.

"I'm sorry, sweetie. I've been picking up as much work as possible to make ends meet. Let's order dinner from your favorite Chinese place and then watch a movie. You can choose which one."

Biting my tongue, I slowly nod at the typical night we have together. She'll be on her phone most of the time until she decides to go to bed early, leaving me to clean up and sit in silence by myself.

But just like those other times, I choose not to say a thing, because if that's all the time I get with her, I'll take it.

"Sure, Mom. I'd like that."

Chapter Ten

CALEB

THE FIRST FEW WEEKS of the semester fly by faster than I anticipate, considering my life is a stream of constant school assignments, work shifts, and hospital visits. Each day blends into the next, with the same sleep deprivation, caffeine addiction, and heavy anxiety weighing on me as Dad gets worse.

Before I know it, August turns into September and the crisp air leading to fall is the only thing that seems to give me a boost of energy when exhaustion weighs me down.

That and coffee, which I haven't gotten as often from Bea's because I'm a chickenshit. Ever since I discovered Raine works there, I've been hesitant to go at all, which means making shitty coffee in the cheap machine I bought for my apartment. It hardly hits the spot like the bakery's dark roast, but there are some things I don't want to deal with—my mixed feelings for my ex being one of them.

Almost as if I manifest it, a cup of coffee is set on the store counter in front of the textbook I'm reading. Matthew

Clearwater, another one of my former teammates, is standing there with the same look most of my friends have been giving me lately. "Dude, you need to stop."

Stop. I don't know what that word even means anymore. "Stop what? Trying to pass grad school? Trying to keep a roof over my mother's head? Living?"

Matt's lips twitch downward at my melodramatic reply before he sighs and pulls my textbook away. "Let's be real, man. You're not doing any studying when you've gotten, what, a few hours of sleep at best? DJ said you dozed off in business economics the other day and it took him kicking you awake before you came to."

I'd spent the night before with Dad because he wasn't doing so hot. The nurses normally don't let people stick around after visiting hours, but Emma was working and managed to convince her shift supervisor to let me stay so long as I was quiet and out of the way. I woke up with a blanket draped over me that definitely wasn't there when I fell asleep and a second tray of food with my name on a piece of paper in Emma's handwriting.

Something she wouldn't have done if I'd told her what happened at the hardware store. Not that I wasn't tempted to rip the Band-Aid off and risk losing her too. She deserves better than the half-assed excuses and low energy I give her.

I know that.

She knows that.

But I don't want to let go of this.

"Mom told me I should talk to my adviser about taking a leave of absence," I murmur, scrubbing my tired eyelids. "Dad got talked to about palliative care and hospice yesterday by his oncologist and the team who've been working with him. It was…" No words can describe the mood of the room when that conversation was brought up. I still don't think any of the information they offered has really soaked in.

Matt shakes his head. "I'm sorry, Cal. I don't think your mom is wrong though. Even if you take a few weeks off, you can make it up. Maybe you could talk to your professors about trying to line up some work and notes so you don't fall behind if you want to come back."

Taking the coffee he brought me, I pull back the plastic tab and take a long sip of the liquid that I have a feeling Raine made, based on Bea's logo on the side of the cup. "I haven't really had time to think about my options."

It's not entirely true. I've thought about taking a break from school, but I've never given up on anything. Dad taught me better than that.

"Dad is thinking about coming home and having a team of nurses help settle him in where he's comfortable. He doesn't want to be in the hospital anymore."

"Can't say I blame him," my friend remarks, voice quiet. I remember when Matt was hospitalized freshman year with a burst appendix that turned into a bad infection, so he was stuck at the hospital. The only thing that got him through it were the cute nurses who entertained his cheesy flirting for the period of his stay. He asks, "What does your mom think about all this? My aunt said she's sad she doesn't see her at their Tuesday book club meetings anymore, but she isn't sure if she should drop by the house to say hi with everything that is going on."

Mom could use the company, but I get why people might be hesitant. Nobody knows what to say to us anymore. If it's not "sorry," it's nothing at all because they're afraid of saying the wrong thing. "When they started giving us options about how to move forward, Mom looked a little pale. I know she wants him at home, but I can tell there's something on her mind about it that she's not saying."

His eyebrows go up, as if to say *Sound like anybody else we know?*

Lifting my shoulders limply, I stare down at the drink in my hand and blow out a breath. If someone had told me three years ago that I'd be here, watching my father die, after being dumped by my longtime girlfriend, and struggling to keep up with school and work, I wouldn't have believed them. Then again, nobody expects their life to do a complete one-eighty. It's why everyone says to hope for the best, expect the worst, but plan to be surprised.

The number of surprises I'm dealing with lately is just a little too much for any one person to handle, which only adds to the anger slowly bubbling under my skin. I was raised to be tougher than this. So why am I struggling so much harder compared to the man who's dying?

Not wanting to think about it anymore, I decide to shift gears and diverge the conversation. "What's new with you?" I ask Matt. I lean back in the chair behind the store counter and listen to it creak. There's only a small space cleaned off for when customers come to check out, and the rest is covered in paperwork I still need to fill out, organize, and file.

Matt looks around at the items lining the shelves by the register—mostly candy, gum, and a few smaller household items people usually forget to pick up until they see them. "There's not much going on with me," he replies, grabbing a Snickers bar and tossing it onto the counter before pulling out some money.

One of my brows pops up as I give him change for his chocolate before saying, "I doubt that's true since you're still going hard for Rachel. I heard through the grapevine that she's leaving as academic adviser now that she's in her last semester of grad school."

Matt waggles his eyebrows. "Yeah, but she'll still be at Lindon though."

"As a *professor*, Clearwater. It was bad enough you were constantly flirting with her when she was on staff. She's been working hard to get her degree. Remember how excited she was when the school offered to pay for grad school if she'd work for them? Don't fuck this up for her because you want to get your dick wet."

He peels open the snack he bought. "You sound like Aiden," he grumbles, speaking of the former tight end on our team. He takes a huge bite of the candy and, with his mouth half-full, adds, "We haven't done anything wrong. And Lindon can't afford to fire anybody else after the huge scandal with the coaching staff."

I make a face, remembering the forced mass exodus that occurred with the football faculty earlier this year. The administration decided that letting them go was for the best, which surprised a lot of people. "Look, do whatever you want. I would just hate to see anybody take any risks that don't pan out in the end." I sit back, grabbing my textbook again and opening to the page I was on before.

It's a long moment later when Matt breaks the tense silence between us. "We're being careful."

I glance up at him, realizing Matt and Rachel must have already started something they have no intention of ending anytime soon. The former Lindon football team used to work with her enough to know she's determined to make a future for herself. She could still end things with him if he's a threat to that.

I've learned to expect the unexpected.

He drums his hands against the edge of the counter. "I don't suppose I could convince you to close up shop early and come to dinner with me and DJ, can I?"

My eyes go to the time on my phone screen before flicking back to his. I've still got a few hours before I'm supposed to close, but it *has* been quiet in here. A little too quiet for business, if I'm being honest.

"I have to be at the hospital by six" is how I reply, grabbing the keys from where I keep them hidden under the counter. "And I'm taking my coffee."

Matt looks both pleased and surprised, probably the same way I look knowing I've justified taking a break for once. "The crew will be happy to see you."

They have no idea how much the feeling is reciprocated.

~

Dad is sleeping when I finally make it to the hospital, and it gives me time to *really* look at him. When he's awake, he tries downplaying everything as if he's not on the verge of death.

"Hey," a quiet voice greets from behind.

I turn to see Emma there with a small smile on her face. "Hi. Didn't expect to see you here. Did you pick up another shift?"

I've learned her schedule by now, especially knowing she's one of the few people who can get Dad to eat, even if it's pastries that one of her coworkers brings in. At this point, Mom and I don't care what he eats as long as it's something.

She peeks around my shoulder at Dad before nodding toward the hallway. I follow her out, watching as she stops a few feet from the door and lets out a tired sigh. "We've had a lot of callouts today, so I was voluntold to stay until my boss can try getting another person to cover. It's not looking optimistic."

My brows dart up. "How long have you been here?"

She lifts her wrist and looks at the purple smartwatch. When she cringes, I know the answer isn't going to be a good one. "Over twenty-four hours. I dozed in the on-call room earlier, but I could use approximately a ten-year nap when I get home."

I whistle softly. "Damn, that's tough. Do you need anything? Food? Coffee?" I look into Dad's room to see if he's still sleeping. When I turn back to her, I ask, "Do you have time to get coffee down at the cafeteria? I know it's not the best, but…"

Before she can answer, one of the other women working calls out to her about a patient in a different room.

Emma frowns. "I want to, but I can't. I just wanted to check in with you. How are you doing?"

I slowly shake my head, sliding my hands into the pockets of my blue jeans and feeling like a total jackass. This girl is running on no sleep and still checking in on me despite how little of my time I've been able to give her. "I'm okay for right now. Fall semester has been a balancing act that I'm starting to think isn't worth it, but…" I let my words fade before limply lifting my shoulders. I haven't really admitted that to anyone, but pressure eases from my chest once I say it aloud.

She reaches out and brushes her fingers along my arm in comfort, letting me breathe a little easier. "I'm around if you ever want to talk. You have my number. Even if this doesn't go anywhere serious, I don't see why we can't be friends."

I'd be lying if I said I wasn't tempted to use her number

94

a lot more than I have. Something always holds me back from following through. Or rather some*one*. "I know, and I appreciate it."

"Anyway, I've got to go," she says, starting to back away. Flashing me a smile, she gestures toward my dad's room. "Tell him I'll be back later with something better than the cafeteria meat loaf. Nobody should be subjected to that."

I snicker and wave her off, heading back into the hospital room that I've become a little too familiar with. Dad is still snoozing, his soft snores drowned out by the machines he's attached to. I sit there for a while, staring at his paper-thin skin and sunken facial features, before pulling out my phone and thumbing through a few unanswered messages.

DJ: Good to see you today man
Matt: The guys said we should make this a weekly thing
Mom: How's he doing?

As much as I'd love to see my friends more often, I know I can't promise them anything. If I let on how bad Dad is, I know they'd understand. But I can't bring myself to be honest with them about the reality of the situation because that means coming to terms with it myself.

My father is dying.

More and more every day.

And there's no stopping it or slowing it down, which means the only thing we can do is watch as the cancer kills him.

Swallowing, I thumb out two text messages one after the other, to two separate women who have my mind in a constant state of confusion.

Me: If you ever want to take me up on that coffee,
you know where to find me
Me: I'm lost too

Raine: Should we talk about that night?

Staring at the text, I let out a frustrated sigh and put my phone back into my pocket. What did she expect when she told me she felt more lost now than when we were together? Had I suffocated her that much? Made her that uncomfortable somehow?

Maybe DJ isn't too far off about being addicted to her. Should she and I talk about the hookup? Probably. Do I want to tell her that we shouldn't have had sex? That I partially regret it? No. It'd hurt her feelings, and there's no point in that when there's enough damage between us already.

In a hoarse voice Dad asks, "Girl trouble?"

Despite myself, I can't help but laugh at the first words out of his mouth as he slowly wakes up and turns to look at me where I'm occupying my normal seat.

I admit, "You could say that."

He says those three damn words that I'm going to miss hearing from him. "Talk to me."

Fighting back the emotion rising up my throat, I do just that, knowing I'm on borrowed time to get sage advice from the man I've always looked up to and aspired to be like.

Squeezing my eyes closed to fight back the sudden onslaught of emotion, I murmur, "I don't know what to do,

Dad. Raine apologized for what happened. And no matter how much I wish I didn't, I still love her."

"So what's the problem?"

I take a deep breath. "I don't know if I can ever trust her not to break my heart again if I let her back in."

Chapter Eleven

RAINE

THE MENU AT BARTISE'S is unique, and the seafood section makes my stomach growl. "What are you thinking about getting?" I ask Skylar, the sophomore dating DJ. I'm grateful she agreed to have dinner with me because I wasn't sure if she'd stay loyal to her boyfriend's best friend or if she'd still want to be mine.

When Skylar started sharing some of the romance books she read over the summer, it was hard for me to have conversations about our favorite authors. We bonded over our love for smutty books and book boyfriends, but it was difficult getting into the romance mood when my love life was abysmal at best.

"I think I want the chicken," she answers, eyes trained on the short list of poultry options and pointing to one. "The chicken parm sounds delicious, and it's been a while since I've had any that isn't in tender form."

My lips twitch into the ghost of a smile as I remember the first time Caleb asked me out.

"We should get chicken," Caleb says, pulling my focus away from the math homework I'm doing at the counter.

My eyebrows pop up as I remove the green apple lollipop that I bought from the hardware store's display case from my mouth. "Did you say chicken?"

Caleb stops restocking the candy he's been working quietly on for the past twenty minutes. He swipes his palms down his thighs. "Or other food. We could get pizza Friday night after the game. If you're still planning on coming, I mean. You don't have to, of course. Come to the game. Or, uh, get pizza."

I sit back and stare at him for a second, pressing my lips together as they threaten to curl upward. Stifling a giggle, I say, "Are you asking me on a date, Caleb Anders?"

He blows out a long breath and rubs the back of his neck. "Sort of. Yeah."

I watch him for a moment, forgetting all about the Pythagorean theorem in front of me that I've been struggling with since I started my shift this afternoon.

After a moment, I nod slowly and reply with a simple "I like chicken tenders."

Snapping out of it when I hear Skylar ask what I'm thinking about ordering, I mumble a semicoherent "Mongolian shrimp," even though my eyes lock on the chicken tender basket that takes me back in time.

Skylar doesn't seem to notice the distance in my tone when she perkily says, "That sounds yummy too."

Humming, I close the menu and push it off to the side. Grabbing my water, I study the blond, who's still examining the food options.

I'm glad she and DJ have each other, especially after the horrible things that happened to her freshman year.

"Hey, Sky?" I play with my water glass as she raises her

eyes. "Thanks for tonight. I know I didn't reach out much this summer…"

She shakes her head, a soft smile on her face that eases the tension in my chest. "You don't need to be sorry, Raine. I get it. I'm glad you asked to hang out. Olive has been busy with Alex while he's in town, and I wasn't sure if you'd want to hang out after everything."

Her friend Olive is involved with a rookie on a national hockey team who graduated with us in the spring. I didn't realize she and Alex were still seeing each other. I assumed once he left Lindon, they'd call it quits.

I guess it's just me who makes those types of choices.

"Can I ask…" Wetting my lips, I squirm on my seat and clear my throat. "Can I ask if he's okay? You probably see Caleb more than I do. I'd reach out, but…" Would he want me to? He never so much as replied back to me when he texted me last. Just when I thought we'd finally get a chance to talk about what happened at the store, he ghosted me completely.

Skylar's smile doesn't leave her face. "I think he's trying to seem okay considering everything that's going on. But I don't know. I doubt anybody could actually be okay given what he's going through with his dad."

Nodding in agreement, I stare down at the table. I'm glad she's being honest. Most people would probably tell me he's fine and leave it at that or question why I want to know at all.

When the waitress comes back to our table to take our order, I pass her my menu and say, "I'll have the chicken tenders, please."

Skylar is staring at me.

But I don't meet her eyes.

That night after Mom goes to bed, I send another text to Caleb.

Me: Can we talk?

The text goes unanswered, and before I go to bed, I see that he posted a picture online of a table set with two plates and a girl's hand in the corner of the image.

~

My feet drag as I walk along Main Street after a horrible night's sleep from bad cramping and intrusive thoughts. I pointlessly waited for a text from Caleb only to be disappointed. It wasn't until after midnight when I gave up and went to bed, only to toss and turn, hoping anytime I flipped my phone over there'd be a text waiting for me.

Pathetic, I chide myself. I've never lost sleep over whether a guy texted me before.

Especially not one who obviously has the right to move on with his life after I pushed him to do so.

I glance at my watch and wince when I realize I'm a few minutes late meeting my dad. He's always been a stickler for punctuality, not that I blame him. Ever since he got his real estate license a few years ago, he's built a name for himself and the agency he works through in the tricounty area. It's kept him on the go more times than not, which means embracing whatever time I do get with him.

"Sorry," I say as soon as I slide into our usual booth at the diner. It's our favorite place to meet up, and our orders never change. Burgers, fries, and chocolate milkshakes with extra whipped cream. Dad always takes the cherry from mine because I didn't like them as a kid. I haven't told him that's changed over the years because I like our routine.

"Are you all right?" he asks, one of his dark eyebrows arching up as I peel my cardigan off and put it over my purse beside me.

For a second, I wonder if he knows just how much pain I'm in. I was tempted to cancel on him today to take some Motrin and lie down with a heating pad on my stomach, but I knew Dad would be hurt if I didn't come. "Yeah, why?"

"You're five minutes late," he says. "Just thought something might have popped up. You look a little…"

I groan internally, already knowing how rough I look. The medicine I took barely kicked in before I told Mom I was leaving. "No woman wants to hear that she looks anything other than lovely, Dad. I'm having an off day, that's all. We're allowed to have them once in a while."

Thankfully, he doesn't press or lecture me on timeliness and changes the topic. "Okay, princess. I meant no harm."

I simply nod once, moving pieces of my frizzy burgundy hair behind my ear.

"Some good news," my dad says. "I might have a buyer for that Lakeview home over in Decatur."

I smile, knowing that property was causing him a lot of stress over the past few months. "That's the million-dollar home that was renovated last year, right?"

Pride takes over his expression, brightening the greenish-blue eyes I wish I'd gotten from him instead of my brown ones from Mom. "It is. There were a few people interested but only one of them who wasn't offering too far under the asking price or for ridiculous stipulations in the contract."

"I'm glad," I tell him, hoping that'll ease some of his worries. He's got enough going on trying to balance meetings with Mom and the lawyers; he doesn't need other things weighing him down. "Do you think the deal will go through then? I know your boss wasn't sure the price tag was going to work in the current market."

He rolls his eyes, grabbing one of the full water glasses and pulling it toward him. "That's because she didn't see the vision like I did. It's all about how you sell it." There's a pause before he scratches at his clean-shaven chin. "Speaking of selling, I wanted to run something by you."

I lean back with caution. "Okay…"

"The summer cabin is in a great vacation area, and your mother has been debating putting it up for sale."

Sitting up straighter with surprise, I shake my head. "You know that's never going to happen, right? Even though it's in Mom's name, Tiffany would put up too much of a fight. There are a lot of memories in that cabin."

Maybe that's selfish of me to say, considering I've had my fair share of memories there too, but I couldn't imagine my one place to escape going away.

He folds his hands together on the table and leans forward. "I know that. Your mom and I have spoken about how the money we could get for it could help you with college. You're in debt because of the loans you took out, and neither she nor I want to see you drown in them. I can get the cabin on the market and get a great price for it. It doesn't make sense to have it go to waste or get ruined by the people your aunt rents it out to during the offseason. And you're going to be busy with graduate school and earning your certification, so it isn't like you'll be able to visit as much. Keeping it up, maintaining it, will be more money than it's worth."

Rubbing my hands down my thighs, I shake my head.

"Mom and Tiffany love that cabin. *I* love that place. They swore it'd stay in the family after Grandma Maud died because she loved it too. I appreciate you guys wanting to help me, but you don't need to. I can manage my loans. I'm responsible."

"I know you are," he replies. "This isn't a question of whether you're responsible."

My shoulders drop. "Then what is this about? Why do you want to sell it now? Does this have to do with the divorce?"

He glances out the window for a moment before sighing once. "It's not about the divorce. I'm not after the money. In fact, I won't get a single cent of this sale. The whole point of this is to help *you*. I spoke to your mother last night, and—"

I stare at him. "You talked to Mom?"

She was on the phone for a while last night, but she told me it was Aunt Tiffany on the other end of the phone. I didn't think much about it because she and her sister always gossip whenever they can.

He finally says, "Believe it or not, I still want to make her happy. And what would make her happy is showing you how much she loves you by doing this. She's proud of you, Raine. You've been so smart with every choice you make in your life, so she wants to make sure you're taken care of."

Smart. My mother always calls me that, but she never means it academically. I do just fine, getting mostly As for years in school. I *am* intelligent. But no. She keeps rubbing my breakup in my face by trying to make me think it was the best decision I've made. "I can take care of myself, you know. I've been doing it for a while. I'd rather not be the reason there's a rift between Mom and her sister. They're close, but this could make things complicated. And she needs somebody in her life right now, especially after—"

Stopping myself before I can say *the divorce*, I close my eyes and regroup. I have no idea whose feelings I'm trying to save by brushing off the topic at this point—mine or Dad's. Seeing him brings back a lot of memories of when the three of us were a family. Even if those picture-perfect moments were rare, they existed. And it gave me hope for my own future because I knew what *not* to do in my relationship.

Yet here I am anyway, learning how to move forward from the person who could have given me that.

I'd hardly call that smart at all.

"Mom doesn't have a lot of people in her life is all I mean. I'd hate for her to get into a fight with the one person who's always been there. Tiffany seemed really happy at the cabin this summer."

He simply answers, "I get it. I do. I don't want that for her either. All I'm asking is for you to think about this. For your mother. It's not a done deal or anything. We're simply discussing it as a possibility."

I sit back in the booth and absorb all this. "You really do love her still, huh?"

His fingers graze his jaw. "It takes a long time to unlove somebody, kiddo."

Swallowing my words, I glance down at the table and the little scratches people have made into the wood with their initials.

When the waitress comes over a few minutes later, she's not surprised at what we order. And as soon as the milkshakes are delivered, Dad reaches over and plucks off the cherry from mine with a smile and asks, "So how is everything going with you?"

For a moment, I debate what to tell him. The truth or a lie?

When I say "Things have been fine," it's obvious he hasn't learned anything from all the times Mom has said that same four-letter word when it was far from the truth.

All the oblivious man in front of me responds with is "That's good, princess."

Chapter Twelve

RAINE

SLIDING INTO MY USUAL seat for my first class the next day, I groan at the pain-induced nausea twisting my stomach. I raided Mom's medicine cabinet this morning to take anything I thought could help before school, but it hasn't helped.

"You look like you're either hungover or ate the mystery meat the dining hall served yesterday," Charity, one of my longtime classmates, comments, studying the way I wrap my fingers around the ginger ale. "Should I be worried? Because you're a little paler than usual, and I swore to myself I was *not* going to get sick this year."

Charity has always been worried about catching colds when the school year starts. During freshman year, she got so sick she had to miss two weeks of school.

I hold my hands up. "I woke up feeling a little queasy." I want to blame the food from the diner, but I know it isn't that. "It's not contagious, so don't get your Lysol out. I know you carry it."

She eyes me suspiciously. "How do you—"

"Junior year adolescent psychology. Remember what you did to poor Josie? She was terrified of you after that. She literally dropped the class so she didn't have to see you again."

Charity blows a raspberry with her lips in exasperation. "I didn't mean to get anything in her eyes. She'd been sneezing without covering her mouth, and I wanted to clean the air around me. It was innocent."

The noise escaping me is abrupt and unattractive, but I don't care. Just like I don't care about the scathing look Charity gives me for being amused by her germaphobia.

"You probably shouldn't Lysol anyone in the first place, Char," I remind her, knowing she'll more than likely do it again. I refuse to be victim number two.

When I bend down to grab my things from my bag, I suck in a breath at the sharp pain tugging at my lower abdomen and try breathing through it without giving anything away.

If Charity notices, she doesn't say anything about it for the rest of the fifty-minute lecture. It gives me a chance to suffer in silence, praying for the day to pass in a blur so I can curl up in the fetal position hugging my heating pad and a waste basket.

Before we're dismissed, Professor Wild starts going around the room with a glass bowl full of paper. "I want each of you to select one prompt from the bowl. This will be the subject of your final project at the end of the term. You'll be asked not only to conduct interviews with at least two different people as if they're your client but to write a detailed paper on how your subject is vital to the study of psychotherapy. While you *are* allowed to pair up with your peers, I will offer extra credit to those who use outside sources to complete this project so long as they sign off by the deadline printed on your syllabus."

When the middle-aged woman gets to me, I reach into the bowl and pull out one of the few pieces of paper left. Unfolding it, I gape at what's written along the middle and wonder what kind of cruel joke the universe is playing on me.

The psychology of romantic relationships.

Blinking slowly, I look up at the professor, who's moved on to the next section of students. "You're going to take on an angle of your topic as you see fit. Preferably one that you're most likely to see during a counseling session. Get creative. Use your imagination and, of course, some of the material laid out in your textbooks as resources to guide you. Remember, this is essentially practice for the future. What are you most likely to encounter? What advice would you give to them?"

Charity shows me hers.

Psychology of domestic abuse.

I cringe, a little more grateful for my topic. When I turn my paper around to show her, she laughs at the irony. She knows about the breakup. Not the details, since she and I have never really been friends, but most people around here know about the split. How could they not when the proposal happened at the university's graduation ceremony? There are photos and videos of the moment I rejected Caleb and walked away that circulated the first few weeks of summer.

Leaning back against the chair, I fold the paper back up and stuff it into my notebook.

Professor Wild returns to the front of the room and starts writing key due dates for the project on the board for us to copy down. "You will be working on these projects throughout the semester, so I highly suggest you begin brainstorming where you'd like to take your topics and whom you'd like to partner with, because I expect a polished draft by finals week."

Charity leans toward me. "I don't suppose you'd want to be each other's partners? I can play the scorned lover who has major commitment issues, and you can be the docile doe-eyed girlfriend who's on the run from her abusive boyfriend. I'm thinking his name will be Greg because that sounds like a douchebag name, right? We could easily ace this."

I think about it for a second and remember what my grade was on my first assignment a few weeks back. It wasn't great, which means I could use the extra credit.

Closing my notebook and stuffing it into my bag, I say, "As much as I'd love to trash-talk your ex"—I eye her knowingly. She must have forgotten I met her egotistical ex-boyfriend Greg a time or two—"I think I'm going to try finding someone outside class to get some extra points."

She frowns but nods. "Okay. Who do you think you'll ask?"

My options are limited. "I'm not sure. Maybe my mom will help me with it, but that subject might be sort of touchy considering the divorce and all." I shrug. "I'll figure it out. She still owes me for forgetting my birthday and ditching our normal summer plans. I'm hoping I can sucker her into doing it with a guilt trip."

Charity grins. "Evil. I like it."

I wink, even though I'm ninety percent positive that Mom is going to tell me no. I'll cross that bridge when I get there.

As we're packing up, I notice a notification lighting up

my phone. Hope blossoms in my chest as I pick it up and type in my passcode, thinking I'll see Caleb's name, only to be met with a spam text from an unknown number.

Standing up after turning off my phone screen and sliding my cell into my pocket, I sway on my feet and have to grab the back of my chair for balance.

"Whoa." Charity grabs ahold of my arm as I blink back the dizziness that accompanies the next wave of nausea that my ginger ale obviously hasn't touched. "Do you need to go to the health clinic?"

Waving her off, I take a few deep breaths until I feel better. "No, I'm fine. Just..." I take a few more deep breaths, counting to five. "It's nothing. Stress. Thank you though."

As I straighten up and collect myself, I try ignoring all the heaviness building inside me. It'll be a few days before I feel better if it's anything like last time, but I know stress won't help. The more I think about Caleb, the worse it'll be to recover.

I never thought I'd feel sick over a boy again, but here I am. And now I get to psychoanalyze myself and all the reasons why I'm an idiot for acting this way when I have no right to.

Sometimes I worry that I'll make a horrible counselor because I have enough problems figuring out the reasons I do what I do. Like breaking up with Caleb and then being depressed about it. Or feeling sick whenever I think about where I'll be six months from now compared to him. Will he be happy with someone else while I'm still single thinking about him? Will we both be on the same path alone, trying to find ourselves? I don't even know what I'll feel like tomorrow, much less in that much time.

I'm lost too, he texted me.

That doesn't make me happy to know. I wish I was the only one who felt that way. Then at least I'd know I did the right thing for his sake, if not for mine.

As long as he's not like *this*. Rooted deep with every kind of intrusive thought possible.

I grip my backpack strap tighter, knowing I'll never break free from that train of thought if I keep focusing on it.

"I'll see you Friday," I tell Charity, evading her concerned expression by weaving through the other students exiting the classroom.

I skip my other classes because I don't think I'll feel well enough to go to them *and* work later.

~

It's twenty minutes from closing when I finally get a chance to sit down. Elena walks into the back and stops when she sees me clutching a cup of peppermint tea that Bea made for me when she commented on how green I looked. The teenager gives me a once-over before tossing the rag in her hand into the little hamper in the corner.

"Are you still upset over that mishap earlier? It wasn't a big deal." She shrugs. "The guy wasn't even mad about it. His wife was a little pissed, but she always has sort of a resting bitch face whenever she—"

"Enough," Bea cuts her off in a scolding tone, coming into the room with an empty tray that used to have croissants on it. She made them with orange chocolate filling and chocolate drizzle on top to look like spiderwebs since October is quickly approaching. "We don't gossip about customers here. Even if it is true. That woman is a snake no matter how nice you are to her. Spilling a little coffee on her bag isn't the end of the world."

I can't say I feel bad about it now. Not after she lectured me on how expensive the black leather bag was when I accidentally tipped her husband's coffee onto it. He, on the other hand, told me it was no big deal. I refilled the coffee as I was berated by the woman at his side.

Bea turns toward me with her hands on her hips. "That woman is always harping on someone when it comes to her husband. I never understood what he saw in her. A pretty face, I suppose, when you look past the scowl."

I can't help but crack a smile despite how much energy it takes. Between the rising headache in my temples, the stomachache making me queasy, and the constant ache in my lower back, I've had a rough day. Elena has talked my ear off to the point that I haven't had one second of peace since I arrived. And because I didn't want to admit just how off I felt, her nonstop play-by-play on her day worsened the growing throbbing in my skull.

The teen huffs. "I thought we weren't allowed to gossip about the customers."

Sipping my tea to hide my trembling lips, I hear Bea reply with a tart "I own this place, child. I can do as I please."

Her granddaughter grumbles under her breath before heading out to the main room to start to clean up.

I shift in my chair, trying to swallow down the threatening nausea. I've never been a huge fan of tea, and every sip makes me want to gag. But it has eased my stomach, so I power through until the cup is empty. "Is there anything you need help with back here before I go help her?"

Bea stares at me, her eyes narrowing a bit as she scans my face, then down the entirety of my body. She's been eyeing me throughout the day without saying a word, and I haven't asked what's on her mind. "Might as well go out there or Elena will drag her feet to get extra hours. She thinks her first car will be brand new, so she wants to earn all the money she can. Don't have it in me to tell her that her mom will never let her get one."

"A car?"

"A *new* one," she corrects. Shaking her head, she glances toward the girl in question. "I know for a fact that she scratched her mother's car while practicing three-point turns. Then dented her father's trying to parallel park."

I cringe. A new car definitely wouldn't be ideal for her then. "I'll go make sure everything is cleaned up."

I set the cup in the sink and head back out to see Elena aggressively scrubbing the counter like she's got a vendetta against it. I approach her, grabbing one of the coffeepots with barely half a cup left in it and dumping it into the sink. "You good over there?"

For once, the teen is uncharacteristically quiet. It makes me look over my shoulder at her to see if she's okay. Her movement pauses before she sighs and keeps scrubbing. "Grandma doesn't think I'm responsible enough to handle a new car. I thought if I worked hard, I could prove to her and my parents that I deserve one."

I start washing out the pot. "I don't think you have to worry about proving you deserve one, Lena. They just want to make sure whatever you get is...sturdy." I can feel her rolling her eyes at my careful choice of words. "Plus, car insurance isn't cheap for new drivers. They're going to want to make sure you're covered and safe."

"You sound like them," she mumbles.

I move from one machine to the next. "It isn't a bad thing that they care about you. My parents were the same way when I started driving. The day after I got my license,

I hit a deer and messed up the bumper so bad it cost almost a grand to fix."

"*A grand*? Like, one thousand dollars?" she all but gasps.

It still makes me flinch to think about. "It was bad. I thought I was going to be grounded for months, but my parents were just glad I was okay and had insurance on the car."

While I have my issues with my parents, they've never made me feel unloved. The few times I've messed up, like the deer incident, they didn't make a huge deal out of it. They didn't yell or fight or anything I was used to from them. They rushed to the scene of the accident and hugged me tighter than I'd ever been hugged by either of them because they were worried I'd gotten hurt and were grateful I wasn't.

Elena is quiet again. Then, "You haven't said much about them. I know people are talking about their...uh..."

"You can say divorce. It isn't like it's a secret. Trust me when I say that sometimes people are better off without each other. They're healthier."

"Is that why you broke up with Caleb?"

I freeze at the question, hands stilling on the pot handle my fingers are tightly wrapped around. There's no easy way to explain why I did what I did without giving too much away.

It's beyond fear. It's reality.

"Sorry," she says. "People say I'm too nosey for my own good. You guys were really cute is all. I was thinking you'd get married and make adorable little—"

"Elena," Bea chides, cutting off her granddaughter. It's nothing I haven't heard before, but it doesn't hurt any less to hear. "Read the room, child. Enough talking. More cleaning."

My stomach hurts replaying all the times I thought I'd have that future too. That was when I was a teenager, expecting to be like everybody else who was young and in love.

Before the future became *real*. Plausible.

"I don't think that future is very likely anymore" is what I tell Elena before tuning out everybody around me to finish my shift trapped in the depths of my own mind.

Chapter Thirteen

CALEB

SPENDING THE BETTER PART of the last three and a half years living with a bunch of horned-up, cocky football players meant hearing and seeing it all. Whenever one of them would go through a breakup, there'd always be somebody telling them to get under somebody new to get over whoever they're stuck on.

I gave advice to anybody who asked for it that I'd like to think was reasonable, not solely based on sex. Ironically, now that I've moved out and live on my own without anybody pestering me with sage wisdom, I find myself using the physical stuff to get through all the other tangled bullshit inside my head.

Slowly peeling the comforter off my body, I creep out of bed and glance over my shoulder at the raven-haired beauty sleeping soundly on her stomach. The comforter has fallen halfway off her naked body, showing off the small tattoo of an open birdcage on her shoulder and the script running down the length of her spine that's from her favorite Edgar Allan Poe poem.

The first time we slept together, we lay in bed while I grazed my fingertips along the letters and listened to her tell me about the other tattoos she wants to get. She loves literature, flowers, and music, so she wants all her favorite things represented. When she asked if I ever wanted any, I told her I couldn't think of anything permanent that I'd want immortalized on my skin.

It's not entirely the truth.

A long time ago, I thought about going with Aiden Griffith to get some work done when he was getting his Captain America shield filled in by a popular artist in the next town over. I had every intention of getting Raine's name until the guy who owned the parlor talked me out of it. "You never know what the future will bring, my man. I've seen a lot of people come to regret ever getting names tatted on them."

I wanted to get it ten times more just to prove I wouldn't be one of those people. The only reason I didn't go through with it is because it was a cash-only studio and I had none on me at the time. When he asked if I wanted to make an appointment to come back, I told him I'd call.

Guess that was fate's way of stepping in.

Gathering my things, I start dressing on the other side of the room and peeking at the girl hugging a pillow on the bed. I never stay the night. It's why I never invite her to my place. I know I'd feel bad kicking her out when all was said and done. The thought of sharing my space with someone new sends me in a panic spiral, especially because Emma and I aren't exclusive. And as much as I have a feeling she wants to be, the only thing I can promise her is taking it a date at a time.

I'm slipping on my boots by the door when Emma comes to, groggily asking, "Are you leaving already?"

Glancing at the time on her microwave, I wince at how late it is. "You've been asleep for a while. It's almost two. I've got a test in the morning, so..."

She never says if she wants me to stay and never bothers asking. Maybe she knows she'd be setting herself up for disappointment.

Walking over, I bend down and press a quick kiss to her head. "Go back to sleep. I know you're off tomorrow. You could use all the rest you can get."

Emma watches me for a second before sitting up, lifting the comforter to cover her bare chest. She looks like she's about to say something else but settles with "Good luck on your test."

I smile, pecking her lips before grabbing my keys from my sweatshirt pocket. "Thanks. I'll let you know when I get home."

All she does is nod, and I feel those eyes follow me as I make my escape out the front door of her apartment.

Do I feel bad for ditching her every time we hook up? Yes. She's the only person I've slept with besides Raine. And despite the breakup, it still feels like I'm cheating on Raine by sleeping next to somebody else. The ridiculous thought digs its claws in as I drive home, walk into my apartment, and listen to the silence I'm surrounded by.

One of these days, I'll sleep over at Emma's. If she'll let me. But maybe by then she'll be sick of my back-and-forth, and I wouldn't blame her.

I'm sick of it too.

And while I don't want things with us to end, I wouldn't hold it against her if she told me she was done.

This time, I'd let her walk away.

~

The storm echoes throughout the valley, causing me to shift for the tenth time in bed, praying for sleep to come. I've been lying here for a couple of hours, and just when I'm about to drift off, a new boom of thunder rattles the windows and startles me back to consciousness.

I used to stay up just so I could watch the storms from the enclosed porch on my parents' house. Dad would always be outside on the swing he loved rocking with Mom in, and we'd sit there in silence as we witnessed Mother Nature's wrath. It was somehow peaceful to see how the lightning could brighten the otherwise pitch-black sky and how the air had a certain welcoming scent to it as the rain trickled down onto the tin roof.

Dad even talked Raine into sitting out there with us whenever she was over for dinner or to have family game nights with us. He'd always make a joke about how the sky was calling for her whenever it would open up. "The sky is trying to get your attention, Raine," he'd always say, nudging her playfully. "Are you going to answer?"

Once, he convinced us to go out and dance in the rain. Raine was laughing at my horrible dance moves, telling me I should leave all the sideline entertainment to DJ, since he tended to show off his moves during halftime. I remember the day it was pouring down and Raine got my dad to not only go out with her but dance with her too.

It made me think of what our wedding would be like. She'd dance with her father, I'd dance with my mother, and maybe Dad would ask her for a chance to dance with him before I stole her away for the night.

We'd never have that now.

The nostalgic feeling of those late nights on the porch is long gone, replaced by dread over how different everything is now. It weighs down my stomach until I'm giving up on sleep, tossing the thin blanket off me and walking over to my small apartment window to see what mayhem is ensuing outside. The front lawn has a huge puddle in the middle of it, and one of my trash cans is tipped over from the howling wind.

It's late in the year for storms like this, but it's better than the snow we got in October a few years ago. People were trick-or-treating with winter coats on over their costumes, collecting candy in between snow squalls.

When I walk into the tiny kitchen, I hear the *drip, drip, drip* that's definitely not coming from the sink faucet. Flicking on the light, I do a quick examination of my surroundings before turning toward the open living room. The space is crowded by the big couch that was given to me by a friend of the family and a cheap TV stand I bought online with an eight-year-old television on it.

And right above that old piece of technology is a huge water stain with droplets slowly coming through the bubbled ceiling.

"Fuck," I curse, rushing over to unplug my TV and pull the stand away from the leak. I clench my eyes closed before taking a few deep breaths to calm myself down. Mom always told me that getting worked up gets you nowhere fast, and it's obvious that there's nothing to be done about what's already damaged.

So instead of the sleep I desperately need before my first exam bright and early tomorrow morning, I spend the next two hours fixing the leak. Which includes going to the family hardware store, getting materials to patch the roof, and waiting out the storm in order to actually cover the damn thing before it does more damage inside.

By the time five a.m. rolls around, I'm so tired I can't keep my eyes open. I hop into the shower to warm up from the cold air, spend the next twenty minutes trying to dry up the wet carpet, then pass out on the couch.

It feels like seconds later when my phone alarm goes off, telling me to get my ass up for class. And for the first time, I don't. I don't know if it's the exhaustion weighing down my limbs or the fogginess making logic run for the hills, but I don't care about my test. Or about school or about my shift later at the store.

All I want is sleep.

An extra five minutes.

Maybe ten.

Turning my alarm off, I doze back off, not thinking about much of anything, much less the constant noise of my phone going off. Subconsciously, I know I'll regret choosing to ignore my responsibilities when I wake up. But for the first time in a long time, I manage to have a completely undisturbed sleep.

No dreams.

No nightmares.

Nothing. And maybe complete silence is what I need, even if I can only get it in small doses.

When I wake up a little while later, there are eight missed messages on my phone. Since none of them are from my frantic mother, I choose not to go through them. It probably makes me a little bit of an asshole, especially because I saw Emma's name in the mix, but I can't gather enough energy today to care about anything or anyone.

By the time I slide into my usual seat minutes before my

last class starts, I'm getting a few stares from people who I typically beat here.

DJ, who's taking a few of the same classes as me this semester, throws a wadded-up piece of paper at me from the row over. He leans forward once he captures my attention, his brows drawn up. "Everything good?"

I lift my shoulder and nod as if to say *same old, same old.* There are never new updates anytime one of my friends asks how I'm doing these days. The default answer is "fine" or "okay" with an occasional "tired" mixed in if I feel like being halfway honest, but most times I lie through my teeth because I've always been the friend who's had his shit together.

DJ exchanges a look with somebody on the other side of him before turning back to me, slowly nodding. "Okay, well…good."

He's being weird. Then again, that's not entirely abnormal for DJ. "Did I miss anything this morning? I emailed Kroger about the exam and haven't heard back from him. Sort of hoping he lets me make it up."

My friend sits back. "He isn't a total douche, so I don't see why he wouldn't. You've had a lot going on."

I make a face, not wanting to let my father's condition be the reason I blow off school. Realistically, today shouldn't have happened. I realized that when I woke up feeling like shit about skipping class when I could have chugged a cup of coffee or three and made it in. I even studied for this exam unlike others I've gone in and half-assed, hoping for a decent grade.

Cracking my sore neck because of the shitty position I slept in on the couch, I blow out a breath and grab my notebook. "I don't know. Neilson knew about everything and acted like he couldn't give less of a shit this summer. I almost asked him for an extension once, but the man wouldn't let me get the question out. It's like he knew the second I walked up to him."

One of our other classmates, Jeremy, snorts at the drop of the well-known professor's name. "That's because Neilson has a rep to protect. Man was carved from Satan himself. He gave me a C on a project during undergrad. *Me.*"

I'm glad I'm not the only one who rolls my eyes at Jeremy's remark. DJ does too when we share a look. The kid has been full of himself since we've known him, which has been three years. A lot of people who stuck around for their MBA also did undergrad at Lindon and shared a lot of classes together. There are some people, like Jeremy and his big head, I wouldn't mind if I never saw again.

I'd take Professor Neilson over him any day because at least the elderly man who takes no shit also rarely speaks it.

"I'm just saying," Jeremy keeps going, leaning back and crossing his arms. "If I could get a grade like that, it's obvious the man doesn't give a damn about anybody. With Kroger, you're basically going to be handed an A because he'll probably feel bad for you."

Eye twitching, I focus solely on the notebook I'm opening to last class's scribbles.

DJ asks Jeremy, "When you talk, do you ever hear what a douchebag you sound like? Or is it sort of an 'in one ear and out the other' situation?"

I don't hold back the snort as I grab my pen from my pocket and jot down today's date in the corner. I'm tempted to tell DJ to stop while he's ahead because it isn't worth dealing with Jeremy, but hearing the idiot try to talk his way out of this conversation is the most entertainment I'll get all day.

That is until Jeremy says "What? I'm being honest. People aren't going to treat a student whose dad is dying like anybody else. He's going to get some free passes. Not even professors want that kind of bad karma on them."

The room grows quiet.

Deathly quiet.

No murmurs.

No conversations from anybody.

Slowly, I look up at the guy who knows he fucked up. When I lock eyes with him, it looks like he's trying not to shit himself.

The worst part is that people do pity me.

They've pitied me since they heard the news. The number of times I've been told "sorry" has made me fucking immune to the word. I don't even want to hear it anymore in any context, which is probably why hearing it from Raine didn't mean shit the way it would have before Dad's diagnosis.

Their condolences don't change anything, least of all the fact that my dad *is* dying. But does that mean I want to hear people say it aloud and act like I'm asking for a handout? Like I expect one?

No.

Fuck no.

"Jeremy," I say in a low, slow tone, "I'm usually not one to start shit, but I am the one who tends to end it. So for once in your life, I suggest you shut the hell up before I make you shut up. I'm in no goddamn mood today for your bullshit. Understand?"

The tension in the room grows, so much so that the professor walks in and stops to study everybody because he can sense something is about to happen. When he sees the stare-off between me and the douche who might have just pissed himself, he clears his throat and makes his way up to the front.

"Sorry I'm late," he says, still eyeing us in the back. When his focus turns to me specifically, I can't help but feel my jaw clench. "I wasn't expecting you, Caleb. I figured you'd be dealing with…" His words trail off, finally snapping me away from Jeremy.

The confusion on my face must be obvious because DJ cuts in with "The store."

Dumbly, I repeat, "The store?"

More people stare.

My friend's eyes grow wary. "Dude, didn't you look at your phone? I figured that's why you weren't in class this morning. People at Bea's were talking about it. Matt and I tried getting ahold of you too, but you didn't answer, so we figured you were already there with the cops. Raine said she reached out to you after she called the police."

I pull out my phone and notice just how many messages there actually are that I've been avoiding since I woke up earlier.

"Fuck," I say, darting up and collecting my things and ignoring the chair clattering to the floor behind me.

I read one message.

Then another.

Another.

Raine did, in fact, message me three different times before calling. So did Ronny. DJ. Matt. There are a few other people who are friends of the family who reached out, including a retired cop who Dad always played poker with on Friday nights before he was too sick to go.

DJ stands too. "I'll come with you."

I don't have time to argue as I walk out of the classroom, feeling like the biggest dickhead known to man. The one time I take a fucking break, and the hardware store is robbed because I obviously didn't lock the fucking door behind me when I left this morning.

DJ says, "Take a deep breath, man. You look like you're about to explode."

I stop abruptly, turning to him faster than he's expecting. "That's because I am. *One* day, DJ. I wanted one goddamn day where I didn't have to deal with anything. I'm running on little sleep and coffee fumes. And look what happens when I try being selfish. I ignore a shit ton of people who've been trying to get in contact with me for *hours* so that they don't have to reach out to my parents and add more shit onto their plates. The store is my responsibility now."

I swipe a hand through my hair, feeling how shaky my palm is from the anger. From the *guilt*.

Slowly, DJ takes the keys dangling from my free hand. "I'm driving because you're going to rage the entire way there. The last thing you need is to damage your truck or, God forbid, get yourself or someone else killed because you're pissed."

I don't fight him on it because I know he's right. The last thing I want to do is get myself into a bigger hole than I'm already in.

"Caleb!" I hear, stopping me from opening the door to my truck. When I turn, I see Raine jogging over to DJ and me.

I hold up my hand, wanting to avoid any extra mixed emotions right now. "I can't handle any more bullshit today, Raine, so whatever you have to say needs to wait."

She stops abruptly a few feet away, lips parted in shock at my cool tone.

DJ curses under his breath before shoving me toward the passenger door. "Get in the truck, dumbass, before you say more shit you're going to regret later."

Right before I climb in, I see Raine's crestfallen expression as she takes a step back. I get in and slam the door shut with a groan, knowing that was uncalled for.

DJ walks over to her, but I don't know what they say. Her eyes go to the truck for a brief moment before she shakes her head, turns around, and walks away. My best friend walks over, climbs into the driver's side, and shoots me a look.

"I don't want to hear it," I grumble, pinching the bridge of my nose.

He scoffs. "I hope you realize what a dick move that was when you clear your head. She was just checking in on you because she cares. Jesus."

That hits me square in the gut, which I have a feeling he was going for. "I'll talk to her when I can."

The only thing I give him is a noncommittal noise when he replies, "You can't do it all, Cal. You're not a superhero, and nobody expects you to be."

I harrumph, looking out the window as we drive down the main drag and thinking about how much easier it'd be if I were one.

Chapter Fourteen

RAINE

I<small>T'S BEEN TWO DAYS</small> since I spoke to the police officer about the hardware store, and I still haven't heard a single thing from Caleb after trying to catch him on campus. Did I expect a thank-you for letting him know? No. But I figured I'd get some sort of update to make sure he was okay. I was willing to give him the benefit of the doubt for snapping because he was obviously having a bad day, but the silent treatment is hard not to be upset about when he's been using it to avoid talking about us having sex too.

Grumbling over my sour mood, I check my phone for the third time in an hour and a fourth right after just in case he texted me and I didn't see it. When I come to terms with the fact that he wants nothing to do with me, I decide to power off my cell and stuff it into my book bag. I can't spend another day obsessing over the situation. Namely, Caleb.

I spot Skylar walking into the library a few minutes later, her eyes dancing along the sections of seating until they land on me. She waves and walks over to where I've got my textbooks all set up in front of me on the table with a perky smile on her face.

"Hey," she greets. Her eyes study the mess of school material in front of me. "That all looks intense. I'm glad I ruled out psychology as a major if that's the reading material."

I grab the apple-cinnamon flavored coffee I bought from Bea's after my shift this morning and take a sip. "Yeah, classes are a little rough this semester," I admit.

Mom had told me she didn't want to be part of my project in the most Janet Copelin way possible. "I don't need to be part of your little therapy session, Raine. I've got other things to focus on."

It wasn't necessarily a surprising reaction to hear since she rarely helped me with homework in the past, but I would have liked her to at least entertain helping me. "How are you doing?" I ask, gesturing toward the seat across from me. "You can sit if you'd like. I haven't seen DJ yet if that's who you're looking for."

Last time I crossed paths with DJ, he told me to give Caleb time. "He's going through it, Raine," he'd told me. "I'm not saying that what he said was cool, but we both know that's not him. Just do me a favor when he comes to his senses? Make him grovel."

DJ was trying to make me feel better, but it didn't work. Because I know if anyone should be groveling for all the horrible stuff that's happened between us, it's not Caleb.

Skylar's sweet nature and DJ's typical goofy personality have made me feel a little relieved that the people I've known for years aren't just going to drop me out of their lives completely because of my relationship shift with Caleb.

Mom told me not to worry about that stuff before the semester started. "Your true friends will never leave," she said. I guess she'd know. I watched the small group of people who she and Dad hung out with on occasion split between them, like their friends had to choose sides with the divorce too. Mom spent weeks complaining to me about it, and there was nothing I could say to make it better.

Skylar sits down, dropping her things onto the small corner of the table I'm not taking over. "I'm not sure he can come. He told me he was with Caleb at the store. They're doing more cleanup today after the police came to try getting fingerprints and look over the security footage. Did you see who did it? Danny told me it looked bad when they went in the other day."

Knowing he saw the damage and still didn't reach out only makes me feel worse, but I try not to let her see that. "I didn't go in or anything, but it didn't look like there was anybody inside when I passed by. The police got there pretty quickly, and they didn't mention anything either."

She nibbles her bottom lip. "That sucks." A brief pause surrounds us. When she shifts and looks around, I'm wondering what's on her mind. Then she says, "Can I ask you something?"

I already know what it's about. "Sure."

"Do you miss him?"

The question sinks in almost instantly, but not as quickly as the answer. "Every day."

We share a look, and I note the confusion on her face. I understand. It's the same look most people give me over the situation. How could I not miss someone I spent so much time with over the years? Losing Caleb felt like losing a piece of me.

"Did you date anyone before DJ?"

Skylar looks at me, her brow unfurrowing as if she

understands where I'm going with this. "Not anything serious, but yes. I had one relationship before him."

I nod. "I haven't. It's always been…" Well, it hasn't always been Caleb, but if I brought up Cody, people probably would think I broke up with Caleb solely because I wanted to explore other options.

Did I try using that as an excuse when Caleb pressured me for a reason after I told him no? Yes, I did. It was a cop-out that I'm not proud of, but I thought it was better than the truth.

Maybe if he was angry at me for worrying I was settling down with the wrong person, he'd be able to move on with someone who can give him the legacy he's always wanted to build. The children and house with a white picket fence.

It hurts way too much to think about, but that's my burden to bear. Not Skylar's, Caleb's, or anybody else's problem.

"I have a lot to figure out, Sky. Things I wish I could have done before he asked me to marry him and things I'm probably still avoiding a little. But some feelings have to be dealt with on your own without any other influence, and I knew I wouldn't be able to sort them out if we were together. I was scared to tell him yes, and the next thing I knew I was being escorted away from the football field by my family."

I'm still mortified by the experience. I'd rather not think about it, but more times than not it's the last thing that replays in my head before I manage to sleep at night. His face is melded into my mind, the expression he gave me a combination of pure shock and heartbreak.

The blond across from me reaches over and squeezes my hand once. "I'm sure it couldn't have been an easy choice. Do you think you two will ever…?"

That's the million-dollar question that everybody wants to know. Do I have feelings for him? Yes. But has anything really changed since turning him down? No. Because he doesn't know how deep my problems go—the same ones that would inevitably impact him if I were finally honest with him about them. Where would that leave us even if we jumped back in headfirst? Not anywhere healthy.

"It's not really up to me," I admit, rubbing my arm before picking up a highlighter.

We fall back to silence again save the people talking at the tables around us.

Skylar clears her throat after a few minutes and pulls out her phone. "Olive and I are planning on going to this open mic night at Hulbert. I'm not sure if that's your thing, but you're welcome to come."

I nibble my bottom lip. "When is it?"

"Thursday night." She smiles. "I don't know if you've got any other plans since it's Halloween. We were planning on meeting at Bea's, actually, to grab food beforehand. We could all meet up and then head over if you're not working a shift that night."

I won't know my schedule until tomorrow, which I tell her. "I'll let you know," I promise. It might be good to go out. I've had people invite me to things before, but usually Caleb and I would do something else. I never thought he'd enjoy open mic nights. Most of his friends would tease the people brave enough to perform or crack jokes there, and even though he's not like them, I never wanted him to be bored. So I didn't bother going to stuff like that.

Her eyes go down to her phone before that friendly smile grows into something much bigger. "Danny is on his way now. He's trying to convince me that we need a tortoise. Long story. I'll fill you in another time. Anyway, let me know about open mic night when you know your schedule."

I give her a nod before waving her off when DJ walks in a few minutes later. He puts his arm around Skylar's shoulders, tugging her into a frontal hug and pressing a kiss against the top of her head. Those two have been cute since day one. There's still a tiny piece of jealousy that makes itself known when it has no right. When I force myself to look away, I notice the new person who walked into the library after them.

And he's looking right at me.

I expect him to walk away or head toward the table Skylar and DJ have sat down at. Instead, Caleb beelines right for me. I have to swallow the weird choking noise when he stops right where Skylar was sitting only minutes before. He doesn't sit down, simply stands and watches me watch him back.

Then he says, "Thank you."

Two words.

I fidget, feeling eyes on us.

I wanted to hear from him, but I'm surprised it's face-to-face. A text would have been better. A lot less personal.

His lips press together as he dips his chin and picks at his shirt. "Some things are better said in person," he says as if he can read my mind. "This is one of them. I appreciate you calling the cops and getting them there before more could be taken at the store. I know that's probably what you came over to say before I acted like an ass toward you the other day. You didn't deserve that."

"Is everything okay?" For some reason, I feel the need to elaborate. "With the store, I mean. Did they get any money or do a lot of damage?"

He shifts on his feet uncomfortably. "It will be. They couldn't get into the register, but they took some expensive stuff to make up for it." His eyes finally lift to mine before a small sigh escapes those downturned lips. "It was my fault," he mumbles.

My brows pinch. "How?"

"I forgot to lock the door. I was tired and not thinking straight."

I frown. "You can't blame yourself for other people's actions. They chose to rob the place whether the door was locked or not. Do the police have any leads?"

"The cameras picked up a little bit. It's fuzzy, but it's something to work with."

All I can manage is "Good."

His throat clears. "Anyway, I just wanted to say thank you. So…"

"Yeah."

"Okay."

He still stands there.

I still stare at him.

"I know you don't want to," I say quietly, feeling a little awkward for bringing it up, "but I still think we should talk about what happened between us. Just for some clarity."

He doesn't look particularly thrilled at the idea of discussing our hookup, even two months after it happened. Not that I can say I am. "Look, it was a one-time thing. Right? I just assumed we were both in the moment because we're not together anymore. I was emotional. I don't know what else to say about it."

It takes me a few seconds to figure out how to respond, feeling the weight of his uncertainty absorb into my chest. I don't know what I expected him to say, but it wasn't that.

"Right." Why does my heart ache so much right now? "Yeah. It didn't mean anything. I guess I just wanted to clear the air. Make sure you're...okay."

Okay is the last thing Caleb is, and we both know it. The two of us haven't changed and neither has our situation.

Caleb begins to say something else, his lips parting, before he apparently second-guesses himself and turns to leave.

"Wait," I call out before he can walk away again. He glances at me hesitantly. This time, it's me who struggles to find the right words. Shoulders drooping, I shake my head and tell myself to stop being a coward. "If you need anything, let me know. I know we're not together, but I can help clean up the store if you haven't finished yet. I'm still here."

I'm still here for you is what I don't say, hoping he'll read between the lines.

His lips press together before he nods once and says, "Okay."

Okay. That word again. Something tells me he won't be reaching out for help.

From the corner of my eye, I see both Skylar and DJ giving me sympathetic looks when Caleb walks away. I bet that's how they looked at him the day of graduation when I was the one doing the escaping.

~

For the longest time, there were only three places in Lindon that I considered my safe places—Bea's Bakery, the football house where Caleb and some of his teammates used to live, and the campus library. I never told people that my parents' constant arguing was a reason I preferred staying out of the house for as long as I could growing up or why I settled for the sorority house even though the girls were catty and never had anything nice to say about one another half the time. The football house was a peaceful getaway, and I enjoyed spending time there, even when the boys would get a little too competitive playing video games or tease me and Caleb if we went upstairs.

Living back at home is different now. It's quieter without Dad and a little isolating because Mom stays busy with her tailoring gigs that leave us on opposite sides of the house when we're both here. I thought I'd like it that way, but I was wrong.

When I walk into the kitchen, I see a note on the whiteboard on the fridge that says Mom went to meet with Dad and their lawyers.

Grabbing a water, my keys, and my bag, I head out the door and offer a small smile to the elderly man next door. Mr. Applebee barely talks to anybody, but he's always outside working on his beautiful garden. Sometimes I wonder what his life story is, but Mom and Dad always told me to mind my own business instead of asking a million questions like I tend to do.

"Hi, Mr. Applebee," I greet in passing, noting the bright red tomatoes he's picking from what must be the last crop of the season. "It looks like you've got a better crop this year. I heard people saying they were having issues with their tomatoes last year because of the bugs."

When I was a teenager, my parents thought it'd be fun to have our own garden. We spent weeks building a section in the backyard for it, with the help of Caleb and his father at the hardware store supplying helpful tips, tricks, and supplies, only for all the plants to die looking sad and diseased. Mom said she didn't want to waste more time and money trying to grow anything else, so the cute garden bed we spent so much time on is now all grown in.

My neighbor simply nods once and goes back to the tomatoes. I shrug it off and head down the sidewalk, hoping a walk in the fresh air will help me clear my head and get me in the mindset to get some work done. I have a pile of reading to do by tomorrow that I've barely touched because my mind has been elsewhere.

I'm walking toward the entrance of the local park that has my favorite walking trail when I see a dog sniffing one of the garbage cans on the corner. There's no collar on the tiny gray puppy that can't be more than a couple of months old.

"Hey, cutie," I greet, cautiously approaching the friendly dog. It looks like it could be some sort of pit bull mix. Whatever it is, it's adorable. I crouch down and reach out carefully to let it sniff my fingers before a cute pink tongue darts out and licks me. "You're far too little to be wandering out here alone, especially by the busy street."

I glance around to see if anyone is searching for him and frown when I realize it's only me out here. Sitting down on the concrete, I watch as the animal slowly approaches me with a little waddle that makes me smile.

The smile grows when he steps onto my leg and wags his tail so hard his butt wiggles. "Do you believe in fate? I've always wanted a dog of my own, and maybe now is the perfect time."

A cute, high-pitched bark comes from my new four-legged friend currently standing in my lap. It makes me laugh as I scratch between his ears and see him wag his tail harder.

I've always said I wanted to get a dog when I got my own place, but I never lived anywhere that had room for one. Caleb and I discussed what breed would be good or what place we should adopt from, but we never made it to that point.

"*It'd be like our baby,*" I tell Caleb, looking up at him from where my head rests on his lap. "*Corgis are pretty cute. Have you seen the one that's gone viral online? His accounts are all named Conner the Corgi. I spend way too much time watching the videos his owners make of him.*"

Caleb smiles down at me, passing me another handful of Milk Duds and moving hair out of my eyes. "Corgis are cute, but you know what's cuter?"

My face twists in consideration. "A bulldog? Frenchies are pretty adorable too."

He laughs. "I was thinking about an actual baby."

My lips twitch downward at the thought.

The appetite I had is squandered by the baby talk. Not because I hate babies but because I remember vividly what my doctor told me about having them years ago. After it happened. I don't like thinking about that.

Denial at its best.

Staring at the candy melting in my hand, I say, "We're only twenty-one. We've got a long time before we consider a baby. We're still babies ourselves."

He bends and kisses my temple. "You're right. But I think we're going to make some cute kids one day."

Throat tightening, I make a humming noise in feigned agreement. "Yeah. One day."

Maybe I should have just ripped the Band-Aid off and told him then. It was the first time Caleb ever brought up babies, but it definitely wasn't the last time. I'd always find a reasonable response.

We're still young.

We've got our careers to focus on.

We should get a dog first.

We need a house.

What about our student debt?

I knew those excuses would run out eventually. And they did.

I glance under the puppy to see if he is, in fact, a boy. Sometimes when I can't sleep at night, I'll google puppies for sale in my area to see what my options are. The price tags are the only real reason I haven't tried harder to actually get one. That and my mom always being hesitant about pets. When we lost our tiger cat, Murphy, years ago, she swore we'd never get another pet because it was too hard to see them go. Dad thought she was being a little dramatic, but I understood. Losing things you love puts a hole in your heart that never really heals no matter the amount of time that passes.

"Oh my God, you found him!" someone says frantically from behind me. I look over my shoulder to see a girl who looks around my age.

Dark hair, almost black. Tall. Pretty.

She stops beside me and squats down, fussing over the dog who's clearly happy to see her. "He got out of the yard earlier when I wasn't looking. I swear, I knew this one was going to be trouble as soon as he was born. Thank you *so* much for keeping an eye on him."

My chest deflates, along with the possibility of me being able to take this little guy home with me. "What's his name?"

The girl smiles at me, her eyes a unique shade of gray-blue that I haven't seen often. "He doesn't have one, actually. My parents' pit bull had an unexpected litter of puppies with the neighbor's dog, so my family told me not to name them or else I'd get attached. I already am though. How can you not be when you see that face?"

I turn back to the puppy in question. "So he's for sale?"

"Are you interested? My mom isn't sure what to price them at quite yet, but I can talk to her. You're Raine, right?"

My eyes widen at her guess.

"I've seen pictures of you," she admits. Before I can ask where she's seen photos of me, she stands and glances down at the puppy still on me. "Let me ask my mom about this troublemaker. Pitties don't sell well because of their reputation, so she may be willing to give you a really good price."

I carefully pick up the squirming puppy and stand up, passing him over to her. "I'd appreciate that. I can give you my number."

She waves me off. "I'll ask Caleb for it." Lips parting in confusion at the casual statement, I remain quiet until she decides to elaborate. "I work at the hospital. I'm one of his dad's nurses."

Wow. Small world. "That's a tough job, especially if you work with a lot of patients like him." The dying ones, that is. She has to be strong to cope with being surrounded by people you can't save.

She shrugs, her friendly expression not falling or morphing into anything else. "It can be, but I wouldn't trade it for anything. What's that saying? Everyone comes into your life for a reason, a season, or a lifetime. I'd like to think the patients who come into my life are there to make a difference somehow."

I find myself nodding along, a tight smile on my face despite the heavy feeling in the pit of my stomach. "I didn't catch your name," I tell her.

She holds out her hand. "Emma."

We're quiet for a moment before the puppy in her arms starts barking and squirming, demanding to be let down.

"You'd better get going before he pees on you. That'd be about my luck."

Her nose scrunches. "Trust me, it's already happened at least three times since the puppies were born. Pee everywhere. Then again, you never know what fluids you'll get on you in the hospital." She shrugs again. "I told myself it's practice for whenever I become a mom someday. Everyone says to get a dog before you have a kid, so you know what you're in for."

Clearing my throat, I say, "I'm just looking for a dog right now."

Emma laughs lightly. "You just went green. I'm teasing. I should have an answer about the puppies in the next week or two."

I watch her and my potential four-legged roommate walk away after waving them off.

Walking toward the trail, I find myself smiling at the step I'm finally taking to move forward after a little too long of sulking in the choices I made in the past. The hole in my chest is still there, but it doesn't feel as intimidating.

When I get home, I see a basket full of ripe tomatoes on the doorstep and a little note about the best ways to eat them. My smile widens in the direction of Mr. Applebee's house, knowing he's the one who brought them.

For the first time in a long while, I feel hope.

Chapter Fifteen

RAINE

Mr. Applebee is tending to one of his garden boxes when I round the white fence splitting our properties after another long day at work. I'm tired, my back hurts, and stress has given me another headache that makes my eyes ache.

"Thank you for the tomatoes," I tell my neighbor, stopping at the little gate door of his property. "I cut one up for BLT sandwiches."

My fingers smooth along the top of the fence. He built it all on his own. I remember when he and his wife, a cute little woman who couldn't have stood taller than four foot nine, spent two weeks painting it white a long time ago.

The elderly man looks up, pausing what he's doing with the soil. He doesn't say anything at first but eventually glances down at his dirtied gardening gloves with a short nod. "You're welcome."

His voice is gravelly. Nobody really hears it anymore since his wife passed years ago. For the most part, he keeps to himself. He gardens, he goes to the grocery store, and he walks to the cemetery a block away to visit the grave of the woman he loved. I'm not sure he has any family around, but if he does, they don't see him. Does he get any social interaction?

Mom told me not to bother him, but maybe he needs that once in a while. "What do you do in the winter when it's too cold to grow anything?"

Once again, he stops what he's doing to look up at me. Huffing out a sigh, he peels off his gloves and slowly pushes to standing. "Why do you want to know?"

I lift a shoulder innocently. "I like hearing people's stories. Did you know I'm in school for psychology?"

He drops the gloves into the wheelbarrow beside him. "I'm not looking for a therapist, young lady."

My lips curl in amusement. "That's good because I'm not a certified therapist. Not yet anyway. I'm working on it."

He stares at me.

My eyes go to my childhood home, which I'm sure is empty as always. I don't want to be alone right now. That means constantly thinking, and I want to shut my brain off for a little while.

I lean against the fence. "Can I ask you something?"

He closes his eyes for a second and walks around the garden box toward where I'm standing. "Well, nothing's stopped you from asking questions so far."

"Do you have any kids?" I ask, not remembering any growing up. They haven't always lived next door, but this was his home for a long time. "I know it's none of my business, but I've only ever seen you here. It must get kind of lonely. I get lonely sometimes."

Mr. Applebee glances off in the distance, gripping the top of the fence post. "When you get to be my age, loneliness is the least of your problems."

A heaviness weighs down my lips. "What if you didn't have to be lonely?"

His bushy white brows arch up.

"I've got a project for school I could use some help with," I tell him. "It'd be me bugging you with questions about relationships. I'd love to hear about yours with your wife. You two were always smiling no matter what you were doing."

A small smile appears on his face. "That was my Annemarie. She was the happiest soul put on this earth. Didn't matter what we were going through, she always had a positive outlook on life. She had a lot of goals she didn't get to accomplish. No doubt she would have changed the world if she'd had more time."

It makes my stomach fuzzy to hear the love in his voice while talking about her. "What do you say, then? Would you be interested in helping me? We can meet up somewhere. Maybe Bea's Bakery. Have you been? I work there, and we've got really good pastries and coffee. It'd be a peaceful place to work on the assignment."

My neighbor scrubs his jaw. "I don't know. I don't get out much…"

I perk up. "Which means this is the perfect opportunity for you to. Look, this assignment is worth a lot of my grade, and I still need two people to talk to for it. This will be perfect for both of us. And I'd really love to hear more about Annemarie."

He takes one more deep breath and dips his chin. "Fine. But I can't miss *Wheel of Fortune*. Haven't missed an episode yet and won't until the day I die."

I'll give him one thing: he's loyal.

I stand straighter and stick my hand out toward him. "That sounds like a fair deal, Mr. Applebee."

He stares at my hand for a second before shaking on it. "If we're doing this, you should probably call me Leon."

~

A white bag that smells like grease and fries is placed in front of me, making my eyes go up to my mother. "I know I said we'd try cooking something for dinner tonight, but it turns out you need actual groceries to do that," she says.

My lips twitch as I open the fast-food bag and peek inside. "Please tell me the chicken nuggets are for me?"

Mom rolls her eyes as she goes over to the sink and starts washing her hands. "Well, I don't eat them. That was always you and your father's thing. You two used to fight over which sauce was the best."

I grin, remembering all the petty arguments we'd get into. Mom would threaten to take away all our sauces if we didn't behave, and I'd laugh because I thought she was joking. But one time she actually did, and then she and Dad got into a fight about how he never acts his age and that he needs to grow up. The moment was spoiled after that.

"I always thought the barbecue was better until I tried them with ranch," I say, brushing off the thought.

Mom dries her hands and helps me distribute the food. "I don't understand why you're so obsessed with chicken. Especially nuggets and tenders. It's like you're reverting back to your childhood."

There are worse things I can be addicted to, so I'd say my love for all things chicken isn't all that horrible. "Have you heard from Dad lately? I know you saw him the other day."

Mom has Aunt Tiffany to talk to, but I want her to know I'm here too.

She sighs and steals a fry from one of the containers. "I spoke to him on the phone the other day. Be grateful you got out of a relationship, Raine. You're far too young to settle down anyway. You've got your whole life ahead of you. Plenty of time to make dumb decisions that won't cost you a lifetime."

My eye twitches at the passive-aggressive answer, and I wonder if she hears how hurtful it is. I'd hardly say her settling with Dad ruined her life unless she considers motherhood to be that strenuous. Some people could only wish for that kind of life. "Caleb and I are..." What are we? We're not friends, but we're not enemies. "I still have so much respect for him, Mom. Let's not disrupt that."

She unwraps her burger. "All I'm saying is that you did the right thing choosing yourself. It's far less drama, and you can focus on all the things you want to do with your life."

And she couldn't? "What would you have done if you didn't get pregnant with me?"

Her eyes lift to mine. "I don't think about that because it didn't happen. Best not to focus on what could have been."

There's no doubt in my mind that my mother loves me. Maybe she would have preferred having me a little later in life or having a child with somebody else, but she doesn't resent or regret having me. Still, hearing her dismiss her future simply because I exist doesn't sit well with me. It's not what I would want if I were in her shoes.

"You could still do something now," I tell her, picking at my nuggets. "I'm in college, Dad is doing his own thing. You've got all the time in the world to do whatever it is you wanted to before having me. So what is it?"

For a moment, she looks contemplative. I'm not sure she's going to answer when she sits down beside me and

147

picks up her food. "I've always wanted to travel, especially overseas. Get inspiration from fashion in Paris or Milan. I thought about opening my own boutique or thrift shop too, using my own designs and gathering vintage items. Something that showcased all the unique pieces you can't find in any other store around here."

There's a small smile on her face as she thinks about it, which makes me smile too. "I didn't know that. I could picture you in France."

She stares at her food, an absent look on her face. "Like I said, I don't like to focus on things like that. Sometimes we need to let go of our expectations because that's the only way to accept what our actual reality is."

I know it isn't my fault that she feels like she can't travel or buy her own boutique, but there's still a sadness that weighs me down hearing her say that. Her choices may have been what led her here, but there is always more than one piece to a puzzle to get the full image. I'm a factor in that.

Is that why I hurt Caleb and myself? Because I couldn't fully accept my reality? Or was it because I accepted it too quickly?

I suppose the endgame is all the same.

Mom sets down her partially eaten burger and points a fry at me. "I know you still think about him," she says. "It's all over your face. Take it from me, sweetie. Letting go of what's in your past is what helps you build a future. There's nobody to weigh you down that way."

Nostrils twitching, I manage a feeble nod even though I don't want to believe her. I want to tell her about Cody. About the night I woke up in a pool of my own blood. What would she do if she knew I drove myself to Planned Parenthood because I was too afraid to ask her to take me? Would she have scolded me for being irresponsible or comforted me? I wish I knew what the answer was, but I never know which way my mother might lean in the moment.

I know she's not totally wrong, but that doesn't mean I'm ready to release all the pent-up feelings—the sadness, the anger, the pity, the *love*—that I still feel for Caleb Anders.

That night, when I'm lying in bed and listening to the steady rain smack against the tin roof, I get a text that only feeds the rebellious feeling that goes against my mother.

Caleb: I can't sleep

I stare at the three words and wonder if more are coming. Had he meant to send that to me or to somebody else? A girl? Maybe one of his friends?

Eventually, I thumb out a reply.

Me: Me either
Caleb: The sky is calling you...

Swallowing at the words his father used to tell me, I watch as those three bubbles dance along the bottom of the screen as he keeps typing.

In my heart, I know what the next sentence will be.

Caleb: Are you going to answer it?

I sit up and look at the time on my phone. It's late, and I'd be dumb to go anywhere tonight, especially to see Caleb.

But I know when I throw the blankets off, examine my outfit, and glance over at my closest pair of shoes that I've made up my mind.

So I send another message to the boy who knows me better than anybody else in hopes he'll pull through.

Me: Meet me at our spot

If he doesn't come, maybe it's a sign that Mom is right. I'll need to let go. But if he's there…
I don't know what that means.
But it means something.

Chapter Sixteen

CALEB

OUR SPOT HAPPENS TO be the edge of Alden Field on the outskirts of Lindon where they set up flea markets and fireworks displays in the summer, Octoberfest in the fall, and sled races in the winter after the first big snowfall. It's a well-known area, especially to local teens who like to sneak off to smoke weed, set up bonfires near the woods, drink, and hook up.

Raine and I used to come here when we wanted privacy to look up at the stars or watch the storms that would whip through the area. And sure, we'd had our fair share of make-out sessions in the cab of my truck. Once the first move was made, it was hard *not* to make more.

Our first kiss was in this field, weeks after our first date at Birdseye Diner where we each got the chicken tenders basket from the kids' menu and an extra order of fries. Long gone was the version of me who could barely string together a sentence asking her out coherently, because Raine made everything so…easy.

That's always been part of her personality. There was comfort in any conversation I had with her back then. When did that stop? I've been racking my brain trying to come up with an answer, and I draw a blank every time. There were moments in the beginning of our relationship that were rocky because of how new it was, but by the time we went to college, I thought we were stable.

Caleb and Raine against the world.

Maybe it was the other way around.

I scope the area out as the rain comes down, splattering large droplets against the windshield of my truck. Was Raine up watching the storm too? Was she thinking about me, or trying not to the same way I've attempted to stop thinking about her? Turns out that's a hell of a lot easier said than done.

I probably should have left, knowing she was coming here, but this is one of my favorite places. It's calming despite all the memories I've shared with Raine here. It's where I come to think and be by myself whenever I have a spare moment when my apartment seems too daunting.

Still, temptation sinks its claws in like it always does when she's involved. And despite all the reasons why I should fight it, I let her back in.

A drug.

A weakness.

That's when I see her running across the muddied field in the rain, and my heart does the same damn thing it always has. It beats a little bit faster than the moment before because it doesn't know any better.

"Christ," I murmur. She has no umbrella, rain jacket, or boots.

I get out of the truck and jog over to the passenger side

with the hood of my jacket up, protecting me from the downpour, and open the door for her as she gets closer. "Are you crazy? Why didn't you drive?"

Raine doesn't get in right away. Hair wet and sticking to the sides of her face, she looks at me and lifts one of her shoulders. "I needed the fresh air. Plus, the car has been acting up, so it probably would have woken Mom up."

Heaven forbid Janet knows her grown daughter is leaving to see me. "Yeah, what a shit show that would be," I grumble.

I don't miss the frown weighing down my ex-girlfriend's face before she climbs into the truck. After closing the door behind her, I walk around the front again and get in the other side. Once my door is closed, we're bathed in silence with only the muffled sound of the rain pelting the metal sheltering us.

"Do you remember the first time we ever came out here?" she asks, voice quiet as she stares out the windshield.

Does she know she's shaking? I reach into the back to grab one of the spare shirts I always keep in here and pass it to her. "Dry off. It's cold out tonight."

I lean forward and turn the heat on, hoping it actually works. You never know what you're going to get with this twenty-plus-year-old Ford.

When I lean back, I watch her use my shirt to wipe off her face and arms, then squeeze her hair dry. "We were invited to a party out here," I finally recall, looking toward the spot where people still tend to congregate. "It was the first time you ever drank. You puked in your neighbor's bushes when I was trying to sneak you back inside your house."

She cringes. "Poor Mr. Applebee had to hose it off the

next day. I watched him from the living room window, too embarrassed to tell him it was me. That wasn't my proudest moment. I'm not sure why I kept drinking that night anyway. The beer was terrible."

My lips twitch upward despite me trying to fight the amusement. "It was room temperature and the cheapest kind they could find. But you stop tasting it the more you drink."

Raine fiddles with the borrowed shirt she's holding. "We kissed that night. Before the whole puking-in-the-hedges thing."

I lose my small smile. "I remember."

"Dance with me?" I ask Raine, pulling her off to the side. There are other people coupling up and dancing, some leaving to find a private spot, and a few others pouring more drinks.

We slow dance for a few minutes with her arms around my neck and my hands on her hips. Neither one of us can look away from the other.

I move first, only a little hesitant when I brush my lips against hers. They taste like beer and the reminiscence of the watermelon Chapstick I saw her put on earlier. It's a small kiss, minuscule really, but it doesn't feel that way.

It feels so much bigger.

Bigger than two fifteen-year-olds.

I would have kissed her longer, but then some of the guys I play football with whistle and catcall at us, making Raine's cheeks pinken.

I know in that moment I want a lifetime of kisses from this girl.

Raine lowers the shirt onto her lap. "I was so nervous that night."

My brows pinch. "Why?"

"Because I was worried that you were going to kiss me and I'd be bad at it since I'd never..." There's humor melded into those words that has her smiling at the memory. "I guess I drank so much for liquid courage in case you were going to make a move."

I snort. Maybe that was a sign all along. Anybody who needs to get drunk to kiss somebody else probably isn't going to last with them long-term.

Resting my head back against the seat, I close my eyes and heave out a deep breath. "This is probably a bad idea. Us here tonight."

I'm met with momentary silence. "If you think that, then why are you here?"

Pressing my lips together, I turn my head to look at the girl I can't stop thinking about no matter how hard I try. My first kiss. My first everything. What she doesn't know is that I was nervous as hell to kiss her that night too. I'd wanted to since the night we were put in a closet together all those months before.

She fidgets the longer I study her. Her hair isn't sticking to her cheeks anymore but pulled behind her ears. It always looks darker when it's wet, almost brunette, similar to the color of her eyes.

She's effortlessly beautiful no matter what, even without makeup and looking like my parents' dog Frank when he gets stuck out in the rain.

It hurts to be this close to her and still not have her at all.

"Caleb?" she asks.

My nostrils flare with a sudden burst of emotion that I try swallowing. Because I don't want to think about how beautiful she is. I want to remember how much she hurt me. How I'm with Emma now. How much easier it'd be if I could let everything we've been through go.

"My dad is dying," I say, voice cracking with weakness.

"And it feels like I can't keep my head above water long enough to breathe. Every time I think about him leaving us, I–I—"

I swipe at my face and try collecting my shattered thoughts before I start crying. I feel the tears pricking my eyes and heat creep up the back of my neck the longer I hold it in.

Crying shows your weakness. That's what's been drilled into my head by society. By all my football coaches who've ever told me not to let people know they've defeated me. I can be angry, but I can't give in.

Forcing another deep breath, I say, "I try not to think about it by keeping busy with school and the store, but there's always a reminder because everything I do is *because* of him." Closing my eyes and squeezing them shut, I whisper, "And I just need the thoughts to turn off for a while. So I shouldn't be here. But…"

But I don't have anywhere else I can go.

That's the excuse I make.

I *could* be at my apartment.

I *could* be with Emma.

I'm not though.

I'm with the one person whose touch physically calms me. One single brush of her hand against mine, and I melt into nearly a decade of memories. I've always been comfortable enough to tell her anything because she was the one person I could talk to about whatever weighed me down.

Now is no different.

Her fingers tug at mine until our hands are molded together so tightly nothing can get in between them.

"I meant what I said at the library," she tells me. "I'm here for you. For whatever you need."

Those words sink into my chest, jump-starting the tight organ in my rib cage that feels like it's going to explode the second her fingers dance up my arm and massage the tense muscles along the way.

Whatever you need.

What if I told her all I need is her?

I could risk it, but I don't know how much more disappointment I can take in this lifetime.

Suddenly, there's nothing innocent about the touches that we share. I lean in first, but Raine meets me halfway. That's when touching turns into kissing, which turns into moaning. One second she's in the seat beside me, the next she's straddling my lap.

Her damp shirt is off.

No bra.

My jeans are unbuttoned with the zipper pulled down.

Her leggings disappear.

No panties.

She hates wearing anything under her leggings because of panty lines, and it drove me fucking crazy. It was rare, but there were times we would sneak off for a quickie whenever she wore them because I knew all I had to do was peel down the body-hugging material.

My fingers grip the back of her head as the kiss goes on, her tongue twisting with mine and her body moving along the hard length freed from my boxers. I can feel how wet she is, how her breath shudders every time she glides along my shaft.

There's a brief nudge in my consciousness that tells me I should stop this from moving forward. For me. For Raine. For Emma. But do I?

No.

I bite down on her bottom lip when she grabs ahold of me and tries inching down my shaft. She's tight as hell, squeezing my cock and making it impossible not to groan as she works her way to the hilt. A pinch of pain tweaks her face, followed by a sharp intake of breath as she sits there for a few seconds, then starts to move.

"Wait," I tell her, squeezing her hips once. "Do I need to get a condom or...?"

We rarely ever used them because she was on the pill, which was why we got lost in the familiarity at the hardware store. But I know it's better to ask considering our situation now.

A flicker of sadness sweeps over her expression as her lips twitch downward. "We don't need one."

It's the answer I expect, but it doesn't match the dullness in her eyes where lust usually is whenever we're like this. "Raine—"

"No more talking," she tells me, cutting off the conversation before logic can seep in.

My body listens, shutting off my brain despite the warning alarms in my head.

It's a haze of desperation from there. The truck rocks, the glass fogs, and everything else around us fades away until all I hear are the little noises that escape her as she moves on top of me.

I let her take the lead, resting my hands on her hips and groaning every time she grinds and swivels until I'm jerking inside her.

"Going to come," I warn her, fingertips tightening into her flesh as she rides it out, gripping the seat behind my head and letting hers tilt backward as she lets out the sexiest moan that has me letting go.

I can feel her clenching around me, milking me of every last drop that spills inside her as she breaks apart when I work her clit.

It takes a few minutes to catch our breaths, her eyes dropping to mine to see one solitary tear roll down my cheek.

That tear holds a lot.

Says a lot.

Feels like a lot.

Weakness, weakness, weakness.

Swiping it away, I grab the shirt she used to dry off with and wipe both of us clean once she climbs off me, then toss it onto the floor and watch her redress. "Here," I tell her, passing the hoodie she took off me. "You shouldn't put your wet clothes back on or you'll get sick."

She stares at the offering like she can't believe we're here again but eventually takes it. "Thank you" is her whispered reply.

I want to say something, anything, but don't know what there is to say at all. I clear my throat and fight back the other tears that build in the backs of my eyes.

"You can cry around me," Raine tells me softly. "You're going through a lot right now."

All I can manage is a hoarse "I know."

I don't let myself be any more vulnerable than I already have been with her. I've given enough of myself to her tonight. I need to hold on to what's left.

"We shouldn't have done that" is my reply, clenching my eyes closed and pinching the bridge of my nose.

She's silent, causing me to open my eyes and look at her. Her lips are parted, her eyes distant as they quickly move toward the window.

We go back to silence, waiting until the windshield defogs before I drive her back to her parents' place.

I put the truck into park at the front curb. "We should have at least used protection," I murmur, not that it matters now. "I still want kids, but..."

She doesn't need me to tell her why that'd be a bad idea for us now.

Raine takes a deep breath before turning to me in the borrowed sweatshirt. She reaches over and cups my cheek, brushing her thumb along it. "I know you do."

My chest hurts as she drops her hand, opens the door, and slides out without another word. I watch in silence as she escapes into the house, shaking my head in disbelief.

Before I pull away, I get a text from Emma, drawing me back into the piss-poor reality I've created for myself.

Emma: Miss you xx

Chapter Seventeen

RAINE

THE GIRLS' NIGHT AT Hulbert with Skylar and Olive, Skylar's best friend, reminds me of what it's like to be a normal twenty-three-year-old girl again—the kind with friends who can talk about anything from potential puppy names to the current hockey season and everything in between. And despite the girls being careful not to broach the topic of boys, it still leaves me thinking about the brown-eyed one who's often in the forefront of my mind, especially after the night in his truck.

The first time I ever felt like I finally had some semblance of balance in my life was when Caleb and I were sixteen and sneaking around because my parents didn't want me dating. I had a friend *and* boyfriend wrapped all in one person. Somebody I could enjoy myself with even in the most boring situations. Like when the hardware store was dead, and we'd find innocent ways to pass the time that'd leave us laughing so loudly people would come in just to see what was so funny. Or little study dates doing geometry or biology that would end in little brushes of the hands, knees, or feet because we were both too shy to actually make a move.

Well, until the night at the field.

He was *my* person.

Nobody else's.

It wasn't until we were eighteen and both attending Lindon University that we realized nobody could stop us from being together. My parents always had something to say about it because they were worried I'd get distracted, but I knew myself better than that. And I knew Caleb would never stop me from achieving all my dreams.

We both wanted the best for each other.

That was why it felt empowering when those afternoon study dates at the pizzeria suddenly were being held at the campus library, and the house parties we'd sneak off to with almost-kisses in closets turned into campus bashes at one of the frat houses. There, a lot more liquid courage led to real kisses on the dance floor. But nothing could even begin to compare to our first kiss at Alden Field. We didn't have to hold back or have moments alone in his truck. We could just be…us. Anywhere. Everywhere.

Because of that all-consuming feeling, I don't regret hooking up with him again. If anything, it felt right. I wanted him, maybe even needed him in ways I didn't want him to know.

The moment we touched in his truck, we were us again, even if for only a small fraction of time.

Before college, it was hard to feel like everybody else because I'd be stuck at home listening to my parents bicker nonstop about the tiniest things. I didn't invite friends over because I was too embarrassed about Mom and Dad making a scene, and dating was a sore subject since the day I hit puberty, which meant not bothering to ask about boys because I knew what the answer would be. While everybody around me had a social circle that they'd have sleepovers with or go to birthday parties for, I was dreaming of the day I'd go off and carve my own life.

Caleb was always part of that because he'd always been there as my saving grace. He was the one consistent person I could depend on when I needed a break from my parents. He'd hold my hair back at parties when I decided to drink too much or carry me inside when I fell asleep during long drives. I barely missed a football game when he signed on to Lindon's team and still spent summers working at the hardware store with him and his parents.

His family became mine.

A healthier one that I wasn't used to.

But the problem with putting all your eggs in one basket is what happens after you drop them all.

I still love Caleb.

I love his heart.

I love his family.

I love everything he's ever done for me.

That's why I said no, so that I could give him the world back.

I still want kids...

I know you do.

"I don't think Raine is listening," Olive muses, tossing a balled-up napkin at me.

Skylar laughs. "She probably checked out after your ten-minute summary of *Star Wars* and why it's better than *Star Trek*."

Olive waves her off. "Ten minutes is impressive

considering how many movies there are in the franchise. And you obviously weren't listening because the whole point of my rant was that you *can't* compare them."

"Sorry," I apologize, rubbing my eyes. "It was a long day. Bea offered discounts on certain coffee and pastries for anyone who came in dressed up between twelve and five. The place was swamped."

It's hard to believe it's Halloween already, but here we are. When I walked in for my shift and Elena saw me without a costume, she made me wear cat ears and drew whiskers on my cheeks with eyeliner. She, on the other hand, was dressed to the nines as some sort of badass leather fairy that's supposedly based on a book series I haven't read.

"It's fine," Skylar reassures me. "We're glad you were able to come tonight."

"You still haven't answered the question. What color is the puppy?" Olive cuts in, sipping the Shirley Temple she ordered from the waiter dressed as Baby Yoda. "That could impact the name."

Skylar scoffs, peeling a piece off the blooming onion that's sitting in the middle of the table. "Says the girl who names everything after Marvel characters no matter what they look like."

"You can't tell me that my betta fish didn't look a *little* like Steve Rogers," she argues, causing me to smile.

"How can a fish look like Captain America?" I ask.

Skylar gestures toward me. "*Exactly*! See, she gets my point. Your fish looked like a fish. You should have named it Bubbles or Nemo or something."

Olive crosses her arms over her chest, which is covered in a Rangers hockey jersey that still somehow does little to hide her double Ds. Her brother signed on with the professional team after he graduated and has been getting a lot of airtime recently. She said she was dressed as his biggest fan for Halloween.

The hockey fanatic says, "I refuse to name any pet something that unoriginal." She focuses on me. "Don't let Skylar name your dog. It'll probably be something like Spot or Rover."

"Hey!" Skylar laughs, clearly not fazed by her friend's assumption. "I'd like to point out that your name is Olive. I don't think either of us are in the best place to name anyone or anything."

Olive starts to argue but stops herself, lifting her shoulders as if to say *true*.

I play with the straw wrapper I folded accordion style. "The puppy I saw was gray, but I haven't heard from Emma yet. So I might not even be getting him."

Both girls frown at me. Then Skylar says, "There's still time. Maybe she's busy. You said she knew Caleb, right? You could always ask him to put in a good word for you or something."

We didn't do a whole lot of talking the last time we saw each other, so I don't know if that's a good idea. Would I have a right to ask him for a favor? I'm not even sure I want to bring her up since she's helping take care of his father. It might be a sensitive topic. "No, I'll let it be. What's meant to be will happen, right?"

Each of them nods, but they look at me like I might break down at any second.

Thankfully, Skylar decides to change the subject. "I think you should come with me to the football party. Olive is coming, and Danny will be there. It'll be fun."

Clearing my throat, I grab my water and take a long

sip to quench my dry mouth. "I don't think that'd be a very good idea. I've been trying to give myself some room from…all that. Find my own people and give the guys some space. You know?"

Even though she doesn't seem happy about it, Skylar nods. "That's understandable."

"Agreed," Olive chips in.

Still, Skylar says, "But if Caleb is there, maybe it wouldn't be such a bad thing. You two are both on campus and the town is small. There aren't any rules saying you can't both be at the same place at the same time. Plus, Danny misses having you around. You're the voice of reason, and he really needs it sometimes."

My lips twitch. "Still trying to get you to agree to a tortoise?"

She blows out a breath. "Yep. I think it may be a losing battle at this point. He's hell-bent."

That's a conversation for another time, I guess. "All I want is to make sure Caleb is happy. And I don't know if he can be if I keep showing up places. I already took over Bea's. It's obvious he tries to avoid the place when I'm working. I know DJ and Matt like the coffee, but they don't drink two cups at a time, especially not one that's specifically Caleb's order."

Skylar winces. I'm sure she knows her boyfriend has been sneaking coffee and snacks to Caleb so he wouldn't have to see me. I get it. I'd probably do the same if I were him.

Olive decides to change the subject back to puppies. "I still think that you should consider something cool for your dog's name when you get one. Like Kylo Ren or Darth Vader."

That has me smiling for real this time, grateful neither of

these girls are giving me a hard time for the decision I made about Caleb.

They probably accepted I've made up my mind.

Now I just need my own mind—and heart—to accept it.

~

Elena is sitting on the counter during a slow time at the bakery and swinging her legs back and forth while hounding me with questions. "Why not? I could be a great test study."

I pull apart some of the croissant I took from the display and pop it into my mouth, praying I'm able to keep it down. After my night out at Hulbert with the girls, I went home and researched everything I'd need to get for a dog while nibbling on some of Mom's leftover Thai food. Since neither of us cooks, our fridge is full of takeout boxes. Now I'm guessing they had some old food we should have thrown out a while ago.

Regret has definitely settled into my stomach because I've been fighting the urge to vomit since I heated up the mango chicken. I couldn't afford to miss work, especially since I'm picking up my four-legged friend in a few hours. When Emma texted me before I left the open mic, it felt like fate was finally on my side.

I don't have Caleb anymore.

But I'll have *someone*.

A dog of my own like I always wanted.

Something else to focus on.

Shaking myself out of my thoughts, I pop another tiny portion of the croissant into my mouth and answer the teenager. "You're seventeen, Lena. What do you know about relationships?"

She scoffs, putting her hands on her hips in offense. "I watch reality TV, Raine. It's basically all the research I need. I could make something up for your project that would blow your teacher's mind. What better case study is there than something based on those awful reality dating shows that are nothing but drama?"

Even though that'd be entertaining, I shake my head. "I appreciate the offer, but I don't think your extensive knowledge on *The Bachelor* and *Love Island* is going to help me with this assignment. Plus, I already asked someone, and I think I may still get my mom to change her mind about doing it."

She blows out a raspberry and glances at the window where a few college kids are walking by in groups. "Did you ask Caleb?"

Her question gives me pause. "You think I asked my *ex-boyfriend* for help on my project about *romantic* relationships?"

She's quiet for a second before shrugging as if there's nothing wrong with that. "I don't see why you couldn't. He'd probably agree if you asked him. He still loves you."

I'm staring down at my snack absentmindedly, so she doesn't see the doubt on my face. After my last exchange with Caleb, I'm not so sure she's right. And I don't know if I want her to be. He deserves to have somebody be sure about him, and it'd be unfair for me to go back on everything I've put him through only to change my mind. While I don't regret making love with him, I know it was a mistake because it puts us back to square one where we're both as confused as when I told him I couldn't marry him.

"It's not going to happen" is all I say as I push off the counter and start working on the project Bea gave me earlier. She and Elena made cute little item tags to put in the display case so people could see what everything is instead of trying to look on the chalkboard above the coffee machines to figure it out.

"Why not?" the stubborn girl behind me pries, not seeming to care that I don't want to talk about it. "If it's not Caleb you asked, who is it? Is it another man?"

"Lena—"

"Look!" She smacks my shoulder a little too hard, causing me to cut into my flesh with the sharp pair of scissors instead of the paper I was supposed to slice. "He's coming in right now!"

Hissing at the pain as blood instantly starts dripping down my hand, I back away from the counter and watch as the teenager's face pales beside me once she sees the red droplets.

"Oh my God!" She jumps down and races over to where one of the dishcloths is before running over and pressing it against my bleeding hand. "I'm sorry! I'm sorry! I'm sorry! I didn't mean to do that. I just got excited."

The cloth pressing against the cut looks stained and smells like coffee. "Did you give me a fresh cloth or a dirty one?"

She gapes at the stained cloth. "I–I don't know. I panicked."

I put as much pressure as I can stand on the wound that hurts like hell before staring down at the mess on the countertop and floor.

"What happened?" a rushed voice behind us asks. I know who it is without turning around. I've heard the tone a time or two in the past when my clumsy self would accidentally trip or fall. Like when I was seventeen and slipped on a

169

patch of ice at Lindon High School on the way to my car and bruised my butt *and* my pride in front of a group of classmates. That was the third time I'd fallen that winter, and Caleb's dad teased me about having the kind of talent to trip over painted lines.

Elena says, "She cut herself. Oh God, there's so much blood." She backs away, making a face that tells me she doesn't do well with it. "I'm sorry, Raine. I saw Caleb walking in and wanted to let you know."

I don't have time to worry about what the man in question must think of that because red is quickly seeping through the dirtied white material that's getting God knows what into the wound.

Suddenly, Caleb is by my side, grabbing my wrist carefully and pulling the cloth toward him like the mother hen he's always been. He peels back the cloth to check the injury and curses under his breath when he sees whatever I'm too scared to look at.

"This is going to need stitches or glue," he tells me gently. He points to Elena. "Get a new cloth for her. I'm taking her to the hospital."

"Caleb, I'm—"

"Don't say you're fine. You aren't. We both know this is going to need to get checked out or you could get an infection. Let's just set things between us aside for right now and get you taken care of."

Set things aside. As if it's that easy.

Elena jogs over with a fresh cloth, this one definitely clean, and gives me another apologetic look. "I'm sorry again, Raine. I'll tell Grandma Bea to take money out of my paycheck to make sure you get the rest of your pay."

It's a sweet thought, but I don't have time to tell her

not to worry about it before I'm being pulled around the counter and toward the front door where people are starting to walk in.

"Caleb, Lena can't be here by herself."

He doesn't seem to care as he takes his jacket off and starts putting it on me before the cold air hits us. "How much help are you going to be when you're bleeding half to death?"

It's a logical question, albeit a tad bit dramatic. "I'm not bleeding to death. Can you at least call Bea? Or let me call her to make sure Lena will be okay?"

I don't have to look at him to know the sigh is one of exasperation. "I'll call Bea when we get you to the hospital. Lena has run things on her own before. She'll be fine. And *don't*"—he pins me with a serious expression—"argue with me right now."

Pressing my lips together, I nod once and let him help me into the truck. He's being excessive, careful not to touch me but there in case I lose my balance. People always joked that he was the parental figure in every situation—the DD when the boys went out drinking, the person who collected keys at house parties, and the go-to to call on whenever somebody needed help. I don't know whether to believe he's being helpful now because he still cares for me or because this is just who he is as a person.

The ride to the hospital is short since it's only a few blocks from here. We could have walked if Caleb didn't think I would keel over at any second from blood loss.

It isn't until we're inside the emergency room at the check-in desk that I trust myself to face him and say, "You don't have to stay."

One of his brows pops up as he accepts the clipboard with paperwork on it. "How are you going to get back?"

It's hard not to smile. "It's not even a ten-minute walk back to Bea's. Less than that if I cross over on Pine from Maple Avenue."

"First of all, it's November and cold. You're freezing even in the summertime. You'd be half-frozen by the time you made it back to the bakery. Second, do you honestly think Bea is going to let you work the rest of your shift after you get back?"

I'd most likely get double-teamed by Bea and Caleb and told to go home and rest.

"It's a little cut," I argue, my good hand gripping the jacket that's too big for me.

He grumbles, "We'll see about that."

And we do.

Because despite me telling him, on three different occasions, that he can go home instead of staying with me, he helps me fill out the paperwork and comes back to the room with me. His eyes are trained on me from where he sits in the corner—on my hand and on every little movement that the nurse, Salvatore, makes as he examines what's under the saturated cloth.

"All right, I'm going to have you keep this wrapped up. One of the doctors will come check it out too, but I'm pretty sure it's going to need some glue. The nick isn't too deep, but it's in a sensitive spot, which is why it's bleeding so much. The doctor on call tonight will confirm when he's done with his other patient." Salvatore grabs a plastic cup with an orange cap on it, passing it to me. "I'll need you to try giving me a urine sample too, to rule out pregnancy. If stitches are necessary, we'll give you medication to help with the pain."

My stomach drops at the P-word. "I'm not," I tell him

quickly, too afraid to even look in my ex-boyfriend's direction. What would he see on my face if we locked eyes?

Too much.

The nurse gives me an empty smile, as if he delivers this speech all the time to the frantic women who have to provide samples before treatment. "It's hospital policy."

From the corner of my eye, I see Caleb shift as he stares down at the sample cup. He remains silent, his hands tucked into the crooks of his arms from how they're draped tensely over his chest.

Shoulders dropping, I accept the cup and head to the bathroom across the hall.

I wish I could have told the nurse that this was pointless, and it only irritates the anger that I've had to bury deep, deep inside me since I was told by my gynecologist that I had a future of struggles ahead of me.

"It'll be a very hard journey, and you may need to make some tough decisions," Dr. Fields says, giving me the sympathetic smile I'm sure she gives all the patients she tells bad news to. "This isn't the end of the world, Raine."

But it was.

I knew the day I was told I had advanced endometriosis it was the end of *my* world. The one I'd get to share with Caleb for the rest of our lives. And that ugly green monster still lives inside me whenever I think about what could have been if things were different.

I'd be happier.

Healthier.

With the love of my life.

Instead, my body decided to revolt against me and ruin the one chance I got.

I debate on putting my hand through the mirror so I don't

have to look at the reflection of the broken girl anymore but decide I've already done enough damage to myself for one day. So, nostrils flaring, I wash my hands as best I can after filling and putting the cup where I was told to and head back to where Caleb is waiting for me.

"You okay?" he asks after I settle back onto the stiff hospital bed.

I lift a shoulder, not sure how I am. I'm tired. Upset. Pissed off. An array of things that I can't tell him. It's better to be silent than lie. How could I possibly explain to him that I'm upset because I had to pee in a cup despite knowing there's a high probability that I'll never get pregnant?

Dark, heavy emotion hurts me at every corner.

It burns my eyes.

Prickles the back of my neck.

Tightens my throat.

I have to keep my gaze pointed at the floor so he won't see all that taking over, because I want nothing more than to scream.

After a few minutes of silence, save for the loud patients and machines in other sectioned-off areas of the cold emergency room, Caleb asks, "Why was Elena trying to get your attention about me anyway?"

Internally, I flinch as I toy with the zipper tab of his jacket that I'm still wearing. "It was stupid."

"Tell me."

After taking a deep breath, I turn to give him an uncertain look. "Caleb…"

"We're going to be here for a while."

Sighing, I lean back and attempt to make myself comfortable. "It's for a school project I have to do with a couple of people. I was telling her I found someone outside of class

174

to help me already, and she was grilling me for details. But before I could tell her about him, she started hounding me about why I didn't ask you."

His lips purse. "Him, huh? Who *did* you ask?"

Before I can tell him, Salvatore walks through the parted curtains. "Ms. Copelin," he says, his eyes going to Caleb for a moment before darting back to me. "I'd like to talk to you for a moment. Would you like him to stay or...?"

Alarm coats my insides, causing me to slowly turn toward Caleb for a moment. "I don't understand," I say slowly, eyes trailing back to the nurse. "Um, I guess he can?"

"What is it?" Caleb asks, concern weighing down his words. He's on high alert, maybe more so than I am. And I wonder if it's because of the news he'd gotten about his father that turned his life around or if it's something else. We haven't used protection, and only I know we're safe from the repercussions. He's a smart guy who could easily assume that's what Salvatore will tell me.

Despite whatever the nurse needs to share, I could use someone in my corner right now. Caleb has always been my person for comfort when my nerves get the better of me just like I've been for him. So, a little more confidently, I say, "He can stay."

Salvatore presses his lips together. "There's some blood notable in your urine sample, so we wanted to know if you're on your period, finishing your cycle, or have a potential injury that could be leading to the trace in it."

My nose twitches as I rub my legs. "No, I'm not on my period right now. I don't start it for another couple of weeks."

He nods. "Well, I'm sure it's nothing concerning. If you're open, the doctor can go over your file and maybe do some bloodwork after we get your hand taken care of just to be sure."

A small, shuddered breath escapes my lips as I take in those words, because I know what they'll find when they start digging. If they do more image testing, they'll probably find more cysts and scarring. More reasons for the backaches and cramping. I don't need them to confirm anything, but I can't tell them that either.

Voice quiet, I say, "Okay."

I'm only brought back to reality when Caleb stands up and stares at me with narrowed eyes that I can't read.

"Caleb?" I ask, brows pinching at his darkened expression. "Are you—"

"Fuck," he curses, walking out of the tiny room before I can finish the question, fists tightened into balls on either side of his body as he goes.

He doesn't look at me. Doesn't say another word. It leaves me gaping at the nurse, who only offers me a sympathetic smile.

What the hell just happened?

Chapter Eighteen

CALEB

She's got to be pregnant.

The thought rips through every single barrier I put up as I remember each time we've had unprotected sex. She told me it was fine. Why would she lie about that? Why else would she not look me in the eye when she was told to pee in that cup or when the nurse came in asking questions? I've seen her panic before, so I know the look well at this point. But this isn't because she forgot to do a homework assignment or study for an exam.

Fuck.

It takes me a few minutes to cool down in the hallway, with a few cautious nurses staring at me from the far side of the reception area, before I'm calm enough to go back into the room my ex is still sitting in.

It's just Raine when I enter through the parted curtains, her face still as pale as when I walked away, except her eyes stay locked on the floor and one of her hands gently cups her lower stomach.

I ask one thing: "Whose is it?"

It's only then her eyes slowly, *so slowly*, lift to mine. The deep brown color is full of distance and shock.

Then she blinks. "What?" she whispers, another blink doing little to clear the cloudiness. Her voice is so quiet I almost don't hear it, but what I do sense is the crack in her tone.

Is she really going to play dumb right now? There was a reason she ended things, and it was obvious that caught up with her.

"Chris texted me over the summer," I tell her, eye twitching at the memory of the message I got from the douche who was obviously trying to get a rise from me. It worked. It stung then, and it's ten times worse now, considering the current situation. "He basically told me what happened."

Is it hypocritical to be pissed that she was involved with other men this summer when I've been seeing Emma? Yeah. But it doesn't suck any less knowing it was somebody I knew. Someone I hung out with, *with* Raine.

It's never fun having to accept that someone you love has moved on without you.

Chris: Tell Raine I'm sorry about what happened between us

Chris wanted to piss me off by sending that text, especially since I—along with everyone with fucking eyes—know he's had a thing for her for a long time. The quiet ones will always be the sneakiest, so I'm not shocked that he made a move as soon as he could. I just didn't think she'd be that stupid to fall for his nice guy routine. There was always something a little sleazy about him, and I doubt I was the only one who thought so.

"Chris?" she repeats, shaking her head as if she has no idea what I'm talking about.

"Chris," I confirm, fists tightening again.

"Caleb, I don't know what you're talking about or what you must be thinking. What did Chris say happened?"

What I'm thinking is that my ex-girlfriend dumped me to date other people because she was worried she'd be settling for me without knowing what and *who* else was out there. Does that hurt like hell knowing I would have given her everything she could have ever wanted? Yes, it does. But would I be naive not to put some sort of barrier back up to protect myself now that she's back?

I don't want to think the worst of her, because there's not a bad bone in Raine's body. But I can't ignore what's happened since I got down on one knee. It's not too far off to assume that she got into something this summer that's going to be one hell of a problem to get out of.

Loosening my fists, I admit, "I'm not sure what to think anymore, Raine." I scrub the side of my face and close my eyes for a moment. "I used to think this would be *us*. We'd be here, excited about a baby. It could have been, before you dumped me for anyone else to make sure you had a taste of something different just to be sure."

A sharp breath comes from her that has me opening my eyes. "You could not be more wrong than you are right now, and I don't like what you're implying, Caleb. You're upset, I get it. But I suggest you take a breather before you say one more thing."

Take a breather? A dry, disbelieving laugh escapes me that has her eyebrows rising in inquiry. "Answer me this. Was it worth it?"

There's a brief pause where we stare at each other, hurt

shadowing her features. It no doubt mirrors my own. "Was what worth it?"

Pathetically, I whisper, "Breaking us up. Hooking up with people. Was all *that* shit worth *this*?" I gesture toward her stomach, eyes focusing a little too hard on her torso hidden beneath my unzipped jacket and a typical tee with Bea's logo on the corner pocket. The baggy material offers no insight as to what lies underneath.

Raine stares at me for a few long, tense seconds before she repositions herself so she's facing me. "Listen to me right now, Caleb Zachery Anders, because I'm only going to say this *one* time."

My eyebrows shoot up at her hard tone and angry gaze. I'm smart enough not to say anything before she enlightens me on whatever I need to hear. I've learned a time or two in the past that it's not smart to cut in when she's feeling feisty, especially when the middle name is dropped. Except those times typically led to something a lot more fun in apology than what I anticipate this conversation will lead to.

"I've had sex with *one person*"—she sticks up her good hand with only the pointer finger up, though I'm sure that's not the one she'd prefer using—"since the breakup. *One.* If you're as good at math as you used to be, you can figure out who that person is. And even if that were different, you have no reason to judge me for sleeping with anyone else when we're not together.

"I was *confused* and *lost* when you asked me to marry you. That's the truth. I had a lot to think about that would impact *both* of our lives if I agreed. I hurt you, and I've already told you how sorry I am for that. But this? This temper tantrum you're throwing is ridiculous. You have no idea what you're talking about right now. I'm not pregnant, you *goddamn* jackass." She looks at me with tears springing into her eyes that she quickly blinks away. "This conversation is not helping anything. I know you're going through a lot right now, but I am too. I don't need you being mean to me to add to it. So I think you should go."

She's really only ever been with me?

The thought comes crashing into me.

Because I haven't just been with her.

My throat thickens. "Raine—"

"I said *go*, Caleb. You don't need to be here. Thanks for the ride, but I'll figure out how to get home. You've done enough."

The curtain moves behind me, and a throat clears, turning my attention over my shoulder to see Emma standing there. Her eyebrows arch as she looks between Raine and me and says, "I think you should listen to your…friend. Come on."

She doesn't work on this floor, which means one of her coworkers must have paged her to come down and get me before I made more of a scene. Great. That means the chances of Dad hearing that I'm here with Raine are pretty likely. Whenever he's not sleeping, he's listening to the gossip surrounding this place, whether it's with patients or staff.

Raine looks between me and Emma, whose hand is on my shoulder, trying to get me to turn around and follow her out. There's surprise on her face that I can't figure out. They wouldn't know each other, would they?

My ex's expression drains, turning into an empty void that offers little emotion. "It looks to me like I'm not the one who's been busy after graduation. So don't be a hypocrite. It's not a good look on you."

Swallowing, I feel a lump in the back of my throat that

makes it hard to talk. My voice is hoarse when I say, "I just assumed that you…"

Emma squeezes my shoulder. "Come on."

"The fact that you assumed I screwed *Chris* says a lot more about you than it does me. And you know what? Just so we're clear, he kissed me. I never kissed him back though. If he claimed anything else happened between us, it's his hurt pride talking."

"I made a mistake. I—"

"I did too, by having sex with you again," she says, cutting me off coolly, looking away from me to end the conversation. "So much for it being a one-time thing, huh? I was dumb enough to think that it somehow would help you. That it would make both of us feel better, like our company always did before. We were *both* emotional that day, and that night in the truck. And look where it led us. Fighting. Pointing fingers."

Heart tightening, all I can do is stare.

I guess she's not wrong though.

The sex should have never happened, especially with this outcome. But there's nothing we can do to change that now.

I step toward her, lowering my voice and asking, "You're really not…?" My eyes dip down to her stomach again.

Her eyes stay focused on the section of curtain in front of her. Weakly, she replies, "No, I'm not."

Lips pressed together, I heave out a heavy sigh, feeling like a complete asshole. "What do we do now?"

"I'm going to get my hand fixed up, and you're going to go with your friend." She says "friend" like she's in pain, still not bothering to so much as glance in my direction for a heartbeat too long. Then she lets loose a sigh, clenches her eyelids closed for a moment, and opens them in my direction. "But there is no 'we,' Caleb. Because the man I knew wouldn't have said any of that to me."

My stomach drops. "I didn't mean it."

She leans back. "Yes, you did."

Knowing there's nothing I can say right now, I let Emma guide me out, realizing she more than likely heard what Raine said.

"I'm sorry," I tell the woman walking silently alongside me.

She shakes her head. "Don't."

"Emma—"

She stops walking and looks at me. "I knew in my gut that starting anything with you was a mistake. I went against that feeling. That's on me. Everything else is on you though. You shouldn't have led me on or spewed all that bullshit. It was messed up, Caleb."

I know she's right, so I don't bother refuting her. And I watch as she contemplates what more she wants to say before she gives up and walks away.

When I get up to Dad's floor, I see him standing by the window, leaning heavily on the IV pole tight in his grasp. As soon as I walk in, he slowly turns and offers me a shaky smile even though he can see the scolding look on my face.

"You shouldn't be out of bed on your own," I start in on him, walking over and putting a hand on his back to help stabilize him as he turns around. "What if you fell and nobody was around to hear or help?"

He laughs, but it quickly turns into a dry cough that shakes his entire torso. I manage to guide him to the chair in the corner and help him sit down until he waves me off. "I'm fine, I'm fine. What are you doing here anyway? I wasn't expecting you until later."

I shift on my feet, still feeling the weight on my shoulders from the conversation I had only minutes ago downstairs. "It's sort of complicated. I'm not sure..." Swallowing, I have no idea what to tell him. There's a lot I need to process, and I haven't had time to do that yet. "I fucked up big time," I mumble, threading my fingers through my hair as I start pacing across the room from him. "I don't know what the hell to do, Dad."

"Why don't you tell me about it," Dad says, voice gentle.

I close my eyes for a moment, tipping my head back and then staring up at the ceiling. "I thought Raine was pregnant. And I thought...it wasn't mine. She's downstairs getting stitches in her hand. She'll be okay though."

Dad is quiet. "That's a lot to take in. I'm glad to hear she'll be okay." Another pause. "I take it you two have seen each other since the breakup then? Heard you might have been seeing each other, but you didn't bring it up. Especially since you're seeing Emilia."

My lips twitch. "It's Emma," I correct him. I don't typically tell my parents about my whereabouts these days, but there's no point in denying it. "She and I weren't really dating. Not exclusively anyway. I know that doesn't justify me seeing Raine though."

He hums.

Rubbing the back of my neck, I say, "If she *were* pregnant, it would have been mine. And that messed me up because I always wanted to be a dad. But if she were and it wasn't my kid...I would have had to see her live out the dream I always pictured with her but without me in it. I got so fucking *angry*."

Dad nods in understanding, but I doubt he truly gets the irritation and guilt threatening to bubble over. "I have no doubt you'll get that future someday. But if it's not in the picture right now, then that's for the best. You have more important things to focus on."

I look at him, studying his glassy eyes as they watch me and his narrow frame that seems even smaller than it did a week ago. He's deteriorating in front of my eyes, and there's not a damn thing I can do about it. "How do you do it?"

"Do what?"

I look at him with wary eyes. "Be a father. Be a good man. How do you do that when there's always something trying to hold you back or test you? Because I don't know how to balance everything right now, Dad. It feels like…" How can I tell him I'm drowning? I'm being suffocated by the weight of all my responsibilities, yet I still would have added a baby to the mix if it came down to it.

Because it'd be with Raine.

Because it could have given me the future I saw for myself a long time ago.

He's quiet for a moment before letting out a small sigh. "I don't know."

I look up at him in confusion. "You don't know what?"

"I don't know how I did it. Be a father. Be a good man. It's just something you figure out along the way. I'm by no means perfect. No human ever is. Anger still gets to me. There are days, long before now, when I felt defeated. You think you fucked up now? Just wait. You're going to keep screwing up, but you'll learn from those mistakes and grow from them. But, son?"

All I do is stare, his image becoming blurry from panicked tears. Tears that I can't find the energy to fight anymore.

"If there's anybody who can make the most out of life no matter the obstacles," he tells me, voice the same gentle tone that it is when he offers me sincere advice, "it's you.

The only thing somebody needs to know how to do is love, and you've always been full of that. At the end of the day, it's how you express it, accept it, and distribute it despite all the challenges that makes a difference."

I don't know what it is about that statement that makes me break. But it doesn't take long before I'm sitting on my father's hospital bed crying while the man who raised me makes his way over slowly to comfort me despite his own battles. For once, I don't feel bad about showing any weakness, because my father is here to help me through it. His belief in me eases some of the pressure that'd been sitting on my chest for far too long.

A man's love. A father's love.

If that's the secret to being a good person, then I've had the best role model.

~

I know what's coming when I see Emma approach me as I'm putting a lid on my coffee cup in the cafeteria a few hours later. I asked one of the nurses on staff if Emma was still working, but they didn't seem interested in giving me any details. They're loyal to their coworker, and I respect that. I asked if they could let her know I was looking for her, and I'm pretty sure one of them rolled her eyes.

Fair.

"Hey—"

She holds up her hand, looking more tired than normal. "You told me you wanted to move on. That you were ready to do that."

I didn't mean to lie to her. "I thought I was" is my quiet reply. Even though I know she's not looking for details, I feel the need to explain. "Raine and I were talking, and a lot of emotions came up. She's...familiar to me. It's a hard pattern to quit."

It's a shitty reason to do what I did, but at least I'm being honest.

Emma can't look me in the eye as she crosses her arms and lets out a breath. "I told you before that I didn't think dating was a good idea because of everything you're going through, but *you* told me you wanted to give it a chance. *You* convinced me to not let this end."

All I can say is "I know."

Both women have a right to tell me off, so I accept everything they say. Do I like what I've put them through? No. It makes me feel like a jackass, especially considering I accused Raine of sleeping around.

"She wants a dog," Emma tells me, causing my eyes to lift to her in curiosity.

"What?"

Emma lowers her arms to her sides. "She wants to buy one of the dogs from my family's litter. I saw her in town the other week with one of them that escaped through the fence."

I stare for a brief moment. "I didn't know you two knew each other..."

"Your phone background is of you two," she points out, making me feel like an even bigger dick. I'd meant to change it, but I couldn't. "I recognized her right away but didn't tell her how close you and I have been."

That must be why Raine kept staring at Emma when she walked into her hospital room earlier. "I'm sorry, Em. I wanted to believe I was over the relationship."

She gnaws her lip and nods once before standing straighter

and finally looking me in the eye. "Yeah. I obviously wanted to believe that too. I guess we're both idiots."

As she starts to walk away, I reach out to gently grab her wrist. "Wait."

Her wary eyes look over her shoulder at me before she carefully takes her arm back.

"How much are you selling the dogs for?"

Emma blinks slowly, staring at me as she soaks in that question. Then she says, "You want to buy it for her, don't you?"

I cringe, realizing how fucked up that is.

She scoffs. "Of course you do." Wetting her lips, she shakes her head and rubs her tired eyes. "You're such a dick, Caleb."

Then she walks away.

Chapter Nineteen

RAINE

CALEB'S REACTION IN THE hospital is the exact reason I chose to end things in the first place. He *wanted* there to be a baby, but there isn't. He *wants* to be a dad, but he can't be. Not with me. I saw it clear as day on his face just how devastated he was the second it soaked in that I wasn't about to give him what he dreamed of.

I'm not pregnant.

Not with his baby.

Definitely not with Chris's.

Every fear I had about saying yes to his proposal was solidified in the middle of the emergency room. I hate that I was right because that means there's no chance for us. Not again. But at least I got some justification knowing I wasn't completely out of hand with my choice.

It's for the best, I tell myself for the billionth time. If not now, it would have happened someday when things became too much.

That realization smacks me head-on as I sit in my

bedroom surrounded by silence, knees drawn to my chest as I stare at the corkboard full of a collage of pictures from over the years.

My light-pink room, with frilly curtains, decorative pillows, and random stuffed animals lingering on the dresser, shelves, and bed, screams innocence when I'm anything but. I'd like to think the good intent behind the reason I'm not a saint makes up for the feelings I hurt along the way.

I'm not sure that's enough though.

Lowering my feet to the floor, I walk over to the corkboard and touch one of the pictures hanging there. It's ripped down the middle because I didn't want to see the other person whose arm is still seen around me next to the pool in Radcliff.

It was summer, and I'd been excited to see my friends in Virginia but sad that Caleb wasn't going to be there. We were new, nothing serious, so I told myself it was good to miss him, good to have our space. People who are always near each other tend to get on each other's nerves from what I can tell.

"Come on, Raine," Collin teases, lowering his phone to look at me. "I know you can smile. Let's see it."

The boy next to me, Cody, puts his arm around my shoulder and tugs me into his side. He's more muscular than Caleb, and it makes me wonder if he plays sports too. Is he a football player? He seems like the baseball type. I think I heard him and Chris talking about the Yankees and Red Sox game earlier.

I also notice that he smells nice. Whatever cologne or body spray he's wearing isn't too strong. I can't help but take a small breath to try figuring out what scent is coming from him. It's woodsy and floral at the same time. New compared to what I'm used to.

"Did you just smell me?" he asks, a lopsided grin on his face.

Instantly, my face blossoms with heat. "I...uh... Sorry."

He winks, causing my face to pinken even more. "Don't be. You can do whatever you want to me."

There's no doubt he's flirting, which makes a nervous laugh bubble past my lips.

I think briefly about Caleb. We aren't officially dating yet, so flirting isn't against the rules. Right? I see girls flirt with Caleb all the time, especially the cheerleaders who go up to him after the games. It doesn't make me feel great when I see him laugh at whatever they're saying, but I know I've got no claim to him.

Maybe that's why I settle into Cody's side and grin at Collin as he lifts his phone to snap more photos of the group.

Cody is cute—a blond surfer wannabe compared to Caleb's dark-haired, dark-eyed, all-American thing. They're both cute in their own ways, and they both seem to like me. It strokes my ego a little because there's nothing particularly special about me. My hair is a frizzy dark red mess that I usually don't know what to do with, I barely wear makeup because I have no idea how to apply it much less make it look good, and I'm not the best at making conversation without coming off as awkward.

Yet here's an attractive boy who keeps smiling at me, finding tiny ways to touch me whenever we're near each other, and flirting enough to make me blush regardless of how I see myself.

It feels good to be wanted, and that makes me feel like any other teenage girl. Suddenly, I understand why those cheerleaders want the athletes' attention so much. It's fun.

That's why after a while I stop thinking about Caleb altogether and stay in the moment with my summer friends.

Which is why I follow Cody inside that night when he asks if I want to go somewhere quieter to talk. And we do. We talk about our favorite music and listen to some of their best songs on YouTube, talk about movies, hobbies, and everything in between.

We never bring up what our lives are like outside summer—what or who we're going back to. It's easier that way. Safer.

That night, I lose my virginity to the smooth-talking summer boy who I'd never see or speak to again.

It was awkward and fumbled, and it'd hurt. When all was said and done, I lay in bed alone after he got dressed and left, claiming he couldn't be caught out past curfew again. I wondered if anybody would notice the difference in me. I heard sex could do that to people.

A few months later, I did notice a change. When I woke up in my own bed at home in an excruciating amount of pain and blood covering my sheets and legs. I'd had bad periods before, but this didn't feel the same as normal, and I'd had plenty of experience since starting my cycle at eight years old. Then again, it'd been over two months since I'd had one at all, which I chalked up to stress.

I'd felt horrible for sleeping with Cody—for giving him what I should have given Caleb.

But when I drove myself to Planned Parenthood the next morning all by myself because I didn't want to ask Mom or Dad to take me to the doctor, my world completely stopped.

"You suffered a miscarriage. I'm sorry for your loss," the woman in the lab coat tells me, putting her hand on mine in comfort.

Life hit me harder than it ever did that day, and I couldn't tell anybody. Not Mom. Not Dad. Definitely not Caleb. And there'd been no way to tell the boy who was the father to my unborn baby, because it wasn't as if he was in my life. I didn't have his number. Didn't know his last name. One decision with him led to a life-altering reality for me.

It was all downhill from there. I just didn't know it yet.

Blinking slowly, I grab the picture from that day in Radcliff, study what's visible of Cody's arm, and grind my teeth. I crumple the print and toss it into my wastebasket. Then I do the same with another picture from that summer.

And another.

And another.

Until I'm tearing the corkboard off the wall and throwing it onto the floor with hands shaking from anger.

With blurry eyes, I stare at the ruined images scattered on the carpet. "Stupid," I whisper to myself. "You were so *stupid*."

Clenching my eyes closed to stop the tears from falling, I inhale deeply and kick the corkboard before dropping onto the edge of my bed and staring at the mess I made.

My whole body is shaking, making me wrap my arms around myself and squeeze.

I'm *angry*.

For the losses I've suffered.

For the sacrifices I've had to make.

I endured so much and had nobody to help me get through it. And the worst part? Nobody can, especially not now.

My body *failed me*, and I have no control over it. No answers. No relief. I've had to silently grieve the loss of two different lives—the one of the baby I'd never get to know, and the one of the person I was before I ever found out. Because the moment I heard the news, I realized I'd never be the same.

Standing, I sniff back tears and step on the pictures as I walk out of my bedroom.

Mom is gone again.

No note.

No text.

No phone call.

She's probably with Dad.

Feeling suffocated in the house, unable to be on my own

right now, I walk outside to see an unfamiliar vehicle pull up at the front curb. My eyebrows dart up when I see Emma step out of the driver's side and round the front of the car. When she sees me, she looks as on guard as I am, and that's when I know we're aware of the other person's involvement with Caleb.

Rubbing my arm with my good hand, I take a deep breath so she doesn't see the breakdown I'm on the verge of and walk over to her. "Hi."

Her gray eyes go from me to the house, then back to me again. Does she see the defeat in my eyes? The exhaustion? Or does she see someone who helped hurt her with the boy she obviously has a thing for? I could see it when she touched his arm to walk him out of the room.

"I asked around to get your address. Hope that's okay."

Biting down on the inside of my cheek, I release it and say, "I guess that depends on if you're here to hit me or not."

Emma smiles faintly. "You're safe. I've never been much of a fighter."

Me either. I guess Caleb has a type.

We're quiet, staring at each other.

Then I say, "I didn't know."

She doesn't need me to elaborate.

"Neither did I," she replies. There's a pause, more shifting in discomfort. "Or maybe I did in a way. Subconsciously, I knew Caleb still loved you."

I don't tell her about my cluelessness to her presence in his life because it wouldn't do any good now. Why keep hurting people's feelings with the truth if a lie could save them even the slightest bit of pain?

"I have something for you," she tells me, walking over to the back door of her car.

I gape at the wiggling gray puppy she takes into her arms that's licking her face. "Oh my God," I whisper, walking over to get a better look. "I didn't think you'd still sell me one after the hospital. I wouldn't have blamed you."

She looks down at the dog before passing him to me, watching as I quickly wrap him up in my arms. "To be honest, I was debating on keeping him out of spite. But what happened wasn't your fault. Not entirely. I'm not going to be petty because of everything that went down, especially when I promised my parents I'd help find good homes for these little guys."

The softness in her voice makes me realize she's being genuine. "Thank you."

She doesn't look at me but at the puppy when she says, "I figured you could use a good, stable companion now more than ever." Reaching over to scratch the dog's back, she lifts her gaze upward and adds, "We both could. Because I don't think Caleb is capable of being that for anybody right now."

Is that her way of saying things with Caleb and her are over? Because I may not know the specifics, but it's obvious that there was *something* there. I choose not to ask. It's safer that way.

Probably for both of us.

"How much do I owe you?"

Emma steps back, sliding her hands into her jacket pockets. "Nothing. It's taken care of already."

My brows pinch in confusion. "What do you mean?"

The girl standing in front of me, still in her scrubs, sighs. "I'll never know what happened between the two of you, but it's obviously not big enough to make him care any less. I'm looking forward to the day I can experience that kind of loyalty, even after heartbreak."

Is she saying what I think she is?

I look down at the dog, whose tongue quickly finds my chin in happy kisses.

Emma walks back to her car, stopping before she climbs inside. She watches me for a second before shaking her head. "Good luck with...everything."

I'm too slow to respond before she gets inside and drives away.

When I walk up to the front door, I see Mr. Applebee outside his house with a rake, working on the fallen orange and yellow leaves coating his otherwise green lawn. "Got a new friend there?" he asks, nodding toward the squirmy puppy who clearly wants to be set down.

I force a smile, but it feels too heavy to be believable. "I'm trying to avoid the loneliness thing. What better way than with a dog?"

He leans against the rake handle. "My Annemarie used to say that the times we're feeling loneliest are typically when we need to be by ourselves the most."

My brows pinch. "That doesn't make any sense to me."

One of his shoulders lifts as he fights off what I imagine is almost a smile. "Well, she also told me that bacon was going to kill me someday. She switched us to that nasty low-fat, low-sodium turkey alternative, so maybe she had no idea what she was talking about."

That gets me to crack a smile of my own.

Scratching the puppy between his ears to get him to calm down, I gesture toward my house. "I should go in and get him settled."

I guess I also need to buy him some things since I never got around to it. Mom isn't going to be very happy, but I'm sure he'll grow on her.

"Are we still meeting tomorrow afternoon?" he asks, taking up his rake again. "I've been thinking a lot about those pastries you've told me about."

I want to ask him to reschedule, but I don't want to risk him backing out of the project. Enough of my life is at risk because of my choices; I don't need my grade for this class to be at risk too. "Tomorrow. Right, yeah. Pastries are on me. Unless Annemarie said something about them being bad for you too."

Leon pats his stomach. "Only for the weight, but I clearly don't care about that. Too damn old to care about the little things."

Snorting, I murmur, "Yeah, I've definitely gained some weight since I started working there." I brush the thought off and force a bigger smile. "See you tomorrow, Leon," I call out, carefully opening and pushing the door wide with my injured hand.

After setting a few towels down on the floor for my unnamed new family member, I pull out my phone to see a few unanswered messages.

Mom: I won't be home until late tonight. There's money on the counter for you to order pizza
Caleb: I'm sorry about earlier. We need to talk about all of this

Choosing to ignore both like they've ignored me in the past, I turn my phone off and sit on the edge of my bed, staring at the empty corkboard. It seems appropriate. It's a clean slate wiped away by a tsunami of regret. The only way to move on is to rebuild from the ground up.

The whining coming from the floor has me moving my

gaze from the trash bin full of old photos and toward the puppy that's officially a fresh beginning for me. "What am I going to name you?"

~

Grabbing the two plates with heated muffins on them from Elena, I head over to the corner table where Leon is waiting for me. He's got a walking cane leaning against the wall, a steaming cup of tea in front of him, and a curious expression on his face as he studies the other tables of college students having lunch.

"Here," I say, putting his cheesecake muffin down in front of him.

Sliding into the seat across from him with my chocolate chip muffin, I set it to the side and move my water to make room for my notebook.

I'm a little scatterbrained as I search for a pen in my bag, and my neighbor notices my flustered movements. "Is everything okay?"

Pausing, I let out a tiny breath. "Not really." Cringing internally, I grab the writing utensil from my bag and drop it back onto the floor beside my feet. "Sorry, it's not your problem. There's a lot going on is all."

Leon drags his muffin closer. "I don't suppose it's anything I can help you with, is it?"

We'd be here all day if I started listing my problems, starting with Mom being gone again when I woke up. If I hadn't noticed the empty wineglass with a lipstick stain on the counter or the missing slice of pizza from the box, I would have assumed she never came home. But between that and the Post-it she left on the fridge asking why she had to clean up a pee stain on the kitchen floor this morning, I knew she snuck in late before whatever meeting she had with a client this morning.

I wanted to tell her about the new addition to our household last night and get it out of the way, but maybe it's a good thing we avoided it. Then she would ask what happened to my hand and why I looked like I had been crying. Because I had been. Not because my hand hurt, which it did, but because my heart hurt. Then I'd need to explain the argument I got in with Caleb and how he bought me a dog, which would take the conversation in an entirely new direction that would probably lead to an argument with Mom about why I need to get past my feelings.

I'm not ready for all that.

The smile I give my neighbor is genuine. "Helping me with this project is more than enough. Trust me. I asked my mom, but she wasn't comfortable with the topic or having her business out there. Plus, she doesn't spend a lot of time at the house anymore, so finding time to work with her on it would have been difficult."

Leon nods in acknowledgment as he pulls the top of the muffin from the body, just like my father always does. "It must have been hard when they split."

I'm quiet for a second. "It's...different. But I think this is what's best for everybody. They fought too much to make it work for the long term."

I remember when Mrs. Applebee, Annemarie, once asked me if everything was all right when she heard the yelling match going on inside the house. I'd been staring at the front door, wondering if I should go inside and break it up after a long day of school or if I should do another lap around the neighborhood in hopes they'd be done by the time I got back.

I was twelve.

Shaking it off, I clear my throat and click my pen open. "How long were you and your wife together?"

He lets the subject change easily. "This year will be fifty-eight years together. We met at seventeen, got married at eighteen, and have been together ever since."

"You still count them?"

His nostalgic smile grows. "Even though she's been gone for four years now, she'll always be with me. She was my soulmate. I still feel her presence even on the bad days."

"How did you know she was the one? That's a long time to be together with one person." I made it seven years before messing it all up, yet they spent *decades* together. "Were you ever scared?"

Those eyebrows pop up. "Of what? Losing her? Sure. Thought that was a possibility a time or two. Have you seen me? I'm no Cary Grant—that was her favorite actor. Had the biggest crush on him. But my Annemarie...*shoo*. She was a looker. I always thought that woman was the prettiest thing no matter what she looked like. Bedhead, bad breath, and all. Never quite understood why she fell in love with me."

"But you never doubted it?"

The older man scratches at the white scruff on his chin. "Our relationship? Nah. I was in it with her one hundred percent, and I knew she was in it with me. That's what love is. It's not about giving fifty-fifty to somebody. Who wants a half-assed kind of love when you could each give it your all no matter the circumstances?"

My stomach dips as I stare at the little notes I've been jotting down. Had I given it my all with Caleb, or was I only ever offering him half of myself, hoping he'd meet me halfway? I didn't even try telling him about my diagnosis. There were a few moments it'd been on the tip of my tongue when he mentioned kids, but I couldn't bring myself to tell him the truth. Then it was too late, everything had boiled over, and I couldn't say a thing. I hadn't given him my all, because I justified to myself that I couldn't.

After what happened with Cody, I'd pulled back a little from Caleb, wondering if it would turn into love at all if I was willing to be with somebody else in the first place. Maybe that was the first sign that I was going to self-sabotage early on.

"Can I ask you something?" I say to Caleb, tapping the eraser of my pencil against my marked-up math homework.

He looks over from where he's typing something on his dad's computer. "If it's about the trig homework, I don't know how much help I'll be. I'm pretty sure I got half of the equations wrong even though I followed the example problems she gave us."

I stare at the assignment for a second before setting my pencil down. "It's about what your dad said at dinner the other day. About how he knew your mom was the one the first day he met her."

Caleb's full attention is on me now, interest piqued. "Yeah, he's said that for years. He always talks about the color of her lipstick and how her hair had so much hair spray he was afraid it'd ignite if she got too close to the fire they were at. What about that?"

Wetting my lips as I scrape my palms down my jeans, I say, "Do you think that sort of thing is true? My parents have never said anything like that about each other before."

In fact, they never talk about their past. Unlike Caleb's parents, who love reminiscing about their dating days, my parents seem to avoid the topic as if it's the last thing they want to remember.

Caleb turns to me, his cheeks turning pink when he admits, "I think it's true. I knew I wanted you in my life the day I first saw you. It was the first time I ever came up to you in the hall at school."

I make a face. "But the day we started talking, I had spitballs in my hair from Sean Puglisi. They were so tangled I nearly cried. Mom even found a few in my hair later that night."

He shrugs easily. "Yeah, but you didn't cry. And you didn't make a scene or be mean to him either, like Katie did when he did it to her. You just asked him to stop. You were always nice to everyone, and I liked that."

Sean had started acting out after his grandpa died that year. Most people knew his grandparents were the ones who raised him. I figured he was probably hurting and that was his way of showing it. Mom said Aunt Tiffany did that when their father died. Grief does funny things to people.

"So you wanted me in your life because I was nice about the spitballs?"

That pink in his cheeks deepens as he goes back to staring at the computer screen. "I wanted you in my life for a lot of reasons. Spitballs and all. I just…knew."

My hand goes to a lock of my hair, absentmindedly touching the strands as if I'd find something gross tangled in there. When I don't, I make myself lower my hand and move on to the next question. "Was there anything you two disagreed on that threatened your relationship?"

He chuckles. "Of course we disagreed. There isn't one couple who doesn't have their fair share of arguments. If that threatens the relationship, then you're not with the right person."

I find myself nodding, jotting down a single word and underlining it. *Secure.*

It makes me start to evaluate all the little things about the way I was with Caleb, knowing that's the last word I'd describe myself with. I don't envy Leon though, because he lost his wife. I may not have Caleb anymore, but at least he's still here.

"You look deep in thought," he notes.

I snap myself out of it. "Sorry. Thinking."

"About?" he presses with interest.

Sighing, I reach for the muffin I have no appetite for. "Life. Love."

Leon's eyes glint with amusement. "Those are two things we can get a little too lost in trying to figure out the answers to."

My head tilts as I take that in. "Isn't it human nature to want the answers?"

A thoughtful noise comes from him. "I suppose. Take it from an old man with a lot of life experience. The more we search for answers, the more questions we have. That's no way to live your life, kid."

Chapter Twenty

CALEB

"Dude," Matt groans, setting his pen down on his notebook and leaning back in the chair. "That's the fourth time you sighed. Is your infrastructure homework as boring as it sounds or what?"

I stare down at the highlighted section of text I marked up fifteen minutes ago. I've read it three times, and nothing seems to be sticking. "I have some shit on my mind."

"With your dad or…?"

None of my friends have asked about Raine, even though we've become the talk of the town since I escorted her from Bea's with her bloody hand wrapped. It hasn't escaped people that we showed up to the hospital together but didn't leave together. Have I been avoiding people so I wouldn't need to talk about the events of that day? Yeah. But I can't keep doing it forever.

"Life," I finally reply to Matt. Talking with Dad made me feel calmer than I had been in a while. All the shit piling on me is still there, but I know I have people to talk to about it with who won't judge me. Dad. Mom. My friends. "Can I ask you something? No bullshit answers either."

Matt's brows arch. "Uh, I guess."

"You never really talk about your parents, so I don't know what your situation is with them. But do you ever worry that something you do is going to fuck everything up with them?"

He stares at me for a second. "Wow. Wasn't expecting that." My buddy scrubs his neck. "My parents are good people. Blue collar. Keep to themselves. I guess when you have something healthy with people, there's never really anything to talk about. I never think to bring them up. But they…yeah, they made my life good. Better than it probably would have been if I'd had any other family."

My brows pinch at the odd choice of words, and then they relax when he sees the confusion on my face and says, "I was adopted. It was closed. My parents are the only ones I know. Like I said, good people. Great people, actually."

Wow. Nobody would have known that if he didn't say something. He even sort of looks like his dad.

Matt's shoulders lift nonchalantly. "And isn't it sort of our jobs to fuck up once in a while? I mean, nobody is perfect. Our parents know we're going to do stuff that they don't approve of at least once in our lifetimes. I think how they react depends on what your relationship is with them. My dad isn't exactly going to be high-fiving me if he ever finds out about Rachel, but he's going to tell me to be careful, just like you and a few of the guys have, because he loves me."

Does that mean he isn't in it for the long haul with her? "You don't plan on ever telling them about Rachel? Not even in the future?"

Out of our friend group, I was one of the few who

always looked to the future. When we were all freshmen, I'd talked about life after graduation with Raine when everybody else was focusing on whatever party was coming up. Matt told me once I was going to scare her off by talking about marriage, babies, and the future so much, but I told him he was wrong.

I guess he wasn't.

Matt grabs his pen and twists it, staring at his notes. "I don't know. I don't want to hide Rachel forever, but it's not really up to me."

"For what it's worth, I hope you don't have to hide her," I tell him. "Nobody should have to hold any part of them back to save face."

He nods. "Thanks, man."

I feel my knee bounce under the table. "I've always tried doing what I knew was right my whole life. I've been training to take over Anders Hardware, I've studied my ass off to get good grades, and I'm doing my fucking best to make sure Mom is as okay as she can be while Dad is at the hospital. I spend more time at my parents' house than at my apartment because I don't want her to be alone. I've never been worried about disappointing my parents because I could handle whatever was tossed my way. But I haven't been able to say the same for a while and chalked it up to being weak."

"The last thing anybody would call you is weak, Caleb."

Why doesn't it feel that way then?

"Whether you want to believe it or not, there are people on your side no matter what you're going through. If I were in your shoes, I'd probably be bawling my eyes out or drinking myself to death. There'd be no in-between. I'd say you're doing a lot better than most people would. So don't think you feeling twisted up about life makes you any less of a man. It doesn't. I'm sure your dad would say the same thing."

He would. "I just hate how much everything has changed. My life was going exactly how I wanted it to, and it did a one-eighty overnight in every way possible. Ever since Raine and I broke up, I haven't felt settled. There's something she isn't telling me, Matt. I know it. The reason she gave me for ending things doesn't make sense. I thought if I moved on or if I just tried something with somebody else…"

Well, that was obviously a shitty plan because it only dragged somebody innocent into my bullshit.

Shaking my head, I swipe a hand down my tired face. "I hurt somebody who didn't deserve it by trying to get over the girl who did the same to me, and I know my parents don't approve, which sucks. They've always been on my side with every choice I've made. But they want me to be alone to process things, and I…" I make a face. "I don't know how to be."

It's never just been me. I've always had a strong support system. Great family, friends, and girlfriend. Why would I need to learn how to be on my own when I had everything I could ever want?

Matt watches me for a moment before nodding once. "You've always had a great relationship with your parents, and you guys have gone through a lot together. There's nothing you're going to do that makes them love you any less, even if they don't approve of what you're doing with this girl. I'm telling you, dude, you're beating yourself up way too much about this. Everything will work out how it's supposed to if you give it time. But if you need to talk to

Raine to get things off your chest, do that. Follow your gut. Nobody but you knows what that's telling you to do."

He's got a point. If I just knew whatever she was holding back, maybe I'd feel better. I could let go. Maybe it could be that easy. Closure. Who doesn't want that? It'd give me a chance to focus on the other things in my life that *should* take precedence.

"Now," he says, "enough of this fluffy shit. It's not my thing. If you want a softy, find DJ. That man is a fucking marshmallow."

Snorting out an amused laugh despite feeling anything but good right now, I shake my head and try getting back into my homework.

"Thanks for the advice," I tell him. "Hey, maybe we could get the guys together sometime soon to do something. Watch one of the upcoming games."

Matt snorts. "As long as it's not a Penn game, I'm sure DJ would be down for that. Let us know your schedule."

Blowing out a breath, I nod and think about how my schedule is going to change a lot, sooner rather than later.

Because of Dad.

Because of Raine.

Raine.

Closing my textbook, I shove it into my bag and push the chair back, knowing I won't be getting anything done if I can't stop thinking about her. "I've got to go talk to someone. I'll see you later, man."

He looks up in surprise, but those lips curl up at the corners as if they know exactly who I'm ditching him to talk to. "Good luck."

~

When I was sixteen, I nearly pissed myself when I showed up at Raine's house with a bag full of all her favorite candy and a card with a cheesy message inside asking her to the winter formal. I had to face her father who'd answered the door, and I knew his stance on dating. *Both* her parents were against her seeing anybody, which made it twice as hard getting them to agree to me taking her anywhere. While we were already seeing each other in secret, I wanted to officially ask her to be my date for the dance that was second best to prom.

I was a little uncertain about asking her because she was acting strange after she got back from Virginia, but she told me she was fine and that nothing was wrong. When she started acting like herself again, or some similar version anyway, I figured it couldn't hurt to shoot my shot. If I could win her parents over, I could win her over too.

That similar feeling of panic is back as I watch Raine behind the counter at Bea's through the front window. I've been debating on going in for the past fifteen minutes but find myself backing away from the door every time I reach for the handle. At least eight people have passed through the door I've held open.

"What are you doing?" a familiar voice asks behind me before Skylar pops up by my side with a smile on her face. I look around to see if her boyfriend is with her, but it's just us.

"I'm just...enjoying the fresh air," I lie, knowing damn well she knows it's bullshit.

Her eyes roll. "Is that why you've been pacing as you stare at your ex-girlfriend like a creep? Because a lot of people would get arrested for that sort of behavior."

I eye her, not as amused as she is when I see the giant grin plastered on her face. "Are you going to call the cops?"

She hums in contemplation. "Nah, it's too amusing to watch you all nervous like this. What exactly *are* you doing?"

Rubbing the back of my neck, I glance at the window. Raine isn't anywhere in sight, making me blow out a breath. I turn back to the girl with curious eyes who's waiting for my answer. "I need to talk to Raine."

Skylar slowly nods, but there's obvious skepticism on her face. "I was wondering if she was all depressed because of you," she murmurs, turning to look for the redhead inside.

Raine's been depressed?

She doesn't give me a chance to ask for more info about that casual statement. "So, what? You suddenly can't talk? You open your mouth and words come out. It's basically magic."

Wiseass. "What are *you* doing here?"

"Do you mean on the public street or at the town's best bakery? Because I'm here for coffee and doughnuts so I can hate myself later for eating carbs after bitching to DJ about how I've gained ten pounds since moving here."

I don't bother giving her a cursory glance out of solidarity. There's nothing wrong with her body, regardless of what food she uses to fuel it. "I'm sure DJ told you not to worry about shit like that. That boy is lovestruck, so I doubt a doughnut will do any harm."

"What about pie? I can buy us a couple of slices and we can catch up. I want the details on whatever is going on with you and Raine. She and I haven't gotten a chance to hang out recently." I'm about to answer her when she points at the window. "Look! Raine sees us. Wave at the cute barista, Caleb."

She grabs my hand and starts waving it for me, drawing my attention to Raine. She stares between me and Skylar with a distant look on her face before turning to help someone at one of the tables.

"Come on," Skylar says, tugging me toward the front door.

"Sky—"

She stops, turning to me and giving me a don't-mess-with-me stare. "I've never taken you for a coward. Man up and go talk to your...er, well, Raine. Go talk to Raine."

"Great pep talk. Really."

She pats my shoulder and gives me her back as she opens the door. I know if I don't follow her, she'll probably pull me in, which I'd rather not have people witness.

A few of the town boys are in the back, calling out to me with friendly waves and raised coffees in greeting. Following my best friend's girlfriend over to the counter after waving back to them, I stuff my hands in the pockets of my jeans and wait for Raine to turn around.

Chest tightening, I think back to the breathing exercises I had to do back in high school when I was worried about passing out in front of the father of the same girl standing mere feet away from me.

Elena shoves Raine forward when she sees us waiting, earning the teenager a dirty look that she simply grins at. When the redhead turns to me, my eyes go down to her hand, which isn't wrapped like it was the last time I saw her.

She lifts her hand, bending her fingers and wincing slightly at the sensitive skin. "It was hard to work with all that gauze, so..." Her eyes go to Skylar, and she smiles briefly before turning back to me. "Do you both want your usual orders?"

Her eyes refuse to meet mine, and her evasion of the

elephant in the room doesn't sit right with me. Ironic, I guess, since I avoided her after our first hookup. Payback's a bitch.

Skylar elbows my rib cage with a little more force than necessary. "We do, but first Caleb wants to talk to you about something."

Jesus.

Raine's eyes lift to mine with a brief flicker of panic. Her eyes dart nervously to Skylar again before she nods once, wiping her hands on the apron tied around her waist. "Okay." She starts putting my usual order into the register until the total comes up, then glances at the girl beside me. "Want me to add yours to his, Sky, or separately?"

I don't ignore the distance in her voice, and neither does Skylar, who gives her a casual shrug and pulls out a credit card. "It's on me" is all she says, winking at me.

"You don't have to—"

"Duh. I know that, but I am anyway. So say 'thank you, Skylar,' and move out of my way so I can pay for this."

Sighing at her theatrics, I murmur a grateful yet dry, "Thank you, Skylar."

Raine peeks up at me through her lashes before quickly glancing back down again to tear off the receipt being printed for the bubbly blond who's getting far too much enjoyment out of the tension between me and my ex.

"Here you go," Raine says. There's a pause before she heaves a sigh, picks her head up, and looks at me. "I've got a few minutes to talk. Lena can get this stuff ready."

Raine guides us to a table in the back that's relatively private and sits in the chair farthest from the other. I try not reading into that as I take the other seat and watch her fiddle with a straw wrapper that was left on the table.

"How are you feeling?" I ask.

She shifts uncomfortably. "Still not pregnant, by you or anybody, in case that's what you're getting at." The coolness of her tone is well deserved on my end.

"That was a fucked-up thing I said," I murmur, knowing there's little I can say to make up for it. "I truly am sorry."

Her lips press together, but she doesn't say anything right away. Instead, her eyes scan the bakery and all the people chatting at their own tables. They laugh, smile, and look like they're having a good time. Then there's us.

Eventually, she says, "I'm tired. That's how I'm feeling. Because somebody got me a puppy that needs to be house-trained."

I'm grateful Emma gave her one after what I put her through. "What did you name him?"

Raine slowly moves her focus back to me, watching me for a moment or two. "Sigmund Freud. I definitely disappointed the girls. Olive was dead set on Darth Vader, and Skylar thought Brody would be cute for him after Brody Jenner. I guess she and DJ have been binge-watching *The Hills*."

My lips twitch. "I like it. It's very…you."

It's a foreign statement considering there have been moments over the past few months that make me wonder how well I really know her.

"What are you doing here, Caleb? Didn't we say what we needed to at the hospital?" Her question isn't unwarranted, and it's filled with caution.

But I'm not letting her get out of this. "I'd say there's a lot left unsaid between us."

She closes her eyes for a second before shaking her head. She clearly hears the shortness in her tone too. "We've both made poor decisions, especially when it comes to each other. I'm trying to figure things out."

Have we though? "And where do I fit in with that? It's not just you who's responsible for the choices we've made."

She gives me a look before her eyes go elsewhere. "I don't know why you think you'd fit anywhere at this point. If you're here because you feel bad, then you don't need to. What's done is done."

I lean forward. "I don't buy that. You just want me to drop it, but there's a reason why we keep coming back to each other."

"It's because of our history. Please don't read into it."

Too late. "It's true that I feel bad," I admit. "It was wrong for me to involve myself with Emma and you at the same time. You two didn't deserve that."

When she nods, I know she must agree even though she doesn't say so.

"Let me make it up to you," I offer. "I bought those fish sticks you love so much. Come over to my apartment tonight so we can talk."

Raine crosses her arms on the edge of the table. "You got my favorite fish sticks?"

I nod.

"But you hate them."

"Well, *you* don't," I counter easily.

We stare at each other in silence.

I'm the one who decides to break it when I notice Elena passing Skylar the drinks and a bag of our pastries. "I'll help you with your project," I say, hoping school-work could be common ground for us. We always studied together in the past. It could be a good way to spend time together now.

"I already found someone to help me," she replies. "Leon Applebee."

After racking my brain for the familiar name, it clicks. "Applebee? Your neighbor?"

She nods absently, looking at something behind me. "I appreciate the offer, but I think you and I have more than enough on our plates. We don't need to add business to ple—"

Pleasure.

A faint shade of pink coats her cheeks. "I didn't mean it like that."

"Of course not," I murmur, brushing off the sting of rejection that has no right settling into my chest cavity. "Why him, anyway? The man is a hermit. I didn't even know he spoke to you before."

All she asks is "Why not him?"

Why not him? The question is innocent, but it strikes me the wrong way. Because I used to think that's how she thought of me whenever her parents would ask her why we were together. "Why not Caleb?" she'd asked her mom.

"I would have helped you if you'd asked me to," I tell her.

She huffs out a quiet laugh. "Would you have? Because I've tried talking to you without much luck before. We've gotten good at fighting but not much else."

"I'd say there's one other thing we've gotten good at," I press not needing to point out the times we've spent alone. The color of her cheeks says she's thinking the same thing. "A lot has changed for us, trust being the biggest reason I couldn't answer your texts or figure out what to say when I should have talked instead of pointed fingers. But one thing hasn't changed. I'd do anything for you, Raine. If you really needed me."

Chapter Twenty-One

RAINE

I'D DO ANYTHING FOR you, Raine. Those words echoed in my head all day. The only thing that snapped me out of it was Mom asking me where I was going a few hours after getting home from work.

"I'm going out," I tell her, taking my jacket off the hook by the door. "Need anything? I saw we were low on creamer, and I know how you get when you don't have any for your morning coffee."

One of Mom's eyebrows pops up. "Why are you trying to distract me from telling me where you're going?"

I pause with my jacket halfway on. "I'm not trying to distract you. But the last time you ran out of creamer, you went on a rampage for the entire day, and I wasn't sure any of us were going to make it."

She gives me *the look*. The unamused one that most mothers give a handful of times in their lives. "It was a limited-time pumpkin cheesecake creamer that the store ran out of. I had reason to be upset."

Popping my lips, I offer a solemn nod. "I suppose. Anyway, I'm—"

"You haven't gone out this late since you were dating. Is this about *him*?" she asks, this time giving me pause as I untuck my hair from the jacket.

I know who she's asking about, but I play dumb anyway. "Who?"

Pushing off the table, Mom walks over to me before I can open the door. "I know it may seem tempting to go back to what's familiar to you, but you've got your whole life ahead of you. Plus, you've got a puppy who's only partially house-trained. What am I supposed to do with him? I told you already that he's your responsibility, not mine."

Gripping the strap of my purse as I haul it over my shoulder, I turn to my mother, trying to keep calm. My mood has been everywhere lately, along with my mind, and patience hasn't come as easily, especially when Caleb is the topic of conversation. I went back and forth on meeting up with him tonight, and truth be told, I'm not sure why I am. I swore to myself that I'd cut him out of my life cold turkey.

For him. All for him. What will it take for him to understand that?

The truth, that pesky voice mocks me. *The one you refuse to tell him.*

I'd rather he assume the worst of me, that I wanted to try seeing other people instead of settling with him, than let him know the real reason. I don't want to admit that I saw Cody, that he got me pregnant, or that I suffered a miscarriage, and I don't want to relive all the moments after—the doctor appointments, the bad news delivered by the specialists.

I want this choice to allow Caleb and me to grieve but to

be grateful in the long run. Because maybe someday we can both be happy, however that unfolds in our respective lives.

Shaking out of the thought, I say, "Sigmund is sleeping in his crate with his stuffed duck that you bought him. I took him out already, and he's got food and water, so he'll be fine until I'm back."

Mom lets out one of her heavy sighs. "I still can't believe you named him after that weird man with the mommy issues. He's too cute for that. It's almost cruel."

I roll my eyes at her theatrics. She was against having a puppy around until she saw Sigmund's face. She fell in love the second his tongue darted out to give her a sloppy kiss. "He's one of the most famous psychologists in the world, Mom. Even if a lot of his psychoanalysis theories have been discredited, his studies have done a lot for modern-day therapy. We wouldn't be where we are if not for his work."

"His *outdated* work," Mom all but grumbles. "Where are you going anyway?"

"Like I said. Out."

"You're avoiding the question, which means it does have to do with Caleb. You're not together again, are you? I thought you moved on from that. You wanted to focus on finishing your degree, finding a practice that would set you up with good benefits and a financial future. I thought there *may* have been someone, but I was hoping it was something fun for you. Not serious or sneaky."

Ew. Mom thinks I've been sneaking out to hook up with someone random? I mean, I guess she's not entirely wrong, not that I'd consider Caleb random. But there's too much history between us, so even thinking about moving on is hard to swallow.

My mind goes to Emma and Caleb, making my stomach

dip, but I refuse to let that hurt sink in when it has no right to. He did what I wanted him to do. He tried finding somebody else who could give him what I couldn't. I can't focus on that right now, or I'll chicken out of going tonight and then I'll be trapped in my room feeling regret. I feel too much of that lately.

"I don't know what you're thinking, but—"

Mom gives me *the look* again. "I'm thinking that you're running back to the only boy you know. You made your choice already. It's not something you should go back on, especially so soon. There are plenty of fish in the sea. Isn't that how the saying goes?"

Irritation bubbles under my skin. "I'm not *running* to anything or anybody. He and I are going to talk and clear the air. And you know what? Who says I made my choice? Why does it have to be cemented?"

"Raine…"

"What?" I cry, voice rising. "What is your problem with Caleb? He's never done anything wrong. He doesn't have a criminal record. He doesn't even speed, for crying out loud. Out of all the people I could wind up with, he's one of the good ones. Shouldn't mothers want that for their daughters? Shouldn't you want someone secure instead of someone like Dad?"

Her expression darkens. "Watch yourself, young lady. I don't like you raising your voice at me or bringing my relationship with your father into this situation. What's gotten into you lately? You've been acting strange for weeks now, and I don't like who you're becoming."

Fists tightening, I reach around her for the door handle. "It's laughable that you think your relationship with Dad has nothing to do with this considering your example of love is all I've ever known my whole life."

I let that sink in a little further, lips parting with the realization I'm not sure I fully thought about until now.

All Mom does is stare at the truth being thrown at her the way it deserves to be. Sure, I've never been in an abusive relationship with my parents. They've never hit me or threatened to and never really yelled at me. But that doesn't mean the emotional toll doesn't swing just as hard as a fist would.

Swallowing down the thick emotion, I ask, "And how would you even know how I've been acting when you're always sneaking around with Dad doing God knows what instead of being here?"

Her hands go to her hips. "I'm a grown woman who can do as I please without my daughter's permission."

"Well, I'm an adult too, last I checked." She starts to say something, but I cut her off before I can stop myself. "You know what, I don't want to deal with this right now. We're not going to get anywhere by arguing about who's right and who's wrong."

"That's good, because you wouldn't like the answer," she informs me.

I stare at her. "One of these days, you're going to tell me why you're so bitter about love. You never liked it. I used to think it was because you weren't in it with Dad, but then you acted the same way with Caleb and me. I get that your life isn't where you used to think it would be, but I'd say you've had a pretty good one so far regardless. You've got people who care about you. Tiffany. Me. Even Dad."

Mom blinks slowly. Whether she accepts it or not is an entirely different issue. "I've never claimed to have a bad life, Raine, or a grudge against love."

I open the door and shoot back, "Well you could have fooled me."

Neither of us says goodbye before I walk out, closing the door behind me and glancing over at Leon's house to see if he's outside. I bet he's watching *Wheel of Fortune* right now because there's a light on inside where I think his living room is.

It doesn't take long to drive to Caleb's, which is good because my car is making weird noises *again* that definitely don't sound healthy. I've been praying it lasts me a few more months, but it may be on its last legs at this point.

Pulling up to the curb in front of the building that sat abandoned for years, I glance around to see the darkened house and empty driveway.

Ever since I heard Caleb was living here, I've found myself driving or walking by on my way home. I'm not sure why it eased some of the tightness in my chest when I'd see his truck there, but it did. What had I expected to find? Someone else's vehicle? Another girl? I'm not sure what I would have done if I had. Seeing Emma touch his arm at the hospital was bad enough. I doubt I would have been reasonable if I saw her or anybody else leave his apartment.

Dumb girl, I chastise myself.

Walking up the two uneven cement steps to his front door, I knock and step back, glancing at the window to see if there's a light on I missed.

Nothing.

Then I knock again. "Caleb?"

I glance at my smartwatch to check the time, but I expected him to be around. He always was when he said he'd be. There were only two times in all the years I've known Caleb when he was either late or had to back out: once when he got a flat on the side of the road and was stranded with no phone service, and the other when he slept through his alarm after pulling an all-nighter the day before during midterms. I wasn't mad at him either of those times, and I don't want to be now.

But there's a nagging feeling on top of the leftover irritation that's been boiling from the brief confrontation with my mother that certainly doesn't help me feel any less on edge.

After a few minutes of standing there, I bend down to peek into the window and confirm that there's nobody home. As I'm walking to my car, I hear a door crack open behind me. Just as I'm starting to let in relief that I wasn't bailed on, I turn to see an unfamiliar face at the door on the other side of the building.

"Are you looking for Caleb?" the older man asks.

Readjusting my bag, I nod and try not to let my chest deflate from disappointment. "Do you know where he is? We were supposed to meet at seven, but his truck isn't here, and nobody is answering the door."

Caleb's neighbor shakes his head. "He's not here, I'm afraid. He left a while ago. I'd try giving him a call. I'm sure he just lost track of time and will be back soon."

Swallowing the swell of emotion rising up my throat, I force out an unconvincing "Yeah. Maybe." I'm about to get into my car when I remember my manners. "Thank you for letting me know."

The man waves me off before going back into his apartment, leaving me to my thoughts as I slam the car door behind me.

He forgot.

That doesn't sit well with me and definitely doesn't lessen the anger that's already burrowed deep in my stomach.

Pulling out my phone, I hit the Call button and raise the cell to my ear. After waiting for the ringing to stop, it goes to voicemail. I close my eyes and say, "I'm at your apartment, but you aren't. Which is obvious, I guess. I hope nothing came up with your dad. Just...I don't know. Text me or something so I at least know you're alive."

The last thing I want is for something to have happened to Mr. Anders. But there's another part of me, an anxious part that has really started annoying me, that wants some sort of answer. One I could justify.

Because being forgotten...well, that's not something I can settle with easily, no matter if I've told myself it's better he moves on without me. I'll always love Caleb, always want him.

That acceptance is my purgatory.

~

I drive around aimlessly for forty-five minutes, only stopping once to get my favorite fast food and another time when the sound coming from the back end of my car scared me enough to pull over and make sure my wheel was secure. I'm halfway through my chicken nuggets and ten minutes from my parents' house when Caleb's name pops up on my cell phone screen. It's an hour and a half *after* we were supposed to meet.

I'm tempted not to answer out of pettiness, but I know better than that. If something happened that he couldn't control, I'd only be adding fuel to the fire between us by assuming otherwise. It's why I pick up.

"I'm sorry" is the first thing he says when I swipe to accept the call.

I take a deep breath and slow down at the stoplight, biting into another nugget. "Is your dad okay?" I ask with my mouth halfway full. I'm hungry, which isn't uncommon when I'm overwhelmed. I've always been an emotional eater.

A pause. "Yes. He's okay."

"Your mom?"

"Yes, but—"

"Was it an emergency?"

His voice is quiet when he says, "Raine. I'm sorry."

I stare down at my food, feeling my appetite slowly fade. "It wasn't an emergency then. You bailed."

The statement is met with more silence on his end, save some light background noise. I grip the steering wheel a little tighter than I need to as I hit the gas once the light turns green. The radio has been off, leaving me solely to my thoughts the entire time I've been out.

I think about my parents. Their poor communication. How often they fought. How long it took them to accept that separating was for the best. If I saw it unfold any differently, would I be different? Maybe I'd trust my gut more—be open to telling Caleb that my love for him has never gone away.

Instead, I saw what it's like for two people to keep each other at arm's length just to avoid talking about the hard stuff.

"It's not that simple, Raine. You'll understand when you're older," Mom says, patting my back and shooing me to another room when I ask her if she and Dad made up yet.

At what age will I get it though? Nothing about life is easy, I've learned that much. But the older I get, the less I understand. Like why I want to hold on to the same man who I know I need to push away for good.

Eventually, I pull myself back to the conversation at hand, feeling the exhaustion of our push and pull weigh me down. "I know you've got a lot going on in your life already, but meeting tonight was your idea. Talking was your idea. Offering to help me on my project, which is a huge part of my grade by the way, was *your* idea, even if I don't need the help."

Which I do.

He doesn't need to know that though.

"I got distracted at the hospital," he explains. "I know it's a piss-poor excuse, but it's the truth. I'm trying to spend as much time with Dad as possible and try not to look at my phone while I'm there. He's not…there's not a lot of time left. If you were in my shoes, you'd do the same thing, regardless of your relationship with your family."

My nose twitches at his tone, which isn't exactly gentle or apologetic. He knows our families are exact opposites, but our love for them is the same. "If I were in your shoes, I would have *let you know* that our plans changed. Or I wouldn't have made them at all if I had other priorities, which I know your father needs to be right now. It takes five seconds to send a text message, Caleb. I wouldn't have cared if you had just told me you couldn't meet up."

Okay, maybe I would have cared *a little*.

I hear a quiet sigh from him. "You're right. I'm—"

"Don't say 'sorry' again," I tell him, not wanting to hear it. "I know you are. All the two of us are anymore is *sorry*."

I don't recognize the sound of my own voice as I squeeze my eyes closed.

"My dad is *dying*, Raine. Isn't that reason enough to be a little absent-minded? He's family. When Mom called me after I got done with work, I thought…" His voice cracks. "I thought the worst. So yeah, I wasn't really thinking about you or anyone else because all I could focus on was what I was walking into or what would happen once I got there. Then the hospice conversation started up again, which put everybody in a shitty mood. And on top of that, Dad got on my ass about you and Emma, and Mom isn't happy about me putting him on edge with my personal-life drama."

"Your dad knows about us?" I whisper.

"Is that really all you got from that?" he asks skeptically.

I slow down at another stop sign, frowning when the noise in my car starts up again. "Your dad has always been nice to me. I don't want your parents to judge me or think less of me."

Caleb doesn't say anything right away, but I hear something murmured under his breath that I can't understand. "Trust me. They're not judging you about anything. It's me they're not very happy with."

I doubt that. When it comes to us, it's a two-way street. Parents like his aren't going to be fans of the people who hurt him. "They love you."

Just like my parents love me, even if they don't say it often. I know that. I just wish I'd hear it more. See it. Feel it.

As I start driving again, I notice thick smoke start to rise from the hood of the car that blocks my view. "What the hell?"

"What?" I hear from the other end of the phone.

I quickly pull over to the side of the road and get out, spilling my chicken nuggets all over the street.

"Raine, what's going on? Talk to me."

"M-my car is smoking."

"Christ. Where are you?" There are muffled noises like he's shuffling something in his hands. "I'm leaving the hospital now anyway. I can come take a look."

I tell him what street I'm on and the nearest number I

see on one of the houses. "I don't know what to do. Should I call the fire department?"

"It sounds like it's overheated. Do you see a fire anywhere?" I hear a door close on his end. "I'll be there in a few minutes. If there's no fire, don't call. This used to happen to Mom's old Hyundai. Remember? The puke-green one that she put neon-orange seat coverings in. My dad taught me how to fix that."

Sniffling back anxious tears, I grab my bag out of the car just in case. "Your mom loved that car," I say weakly.

He chuckles. "Yeah, but she also loves the brand-new one she got after. This one has heated seats *and* a heated steering wheel. She's fine."

"I guess," I murmur.

"Did you know my dad used to want a Bentley? Not a new one but one of the classics—a 1938 in black. He said when they're polished, they look slicker." I can hear the smile in his voice. "Mom still says they're the ugliest cars she's ever seen."

I know he's trying to get me to calm down, and it's working. A little. "What would he have done with a car that old?"

"Show it," Caleb answers. "At least that's what he said. We both know Dad barely took time off work, so it wasn't likely that it would have made it very far. But they put classic cars in the town parades sometimes, especially during the Fourth. Remember when we were nominated prom prince and princess and got to sit in the back of that classic convertible throwing candy to the kids?"

I do remember that. Nobody was surprised we'd won the crowns. Not during junior year or when we won king and queen during senior year. Even back in high school, we were the couple to beat.

"I remember," I whisper.

My anxiety is still spiked, even when I see headlights in the distance and know exactly who it is pulling up to where my poor car is dying on the side of the empty street.

Caleb climbs out and instantly walks over to the hood of the car, which I'm avoiding like it'll blow up at any second.

"You can hang up the phone now," he tells me, which I hear twice since he's only a few feet away.

It only takes him a few minutes of tinkering under the hood, doing something inside the car, and going back to the front before he wipes his hands off on his shirt, closes the hood, and walks over to me.

"Overheated," he explains. "Your radiator needs to be replaced or it's going to burn out the engine. I think there's a leak in one of the hoses too."

Great.

"Hey," he says softly, reaching out and brushing my arm. "It's okay. I think we should leave it where it is to cool off and we can grab it in the morning. It's not blocking anybody's driveway, and vehicles can get by easily. We'll leave a note on the windshield if you want."

I don't know why, but the gentle tone of his voice breaks the barrier I've been keeping my emotions behind, and the floodgates open.

He still cares about me even when I put him through hell. That's more than I ever saw from my parents.

Once the first tear falls, all the others follow suit until I'm bawling in the middle of the sidewalk. Not even a pretty cry. An ugly, snotty kind that has my nose running and my voice hoarse and my body shaking.

And it feels *good*.

Caleb instantly steps closer, then wraps his arms around

me in a tight hug. "Why are you crying, baby girl? I can help with the car. My dad knows people who can get you a great deal."

First a puppy, now car parts?

It only makes me cry harder.

He squeezes me into him, resting his chin on the top of my head and brushing his fingers through my hair. "Talk to me, Raine. Please? I hate seeing you cry. You know that. I know I screwed up tonight, but I didn't mean any harm by it. I swear."

The more I try catching my breath, the more I end up hiccupping. I use his chest as a tissue to dry off my face, which he doesn't seem to mind, before pulling back and running the backs of my hands against my cheeks.

Once I'm able to collect myself enough to speak coherently, I say, "M-my chicken n-nuggets fell on the ground, and I r-really wanted them."

He stares at me.

Blinks.

And then starts laughing.

"All right," he tells me, hooking an arm around my shoulder with another chuckle. "Forget about the fish sticks. We'll go get you some more nuggets and find somewhere to talk."

I sniff back more tears, doing my best to dry my face and fight off the urge to cry again. "I am not sleeping with you again."

He opens the passenger side door of his truck for me. "I didn't ask you to."

"Just chicken nuggets."

"With the sweet barbecue sauce if they're out of the tangy ranch," he confirms with a half grin tilting one side of his mouth as he watches me climb in. Before he closes the door, he stares at me for a second like he wants to say something. His eyes go back to my car, then to me. Even though I'm sure it's not what he was going to tell me, he grips the door and says, "Let's go get you some chicken."

Chapter Twenty-Two

CALEB

THERE'S A THICKNESS IN the air between us as Raine and I sit in the cab of my truck and eat the food I bought us in the drive-through. Our view from the parking lot is nothing like at Alden Field, but I know she's more comfortable here, surrounded by other people getting a late dinner.

"You're moving your hand a little better," I note, looking at the injury in question. "How's it feeling?"

She lifts it, moving her fingers without flinching. "I took some Motrin earlier. It stings a little sometimes, but it's fine otherwise."

I nod, staring at the burger on my lap.

Raine picks up a chicken nugget and offers it to me. "They put some sweet chili sauce in here." She digs out the sauce container and passes that over too, arching her brows when I don't accept either.

"You eat them," I tell her.

Her lips twitch. "You love this sauce."

I love you more is my first thought. I don't bother speaking that aloud though, because it wouldn't get me very far. "You're the one who wanted them. Go ahead and eat up. You look like you've lost weight."

She looks good, but it doesn't stop me from being hyper-aware that her face looks a little narrower than normal.

We go back to eating in silence, save for the food wrapper crinkling under my double cheeseburger whenever I pick it up and set it down.

There's something to be said about people who can sit comfortably in silence. Mom used to tell me that's how you know somebody is the one. You don't have to do anything to feel comfortable around them. You simply exist in the same atmosphere.

"What do you see for your future?" I ask, looking over and watching her stop midway through taking a sip of her fountain drink.

She slowly lowers her drink. "Caleb…"

"Excluding me," I reiterate. She's not going to tell me the reason she called it off without a little pushing. "Who is Raine five years from now? Ten years? What was your plan when you ended it with us? You had to have had one. You always do."

My ex blinks at my boldness, then whispers, "I don't know." Her head leans back against the headrest. "I'm not sure who I'll even be tomorrow at this point. That's a lot to ask of somebody."

Another cop-out. Unlike her, I know my answer. "I see myself running a successful hardware store, one Dad would be proud of. I've already started making plans to build a website that will help people be able to find and order things easier. They can pick it up once it's in. There's going to be competitive prices against the chain stores that they'd have to travel to, which makes Anders that much more accessible to the community." Ignoring my food, I keep going. "I want to buy that plot of land near my parents' house and build something on it. Nothing big or showy, just a small house with plenty of land to settle on. Create a garden, like the one Mom has out back, and maybe do an in-ground pool like Dad used to consider putting in. A space to call my own, with people to call my own. A home. Happiness. That's what I want for my future."

I see her visibly swallow, as if that's somehow too much for her to handle.

"But," I add, leaning back and picking at the fries barely touched between us, "I would have settled for anything that would include you in it, even if that meant you focusing on your career first and us later. If that were the real reason you ended our relationship, I would have understood. You didn't have to lie. You didn't have to make it seem like there was someone else or other options you wanted to explore first."

A tiny breath escapes her, and I'm not sure she'll answer me.

Setting her drink down in the cupholder between us, she shifts her body to me. "How many people have you been with besides me?"

The question is straight out of left field. "Where did that come from?"

"Just..." She wets her lips. "How many?"

For fuck's sake. "I'm not sure I'm in the mood to discuss this, especially since you didn't answer my question."

"I'm trying to."

Confusion has my brow furrowing.

Raine looks down at her lap. "Even in high school, you seemed so sure about your life. What you would do and

233

where you would end up. You never let anything get in the way of the image you built in your head. And that always, always included me." She takes a deep breath and lifts her gaze upward until her wary, dark eyes are meeting my own. "I never understood that. I knew what I wanted to go to school for and hoped I'd find a good practice to work at before opening my own. But anything could have happened. And there were some things that definitely made me wonder if that'd happen. External factors."

External factors. "I'm not following."

"You had football scholarships and girls always after you who would have given you the world no matter what it was, and I never understood why you didn't go after that life," she admits, fiddling with the last nugget in her box. "I'm not like any of them. I used to think that was my parents getting into my head about why it wasn't smart to settle down or be in a serious relationship so young, but that's not it at all."

I know her parents used to get in her head, but she never seemed like she bought into anything they said. It didn't stop her from dating me or sneaking around. That was how I knew she loved me. Because even though she loved them too, she was willing to risk their consequences.

That meant something.

"Your parents fought all the time because they tried making something work between them that wasn't going to. They weren't happy in their relationship." I lock eyes with her, vulnerability seeping through my skin. "But we were. Weren't we?"

Pain instantly lances through her facial features, her glassy eyes saddening as she fidgets with the seat buckle next to her. "Caleb, it was never because I was miserable with you. I thought you knew that by now."

"Then *why?*" I keep asking myself that question, but I've never had the balls to question her answer until now. What's the worst that could happen by pressing her if I already lost her once? "You haven't actually explored other options, and I know the truth has to be more than just being scared of repeating your parents' mistakes. You're smarter than that."

She fidgets in her seat. "It isn't about being smarter. Kids are impacted in a million different ways by their parents. You've always been lucky with the ones you have. Your mom and dad are amazing people who have never been afraid to show their love for you or each other. That's never been my family. It's complicated."

Something bubbles up under my skin that itches to come out. "You know what's complicated? My father living most of his life being physically active, never smoking, barely drinking, and eating fairly healthy ninety percent of the time and *still* winding up with a type of cancer that can't be cured. I'd say that's far from me being lucky, Raine. Complicated is trying to understand the unknown when we'll never really understand it. *This*"—my finger darts between us—"is not complicated. *We* are not complicated."

"I—"

"Turning down my proposal was one thing. We could have figured something out that didn't require you actually breaking up with me. *Complicated* is trying to figure out how we ended up here after seven years together. Almost a decade, Raine. I wanted to marry you. We'd talked about that life together like you were actually going to be in it."

When her jaw starts quivering, I know I'm pushing it. "That life seemed so far away, Caleb. I knew you were up to something at graduation and I just… I couldn't."

Swallowing, I lower my hands and tuck them into the

pockets of my jeans. "I've been going through everything trying to figure out what the fuck happened to us. I thought I missed a sign. Maybe there was something off that I was ignoring. But we were *happy*. So why? Why give it all up? That shit has been gnawing on me for months now even though I've been trying to push past it. To move on like I thought you wanted to do. But when you said you hadn't been with anybody, I was second-guessing the reason you gave me even more. I still want to be in your life. I want to be your friend. Your partner. Your teammate. Hell, I want to be more. But I'm struggling to figure out if that's going to get me even more hurt unless I know the truth."

There were too many nights before things with Dad got really bad where I spent hours replaying every damn memory we shared, wondering what I did wrong. I couldn't pinpoint anything that gave me relief. No closure. No answers. At my worst, I broke down in front of my mother and asked if she saw anything that I didn't—suspected something I never did. Not even she could give me anything to make the grief go away.

All she did was wipe at my tears and tell me I needed to take things one day at a time.

So I did.

I used my friends to deal.

I used Emma.

Then shit with Dad went downhill fast, and it distracted me from my failed relationship in the worst way possible. I'd rather be miserable if it meant keeping Dad alive. What the hell does my happiness mean in comparison to his health?

There's a moment of stretched silence before I realize Raine is giving me time to make sure I'm done before she finally speaks up. "I really am sorry, Caleb. So sorry about your dad, about…everything. There's nothing I can do to make up for what I did at graduation."

"You could tell me the truth."

Her eyes close for a moment. "I told you the truth the day after you asked me to marry you. I said I was scared and confused and worried that there was more out there."

"If that's the truth," I tell her, wrapping up what's left of my burger, knowing I've got zero appetite for it, "then I'd hate to hear what your bullshit sounds like."

Her eyes widen. I can feel her gaze follow me as I toss the leftover food back into the bag and stare out my window.

We don't talk for a long time, and neither of us makes a move or sound.

It isn't until we get to the stop sign at the end of the school's driveway that I notice the shift in her body. Her fists are clenched together so tightly they're white. As soon as they release, she turns to me and says, "It hasn't always been you. I lost my virginity to somebody else and lied when we decided to take that step together."

Everything inside me shatters at her cool tone.

Hope and all.

It hasn't always been you.

Chapter Twenty-Three

CALEB

THE NEXT DAY, I go through one of the drawers in my bedroom and pull out the velvet ring box I've stored since graduation.

Maybe a part of me, deep down, thought I'd get a second chance with Raine.

Because it's always been her.

I knew it from the beginning, even when everyone else said it would wear off. "It's the honeymoon phase," they would tell me.

There was never a point when I believed it'd stop feeling like she was my person. I could never explain to people the reason why. I just knew, and that feeling was one that's had a death grip on me for the better part of the last ten years.

We had our tough moments like any couple, but nothing that ever broke us. Not in ways that I didn't think we could recover from. I can't help but wonder how true that is though.

Looking back, I see that the rose-colored glasses I wore were discoloring the flags I should have seen waving. Like the first time we'd had sex. My mom convinced Dad to close the store and take a trip for their anniversary, leaving me at home alone for the weekend.

I'd asked Raine to stay the night, hoping she knew what the sixteen-year-old version of me was really asking for. It made sense for us to take that next step together, to seal the love I knew we had for each other.

"Do you want to?" I ask, breaking the kiss she'd initiated on my childhood bed.

She blinks up at me, a wariness to her eyes I can only assume is fear.

When she doesn't say anything, I start to move away from her and backtrack. "We don't have to. We can wait."

I see her swallow and wonder what's going through her mind. She sits up and touches my hand, not saying a word.

So I say, "I don't want to hurt you, but I want to share this with you. I've never..." She doesn't need me to tell her that. We're equals here. She gets it.

Wetting her lips, she weaves our fingers together and squeezes once. "I know you won't hurt me."

She never said it was her first time.

Never said it wasn't.

She let me take her clothes off and kiss her and touch her like we'd done before. But when it came to the actual act, I'd felt how she locked up. How her breathing changed. I should have known it was more than nerves because I knew her better than that.

I wanted to tell her I loved her that night, but I didn't. Something held me back. Uncertainty. Maybe that was another sign hinting at our demise all along.

As much as I hate to accept it, I asked for the truth that she'd been holding back all this time, and she gave it to me.

What better closure is there than finding out the woman I've loved for years cheated on me? Lied? *It hasn't always been you.* Fuck me. I bet there were signs I ignored long before she told me she'd admitted what her worries were when I asked.

She didn't *wonder* if there were other people out there for her. She knew from experience.

With the ring in hand, I go to a local jeweler and set the box on the counter. "How much to buy that from me?"

The man behind the glass counter display takes it and inspects what's inside, offering me a sad smile. "You probably won't get back what you paid," he says honestly, plucking out the ring and studying it closer.

The truth is I don't care. "I just want it gone."

I don't think twice about the number he gives me. I simply accept it, take the money, and walk out with what little is left of my dignity intact.

Chapter Twenty-Four

RAINE

FRESH SNOW CRUNCHES UNDER my boots as I follow the little pawprints in front of me that zigzag in every direction whenever something catches Sigmund's eye.

"He's walking better on the leash," Mom says, raising the coffee to her lips. Things were tense for a while at home, especially because she chose to stick around more often after I called her out on it.

The first couple of days following our fight, we kept to ourselves, save the times we'd bump into each other whenever I'd bring Sigmund out for potty training and walks. Then one night, when I was watching my favorite late-night talk show in the living room, she sat down beside me, pulled a blanket over both of our laps, and said, "I just want you to be happy."

It wasn't an apology, but I knew it was as close as I'd get to one. So even though I wasn't sure I entirely believed it, I accepted the olive branch, and we went about our lives. She never asked about that night with Caleb, and I never gave her any information.

What was the point?

I told him what he wanted to hear.

Some truth.

Not *the* truth, but a part of it.

The part that would cut whatever tie he had with me so he wasn't fantasizing about our future. It kills me to know I'd snipped the invisible string still connecting us, but it had to be done. If he hates me, he can't hold on to me or whatever version of us he's building up in his head.

It's safer this way.

And maybe someday I'll believe what I told him—that there's someone else out there for me. Not anybody like him, who could make me happy the way he did. But somebody close.

Hopefully.

The leash tugging me forward and nearly making me slip is what pulls me out of my head and back to reality. "Yeah, he's training faster than I expected."

"Which is good because I don't know how much more pee I'm willing to clean up," Mom remarks, eyeing the gray ball of energy that's sniffing a road sign and cocking his leg. "I thought I was done with that when your father and I got you potty-trained."

At least she hasn't brought up the shoe the dog chewed up. I'm not even sure when he had time to sneak into her room to get it, but by the time I realized what his sharp little teeth were biting into, it was too late to save it. It was her favorite pair of loafers, and I heard about it for days.

"So…" I pop my lips and bury my free hand in the pocket of my coat. "What are we doing for Thanksgiving? I haven't talked to Dad in a little while about it because he's busy closing on that big estate he was working on."

We're days away, and I've been wondering what our plans are. It's the first Thanksgiving since they separated. I haven't wanted to bring it up, but it isn't like we can avoid the topic forever.

"When isn't that man busy?" is her first reply, sighing as she stares solely at her four-legged grandchild. She doesn't admit to sneaking out and seeing him or give away anything about her late-night adventures. And maybe it's better that I am in the dark. There's only so much I want to know about my mother. "I don't know, Raine. Neither one of us can cook, and we've never had a big to-do for this holiday anyway."

She wants to skip it? Disappointment settles into my stomach. "I'm sure we could come up with something if we looked up some recipes online."

It's a weak suggestion, one I already know she'll turn down, so I'm not surprised when she shakes her head. "Honey, let's be honest. You and I can't cook to save our lives, and starting to learn by making a turkey probably isn't the best idea."

"It's never too late to learn new things. I still think we should sign up for a class together."

The look on her face says it all. "Raine, where is that logical side of you? You can't expect every old dog to learn new tricks. Habits are habits for a reason. It takes years to break them."

Gripping the end of the leash tighter, I frown at the woman whose phone goes off in her pocket. Why won't she even give this a shot? Besides basic sandwiches, there's not much else we can put together ourselves.

When she pulls it out, she stares at whatever name is on the screen and sighs. "I need to take this. I'll meet you back at the house. Watch your step. Not all the ice has melted yet."

I watch her walk away, thinking about what she said and hoping she isn't right. Because if she is, that means it's going to take a lifetime to get over Caleb.

~

I stare at the ingredients scattered across Leon's kitchen counter with a skeptical expression on my face. "You want me to do what?"

My neighbor picks up the recipe and passes it to me. "It's an easy one. Annemarie was able to teach even me how to make it without screwing up."

Staring at the paper with pretty handwriting that must be his late wife's, I lower it and ask, "Why don't you just make it then?"

He grabs an apron that's hanging from the side of the refrigerator and passes it to me. "It's almost Thanksgiving. You can't show up without something. That was my wife's one big rule. This pumpkin pie will knock everybody off their feet, so you're going to make it from scratch."

I lied and told him my family was doing something so he wouldn't feel bad for me or offer a pity invite anywhere. But now that means baking a pie from scratch, and all the confidence I had yesterday when talking to Mom about this exact thing has vanished.

While there isn't a long list of steps on the paper, it still feels intimidating. Setting it down on the counter, I notice the way he stares at the sheet with a small frown on his face, and it makes me wonder if he's thinking about Annemarie.

"What are you doing for the holiday?"

His frown turns into the ghost of a smile. It makes him look a lot friendlier when that scowl most people are used to isn't there. "I won't be alone. I'm going to see my daughter and her family."

He's got kids? "You never mentioned a daughter before. How old is she?"

Instead of answering right away, he slowly moves around the kitchen and grabs a few bowls from the cupboard and then a couple of pans hanging above the sink. Once they're in front of me, he lets out a small sigh. "She's thirty-six. We don't talk often. Not nearly as much as I'd like anyway. Her name is Jenna. Annemarie and I adopted her when she was only a toddler. We couldn't have kids of our own no matter how hard we tried, so we decided to look into the local agencies about fostering and adopting."

I stare at the man and wonder if this is fate's way of intervening in my life and telling me how dumb I am. I'd never given Caleb a chance to embrace our potential reality because he'd always been so hell-bent on having his own kids. He'd talk about whose hair and eyes they'd get and which of our mannerisms would rub off on them as they got older.

"Who wouldn't want a mini Raine?" he asks, hooking an arm around my waist and kissing my cheek. "I know we've got time, but I can't wait for that day."

He would have been heartbroken from how long he'd have to wait for that day to come. Science can only do so much for people like me.

Nostrils flaring at the growing anger, I clench and unclench my fists and focus back on Leon and his story.

He busies himself by organizing the ingredients laid out. "The first few adoptions fell through, and it nearly broke my beautiful wife's heart. Seeing her like that…" The breath he releases is full of painful nostalgia as he shakes his balding head. "I never wanted to experience that again. The day we signed the papers and officially got to welcome little Jen into our lives was one of the best days of my life. Because I got to see my Annemarie at *peace*."

Peace. Maybe you don't have to get everything you want out of life to be one hundred percent happy. Maybe you can still find peace in what you're given. If it's with the right person.

Like it was for Leon and Annemarie.

I grab one of the measuring cups closest to me and toy with the glass handle. "Does Jenna live somewhere else and that's why you don't see her often?"

When his jaw clenches, I realize it's probably a conversation he doesn't want to indulge me in. But before I can switch topics, he answers. "Jenna has always struggled with her history. Her adoption was closed, which means we didn't know anything about her biological parents. When she turned seventeen, she wanted to know where she came from. We couldn't help her, and it caused a bit of a…rift of sorts between us. As she got older, she found other reasons to resent us. We always chalked it up to teenage rebellion, but it never got better."

Sadness settles into my chest. "But you see each other still."

His hands pause from grabbing the graham crackers we're somehow turning into a crust. "When Jenna found out she was pregnant with her first child, a little boy, she reached out. She told her mother and me that she finally understood that her past didn't matter."

He loses me. "It didn't?"

Leon shakes his head. "No. She said family are the people who love you even when you're a little shit. Her words, not mine. It's true though. You can't choose who you're related to, but you *can* pick your family. I think finally having one of her own put a lot into perspective for her about what kind of love life has to offer."

One of my hands goes to my stomach. "If you don't mind me asking, did you and your wife ever get angry about not having your own kids?"

My neighbor studies me, his eyes moving down to my stomach before I force my hand to move away before he assumes the same thing Caleb did. "We were sad," he admits. "But we still got a child, even if Annemarie didn't carry her. That doesn't make Jenna any less ours. We're the ones who sheltered her, fed her, and loved her. We're lucky to have had the opportunity and privilege to raise such a wonderful woman. Not everybody gets that chance, even if they deserve it."

Emotion that's nearly impossible to swallow crams into the back of my throat.

"Word of advice," Leon says. "There's no such thing as a perfect family. Everybody fights. Everybody argues. Hell, sometimes people stop talking to each other for a while. But family is always family at the end of the day, no matter how your bond is formed. Flaws and all. That love will always be there."

My fingers tighten at my sides before I dare picking my eyes up. "Thanks for that."

I'm tempted to tell him about everything.

Caleb and me.

Cody.

After Cody.

But as each second passes, I lose my courage to open up to somebody.

Leon hums. "Enough stalling. Let's get this pie done so you can hound me with more questions before your next deadline. I have a story about that time my wife caught me with my pants down doing my business on the side of the road in broad daylight. Woman is a saint for still loving my drunk ass after that one."

I laugh. "I'm looking forward to that story."

Chapter Twenty-Five

CALEB

DAD'S ARMCHAIR IS THREE feet to the right of where it normally sits, leaving me hyper focused on the indentation marks left in the carpet. The living room looks completely different ever since hospice came in with all the necessities they need to take care of Dad. Mom and one of the nighttime aides rearranged some of the furniture to make sure everyone could get around easier. There are tubes and wires and machines scattered in the corner, and the room smells like medicine and antiseptic.

I can tell all the changes are hard on Mom, but she never says a word about how the house has stopped feeling normal since everything was moved around. She puts a smile on her face as though nothing is wrong.

Dad jerks away from the woman working on his arm. "That hurts, dammit," he barks at her.

The woman, Mary, doesn't seem fazed as she offers softly, "Sorry, Rich. I'll try being more careful. Only a few more seconds, okay?"

I know he can't help his temper these days, but it doesn't make it any easier watching him lash out at people when it's so far from who he normally is as a person. "Owen said that they caught the guys who broke into the store," I tell him, referring to his friend who's a retired police officer. "A couple of teenagers with nothing better to do, I guess. They tried breaking into the bank down the street a few days ago, where they ended up being arrested."

Dad raises a brow at the news, distracting him from the nurse. "Who the hell would be dumb enough to rob a bank?"

"*Attempting* to rob a bank," I correct, sitting back on the couch with a grin when I catch the roll of his eyes. "Remember the Nardini kids? It was the oldest boy and one of his friends."

He thinks about it, one of his fingers scratching at the bald patches on his skull from where his hair has fallen out. "The ones who were always getting in trouble for smoking weed in the school bathroom?"

"They've moved on to heavier stuff from what Owen told me." The former police chief heard through the grapevine that the boys had heroin on them when they were brought into custody. "Anyway, Jackson Nardini confessed to a string of robberies around Lindon, hoping it would get him a better deal. Threw his friend right under the bus for it all."

Dad huffs. "Fucking idiots."

I nod in agreement and listen to Mom fuss around in the kitchen. Rubbing my hands down my jeans, I break the silence. "I know I already apologized, but—"

"I don't want to hear it again," he cuts me off, eyeing me firmly. "What's done is done, son. You can't go back and change it. If the cops have them, we'll probably get some sort of payout, if not the actual items they stole back."

I grip my knees. "I know I can't change it, but I've always been careful about locking up. The leak at my apartment just had me a little absent-minded that day."

Dad shakes his head. "It's nothing you can't handle. You're tough. All Anders men are."

Having to look away so he doesn't see the doubt in my eyes, I reach over and scratch Frank's head. The basset hound looks as tired as I feel.

Still, I tell Dad, "Yeah. You're right."

The football game playing on the screen takes up Dad's full attention, leaving me sitting with their dog until I decide to go see if Mom needs anything.

As soon as I walk up to her, she winds an arm around my waist and squeezes me. "Hi, sweetie. Everything okay?"

I nod. "Yeah. Dad is watching the game, so I figured I'd come to see if you need help." I reach over and grab one of the rolls she's putting on the tray to heat up. "He's changing."

The statement gives Mom pause, causing her shoulders to drop a fraction. "They told us his personality would start to change." The smile she gives me is forced. "But he's still there. I see it."

There's so much pain trapped behind her eyes, and I feel horrible because I don't know how to help her.

Mom clears her throat and goes back to spreading out the dinner rolls. "Tell me about Caleb. I feel like we never talk anymore."

I pull apart the bread. "We talk almost every day, Mom."

She gives me an exasperated look. "You tell me that the store is doing fine and that you're passing your classes.

Nothing personal. Do you see your friends? Do you see... other people?"

Her way of hedging for information makes me chuckle. "Subtle."

She cracks a grin. "I thought so. So are you? You went from talking about Raine and Emma to nothing about either of them. I know your father and I weren't exactly fans of what you were doing, but you can still talk to us about it if you need to. What happened?"

Lips twitching, I pop another piece of the roll into my mouth. "I fucked up." I know Mom doesn't like that kind of language, so I lift my shoulder when she gives me a narrowed look and say, "I *messed* up. You guys were right. I shouldn't have gotten involved with Emma. She's a good person who didn't deserve to be sucked into my issues."

Sadness creeps onto Mom's face, and I hate it. Her husband—the love of her life—is dying, and she pities me for *my* love life. "It's true that your dad and I wished you would have waited to start seeing somebody, but we only want you to be happy. Emma seemed to take away some of the stress you were obviously going through."

"Who says I deserve that though?" I question. "You're going through just as much, if not more. Where is your relief from that?"

All she replies is "You."

I blink, confusion twisting my face.

"Seeing you live your life is good enough for me, baby boy. Even if you make some mistakes along the way. Because that means..." Her voice cracks as her gaze roams to the other room where Dad and his nurse are. "That means that you're *living*."

Clearing my throat to avoid the swarm of emotions, I

offer her something that distracts her from the reality sitting in the living room. "I sold the engagement ring. Didn't get a lot of money for it, but I'm thinking about putting it toward the store or maybe a different truck."

When I'm greeted by silence, I have to look up at her to see if she heard me. "Does that mean things between you and Raine are over?"

Haven't they been since graduation? To Raine, it was obviously over sooner than that. I just didn't realize. "Things weren't what I thought they were between us."

"What does that mean?"

Do I tell her? Make her hate Raine as much as I want to? I don't know if that would make a difference one way or another.

"I put too many expectations on us," I settle on. "Too much pressure."

Mom stops what she's doing and turns to me, reaching out to brush my arm. "Sometimes things don't work out the way we want them to, Caleb. But that doesn't mean they don't work out how they're meant to."

What does that mean though? Walking away from Raine is bad enough, but knowing I wasted seven years on her for the greater good is a little too much for me to accept. I don't buy it.

She cheated, I want to tell Mom.

She lied all this time.

She's a horrible person.

If I said those things, I have no doubt Mom would be angry for me. The thing is she's already angry because of Dad. Angry our lives have been turned upside down. She doesn't deserve me piling one more thing on her shoulders.

It's my burden to bear.

"Well, I won't ask if she's with her family today then" is all Mom says, going back to prepping the rest of lunch. "Hopefully the two of you wind up happy in life whether you're together or not. We both know it's too short to be anything but."

Almost as if proving her point, Dad starts coughing from the other room. Then yelling at the nurse for whatever she was trying to do to help.

He's still in there, I remind myself.

It's hard wondering for how much longer.

～

Matt and DJ are waiting for me at our normal table in the back of the dining hall when I drag my ass over to them and drop my notebook down. They exchange a brief look before turning their gaze on me as I sit with a giant cup of coffee.

"Yes, I know I look like shit. No, there's nothing you can do about it. Yes, Dad is the best he can be right now. No, I don't want to talk about it." That should cover the bases of their questions that usually come whenever I see them.

Dad is taking a turn for the worse, Mom isn't handling it well, and there's a growing anger inside me that keeps nipping my consciousness at every fucking turn. I'm exhausted. Stressed. Pissed off. It's a deadly combination because I know I'm going to combust.

The question isn't if, it's when.

DJ shrugs, eyes moving from my face to the coffee I finish. "Whatever you say, my man."

Matt snickers as he pops a fry covered in the nasty mayo and ketchup dip he loves into his mouth. "Does that mean you don't want to hear about the dick that's on your face, or...?"

I straighten. "What the fuck are you talking about?" Grabbing my phone, I turn the camera app on and turn it forward-facing. Sure enough, there's a faded ink-drawn dick on my cheek. "How long has that been there?"

DJ clears his throat and scratches his cheek before passing me a napkin to scrub the drawing off. "You must not remember dozing off in class this morning and basically face planting onto your notebook."

"Where DJ had drawn a dick," Matt adds, grinning when I glare at the guy responsible. "The ink transfer is pretty solid. You can even see the little hair follicles he drew on the ball—"

"Quit it. It's not fucking funny. I've been walking around campus with a dick on my face for the past two hours," I grumble, tossing the balled-up napkin at DJ's face. "You couldn't have told me that it was there before we left the damn classroom earlier?"

The former wide receiver lifts his shoulders innocently. "I wasn't exactly gazing lovingly into your eyes when we left. I didn't even know it was there until now. Skylar was texting me about—" His eyes glimmer with mischief. "Well, it doesn't matter. Point is, I would have said something if I knew."

Matt, on the other hand, says, "I wouldn't have. Didn't you have a makeup exam today with Kroger?"

Now that I think about it, the dude who gave me a chance to take the test I missed was giving me a weird look most of the time I sat there struggling with the material. It didn't exactly give me the boost of confidence I needed as I tried figuring out the gibberish about business analytics and financial datasets on the page.

My phone lights up with a message, pulling my gaze downward at my part-time employee's name across the top of my screen.

Ronny: Sorry man, Sadie is still sick

"Christ," I mumble.

I know it'd bite me in the ass if I gave him shit about taking care of his kid, but I don't know if I can handle a full shift when I already promised Mom I'd be home with Dad while she runs errands.

"You good?" Matt asks, popping another fry in his mouth and watching me send a quick reply to my employee.

I shake my head, knee bouncing under the table as the pressure builds in my chest. "Store shit. Down an employee again. Mom wants me to get home by three. Dad already gave her shit about being babysat considering he's got a whole team of people constantly watching him, but it gives Mom peace of mind knowing I'm there."

My friends exchange another look before DJ says, "Can't you just close early for the day? People around here will understand. Most of them know what's up with your dad anyway."

I don't want to tell them that business is down and has been for a while. I've wanted to try hiring another person to help me and Ronny out since Mom has been gone from the scene, but we can't exactly afford to do that right now because of the revenue we lost after the robbery. Buying a dog for Raine has become a big regret since she admitted what she'd done. That money could have gone to better things. Things for me, for Mom, for the store. We still haven't gotten a payout for the items stolen, and there haven't been as many sales thanks to the new chain store that went in not even twenty miles away. I've already closed early a few times, and Dad has been on my ass about how important consistency is for any business if I want to make money. "Hours need to remain the same no matter what," he told me. "Don't turn me into an excuse not to stay open."

I know Dad comes from a good place when he says he's confident I can handle anything—that I'm strong. So why the fuck do I feel anything but?

Matt grabs his plate. "I'm getting more fries. You want anything before you have to go, dude?"

I wave him off as he goes for seconds. DJ leans back with his arms crossed and watches me a little too closely.

"Don't," I tell him, scrubbing at my eyes.

"I didn't say anything."

"You're thinking something."

"Which *is* scary," he confirms, smirking.

We're quiet for a few seconds.

Then he says, "Once things are quieter for you, maybe we could do a guys' night. *Talk* about things. Get some shit off your chest. No offense, Caleb, but you look like you're about to snap."

He's not wrong. "I can feel it," I tell him, leaning back and clenching my fists together to keep composure. I have an overwhelming urge to scream at the top of my lungs until there's nothing else left. Talking to Matt about shit helped before, so I know it can't hurt to admit as much to DJ. "Everything is about to change. I know it, but I'll never be prepared for it."

"Bro, if there's something I can do to help at any point—"

"Don't you get it?" I laugh bitterly, swiping my fingers through my hair. "Nobody can do anything. The doctors can't

257

save Dad. The bank can't give me more money for the hardware store. And I couldn't save my fucking relationship with Raine."

For once, DJ is quiet. There's no witty comeback or words of wisdom.

Closing my eyes, I lean forward and drop my head. Hand gripping the back of my neck, I let out a long sigh. "She fucking cheated on me, man. I gave her everything, and it wasn't enough to keep her. Just like the doctors couldn't do enough for Dad."

I hate that DJ is blurry when I lift my eyes to meet his, but there's no hiding the tears that form in my eyes as I watch him stare at me.

"She told you she cheated?"

"Not in those exact words," I murmur, using the heels of my palms to wipe my eyes. "I didn't need her to tell me the details. She said everything she needed to."

"Christ," my friend murmurs, shaking his head in surprise. He's at a loss for words. A first for him.

Matt comes back over and drops down, tossing a fry in his mouth. "What'd I miss?"

DJ stares at me.

I drop my eyes.

And Matt says, "Who died?"

Flinching, I shake my head at the innocent question. "Nobody yet."

I think DJ smacks Matt, but I'm not sure because I don't look at either of them.

"Shit, sorry," Matt tells me. "I didn't think about how that sounded."

"Don't worry about it." I push my chair out and stand, downing every last drop of the coffee in the cup. "I need to get going if I'm to get everything done that I need to."

Before I walk away, DJ says, "Hey. Remember what I said. If you need anything…"

"I appreciate it. I'll let you know."

As I'm leaving, Matt follows me out after telling DJ he'll be right back. "Wait up, man."

"I can't talk about it right now," I tell him, knowing I'll break down in the middle of campus. I'd like to hold on to what little pride I have left.

He lifts his hands. "That's fine. I won't push you about what's going on. I just want to tell you that I'm here too. We're family, man. We've always had each other's backs. So whatever you need to get through, we'll be here."

I glance over at him, feeling my jaw clench as I restrain from crying more. "You should head back in before DJ eats all your food."

He presses his lips together and dips his chin once, knowing that I hear him loud and clear. Grabbing my shoulder, he squeezes it and backs toward the dining hall. "Just some advice, brother. Don't hold anything back. The more you stop yourself from feeling what you need to, the more you're going to drown. Don't go down with the ship to save everybody else."

I force another nod and walk away before he sees just how much those words hit.

Chapter Twenty-Six

RAINE

I'M SIPPING MY ESPRESSO when Leon steps up to the table I secured and pulls out the chair across from me. "Haven't seen bags that dark under somebody's eyes since Jenna had colic," he notes, slowly sinking down into the seat and letting out a long breath.

Setting the tiny cup down onto the saucer, I peek up at him through my lashes. "I had trouble sleeping last night."

I was in so much pain when I curled into bed that not even Motrin and a heating pad could help the cramps and pressure building in my back. It was so bad I debated asking Mom to take me to the hospital. But then she'd ask me a million questions that I didn't want to answer.

My neighbor grins. "Stay up late talking to someone?" His lips stretch wider, and a chuckle rises at whatever skeptical face I must be making. "Or maybe not. Sounds like it could be complicated based on that look in your eye."

I've never been good at masking my emotions. "I wish I

was up late talking to somebody," I admit, forcing a smile. It would beat the alternative. "But no."

"Anybody in particular?"

This time, I say nothing.

Leon doesn't let me get away from the conversation that easily. "This have anything to do with the Anders boy?"

I toy with my coffee cup. "That obvious?"

"When you've been around as long as I have, you notice things. You two were attached at the hip, and now you're not. Doesn't take a rocket scientist to know you broke up."

Trying to seem unfazed, I grab my notebook and pen out of my bag and set them on the table. "Do you think you can be friends with someone you love? Maybe not right away, but someday?"

"Don't friends love one another?" Leon shoots back, reaching for the Styrofoam cup of tea I bought for him.

He has a point, but it doesn't make me question what Caleb and I are any less. "My dad said it takes a long time to unlove somebody, and that makes me nervous that it'll be like this forever. Even though there's no chance of us being together anymore"—especially over how I severed ties with him, which Leon doesn't need to know—"I can't help but feel hurt. The thought of him not being in my life…"

It's…tragic. More so than I want it to be.

"That's quite the conundrum indeed," he notes, leaning forward and swiping his hand along his jaw. "Let me ask you this. Is there a reason why you can't love him anymore?"

I give it some thought, but the only answer I come up with is "We're not together."

"Neither are me and Annemarie," he counters pointedly. "Doesn't mean I've stopped loving her."

There's an obvious difference there that I blurt out

before my filter can stop me. "But you can't be." I wince at the unfiltered truth. "Sorry. I mean that Caleb and I are still around each other here. We go to the same school. Have some of the same friends. Things are complicated between us now more than ever. We have no real choice but to be around each other for the foreseeable future."

He shakes his head again. "There's that word again. *Complicated.* I think life is only as complicated as we make it. If you don't want to be friends, don't. Can't say I disagree with your father though. Love is love. We can't always help who we fall for. It takes a long time, maybe even a lifetime, to learn how to stop doing that. And quite frankly, I don't think it's worth it."

"Why not?"

He takes his time grabbing his cup and blowing on the steam billowing from the little opened tab. "The kind of love you can't forget about is the real kind. There's a saying out there that talks about how love isn't about finding someone you can live with but someone you can't live without. So what's it felt like being without the Anders boy?"

Depressing.

My nostrils twitch as I hold my pen with a white-knuckle grip. "Sad. Lonely. I thought I'd spend this summer away from Lindon and clear my head and heart, as if it could be that easy. Maybe learn a new hobby that I never thought about before. But instead, I spent it being lectured to about the evils of men by my bitter aunt who went through a horrible breakup a couple of years ago and being surrounded by old memories and past mistakes. I wasn't healing there. I was haunted."

Instead of asking me what ghosts and demons lingered, he asks, "What's one of the things you want to learn to do?"

The answer is easy. "Cook," I admit a little sheepishly. "I don't know how to. My dad always dealt with the meals growing up. Since he moved out, it's been takeout and delivery because Mom doesn't know how to cook either. And when I was with Caleb, he'd take care of stuff like that. He was good at it too."

I used to joke that he should have gone to culinary school and become the next Gordon Ramsay—trade in footballs for five-star feasts.

His answer was always the same. "It wouldn't be the same. Cooking is only fun when it's for people I care about."

The first time he ever told me that, I knew he was destined to be a doting husband and wonderful father. Somebody who would take care of his family and do anything to support them.

"What?" Caleb asks, grinning up at me from where he chops the vegetables at the kitchen counter.

I smile from the stool across from him, propping my chin on the heel of my hand. "I just like seeing you all domesticated. You're feeding an entire house full of football players and actually making them eat their veggies."

He waggles his brows. "It's practice. There are some picky eaters here who test me nine times out of ten, but they eventually eat what I put in front of them. Except for DJ sometimes. He came home plastered last week after celebrating the game against the Hawks and would only eat dino nuggets."

That definitely sounds like DJ. "Well, he's a kid at heart, so that makes sense."

My boyfriend shrugs, focusing back on the carrots he's cubing. "How many do you think you want? Kids, I mean?"

My stomach drops like it always does when kids are brought up. It's been over four years since the unexpected miscarriage. When

263

I went back to Planned Parenthood for a follow-up to go on birth control, they did some tests when I explained the painful periods I got. They noticed cysts on my ovaries and told me it could be nothing.

But it wasn't nothing. Those cysts kept coming back, and not even the hormonal birth control pills they put me on did anything to help.

It became obvious that the cysts were caused by something, *and eventually that diagnosis came with a lot of potential consequences. Endometriosis. I'd done enough research to guess what was wrong before I saw the official word in my medical file, and I hated knowing there could be a day when I found out I wasn't fertile at all because of the condition.*

Then I would have wasted one core memory on the wrong person. And I think that was what hit me hardest. Because if I experienced that moment with Caleb, I wouldn't feel so horrible. He would have been there, told me it'd be okay, that we'd have time. But would he have been upset that I'd lost the baby? Sad that we'd missed the opportunity? If he was with me when I found out I was sick, would he comfort me? Or would he tell me there was still a chance?

Telling him anything would mean admitting I slept with someone else, and that's a burden I plan on keeping to myself for life. Or at least until I can't keep it anymore. I'll cross that bridge when I get to it.

I don't like to think about the past that often, but it's in the forefront of my mind when children come up in conversation. Because there could be a day when Caleb decides that the struggle isn't worth it in the long run. It's better I make that choice before he does.

"I don't know," I tell Caleb, sitting up. "My focus is on school right now."

His smile doesn't falter. "I get that. There's no rush." Leaning across the counter, he brushes his lips against mine. "We're in this together. I'm ready when you're ready. Maybe we'll have a little redhead. Mom says a redhead would look cute with our eye color."

I tighten my hold around the pen in my hand and shake myself out of the memory. I'd blame the pain I'm in for reminding me that my reproductive system hates me, but it's beyond that.

It's the reason I'm here.

The truth.

Because Caleb is going to be a wonderful father someday with somebody who can give him the world.

And that isn't me.

"So what do you say?" Leon asks, drawing my attention back over to him.

Jaw clenching from the dark path my thoughts are taking me down, I ask, "About what?"

My neighbor chuckles. "Learning how to cook. I can teach you a thing or two. Annemarie house-trained me a long time ago, so I can fend for myself just fine and pass down a few essentials to you."

I unclench my jaw and take a silent breath to release the tightness in my lungs. He'd really want to do that? "I'd like that. A lot, actually."

The second he sees the look on my face, he shakes his head. "Don't get sappy on me. You look like you could use somebody on your side right now. Can't pretend to be your father, but I can be your friend. I might be a grumpy bastard, but I'd be lying if I said I didn't enjoy these little outings."

My smile eases some of the weight in my chest that keeps trying to pull me under. "I'm glad I don't annoy you with my questions."

Leon huffs, taking a sip of his tea. "Oh, you do. But it

gets me thinking about what life used to be when the missus was around, so I can't complain. Much."

I laugh under my breath because he complains all the time. But I like it. It makes him real.

"Now, what would you like to discuss for your assignment today? I can tell you about the time Annemarie stormed out of the house after I accidentally ran over her prized rose bushes. Took me two hours of searching to find her, and instead of yelling, she kissed me and told me that I owed her new flowers."

I crack a smile. "Did you get her some?"

His eyes lighten. "Every single year, I bring a bouquet of homegrown roses from the bushes I planted for her to her grave."

Wow. In that moment, I know that that's the kind of love I want someday. The forever kind no matter the circumstances, even though it won't be with Caleb.

~

I wake up in the middle of the night covered in sweat and curled up with a pillow pressed against my stomach. Groaning when I sit up, I wince at the stabbing pain in my lower abdomen and close my eyes to try breathing through the wave of nausea that comes with it.

It's too much.

"Mom?" I cry out, causing Sigmund's head to pop up from where he's sleeping at the foot of my bed. He lets out a little whine when I toss my legs over the side of the bed, attempting to stand despite the dizziness blurring my vision.

Sigmund is on high alert when I stumble, catching

myself on the wall and knocking off one of the frames that was hanging there, the glass breaking when it hits the floor.

"Mom?" I call out again, looking down at the shattered picture of me and Caleb from prom that's lying on the floor.

Why isn't she answering?

I glance at the time and realize it's the middle of the night. Not even three yet. Either Mom is sleeping, or she never came home.

The first tear falls as I shuffle down the hallway toward Mom's room. When I push the cracked door open and see the empty bed, I frown and nearly double over when the sharp feeling becomes tenfold.

I'm barely able to see past the tears by the time I make it back to my room and reach for my phone on the nightstand. I get as far as unlocking the screen and pulling up my contacts to call Mom when the dizziness returns.

Except this time I don't catch myself.

Fingers grazing the screen, I hit the floor.

I have a strange dream, one where the pain almost feels normal when I hear dream Caleb pick me up and tell me it's going to be okay.

And because it's not real, I let myself believe it. I sink into his arms and soak up the warmth he gives me and listen to the soft-spoken promises whispered against the top of my head.

"It'll be okay, baby," he tells me.

There's air on my face. Cold but welcoming on my clammy skin.

"I've got you."

Chapter Twenty-Seven

CALEB

I HATE THIS PLACE. I hate the smell of antiseptic and medicine, the sounds of the equipment and families talking, and feeling suffocated by the other patients and staff lingering. If I never have to be at this damn hospital again, it'll be too soon.

When I woke up to Raine calling, I debated ignoring it. But my gut told me to pick up because she never called this early. Not even when we were dating.

Now I'm here, standing outside her curtained-off room in the emergency room.

Again.

Do I want to be here? No. Did it nearly break me when I saw Raine on the floor of her bedroom, bleeding? There were no words to describe the utter panic I felt thinking she was gone. The moment I sank down beside her, I had no idea what I'd find.

The thought of losing her physically destroyed me, regardless of what she did in the past. I'm not sure how to feel about that. Because I want nothing more than to cut ties with the girl sprawled on the hospital bed under the heated blanket the nurse gave her.

I want it to be over.

I want to forget her.

To move on.

But one look at her pale face, and that stupid fucking invisible string that attached us at fifteen was back, wrapping us together all over again. When would it end?

"Caleb?"

Head snapping up, I straighten when I see Emma's pinched brows. Of course she'd be working an overnight. We haven't spoken since I paid for Raine's dog. I told her I was sorry, she told me she knew, and that was it. She didn't accept my apology, and I didn't blame her.

"Is your dad okay?" she asks, genuine concern all over her face. I know she cares about him because they spent a lot of time together. Dad always struck up conversations with her whenever she came to check on him and sneak him food or snacks so he wouldn't have to eat the garbage that the hospital served.

She didn't do it for me or because we were seeing each other. It was because she was a good person. Innocent. Loyal.

I glance back at Raine to see her still resting her eyes while the IV gives her fluids. The doctor hasn't been in to see her yet, but a few nurses have come and gone to make sure she's comfortable while she waits.

Walking over to Emma, I say, "I'm not here with him. He's at home."

Those haunting gray eyes move to the room behind me before nodding in understanding. "Is she okay?"

I lift a shoulder. "I'm not sure, but I'm sure she will be."

Emma shifts on her feet. "Good."

We're silently standing and staring at each other while people walk around us.

"How are y—"

"Were you with her?" she asks at the same time as I start my question.

My head shakes. "No. I was sleeping." Another pause. "Alone."

I don't know if it's relief or something else that floods her face. But she says, "But she called you and you came."

All I can do is nod. "Yes."

Once again, those eyes move away from me. This time in a different direction than Raine's room. "I'm glad she has you."

Those words sink in, weighing me down. I could tell her it isn't like that, but isn't it? It's obvious I'm still there for Raine even if she may not deserve it.

So I choose not to say anything at all.

Emma squeezes my arm and lets go, backing toward the nurse's station. "Take care of yourself, Caleb."

I know that's goodbye, so I return the sentiment and walk back into Raine's room to find her awake.

All the redhead lying there pricked by needles says is "She's nice."

There's no way I'm talking about Emma given how our conversation about her last time ended. "How are you feeling?"

Her eyes drop to her lap. "A little better since they gave me pain meds." She rubs her arm and fidgets with the heart rate monitor attached to her finger. "I called my mom. Or…I meant to."

But she didn't. She called me. Whether subconsciously or on accident. "She wasn't home."

Raine shakes her head. "She's out a lot."

We're quiet, save for the machine beeping between us.

My ex breaks the silence. "I'm sorry you're here."

One of my brows arches. "I'm pretty sure that's supposed to be my line in this scenario."

Her lips quiver at the corners. "Still…"

More silence.

We sit like that for a few minutes, staring at the curtains as if we're both willing the doctor to come. When another minute or two goes by and nobody saves either of us from the awkwardness, I shift my body toward her.

"Who was it?"

Her eyes shoot to me. "Who was—"

"Who did you sleep with?"

I see her throat work with a nervous swallow. "You don't know him, Caleb. Does his name really matter?"

It does to me.

I don't know why, but it does.

"His name is Cody," she tells me, taking me by surprise. I guess I thought she would bullshit me. Lie. Tell me it didn't matter. "I met him in Radcliff."

Of course. That's the only place she could have met somebody without me knowing.

Sitting back in the chair, I cross my arms on my chest and process this. *Cody.* Guess she has a thing for C names.

"And no," she adds, causing me to look back over at her. "To answer your question from the other day in the hospital. It wasn't worth it. None of it was."

I'm about to ask what she means when the doctor finally walks in. "Ms. Copelin? I'm Dr. Matthews. I'm on call tonight."

When Raine glances nervously at me, I don't know what

271

she's going to say. But it doesn't surprise me when she asks, "Can you go get me something to drink from the vending machine?"

She doesn't need any more fluids, but I stand anyway with a dip of my chin. Being a dick to her wouldn't get me anywhere right now, so I'll comply. "I'll come back in a bit."

Her smile is tight, but I know there's appreciation in her eyes when they meet mine.

The entire way out of the room, I can only think of the name she gave me, wondering if she ever brought it up in the past without me realizing its significance.

"Fuck," I groan, scrubbing my tired eyes.

I really need to stop asking questions that I don't want the answers to.

~

A few days later, I walk up to Anders Hardware to see DJ waiting for me to unlock the front door, with two cups of coffee in his hands. "I had to sweet-talk Bea for these bad boys. She was cranky this morning because of something Elena did. Don't ask me what. I could barely hear anything besides her grumbling under her breath. Something about a dented car. I even tried my famous smile that Skylar says gets me everything. Apparently, it doesn't work on Bea."

Helping me turn on the lights, he sets one of the drinks down on the counter while I get the computer started. "I'm pretty sure Aiden is the only one who could get a reaction from her with a single smile."

DJ makes a face at the statement we both know to be true, even if he's bitter about it. "That's because Aiden *never* smiled. It made anyone feel special when they got one."

"Jealous?" I ask, lips twitching into an amused smirk.

He lifts a shoulder. "Maybe a little. How could I not be when a stud like that chooses a hottie like Ivy over a sexy beast like me?"

I shake my head at his nonsense and fire up the computer, taking the coffee. "Don't push it, *beast*. What are you doing here anyway? It's Sunday. Shouldn't you be sleeping in or spending time with your girlfriend?"

My friend rounds the counter as if he works here and pulls out the only stool for himself. "I would if Skylar didn't decide to have a sleepover at Olive's dorm. Apparently Olive is in some type of boy crisis, which required McDonald's and eighties chick flicks to resolve. When I called to say goodnight, I heard *Sixteen Candles* in the background. They'd already watched *The Breakfast Club* and *Pretty in Pink.*"

I work around him, gathering a few of the things I need to do before opening the store. "Is she okay?"

"Olive? Yeah. That girl is made of steel. O'Conner probably did something dumb." He's referring to the newest rookie on Pittsburgh's national hockey team, the Penguins. "He's a dude after all. He's bound to fuck up. We all do."

Do we though? I'd like to think I did everything I could to make sure I didn't screw things up, yet here I am.

Brushing it off, I think about his girlfriend's friend and former Lindon U hockey star. I didn't even know O'Conner was still doing shit with Olive since he graduated. I heard through the grapevine that they had some sort of casual fling during his last year at Lindon that I assumed ended when he went off to play professionally. Playing for the big league changes people. He's on ESPN all the time getting coverage on what little ice time he gets.

"Is Sky liking her classes this semester?"

My friend stares at me, amusement coating his face. "You're really not going to tell me, are you?"

I play dumb as I organize the receipts I have to log and file. "Tell you what?"

"About you and Raine."

"What about her?" I ask, feigning innocence as I start organizing tasks for the day that have been piling up around here.

Dry humor sparks his eyes when I look up at him. "You suck at playing dumb. I'm telling you, dude. You're addicted to that girl despite what she's put you through."

This time, I shoot him a look. "Quit it. I'm not talking about it with you right now. I don't want people butting into my business when I'm barely processing it on my own."

"Does that mean there's something there to butt into that you're not telling me?"

I eye him. "Seriously?"

He holds up his palms. "It's a small town. People talk. Especially when you were seen carrying Raine into the hospital. Most exes don't go out of their way to do that for each other."

It's not surprising that people were gossiping about us again. That nagging feeling in the pit of my stomach is back the more I think about her, which is annoying as hell given the circumstances. "Has Raine said anything to Skylar about health issues?"

The question has him slowly shaking his head, obviously concerned. "No. And even if she did, what makes you think I'd know anything about it?"

My eyes roll at his bullshit. "Let's be real, bro. You and Sky tell each other everything. If Raine said something to her, she'd tell you."

"Which means I'd be sworn to secrecy," he informs me.

Does that mean there's something going on that I don't know? Something else that Raine hasn't told me again? Another half-truth that she thinks will sate my curiosity instead of feeding it? It's screwed up. "What ever happened to bro code? Just because Raine and I aren't on great terms doesn't mean I don't care. That's the damn issue. I care way too much. So if you know something..."

DJ swipes his hand across his face. "I'm telling you, Caleb, I don't know anything. They haven't even hung out recently, and last I knew, their phone conversations were about school."

This time, I don't say anything.

"Are you really that worried?" he presses, voice softer than before.

Pressing my lips together, I shrug limply and lift my eyes back to him. "There's something going on. I feel it in my gut. But she won't tell me what it is, like fucking always, so I don't know what to think."

This girl used to bring me peace, but ever since we broke up, it's been nonstop questions because she won't be honest with me the way I truly need her to be. I thought she could trust me with anything, but I was obviously wrong.

DJ watches me stare at the computer screen, letting me process all the thoughts swirling in my head.

I can tell he's trying to figure out what to say, but I don't let him say anything. "If you don't mind, I've got stuff I really need to do that's going to require my focus today. I promised Mom I'd be back for lunch to help her with a couple of chores around the house while Dad naps."

I had to sneak out of the apartment at nearly four this morning after listening to a voicemail Mom left that broke my fucking heart. Hearing her sound so tired killed me, so I left without thinking about all the shit I have yet to do.

I'm tired.

Worried.

On edge.

It makes processing anything outside of Dad hard already, especially when everyone wants to talk to me about what's going on in my life. When I'm feeling too much, it's difficult to properly express what's happening in my head. I try, because that's what I'd want from them. Effort.

The truth is I'm fucking *angry*. But that's not on DJ or Matt or anybody who simply wants to help make things better.

"That's why I'm here, boss," my friend pipes in, grinning at me.

I stop what I'm doing and turn to face him fully with a skeptical expression twisting my face. "What are you talking about?"

He sets his coffee down on the counter and pushes his chair in. "I saw your mom the other day and told her if there was anything I could do to help, I would, since I knew you weren't going to accept the help. You and I are both majoring in the same thing, and I'm good with numbers. She mentioned that you needed to get the books updated and handle the inventory sheets because things with your personal life have kept you busy. I can do some of that stuff."

I swipe a hand down my face, wondering why Mom didn't mention any of this to me this morning. "We can't pay you shit right now."

"Your mom already promised to make me a ton of those pepperoni rolls that I love so much. It's only a day here and there to take some of the load off your back. I don't expect money." Before I can argue, he adds, "Hell, you could probably ask Raine to come in again if you really needed the help. Jeff is the one who's telling everybody about you two at the hospital. His new girlfriend is one of the nurses who works in the emergency department."

Jeff is one of the town boys who loves to gossip about everybody, and apparently, his girlfriend is no different. "Jeff needs to mind his own business for once or I'm telling my mom not to keep sending them Christmas cookies every year."

DJ smirks. "That may shut him up."

We could only hope. "All I want is some privacy while I figure my stuff out. With myself. With Dad. With..." *Raine.* Because ever since I dropped her off at her parents' house from the ER, I knew there was more to the story than she was letting on. Something big.

But because DJ knows this area almost as well as I do at this point, he snorts. "If privacy is what you want, then I hope for your sake you get it."

Humming, I smack him on the back of the shoulder and head toward the back room. Pulling my phone out of my pocket, I hit Mom's number and put my cell up to my ear, waiting for her to answer. She always does, so when it goes to voicemail, I know she's purposefully ignoring me since she didn't bring up my friend's sudden appearance here.

Sighing, I deposit my phone back into my pocket and grab the closest pile of papers for my helper of the day. "Look, I feel bad that she got you in here, but there's no point in convincing you to leave because I know you won't. And I..." Taking a deep breath, I say, "I appreciate that you're here. Really."

His grin turns into a soft smile. "Anytime, man. You know that. All you have to do is ask."

I poke the top paper. "These are receipts from the past two months. I usually try getting them counted and filed at the end of the month, but I got behind. Dad has a system that he explains in writing right here." I point toward the aged Post-it taped onto the counter with faded handwritten instructions on it. "I swear, the second I don't do something the same exact way, he instantly knows, whether he's here or not."

"Spidey-senses," DJ remarks, wiggling his fingers theatrically.

I huff out a dry laugh. "Or he checks the video cameras." Which I've made sure to erase certain footage from since Dad nonchalantly told me to. We haven't spoken of the incident since, and I think a big part of that is because his memory isn't what it used to be. In this case, that's probably not a bad thing. "Look, if you can get that done, I can do some things in the back before it picks up. Ronny is supposed to be here around two unless he calls in again."

"What about asking—"

"No. Just…no."

DJ sighs. "Look, I know you want to play hero, especially *her* hero, no matter what you feel about her, but the A-Team is a thing. They worked together even when they pissed each other off. Probably. I never actually watched that."

I roll my eyes at him.

"Plus, Raine never needed anybody to save her, so you can save the hero theatrics and use the energy to focus on yourself for a change."

The…? "Did you smoke something before you showed up? The A-Team? I have no idea what you're trying to get at."

"The Justice League" is his reply, as if that's supposed to bring his point home.

I'm quiet.

"Avengers?" he offers when I make no point to speak. "Get a clue, Anders. They're all teams that work together to get to a common goal. Kicking ass, taking names. What's that one saying? Teamwork makes the dream work. That's what we are."

"Are you comparing us to superheroes?"

He takes another sip of his coffee before making a bitter face and staring at it. "Man, this shit is strong. But yes. Yes, I am. You could probably pull off the Captain America angle. Which would naturally make me Stark."

"I'm not following your logic."

DJ flattens a palm against his chest. "I come from money. I'll have to figure out how to fake being a genius though, because I failed a couple of my science classes my freshman and sophomore years of college. Maybe I should be Batman instead. Can we switch universes? You could be my Robi—"

"I'm not going to be your anything, Batboy. If you're sticking around, do me a favor and don't be a pain in my ass. Including bringing Raine up or however you'd include her in this little hero dynamic. Think you can handle that for a few hours?"

The long, heavy breath he releases is dramatic as he picks up the first receipt. "I'll do my best, boss. But I'm just saying she could be your Catwoman if you wanted her to be."

I glare.

"Okay, okay. If you need any entertainment, you know where to find me."

"All right. I'm out." I shake my head at his antics and walk into the back room. I don't want to feed into his sarcasm because I'm not in the mood to deal with it.

A few minutes later, I get a text message from my mother that breaks the tension buried in my chest and makes me chuckle.

Mom: I'll make him share the pepperoni rolls I'm making for him. Play nice

Chapter Twenty-Eight

RAINE

SKYLAR HOLDS THE PLASTIC cup full of whipped cream to Sigmund's greedy mouth, giggling at the noises he makes as he messily licks up the dessert that we picked up from Bea's. Usually, she doesn't like offering things like that because it's a waste of toppings, but I know my loving pit bull has grown on her more than she admits.

"So," Skylar says, peeking up at me through her lashes. "How's the project coming? Are you almost finished with the first draft?"

Leon has been sick for a few days, so he hasn't been able to meet up for our next interview. He offered to do it over the phone, but I could hear how tired he was. I dropped off a basket of goodies at his doorstep, including some hot chocolate I made from scratch from a recipe in Annemarie's book, and added a note telling him to feel better soon.

We may only see each other once a week, but I've gotten attached to the elderly man and his stories. I can only hope they continue long after my project ends.

"I haven't really had a chance to work on it," I admit, flinching at the impending deadline in a matter of weeks. The end of semester is quickly approaching. "I've gotten behind on work after taking some days off school to rest."

Skylar's eyes turn sympathetic. "How *are* you feeling? I didn't want to pry, but…"

I didn't have to tell anyone I was in the hospital because half the town knew before I was even out. I learned that after getting a few texts from Skylar, Olive, and DJ to see if I was all right. I gave them variations of the same response.

That I was fine.

Under the weather, I think I said.

"I'm better than I was. I'm on some medication for—" I stop myself, realizing I haven't let anybody in on this new phase of life.

"We're going to do some scans," the doctor on call tells me after we go over my file. "Chances are if the endometriosis has become more advanced, then you'll need to talk to your gynecologist about medication and maybe even surgical treatment options. We'll know more when we get the results."

There was a weight in my stomach as I was wheeled down to radiology because I had no idea what they'd find. All I knew was my worst fear when I heard the mumblings of the technicians as they were bringing me back to my room, telling me I'd hear from the doctor soon.

And I did.

"I'd call your gyno first thing in the morning to schedule an appointment," she says with a smile that doesn't quite reach her eyes. "There's a substantial amount of scarring showing on your ovaries and fallopian tubes, which I'm sure you know is common with advanced endo. I'm not a specialist in that area, so you're better off having your doctor go over that with you when you can."

I knew what she was telling me without actually saying it. It was the same thing my gynecologist had warned me of the moment I was diagnosed. The more scarring there is, the harder it'll be to get pregnant. Medicine only helps the pain, maybe slows the progression. But it doesn't stop it.

When Caleb dropped me off from the hospital, I'd only mumbled a soft "thank you" before Mom rushed out of the house. I was grateful for her startled interruption because I didn't know what else to say to the man behind the wheel.

He didn't ask what the doctor said, but I know he wanted to. It was in his eyes as he scoped me out, studied me from my frizzy bedhead down to my socked feet that he was too frazzled to grab shoes for.

Caleb worried for me.

Because he loves me.

And I love him, which is why I didn't offer the explanation.

Hate me, Caleb, that voice in my head pleads, hoping he'll somehow hear it.

He won't.

He never does.

I jump when a hand taps my arm. "Raine? You okay?" Skylar asks after I space out on her.

Refocusing, I offer her a smile. "Yeah, sorry. It's been a long night. What were we talking about? The project. Right. I have some stuff from my mom that I'm using from our conversations about my dad and their marriage, not that she knows. It'll help counterbalance the things Leon has said about his wife. Show the full circle of what relationships can be like since they're all different."

Skylar stares at me, slowly nodding. I know I'm giving

her the runaround on what we were talking about, but I need the out.

I reach down and pet Sigmund. "Good boy," I coo, taking the empty cup from Skylar and setting it on our table outside Bea's.

Eventually, she speaks up again. "Can I ask you something? It's personal. You don't have to answer or anything if you don't want to."

Nerves prickle the back of my neck, but I nod anyway.

"Did you really cheat on Caleb?"

Her question is asked quietly, almost as if she's uncertain if she truly wants an answer. And I'd be lying if I said it surprised me to hear. I know how this works by now. Caleb probably told DJ about the boy I was with, and DJ told the girl in front of me. It's a natural progression in a relationship. It's healthy when people tell each other everything.

Swallowing the lump in my throat, I wiggle on my seat and fuss over the dog who's grown so much since I got him. "It's complicated," I tell her, not knowing how much I'm willing to divulge.

Will she go off on me like Caleb did? Tell me that I'm making it more complicated than I need to?

"I don't believe it," she says. "Not that it really matters what I think. Cheating just doesn't seem like something you'd do. But *telling* Caleb that you did would definitely be something you'd do to get him to let go."

Am I that predictable?

Not to Caleb apparently.

Then again, it's easier to let emotion get in the way of everything else. Skylar is removed from it all. An outsider looking in without the rose-colored glasses.

"Skylar..." I sigh, gripping the leash in my hand a little

tighter. What can I do other than give her the same speech I gave Caleb? A partial truth to combat all the white lies. "I was with somebody other than Caleb a long time ago. And it's something that I need to live with for the rest of my life."

She frowns. "Raine, it's not like you murdered somebody. If you were with a different guy, it's not the end of the world. I just thought you and Caleb were always together."

I stare at her, wondering if I should come clean. Will my conscience ease? Will the weight on my chest lift, even if it's only a little bit?

In my short time to decide, I make my choice and nod once. "It depends on who you ask. Caleb and I weren't even officially dating until we left for college because my parents didn't approve of me seeing anybody in high school. We dated, but..." I lift a shoulder. "If you want to be technical, we didn't really have the whole exclusivity talk. We were just...together."

Does that make what I did with Cody right? Probably not. But I was young and dumb. I made a mistake simply because a boy was paying attention to me, and I soaked it in.

"I was sixteen when I met Cody during summer vacation. It was one time, and I've never seen him again. But..." When I feel my throat constrict, I decide not to dive into the details. "Well, that's it. I lost my virginity to some random boy and never spoke of it again. A lot happened after that, things that make it so much harder. I didn't tell Caleb until now because I told myself he didn't need to know. Told myself it didn't matter."

I knew better.

It mattered.

It did then.

It does now.

Clearing my throat, I sit straighter. "So yeah. I guess I sort of cheated on him. We'd been seeing each other, but not seriously. We hadn't defined anything. Hadn't shared rules or boundaries. I'm asking you not to tell him, Sky. Can you keep this between us?"

When I eye her, I wonder what she's going to say. Will she tell DJ as soon as we leave here? Will he tell Caleb? It's a game of telephone, but how much of the information will be right by the time my ex picks up the phone?

Skylar sits back in her chair. "Raine, I think you need to tell him. You didn't do anything wrong. Do you really think it's fair to put yourselves through all this? Especially Caleb when he's going through enough?"

The one thing I've learned about life without needing to study the psychology of it is that it isn't fair. We're tested every single day by the choices both we and other people make. Maybe if that were different, if I didn't take the easy route out, I would have been tempted to make things work with Caleb.

That's not the path I chose though.

So I answer honestly. "No, it's not." I press my lips together and stand, tugging on Sigmund's leash to get him to stand. "But that's life sometimes. Right?"

All Skylar does is frown.

"I'll talk to you later, okay? I should probably get working on this project before I get any more behind."

She nods. "Okay. Talk later."

I don't know if I trust she'll keep quiet, but I don't have the energy to care.

~

The next few days are more of the same. I don't call my doctor because I'm afraid to. Mom sneaks out and sneaks back in from doing God knows what. I work on the end of semester assignments and try compiling all my notes into a cohesive paper, work my shifts at Bea's, and try keeping to myself.

Key word: try.

Mom is quiet at breakfast as I slide some of the scrambled eggs I make onto two separate plates and place some of the pancakes I made onto one for us to split. I burned the first three, but it's better than the entire batch I butchered the first time I attempted to make them a few weeks ago for us.

When I turn to place her food in front of her, I frown when I see the pinched look on her face as she stares at some of my homework sprawled across the other half of the table.

"I never understood why you loved this stuff so much," she tells me, shaking her head. "It was like overnight you decided you wanted to help people with their problems."

I sink into the chair I pulled out for myself. "I don't know if it was overnight, but I like helping people. You know that."

I've always been that way—holding doors open for people, offering a listening ear, being the mediator between Mom and Dad. I know they're the biggest reason I am where I am.

It could be worse.

"Well, when did you know?" she asks, causing me to arch my brows. I didn't expect her to wonder because she rarely asks about school beyond the basic "how was your day" in passing.

I never cared. It was easier not to get into the details when she was such a big part of everything. Picking up my fork, I move around some of my eggs and say, "I guess it was when you and Dad started fighting more."

They always bickered about something, no matter how small. Dirty clothes or dishes, not having any groceries, the house being messy, the lawn not being mowed. I used to think it was normal. Because it was to me.

I can't look Mom in the eyes when I add, "It was the day we were supposed to go see that new musical in the city. I remember being excited because we hadn't been since *Cats* came out, and you guys said we could go see the Statue of Liberty and Empire State Building. But then Dad got a work call about something that couldn't wait until we were back, and we never went."

It was one of their worst fights. I'm not sure what all was said, but it was *loud*. It wasn't the first time I heard them argue, but it was the first time Mom left and didn't come home until the next day. She was crying when she walked out the door, that much I knew for sure. She tried hiding her blotchy face and red eyes, but I was sitting on the other side of the bookshelves that faced the front door, so I saw everything.

When Dad found me hours later in the same spot to tell me dinner was ready, he promised that she'd be back.

"She always comes back," he told me.

And I remember thinking to myself, *but why?* That question led to the next five, which turned into hundreds of questions about why anybody does the things they do. I wanted to help Mom and Dad, but I knew I wasn't the fix for their main problems.

"We weren't that bad," Mom tells me, rolling her eyes. "Don't be so melodramatic. You were never abused. You had a roof over your head and food in your stomach. We rarely told you no. I'd hardly say you had it bad growing up because of us. There are far worse people you could have wound up with as parents."

Typical. "You always do this," I exclaim in exasperation. "You complain that I don't talk to you about things, but the moment I do, you accuse me of being dramatic. Just because you never beat me as a child doesn't mean I was in a stable, happy environment. You and Dad had a lot of problems, and I got to be the witness to them all."

"I find it amusing that you don't think you're dramatic considering you're making a big production right now."

I blink, absorbing her tone. "Wow. Okay. I'm just trying to answer your question, Mom. I'm sorry if you feel attacked—"

"*Attacked?* You know what, Raine? I do feel attacked. Your father and I have done so much for you. We've always cheered you on and rooted for your success. And now you tell me that you're studying all this nonsense because of him and me? No. We shielded you from so much growing up, so don't pin this on us."

I take a deep breath to calm my tone so this doesn't escalate more. "I love you, but that's not true. I saw it all. Heard it all. Even when you didn't realize I was paying attention."

Is it so bad to be the reason I'm so motivated? I'm building a future for myself because of them. There isn't any blame, only gratefulness.

I don't get a chance to tell her how much she's influenced me because she decides to take this conversation one step further. "Before you cast yourself in such a good light, think about how close you were to making the same mistake I did. If you hadn't broken up with the Anders boy, then you would have wound up exactly where I am. Miserable and divorced. Be grateful you never got pregnant to add single mom to that list."

All I can do is stare in disbelief at how quickly this turned around.

She locks eyes with me. "You are more like us than you want to admit, always so close to making choices that will ruin your life."

It's hard to restrain myself as I move my chair back. "I'm so sorry that having me was such a huge inconvenience to your life plans, Mom. Truly. It must suck to have settled with two people you didn't really want all these years. Some people would feel like the luckiest people on the planet to have what you did."

Me included.

Tears prickle the backs of my eyes as I grab my plate and walk over to dump it into the garbage bin. Before I walk out of the room, I hear Mom say, "The eggs were rubbery."

I manage to hold in the tears long enough to get Sigmund and his leash and leave the house to go anywhere but here.

It isn't until I'm down the street that I feel my phone buzz in my back pocket.

Mom: I'm sorry

She never was good at saying that in person. Which is why I choose to accept the apology, knowing it's the best I'll get.

Me: It's okay

It isn't. But it'll have to be.

Chapter Twenty-Nine

CALEB

DAD ISN'T EATING. BARELY sleeping. Not even talking much, which is especially concerning. This is the same man who could befriend anybody he passed on the street. I watched him have conversations with anybody he came across—bag boys, door greeters, customers at the store, even the sour old woman down the street who hates everybody.

That man no longer exists.

I don't know the one who took his place.

Last week, he called me Jake.

We don't know who that is.

He didn't recognize Mom last night.

I heard her crying in her room.

The nurses say it's almost time.

Almost time. As if we're getting close to a big event. Like some sort of fucked-up deadline.

"Cal!" I hear called out from behind me as I walk through campus like a zombie. I'm on no sleep and failed melatonin. I'm terrified that I won't wake up if Mom calls me about

Dad, so I choose exhaustion. It's not ideal for the remaining weeks of the term, but it is what it is.

I turn, noticing a skinny kid wearing a Lindon football jersey jogging toward me. He's one of the newbies on the team—a sophomore who started training with us last spring to prep for the new season.

He stops a few feet away. "Hey. I don't know if you remember me, but I played with you before you graduated. I'm—"

"Wells," I say for him. "I know."

His face lights up. "Shit. Awesome. A few of my buddies said not to bother you because of—" He abruptly cuts himself off. "Er, well, I saw you and wanted to see if you got the invite."

I blink. "What invite?"

"To coach."

To...? "I have no idea what you're talking about."

Wells, the delusional sophomore, nods enthusiastically. "A bunch of us were talking about it, and we all agreed you'd be a perfect addition to the new staff they're trying to grow here. You know the game, the turf, and all the old plays. Plus you're familiar with the team. It'd be perfect. Better than the fuckwads they've got wandering around scratching their balls and acting like they know what they're doing. I don't think the new staff knows what the hell is happening half of the time."

"Look, Wells. It's nice I was brought up for consideration, but that's the last thing on my mind right now. I'm sure whomever they've hired will do the job just fine." I don't bother pointing out that we're not exactly a Division I school or anything. The staff that comes in is going to be subpar at best.

Hell, they can't be any worse than the people they let go, considering the major lawsuits that could have been on the school's hands otherwise. Coach Pearce, who'd been an exceptional coach who earned Lindon a lot of trophies over the years, didn't have the best moral compass. He was willing to look the other way when one of his players was accused of doing some sketchy shit to women at parties because he wanted to make sure he was kept on the team. Who knows what else he let some of the guys get away with?

Wells's shoulders drop defeatedly. "I know you've got a lot going on, but maybe after…" He stops himself again. "I just mean when things die down—" He winces, face turning red at the poor choice of words that definitely hit me straight in the gut.

"Wells?"

"Yeah?"

"Stop talking while you're ahead."

He presses his lips together, the color on his cheeks darkening before he nods.

I glance at the time on my watch. It's old but the band is new. It's one of Dad's old watches that Mom kept in her jewelry box after he stopped wearing it. Mom gave me the band and told me to keep it the other day. I didn't want to because it felt wrong to take anything of his. It felt…final.

But having it on my wrist oddly makes me feel like I'm close to him.

Backing up, I say, "I'll think about it, but don't hold your breath."

Will I actually think about it? Probably not. I've had enough on my mind lately that's left me too preoccupied. I've been debating even staying at the school or if I should consider other options.

Dad was insistent that I let go of some of my classes because he didn't think I'd need them to run the store, and I know he's not wrong. Maybe it's time to really think about where I'm going with my life since shit is about to change.

Wells nods, stuffing his hands in the pockets of his sweatpants. "You got it. But just so you know, they're willing to pay for staff members' master's degrees while you're working for them as long as you get your degree here. And I know you're studying for your MBA, so…" His shoulders lift. "I don't know, man. It's just something to consider before you turn it down."

I look back to Wells. "Like I said, I'll think about it."

~

Mom is stress baking again. I can smell something sweet and fruity as soon as I walk in the front door, and it gets stronger as I walk down the hall to the kitchen. I check in on Dad, who's sleeping in his chair, and twitch when I see the color of his skin.

Closing my eyes, I collect myself and head into the kitchen, where Mom is pulling a pie out of the oven. As she sets it down on the stovetop, I say, "He's turning yellow."

Mom tries to smile, but it doesn't hold. "I know, sweetie. They did bloodwork and it's in his liver. We knew it would happen though. Things spread in this stage."

My nostrils flare with anger, but I force myself to breathe through it. "Why do bad things happen to good people?"

My mother is quiet for a long time, staring at Dad's favorite dessert. She's been doing that a lot, even though he never eats any of it. It makes her feel better. She gives it to the nursing staff or our neighbors and sends some home with me to give to the boys.

"I don't know, Caleb. I really don't."

Leaning against the counter, I prop my chin on my hand. "How are you holding up? No bullshitting me."

She eyes me, still hating me using bad language around her. At least there's a little normalcy in our lives. "I'm not sure. It's always going to be your father. I'm...processing, I suppose. For what comes next."

Next. A heaviness settles into my stomach. "What *does* come next?"

The woman who's always had my back shakes her head. "I don't even know what I'm going to make for dinner. So I guess what comes next is that."

I reach over and grab two forks from the tray they're in, then pass one to Mom. "Well, you already made pie. Nothing against dessert for dinner."

Her sigh isn't defeated or approving. "It's hardly nutritious."

I stab into a piece of apple. "It's got fruit."

Mom's laugh sucks up some of the tension in the room. "You're not wrong. And it's not like your dad is going to eat any, so more for us. Right?"

She's trying, and I respect that.

"When you said it was always Dad," I say, staring at the steaming dish in between us. "How did you know? Was there any doubt?"

Raine asked that once upon a time.

I have no doubt Mom knows why I'm asking when she pats my hand. "I wouldn't say there was doubt, but that doesn't mean we didn't have our hardships."

"Really?"

She nods. "We wanted kids at different times. Debated moving somewhere else instead of settling here. We couldn't figure out the timing of it all but had to trust it'd wind up exactly how it was meant to. Once we accepted that, we were okay."

All I can do is nod slowly.

Mom reaches over and knocks her knuckles against my skull lightly. "What is going through that thick head of yours, baby boy?"

The same thing that always is. "I just feel like I need to talk to Raine. Maybe after finals so I can be clearheaded for them."

I don't miss the tiny smile that begins curling her lips. I'm afraid she'll get her hopes up, but I can't stop it. "I think that's a good idea."

The fact that's all she says tells me nothing, and I don't know if I should be grateful or upset for her lack of insight. She's trying to make me figure it out on my own like any loving mother would for her son.

"Caleb?" I hear called out in a raspy tone from the living room.

I perk up at Dad's voice.

"Let me know how it goes," Mom tells me, but I don't know if she means with Raine or with Dad. Because they're both unstable relationships.

When I walk into the room where Dad is, he's propped up in his chair trying to adjust a pillow behind his back.

"Here," I say, stepping over to help him get comfortable.

"I've got it. I said I've *got it*," he snaps, all but smacking my hand away from him.

I hold up my hands and back up. "Sorry. I was just trying to help." Sitting on the edge of the couch cushion closest to him, I brush off the hurt clinging to my rib cage. "What's up? Do you need anything?"

Dad stares ahead, not seeming to focus on anything in particular before his eyes slowly move toward me. "Everything is going to be okay, son."

I blink at the unexpected words. How could he say that? "I don't know if I can agree with that, Dad."

"You don't have a choice."

Jaw twitching, I clench my hands together and squeeze them. "Everybody has a choice. Maybe mine is to be pissed off."

He shakes his head. "That's no way to live your life. You have so many years ahead of you. Don't waste them being angry."

Despite myself, tears prick the backs of my eyes. Hot, angry tears that burn the ducts. I try blinking them away.

"Christ," I grumble, swiping at my face. I never liked crying, especially in front of him. If he can be strong, I need to be too. "Don't do this to me. I can't..." My voice cracks.

He's slow, but he manages to reach over and touch my hand. Inching closer to him, I soak in the warmth of his palm. "I'm real proud of you. Need you to know that. You've gone through hell and have come out of it. That's all I could ever ask of you."

Sniffing back tears, I suck in a deep breath and let it out. Dad is proud of me despite all the ways I've struggled these past few months, and that's more than enough. "I appreciate that more than you'll ever know. And..."

I'm going to miss this, I say silently.

He doesn't need me to tell him that.

He knows.

And the longer we sit there like that, simply holding on to each other for dear life, I process his words.

No more anger.

Chapter Thirty

RAINE

LEON FINISHES READING THE final draft of my paper that I printed for him before putting it down and setting his glasses on top of it. "It's good, kid. You sound like you know what you're talking about, so I'm sure you'll ace it. Hell of a lot smarter than I am, that's for damn sure."

I roll my eyes as I grip the cup of coffee he poured for me. "Trust me, I'm not that smart. I think it's a solid B, but we'll see. We get our final grades sometime next week."

It took me a few sleepless nights to finish writing this because I kept procrastinating. Writing Leon's interview was easy, but delving into what I put down for Mom...

Leon's eyes roam downward. "Has your mother read this yet?" The flinch he's met by has him sighing. "Does she know you wrote her into this? Last you said, she didn't want to help."

I *may* have forged her signature on the initial proposal I submitted to Professor Wild. I was running out of time to find somebody, and she was saying things about her divorce that contributed to a well-rounded project. It would have been silly to pass it up. Plus I've done it plenty of times growing up when she'd forget to sign things for school. I know her signature by heart. "She hasn't read any of my homework since I was in elementary school. And even then, she hated doing it. It isn't as if she'll know."

He eyes me in disapproval. "Don't know if I condone that, but it's your life. How are the two of you doing?"

I told him about our argument and said we made up, but there's still tension in the house. If I don't censor topics, like Dad or Caleb, then everything gets murky. I've learned it's better not to talk about it than deal with the repercussions of the fallout.

Maybe that's why I added our conversation to the paper, posing it as one between her and Dad to fit the paper's topic guidelines. Did I feel a tiny bit bad when I was doing my final readthrough? A little. But I keep telling myself there are worse things I could have done.

Right?

"We're okay," I say, staring into my coffee and watching the steam billow from the top. "She's taking me for a procedure in a couple of weeks. It's minor, nothing to worry about."

That doesn't seem to relax his arched brows as he stares at me. "You feeling all right?"

Wetting my lips, I raise the cup to take a sip when I remember what my gyno told me during our visit last week. Coffee can trigger endometriosis flares. So can half the things I love eating, which I've tried cutting back on despite Mom telling me I'm being overdramatic.

But Mom doesn't know the extent of my diagnosis because I've always played it off like it's nothing. When I told her about the laparoscopic procedure I'm being put under for, her tune changed. After she gave me crap for keeping all my problems from her. Gone are the "it's just a period, eat some chocolate and toughen up" pep talks she used to give me whenever I'd tell her I was in excruciating pain during my cycle, and in their place is someone who seems to actually care.

I know she isn't happy with me keeping things under wraps instead of telling Dad and my friends, but it's easier this way. The fewer people who worry, the better it is to handle.

Putting my coffee down, I lean back in my chair and debate just asking Leon what I've been wanting to know since he said his wife struggled to have kids. I know if I ask for information, it's only fair to offer it.

Out of anybody I could tell, wouldn't Leon be the safest because he's the most removed?

Weighing my options, I make my decision and ask, "Is there a reason Annemarie couldn't have children? Was she sick? I only ask because *I'm* sick with something that's probably going to ruin my chances of ever having kids. I'm not telling you that for pity or anything. I just don't want to pry unjustly."

He frowns. "I'm sorry to hear that. We were never given a reason, unfortunately. Once upon a time, we would have liked one. At least then we had a reason for it. But no. It's a mystery to this day."

Would it be better that way? Or am I the lucky one for at least understanding why I am the way I am?

"If you don't mind me asking," Leon speaks up, "is that the reason you and the Anders boy split up? Was he unhappy with that possibility?"

There's a fire in his eyes that I can tell is directed at Caleb, so I'm quick to extinguish it. "I never told him. I broke up with him because I love him too much to put a hold on his happiness. He wants kids so bad, Leon. He used to bring it up all the time, and it'd freak me out knowing there'd be a day he could resent me for not being able to. I mean, he loves me—*loved* me—so maybe it wouldn't have been that bad. But...I didn't want to take that chance." Saying it out loud sounds stupid now, but fear can make people do a lot of silly things. "I already know what I'm going to be told one day. It's a gut feeling at this point, and my gut is never wrong. I figured it was better to let him go now before we couldn't turn back in the future."

My neighbor stares at me for a long time before shaking his head. "I take back what I said. You're an idiot. Because that might be the dumbest thing I've ever heard."

There's a brief moment when I'm silent as I stare at him.

Leon breaks it with "But I suppose it's also one of the sweetest things I've heard. You love him so much you'd give up your happiness for his. That's something I can see Annemarie doing."

But she didn't. "She stayed though."

He gives me a lopsided smile. "Poor woman was stuck with me by then. Divorce was frowned on by the time we had our problems with children. Maybe if we'd known sooner, she would have let me go too. Someone who loves you that much is willing to do anything, I suppose. No matter how drastic."

I can't look him in the eyes.

"Do me a favor though," he says, pulling my hesitant gaze back to him. "Don't settle for less than you deserve. Annemarie was my forever, and I wouldn't change a thing. Can't picture myself with anybody else. You need to ask yourself the same thing about your boy."

My boy.

I swallow. "He's not mine anymore."

All Leon does is hum, as if he doesn't buy it as much as I do. Then he switches gears. "Why haven't you brought that crazy-ass dog of yours over in a while? Been thinking about getting a pet myself lately. Annemarie wanted a cat, but I've always been a dog man."

And just like that, we move on.

Like I should do with Caleb.

Should.

~

Dad waves at me from the table in the back corner when I walk into Birdseye Diner. A few people turn my way with big smiles as I walk over to the man who's standing with one of his arms out to hug me. "Hi, pumpkin."

He pulls my chair out for me and waits until I'm sitting before going back to his seat. That's when I notice the milkshakes already on the table, next to the glasses of water.

"I already ordered our usual," he admits, looking a little sheepish. "I hope that's all right. Figured even though we're celebrating the end of term, we'd still be getting the same thing."

My eyes go to the cherry still perched on the top of my milkshake. "You didn't take the cherry," I note stupidly, wiggling out of my jacket and letting it drape across the back of the chair.

Dad grins, tugging his milkshake closer to him. "Of course not. You like cherries."

I blink at the statement. "I do." My brows pinch when that soaks in. "You knew that this whole time?"

His chin dips as he takes a sip of his drink. "I'm not always the best at picking up on things, but there are very few things that I *don't* notice about you, Raine."

A ball of emotion swells inside my chest, tightening around my heart. "That's…" I'm not sure what to say. "Sweet. Thanks."

Dad laughs. "If something as small as realizing what food you like makes you emotional, I've clearly failed as a father."

"Don't say that," I tell him, moving hair behind my ear.

A small smile curves upward on my father's face. "Look, I know my faults. I obviously wish I could have changed how certain things happened over time, but I can't. I can only try to make up for it. Which means being present when I can now. Supporting you however I can."

I'm not used to this side of Dad. "You don't need to make up for anything."

"I do," he says. "Your mother and I didn't agree on a lot, but we both have always wanted you to be happy."

I grab the cherry from my milkshake and stare at the bright red color. "I know that."

He slowly nods, almost as if he's trying to figure out what to say next. It isn't like he's ever been a sappy person. Talking about feelings isn't his forte. So this is…weird. Nice, but weird.

The moment is broken only for a brief pause as the waitress comes over with our food and a friendly smile.

Once she leaves, Dad reaches into the inner pocket of his jacket. "There's something I need to give you."

When he slides a check across the table, I nearly choke at the amount it's made out for. "I don't understand. What is this?"

"Money," he answers simply, grabbing his napkin

and tucking it into the collar of his button-down. "Your mother and I have been spending some time together"—I sit straighter and stare cautiously at him—"because we've been working on selling the cabin in Virginia. It didn't take long to sell once the posting went live, and we just recently got the money. Your aunt Tiffany agreed that the money was better spent on you after a couple months of back-and-forth. You can use this to pay your debt and do whatever else you please with it. You should consider getting a new car so you're not constantly nickel-and-diming yourself on the one you have. Even Dale said that thing needs to be put out of its misery, even with the work Caleb put into it."

Caleb? "What are you talking about?"

Dad's brow furrows "Caleb went over to Dale's and checked it out. Worked a few hours on it with Dale's brother during the off hours because they were so backed up. He didn't tell you?"

Swallowing, I slowly shake my head. Why would he do that for me? "I didn't know." My focus goes back to the steep number, double-checking if I'm seeing where the comma is correctly. "I don't know what to say. I never in a million years thought Tiffany would agree to selling the Radcliff estate. We have so many memories there."

"Neither did we," he admits. "It turns out she's been wanting to move closer to family, so your mother loaned her some of the money from the sale to get her up here."

It's been a long time since my family has been this close together. "Aunt Tiffany is moving to New York? I thought she hated it here."

Dad reaches for the ketchup bottle, opening it and putting some beside his fries. "I guess she hated being alone more," he reasons, carefully capping it and setting it in front of me. "She wants to be closer to your mother. It'll be good that they'll have each other. Your mother has been missing her."

A sinking feeling settles into my stomach over the cabin being gone just like that. It was the one place I could go to when I needed an escape. Somewhere to go in the summers when I needed time to think. Then again, it became the very place that suffocated me with poor choices that are better let go of.

I guess having nowhere to run to isn't such a bad thing.

Picking up a fry, I study it and sigh. "This still seems like such a huge deal that I can't wrap my head around. You and Mom don't owe me anything. If this is Mom's way of trying to make up for some of the tension between us—"

"That's not it," Dad cuts in, shaking his head firmly. "This has everything to do with the fact that you're her daughter—the one person she's ever truly loved."

There isn't any sadness in his tone when he says that, but I can see it clear as day in his eyes.

"I don't think that's true at all. Look how much time she's spent with you lately. To be honest, I assumed you guys got back together. She wouldn't spend time with you if she didn't love you."

His smile is empty. "We're not getting back together, princess. The paperwork was finalized a few weeks ago. We're officially divorced. We spent so much time together because we genuinely wanted to figure out how we could help *you*. That sort of support isn't something either of our families gave to us, which is another reason our relationship was doomed from the beginning. Your mother wants to make sure she's always part of your life, even if she's being difficult. So do I. We all need to get along to make sure that happens."

305

I have no idea what to say. My throat thickens as I try swallowing. Gaze blurry as I glance up at him from the check, I shake my head. "You guys didn't have to do this."

"We know."

A single tear escapes the corner of my eye that I quickly swipe away. "I love you, Dad."

Dad passes me a clean napkin for my eyes. "I love you too, kiddo. Always have, always will."

The fact that Mom and Dad get along better when they're divorced isn't lost on me. It gives me hope that a split isn't the end for everybody.

It could be the beginning.

And maybe that means the "curse" I was told about for so long doesn't really amount to anything. My parents might not be totally happy, but they're building something for themselves anyway. They're at peace with their choices.

That counts for something.

Dabbing my eyes, I clear my throat and try changing the subject before I start bawling in front of everybody in the diner. "So tell me about the new property you started showing."

Chapter Thirty-One

CALEB

RAINE'S HAND IS BRACED against the side of the West End Anthropology Building, with her head bent down and hair falling over her shoulders. There's no hesitation before my feet turn me away from my typical path to my last final and right toward the girl in distress.

The image reminds me of one of the first frat parties we went to during college. She swore up and down that she wasn't going to drink again after the party we went to in high school that led to her becoming well acquainted with Leon Applebee's hedges.

"I mean it this time," she slurs, wobbling on shaky legs as I walk us to the football house. "No more, Caleb. Alcohol is gross."

"I know, babe," I muse, trying not to laugh as she groans. We stop every so often when she thinks she's going to puke but manages to keep it down.

The second her head hits the pillow, she's out like a light. I manage to get her shoes off, pull the blanket over her, move the waste basket by the side of the bed, and put two painkillers on the night-stand next to a glass of water she'll need in the morning.

When the sun comes up, I'm there with a stuffed bear wearing a mask and holding a sign that says GET WELL SOON. *I found it at the drugstore when I ran out to get us something greasy to eat to help the hangover.*

She stares at the bear for a long moment before moving her eyes upward to me. "I don't know what I did to deserve you."

I smile. "I love you too."

Stopping next to the girl in distress, I ask, "What's wrong?" and let my hand fall between her shoulder blades. She stiffens underneath my touch for a split second before relaxing when she looks at me with glassy eyes.

Moving hair behind one of her ears helps me see how pale she is. Only her cheeks are flushed as she straightens and turns her body away from me, letting my hand fall back to my side. "Just don't feel well. I walked past the dining hall and smelled something foul. What's new, right?"

"I'm sorry," I say half-heartedly, giving her a quick once-over and seeing the way she cradles her abdomen. "I can grab you some water if you need."

There's a tired glaze to her eyes as they meet mine again. "I'll be okay. I finished my last exam, so I'm on my way home to rest anyway."

I jab my thumb behind me. "Do you want me to walk you to your car?" I'd feel bad if something happened to her. She's unsteady on her feet as she straightens out and presses her fingers to her temples.

"I walked," she admits sheepishly. "I haven't gotten my car back from Dale's. Thanks for looking at it, by the way. You didn't have to."

I should have known she'd find out. "I told the guys at

the garage about it and asked if I could take a look. It was no big deal." Dale's brother often stays late to tinker on an old convertible he's restoring, so he was more than happy to let me stick around when I couldn't sleep.

"It is," she counters quietly. "I didn't deserve that courtesy."

Choosing not to comment on that, I tell her, "I'll drive you."

She looks at me for a second, probably wondering why I didn't want to talk about her car, but eventually nods. "If you're not going to be late for class, I'd appreciate it. I'm hoping the garage will get my car in this week so I can get it back before the big storm rolls through next week."

The sidewalks are cleared off fairly well right now, but I know by the time she would have needed to leave to get here, the town wouldn't have come by to shovel or salt them.

"I've got some time to kill before my next test, so I'll drop you off and see about going over to Dale's. If he can't get it in anytime soon, Ed's might be able to."

As we're walking toward the parking lot, I can't help but notice the white-knuckle grip on her bag strap that she loosens for a moment before tightening her hold again. There's something on her mind. She always fidgets when she's deep in thought.

Falling into step with her, I decide to try lightening the mood. "How are your mom and dad doing?"

If she's grateful for the subject change, she doesn't really give it away. Her shoulder lifts weakly as she stares straight ahead at the line of parked cars in the commuter lot. "Okay, I guess. I think Dad may have been over before I got home from Bea's. It smelled like him—his cologne. I sort of missed it. Their situation is confusing. For a while, I even thought they might get back together."

Mom mentioned seeing Raine's parents together around town and asked if they were still going through the divorce. I think a lot of people are confused about their situation since it seems like they like each other more now than they have for years. "Would it be such a bad thing if they did get back together?"

The question has her lips pressing together for a moment in contemplation. "You and I both know that their marriage was never going to last. You've witnessed the fights. It was a long time coming. Nothing would change if they decided to try again."

She hasn't always been the closest with her parents, which is why she loved spending so much time with mine, but she values her time with them even when she has to endure them complaining about each other to her. I don't envy her. If my parents were like that...

Well, no. Maybe I'd prefer it if they were.

If all I had to deal with was their separation, then at least they'd both still be alive. Not together, but existing. That's better than the reality I'm facing instead.

I'm sure Mom would have chosen that fate for them over what she's dealing with now. Who wants to see the love of their life fade away? They've spent a lot longer together than I did with him, and it's hard watching her watch him knowing what the outcome is going to be. When he lashes out, I see her shrink. When she sneaks away to the kitchen feigning some chore, I hear her little sobs that she tries silencing with running water or other house chores.

So yeah. If I could choose, I'd definitely want a redo. Awkward divorce and all.

Swallowing down that envy, I can't help but wonder

about the past I share with the girl climbing into the passenger side of my truck.

Eventually, the admission that breaks our silence has my posture loosening a fraction. "I was jealous of Emma, even though I had no right to be." She shifts, hands fiddling in her lap. "She seemed really nice when we talked. And she's pretty, smart, and kind. On paper, you two make sense. And that…hurt."

Why is she telling me this now? "I'm not with Emma anymore. So none of this matters. It's moot."

Her body turns toward me. "But don't you get it? It *should* matter. We're stuck in a cycle that neither of us seems to know how to break. I have no hold on you, no right to be jealous or act like you being with someone like Emma isn't okay. Not after what I did in Radcliff. You're not mine because I let you go."

Those words strike me right in the chest.

You're not mine.

"Thanks for the reminder," I murmur, shaking my head as those fucking words echo in my head. As if it needs to be reiterated, I feel the need to tell her, "I'm not Emma's either, even if you think we're somehow a perfect match on paper. Spoiler alert, Raine. There's no such thing. Look at us and this supposed cycle you mentioned. You were with someone else, and I'm still not over you. What the fuck does that say about me?"

The noise coming from Raine is indescribable, but the expression on her face is humorous. "I didn't mean to say that in a harsh way, I'm just trying to say that…"

When she stops, my brows inch higher up my forehead in confusion. "You're trying to say what, exactly? That you'd be okay with me seeing someone someday, but not now? If not

Emma, then some other girl? Are you trying to say you wouldn't be jealous simply because you wouldn't have a right to be?"

Her hands bunch into fists. "I wouldn't have a right to say either way. I was with Cody. You were with Emma. What's done is done."

"Because I'm not yours, right?" I push, not believing that for a second. If we were truly done, wouldn't I have detached myself from her?

Her eyes narrow into slits. "Why are you being like this?"

I pull off onto a side road that barely gets any traffic and put the truck into park before turning toward her. "Because I want to hear you say it."

She throws her hands up, all but growling out a cool "Say *what?*"

I unbuckle and cup the back of her neck, pulling her toward me until our mouths are centimeters apart. Fingers digging slightly into her neck, I say, "I want you to tell me that I'm not yours and *mean* it. Because you wouldn't be getting jealous over someone else having me if you didn't want me at all. You wouldn't be feeding me little half-truths if there wasn't a part of you that wanted to hold on. You talk a lot of talk, baby girl, but what are you *really* saying?"

A sharp breath escapes her, and I'm all too familiar with the sound. She's turned on. Anger be damned, she wants me. Wants this. Her eyes darken with a whole new intent as the top of her tongue slowly drags along her bottom lip.

"Would you let me touch you this way if I wasn't at least partly yours?" I ask, voice dangerously low as I move even closer until the ends of our noses touch.

Her breathing picks up, getting choppy as she brushes her nose along the tip of mine as if she wants to make a move but doesn't want to be the first one to cave.

But I wait. I've always been told I'm a patient man—another trait that I get from my father. In this moment, I can tell it frustrates the woman who wiggles her way closer, hands moving to my shoulders and gripping a handful of my jacket.

"You're not being fair," she whispers, lips ghosting over mine in a barely there touch.

My fingers tighten around the nape of her neck, moving upward to twist in the strands of her thick hair. "What *is* fair anyway? Nothing about what we've gone through is. You made sure of that."

She pulls away just enough to look at me. I expect her to say something witty back, but instead her lips press against mine lightly. Once. Twice. Each swipe becomes a little more demanding as she presses into me, her grip on my jacket tightening and tugging me forward. When our fronts press together, I can't help but slide my hands down her sides and under her jacket to settle on her back.

She stiffens, breaking contact and eyeing me with uncertainty. It takes a moment before her hands find mine, moving them from her back to her hips. "I'm a little sore," she tells me.

I nod. "Okay."

"But other places," she says, lashes fluttering as she grabs one of my hands and places it on her thigh, "I'd be okay with."

My heart picks up, along with something else a lot further south. "Is that so?"

All she does is swallow, moving my hand further upward until it rests on the apex of her thighs. Her mouth finds mine again, her lips opening mine until she teases my tongue and uses my hand to gain friction over the denim between her legs. I hear the hitch of breath when my fingers press against her, causing her hips to arch up against my touch.

Her eager fingers fumble as she works on undoing the button of her jeans, starting to wiggle out of the material enough for my hand to have access to the thin material of her panties.

She says one word: "Please."

That's all it takes before I spiral.

Like she said, it's an endless cycle.

No amount of anger can withstand that one word she whispers.

Taking over the kiss, I use one hand to cup the back of her head, threading my fingers in her hair to keep her face against mine as our mouths fuse with desperation. My other hand goes to her panties, already damp for me, where I move two of my fingers underneath the cotton to tease her until a needy moan escapes her mouth.

Just as I probe her entrance, she freezes as if she realizes where we are and asks, "What if someone sees?"

There aren't any buildings nearby and rarely ever traffic considering this is a seasonal road. I sink just the tips of my fingers inside her and lean into her ear, whispering, "Don't worry. I'll tell them we're just friends. After all, I'm not yours. Remember?"

She gasps when I plunge my fingers farther inside her, making tears shine in her eyes. "H-hurts," she says.

I pause at the stuttered word. "Do you want me to stop?"

One of her arms hooks around my neck until she's hugging us together and moving her hips up to ride my hand in the rhythm she wants, giving me the answer before she says, "No. It's fine."

"Are you su—"

"Yes," she whispers, kissing me again to stop me from asking.

Not another word is said, just desperate noises in between hungry kisses and heavy panting. I feel her fingernails dig into the bare sliver of skin on the back of my neck between where my hair ends and my jacket starts. I know there will be little marks left behind from the bites of pain as her orgasm builds around my digits. Scissoring my fingers and hooking them has her thighs starting to shake and her teeth biting down onto my bottom lip. It only makes me harder, the growing bulge trapped in my jeans painful as hell.

I pay it no attention as a barely audible version of my name comes from her mouth or as she grinds on my hand until I can feel the wetness coating my palm, and I make no move to get any relief when she comes, clenching around me.

Waiting until she rides it out, I watch a sated expression come across her face before I carefully pull out my fingers.

"Funny," I murmur, lifting them to my mouth and slowly moving my tongue over the arousal left behind. "It sure as fuck tastes like you're mine."

A sharp breath leaves her as she watches me, eyelids heavier than before.

One of my shoulders lifts. "My mistake."

Chapter Thirty-Two

RAINE

THE MONITOR ATTACHED TO my finger records my pulse spiking every time I hear footsteps outside the curtain, knowing today is the day I'll know the truth. Whether I want to accept it is a whole different game.

"Relax," Mom tells me, putting her hand on my leg, which hasn't stayed still since I was told to change into the gown and socks by the sweet-faced nurse. "They're going to take good care of you. You have nothing to worry about."

It's not the procedure I'm worried about. It isn't supposed to take long, so I'll be out of here before I know it. What I can't get off my mind is the aftermath.

"What if they tell me worst case?" I ask quietly, staring vulnerably at my mother and hoping she'll be there for me. No theatrics or accusations of being melodramatic.

Right now, I need my mom.

As a daughter.

She gives me that, curling her hand on my leg in comfort. "I have no doubt that *when* you become a mother someday, you're going to be the best one you can be because you're always looking at the positive things in life. That goes a long way, Raine."

Hearing her tell me that means more to me than she'll ever know. "Thank you."

The day I got back from lunch with Dad, I walked into the house and gave her a tight hug. I could tell she was surprised, but it didn't take long for her to return it, wrapping her arms around me and telling me she loved me.

I know we'll always have our tiffs, but I also know she'll always have my back when I truly need her there. Same with Dad.

That didn't encourage me to tell her I saw Caleb again. When he dropped me off after our second truck hookup, Mom was locked away in her craft room finishing a project for a client and that kept her busy all night.

Which was good.

Because I went to my room and curled up with Sigmund on my bed, still feeling where Caleb's fingers had been minutes before and remembering all the reasons that we shouldn't have done that.

How am I supposed to push him away if telling him about Cody didn't impact how he feels? He still cares. Deeply. The same way I do about him. That's why he's still around, helping me. Making his point clear about where we stand. There's only so much I can do before the truth comes out once and for all. Because I'd have to tell him if he doesn't run for good.

Staring at Mom's hand, I ask, "Why didn't you tell me about Caleb's dad? The whole town knew, and I felt like such a moron when I got back and hadn't known he was sick."

She's told me her feelings about my relationship with the Anders family. Even though she never fully admitted it, I think she felt threatened by how close I was to Caleb's mom. It didn't mean I loved mine less, but I could see why it was hard to witness. Especially whenever I'd escape to their house for dinner or board games or *Family Feud* nights by the television.

There's a momentary pause before she finally sighs and releases my leg. "I didn't tell you because you always want to fix things. And some things in life can't be fixed no matter how hard you try."

Just as I'm about to reply, I stop myself with the harsh realization that she's right.

I've always tried fixing people. I tried fixing Caleb's pain that day at the hardware store, and look where it got us. Nowhere.

"Make no mistake, Raine," Mom tells me, eyes firmly planted on my face. "I have never disliked Caleb or his family. I know he's a good person, just as his family are good people. I've only wanted you to live your life before settling down with him, or with anybody for that matter. The thought of you being distracted from all the goals you set out to achieve concerned me."

I have no idea what to say, so I stay quiet.

"You are going to accomplish so many wonderful things because you're strong-willed. I shouldn't have kept anything from you because it wasn't my place. I'm sorry."

Understanding has my head bobbing slowly, even if I wish she'd said something. But what's done is done.

"Thank you for telling me."

She stands up and gives me a hug, right as the curtain opens and two people appear: one of the anesthesiologists who I've already filled paperwork out for and the man transporting me to the operating room.

It's him who asks "Are you ready?"

Mom releases me and takes my hand, squeezing it. "You'll be okay. I'll be right here when you wake up."

Swallowing down the anxiety blocking my airway, I force out a shaky nod to the people waiting for me. "Ready."

And two and a half hours later, surrounded by my doctor and mother watching me sip my apple juice as I fully come to, I listen to the words coming from my doctor's mouth.

"…doesn't necessarily mean it's impossible since you haven't actively been trying. But the damage is significant, so it could be very, very difficult for you. Not to mention the health problems you could have in the process."

There's a sliver of optimism in her delivery, but we both know it's slim at best.

"I'm sorry, Raine," Dr. Ryder tells me softly. "I wish I had better news for you."

I barely register my mother's hand on me.

Or the way I stare at the doctor.

I can't feel anything but numbness and the cool reality blanketing my overheated body.

Not impossible.

I should be grateful for that.

Miracles have happened before.

But I refuse to expect too much.

How many broken hearts can a person survive before there's nothing left to shatter?

Chapter Thirty-Three

CALEB

BEA'S IS BUSIER THAN I expect it to be when I walk in, so it takes a little longer to get to the counter where Elena and Bea are working around each other to grab drinks and food for people.

"Your usual?" Bea asks, already reaching for a Styrofoam cup. "I don't have your favorite in stock right now, but I have fresh blueberry muffins that I know your parents love."

I don't bother telling her about Dad's feeding tube because it's not worth the pitiful looks I'd get. "They'd like that." Especially Mom, who basically only eats eggs, microwave meals, or whatever I make extra of and bring over so she can spend as much time with Dad as possible.

She's lost weight.

Worse—she's lost the light in her eyes.

It's barely even there when she sees me.

When I pass Elena my credit card to run, I ask, "Where's Raine? You guys look like you could use an extra hand."

The teenager glances at her grandmother briefly before

swiping my card through the reader and answering, "She's not working this week."

It's Bea who elaborates as she puts some of the muffins into a bag. "Raine is recovering from a minor procedure. She'll be back next week if you want to pop in then. I think I put her on the schedule starting Tuesday."

Procedure? "Like, surgery?"

Bea hums. "Thought you would have known. Heard you two have been...cozy."

My eyes narrow at the suspicious choice of words, especially given the last time I saw Raine. "Do I want to know what you mean?"

A grin curves the older woman's lips as she sets the bag of goods on the counter in front of me. "All I'm saying is that Steve sees all. Artie hired him to help with some construction over at a building he purchased on Grove Street, and apparently there is quite the view from the side window when certain couples park on the street where they think nobody can see them."

Jesus Christ. First the hardware store camera, now this.

Bea chuckles at my reddening face. "I may not be one to talk, because I certainly had my fun in my younger years, but if you two want privacy, you might want to choose a better place. One where someone as loud-mouthed as Steve can't spy on you. Artie and his entire team knew minutes after he saw you, and you know how fast gossip spreads around here."

Elena turns to her grandma. "That's not fair! I don't even know what happened. Somebody needs to fill me in."

Bea pats Elena's shoulder. "When you're older, dear."

Elena sticks her bottom lip out and passes me my card.

Clearing my throat, I put it away and tuck my wallet

in my back pocket. "Thanks. For, uh, the advice. Do you know if Raine is at her place?"

Bea's hands go to her hips. "Where else would she be, boy? Yours?"

I can't help but snort at her sass. "Fair point. You got me there."

Bea holds up her hand and grabs the bag again before depositing a few more pastries inside it. Molasses cookies, I'm sure. "If you're going to see her, the least you can do is give those to her. Tell her I hope she feels better."

Elena smirks at her grandmother's scheming. "Tell Raine I miss her. Okay?"

Sighing, I nod. "You got it."

No point in denying who I'm going to see at this point, especially if people have seen us in compromising positions.

Bea stops me before I walk out. "Do yourselves a favor and get over whatever is stopping you from being together. Don't you think you owe it to one another to be happy after seeing how miserable you are without each other after all this time?"

I wish it were as easy as that.

"I'll keep that in mind," I murmur, refusing to promise her anything else.

Life is already full of disappointment.

I don't want to add to it.

~

Knocking on the front door of the white house feels just as nerve-racking as it did when I was a teenager. As I wait for somebody to answer, I look around and see the patchy lawn that doesn't seem like anybody took care of before the first frost hit.

"Offered to mow it for them," I hear from somewhere nearby.

I turn to see an older man by the fence of the property next to the Copelins'. "Sorry, what was that?"

Leon Applebee points his cane to the lawn. "I offered to mow it for them before winter hit. Raine told me they'd handle it. Damn near killed me to see them try during the summer. Funny as hell though. The missus, Janet, nearly ran over the garbage cans when she hit the gas a little too hard on the riding mower. After that, she seemed too traumatized to try again."

The image makes my lips curl in amusement. "You're Leon, right?" I walk over and raise my hand. "Raine mentioned the project you helped her with. She likes you."

He shakes my hand. "The kid grew on me. Her and her dog, even if he has a licking problem. Surprised to see you here."

My eyes go to the house behind me to make sure nobody came to the door. Then I turn back to the man currently eyeing me. "I heard Raine was under the weather, so I brought her something."

His eyes go down to the bag, which I lift for proof. "You got pastries in there?"

Lips twitching, I nod. "Yes, sir."

"You gonna share any with me?"

I chuckle and open the bag. "I've got a blueberry muffin up for grabs. My dad won't eat it, so it might as well go to somebody who will."

He reaches in and takes out the food in question before looking back up at me. "I was real sad to hear about your father. Anytime my late wife put something on the honey-do list, I'd make my way down to the hardware store to pick up supplies for it."

Warmth settles into my chest. "We appreciate your business."

His chin dips once. "But I will say, I'm partial to the girl in that house behind you. She's got a real good heart, even if it's a little misplaced sometimes. I'd hate to see anything bad happen to her when she's got so much love to give."

I'm not surprised they formed a bond. Raine has always been good at doing that with people.

"I've got connections, you know," he adds, bushy brows arching. "I know people who could take care of you if need be. Blueberry muffins can only keep you safe for so long, boyo."

This took a turn. "Good to know…"

He gestures toward the house. "Better go. Those girls don't like to be kept waiting."

When I turn, I see Janet at the door watching me and Leon. I wave off the elderly man before walking over to the woman who's trying not to look completely uncomfortable with my presence.

"I come in peace," I offer, lifting the bag of goodies toward her. "Bea sent me with Raine's favorite, and there are extras in there if you want any. If she'll see me, that is."

Raine's mother glances behind her before stepping outside and shutting the door. It doesn't give me much optimism, especially when she crosses her arms on her chest and lets out a heavy sigh like her daughter does when she's stressed.

"I never did say how sorry I am about what's going on with your father," she begins, hesitant eyes meeting mine. "I haven't treated you very fairly, and neither did my husband. *Ex*-husband. You and your family have always been nothing but kind, especially to Raine. I didn't always like that, but I am grateful she's had you."

Straightening, I watch as she shifts on her feet, probably feeling as uncomfortable as I am right now. "My family would do anything for Raine. No matter what happened. I would too."

She glances down at the ground, but not before I see the slightest glaze to her eyes that shows how much she cares, even if she has a hard time saying it. It's the first time I've seen genuine emotion that isn't anger from her. It's progress, even if we're never going to be close. It means she's willing to try.

For her daughter.

"She's vulnerable right now, Caleb" is what I hear next from her. "And I'm trying my best to be there for her, but you may be what she needs more right now. That's not easy for me to admit. I'm her mother."

Her glassy eyes move toward mine.

"But you're her...everything."

I blink.

Repeat those words to myself.

Then blink again.

Janet stands taller and rolls her shoulders back before stepping aside from the door. "I've always been scared that she's going to fall too hard, too fast like I did. But you are not Craig, and she is not me. The last thing I want is for her to struggle with her choices when I played a hand in the ones she made."

I have no idea what to say because this is the last thing I expected when I pulled up to their house. But nonetheless, a tiny part of me feels like a weight has been lifted.

Not because I needed her permission.

But because I have it anyway.

For the first time.

"You two have a lot to talk about. If she's willing to bring it up, hear her out," she concludes. "Maybe if I had, I would have salvaged my relationship with her a lot sooner than I did."

Chapter Thirty-Four

RAINE

I'M LYING IN BED with Sigmund curled beside me when my door cracks open. I turn, thinking it's Mom checking on me for the hundredth time, when Caleb's head pops in. Panic prickles my limbs as Sigmund instantly darts up, tail wagging at the visitor who remains by the door.

"Hey," he greets quietly. "Your mom let me in."

I expected as much since he wouldn't have gotten past the warden otherwise. But why is he here? I've seen Skylar and Olive, who came bearing dog toys and my favorite snacks, and got a phone call from Aunt Tiffany checking in after Mom told her about the procedure. I never expected Caleb though. "Hi…"

He smiles at the dog making whining noises, clearly wanting attention. "He's gotten big, huh? He'll definitely grow into those paws."

Last night when Sigmund was trying to make me feel better, those massive paws stepped on one of my tiny incisions by accident. I could tell he felt awful when I cried out because he chose to stay in his open crate the rest of the night and keep a watchful eye on me from a distance.

"The vet says he'll be at least sixty pounds when he's fully grown," I tell him, trying to match his small talk while sitting up and wincing at the slight pain still lingering in my abdomen.

Caleb watches me prop myself up with a pillow behind my back before gesturing toward Sigmund. "May I?"

All I do is nod, my eyes following him in as he fusses over my four-legged roommate. Sigmund's tail starts wagging harder, shaking not only his entire back end but the bed too.

"You did it," Caleb says, and at first I don't know if he's talking to me or the dog. Not until his eyes pan over to me. "You've always wanted a dog. I remember when you went through a corgi phase and would send me a million pictures you'd come across online, trying to get me to buy us one. But I'd say this dude is a pretty solid start. Your first real baby."

Baby. He doesn't see the way my heart tightens and falls to the bottom of my stomach or the way my chest deflates like somebody stuck a needle in it. Despite how hard I try keeping it in, he can't miss the sob that bubbles from my wavering lips. It has his hand pausing where it strokes Sigmund's back. Then the floodgates open, and ugly, desperate tears begin to fall before I can suppress them.

Caleb moves quickly, suddenly squatting beside me. I don't need to look at him to know those intense eyes are trained on me. I can feel them burning frantically into my face. "What is it? Are you hurting? Should I get your mom? Do you need medicine?"

Maybe it's because he's here with me for the millionth time when he could be anywhere else, but the last barrier I'd built comes crumbling down.

The last thing either of us expects is the blurted, hoarse words that escape my blubbering lips. The truth that can't be contained anymore because it's eating me up inside. I've got nothing left to fight it.

"I c-can't have any babies."

Caleb stares.

And stares.

And stares.

And I cry harder for the words that finally relieve the pressure I've been carrying on my conscience for so long.

Then I hear a whispered "What?"

It's only then that I allow myself to peel open my damp eyes and look at the boy whose jaw is slack with confusion, while mine wobbles with saddened relief.

He's slow to stand. "Raine… What are you talking about?"

I sniff back tears, running the back of my hand underneath my nose and struggling to take a deep breath. My lungs hurt yet feel some sort of ease from each breath I manage to take. The hard part is over—the words are out. "You always wanted kids," I whisper, swiping my hands over my face to dry it. It's pointless. The tears keep coming. "You always talked about what they'd look like and what we'd name them and how we'd raise them together, and I always knew how far away that dream really was."

Caleb's blank expression shadows with every word I say, and he remains silent as I blink back more tears and swallow heavily.

Breathe in.

Breathe out.

We lock eyes. "You wanted the one thing I couldn't give you, so I did the only thing I could think of to make sure you'd be happy. One day."

His head slowly shakes back and forth as if he knows what I'm going to say and refuses to accept it.

"I let you go."

For what feels like forever, there's nothing but silence. We stare at one another with two very different emotions on our faces.

Mine with reluctant relief.

And his...shock. And something else.

Then he says, "What the fuck?"

His hands go to his hair, fingers scraping through the long strands as he backs up and starts pacing. It's his go-to when he needs to process something.

Back and forth.

Back and forth.

Even Sigmund watches, his head moving to follow Caleb's every step.

"Are you telling me that you broke up with me because of this?" he asks, stopping to turn to me. There's a tiny muscle in his temple that's twitching right now.

"Yes."

More twitching.

"How do you even know that you can't have kids? I don't get it."

Tell him, the voice inside me encourages.

There's no going back from it.

My hands shake as I reach for Sigmund, touching his side to feel grounded. "You'll hate me," I tell him.

The question he asks next is delivered in a cool tone. "Wasn't that the plan all along? Why hold back now?"

He's always been too smart for his own good, which is why lying is pointless. It's too tiring to keep it all straight. The half-truths and white lies and partial recognitions of reality.

It's all or nothing.

I give it all.

And I'll get nothing.

Another cycle.

Endless and ugly.

So I tell him. Everything.

All the dirty details.

The sleepless nights.

The fear of realization when I found out I'd been pregnant with Cody's baby and an entirely new fear when they'd seen all those cysts on my ovaries that spread over the years.

I tell Caleb every little doubt that crept into my mind. Could I make him happy if we couldn't have kids? Would he be angry? Resentful? Sad? Could we make it forever after so many promises weren't met?

Deep down, I want to believe we could.

But sometimes you have to sacrifice the comfortable things in life for the good things. It's not always mutually exclusive. I would have preferred Caleb think the worst of me after telling him about Cody, so I didn't let myself hope there was a chance at a future for us.

Because Caleb was always a comfortable thing.

Wonderful. Loving. Attentive.

We were good together, but that didn't mean we always would be. Nothing is guaranteed in life. So you have to figure out what's worth keeping, losing, and letting go of for the bigger picture. It wasn't just my masterpiece that I was painting. It was Caleb's too.

"I want you to know how sorry I am for everything I did. All the things I put you through were always meant for the best. It wasn't that I thought I had to lose you to find me. It was the other way around. I needed to know you'd be happy, even if that meant seeing you build everything we talked about with somebody else. I'm so sorry, Caleb. You've gone through a lot this year, and you didn't deserve it."

I'm greeted by the thickest silence we've ever shared between us. He's not even blinking.

This is why I didn't want to tell him. Because every wave of emotion on his face is clear. Because there's no going back. No more shielding him from anything. No more protection from what fate dealt us.

Eventually, his fists tighten at his sides.

"I can't..." He shakes his head, turning around and cursing.

There's barely any evidence of him in this room because I tucked all the things that reminded me of him into a box in the closet. Safe, for my eyes only when I want to torture myself. And I do. Often. But as he looks around, he must see how much he's been erased from the life I've lived since the breakup.

Caleb abruptly swings around, eyes narrowing as they land on me. "How fucking *dare* you."

My eyes widen.

"How *dare* you make that decision for me," he seethes, fists clenching so tightly they turn white. He doesn't move closer to me or step away. "You had no right to assume I couldn't handle the truth. Do you honestly think you helped? That you made things *easier*?"

Jaw quivering, I shake my head. "Cal—"

"No." He jabs a finger at me. "You don't get to say anything else. You've done enough. All this time, Raine. *All this time.*" More cursing, hair tugging, and pacing.

Sigmund is standing, but his tail isn't wagging anymore.

It's tucked under his legs as he watches Caleb suspiciously, stiff and protective as if he can sense the tension in the room.

When Caleb finally turns to me again, I don't expect his red face or glassy eyes full of angry tears. "You had no right," he repeats, voice breaking with raspiness.

"I really thought I was doing the right thing," I tell him. "I thought if I couldn't have kids—"

"This isn't about the goddamn kids, Raine!" he barks, veins popping in his neck. He grips his hair and stares at me through his tear-stricken eyes. "I *needed* you. And you weren't there."

The second those broken words are out, what's left of my heart shatters. So this time I don't bother saying anything. An apology won't do anything at this point.

I needed you.

I needed you.

I needed you.

"I can't do this," Caleb says. He goes to my bedroom door, gives me one last look as if he's trying to figure out what's real and what's not, and then walks out.

The front door opens.

Slams closed.

Silence.

Mom appears at the doorway. She doesn't say a word when she walks in or when she gets onto the bed and carefully pulls me into her side.

It isn't until I rest my head on her shoulder and let my damp cheek soak into her shirt that she brushes her long fingers in my hair and tells me, her voice uncharacteristically soft, "I know I haven't made things easy for you, but you could have told me. If I'd known what happened all those years ago, I could have helped you. I know it wouldn't have changed what you went through, but it would have changed how you coped with it. I..." She takes a deep breath, pausing her comforting strokes. "I failed you in so many ways, didn't I?"

Squeezing my eyes closed, I whisper, "I failed myself."

Mom is quiet for a long stretch of time before her fingers start moving again. "You've done far better at life than I have, Raine. Despite all the challenges you've faced, especially on your own. I'd hardly say that's failing."

Chapter Thirty-Five

CALEB

MOM STARTLES WHEN I slam the front door closed and storm in. She and Dad are both awake and gawking at me in the living room as I enter, shake my head, and walk into the kitchen.

No words can describe what I'm feeling right now. I don't know if I'll ever find the right way to express everything swirling in my head.

"Honey?" Mom says cautiously, a hand falling onto my back. I'm leaning over the counter, gripping the edges until my fingers hurt. "Caleb, what happened?"

Frustration still seeps into every crevice it can as I look over my shoulder at her. "Raine."

It's the only thing I can get out.

One word.

One name.

Confusion swirls on Mom's face. "I'm going to need more than that. What happened between you and Raine?"

"She—" My hoarse voice is cut off with frustration,

forcing me to clear my throat and stand taller until Mom's hand falls from my back. I take a deep breath. "She lied over and over again. And for fucking what? It could have been different. It would have been fine."

Mom is shaking her head and trying to piece together what I'm telling her when Dad calls out my name.

I look to Mom, wipe my face with my hands, and watch her nod and guide me into the living room again.

He says those three damn words that have me dropping onto the couch with my palms on my wet face. "Talk to me."

If anybody has a right to be mad at the world, it's the man waiting to help me. If there's anyone who needs to be comforted right now, it's the person who reaches over and grabs ahold of my hand. But like always, he's giving everything he has left to me.

So I let it all out.

Every raw admission.

Every hard reality.

Every horrible emotion.

Because I'm done holding it back.

Physically, mentally, and emotionally done.

"She *gave up* on us," I whisper, staring helplessly at my father. "If she had just told me the truth, we could have figured it out. But she chose not to even try."

I swipe furiously at my cheeks, letting Dad's hand fall to the couch arm. All while he watches me with knowing eyes. Studying. Waiting for me to take a few deep breaths and calm down.

"Let me ask you something," he prompts, wincing as he repositions in the chair. "If you got married to Raine, committed to one another for a lifetime no matter the circumstances, without the knowledge you have now, would you care if you later learned you couldn't have kids? Would that information upset you if you struggled with it?"

I blink slowly. "How could you ask that?" How could *Raine* assume I'd be a dickhead about something she had no control over?

Dad gives me a look. "Son, Raine doesn't have a malicious bone in her body. If she thought breaking up with you was for the best, then there was a logical reason for it."

There it is again. Logic. Just because something is logical doesn't mean it has to make sense. "Do I want children? Yeah. Christ, Dad. You know I do. How long have I said I wanted somebody to pass along the store to? To raise them there like you did with me?" I stand, riled up again. "Does that make me an asshole or something?"

"Language," Dad says, coughing. One of his shaky hands goes to his chest, rubbing it until he catches his breath. "Don't you think all that talk is what contributed to her decision?"

Standing taller, my brows pinch at the question. "I don't understand."

Mom steps in from where she's been standing silently at the doorway of the room. "Baby boy, Raine knows how much you want to be a father. You've always been open about what your future looks like. If she thought for a second she was going to get in the way of that, she was going to take herself out of the equation. She did what she thought was best. I'm not saying I condone the way she hurt you, but I can see where she was coming from."

Nostrils flaring, I look away from them and swipe my tongue along my dry lips. Sniffing back the tears prickling my eyes, I roll my shoulders back and let out a harsh breath.

"Best for who? Because as far as I'm concerned, she did it selfishly."

Dad's scoff has my eyes dropping to him in confusion. "I have never heard you spout more bullshit than I did just now. Almost as much as when you tried convincing yourself you stopped loving her."

Mom sighs. "Richard."

Dad shakes his head. "No, Denise. You and I both know those two are meant to be together and too goddamn stubborn to get past shit that's out of their control. You have someone who sacrificed her happiness for yours, kid, whether that was misplaced or not. That's anything but selfish."

I let that sink in.

"She never liked football," he tells me.

My brow furrows. "What?"

"All those games she went to—" He has to stop himself to cough and catch his breath. "I know she didn't enjoy them. But she went for you. Every single time."

Mom's head bobs in agreement. "Actions always speak louder than words, sweetie. There was so much you both did for each other that was meant to enhance each other's lives. Look at how often she'd endure our competitive game nights. She loved being here because you were here, not because she liked any of the board games we were playing."

Raine never said one way or another.

Dad dips his chin. "That girl would clearly do anything for you. You have to figure out if that's enough to get past this or if it's the reason to let her go for good. But you cannot keep stepping on the line. One of you needs to make the final decision."

The final decision.

337

Guilt sinks into my stomach for accusing her of thinking only of herself when they're making a good point. We always did what I wanted, and I never thought twice about it because half of the time it was Raine's suggestion.

But does that mean I can forgive her right now? "I wouldn't have cared," I tell my parents quietly. "About the kids."

Their silence shows their doubt.

"I *wouldn't*," I press. "I'd be...sad. But I'd have her. That's all I ever really wanted." The second that absorbs, my chest tightens.

It was always about Raine.

Not the other shit.

The things we did.

The places we went.

It was always fun because she was with me, right there by my side.

Dad says, "Families come in all different forms. You never know what you're going to get in life. All you could ask for is one full of love. If anything, this proves you'll have a lifetime worth of it from that girl you walked out on today."

Mom comes over and sits on the arm of Dad's chair, putting her arm around his shoulders and smiling at me. "I understand why you're hurt by this," she says softly. "But do you want this to be the reason you can't reconcile?"

Dropping back down onto the couch, I brush a palm down my face before looking to my parents. "At what price though?"

Dad coughs again.

Mom smiles sadly and asks one simple question. "Can you really put a price on love?"

When Dad moves his hand away from his mouth, there's bright red blood covering his skin.

Mom stares at Dad.

I stare at Mom.

And Dad stares at his hand.

Chapter Thirty-Six

RAINE

When I see Leon walk into Bea's with a young, brunette woman beside him, I smile for the first time in nearly two weeks. Ever since the falling-out with Caleb, I've felt a hole in my chest that nothing seems to mend. Not even Sigmund's warm cuddles, the Milk Duds Dad has been sending me, or the cooking class Mom signed us up for together that starts right before the beginning of spring semester. I take each day as it comes and do my best to distract myself from feeling sorry over the choices I've made.

Christmas is in a matter of days, and I don't have the same spirit I typically do. Our tree is up but bare of decorations, and the only shopping I did consisted of gift certificates that I've tucked in holiday cards because it was the easiest route to take.

My neighbor snorts in amusement when he stops at the counter and sees the antlers that Elena made me wear. They have bells on them and give me a headache the longer they rattle, but the sassy teenager insisted we get in the holiday spirit with antlers, ugly sweaters, and Christmas music playing all day long.

"Nice antlers, kid," Leon muses, causing the woman beside him to smile. I recognize her from the pictures he's shown me in the albums he'd pull out when I was over. "This is my daughter, Jenna. Figured it was about time the two of you met."

She reaches her hand out first, which I meet halfway over the counter. "I've heard a lot about you, Raine. Anybody who can handle this grumpy bastard has my respect."

I grin at the man in question. "I like her, Leon."

The old man rolls his eyes. "Of course you do." He gestures toward the seasonal special written on the chalkboard. "Don't suppose you still have some of the warm cider left, do you?"

"Bea bought more yesterday. Two cups?"

Jenna holds out a credit card before Leon can reach for his tattered wallet. "And I'd love it if you could add two apple fritters for here. Dad hasn't been able to stop raving about them for months, so it's time I tried one."

I accept the card. "No problem."

Leon grabs his wallet, which is on its last legs, and pulls out a five-dollar bill to stick into the tip jar.

"You really need a new wallet," I tell him, passing his daughter's credit card back and waiting for the receipt to print.

He scoffs. "There's nothing wrong with this one. Nothing a little duct tape can't fix."

Jenna rolls her eyes. "You're getting a new one for Christmas. It's in your stocking already. Act surprised."

Laughing lightly, I grab two cups and start on their order. "Are you two doing holiday shopping or are you finished?"

"We're almost done," she tells me. "Dad wanted help getting something for the kids, so they're with their father for the day being loaded up on sugar and God only knows what else."

Despite the wary look Leon gives me, I don't feel any sadness hearing about her children. If anything, it makes me happy that he's finding something perfect for them. I guess that's what happens when you accept nothing is going to change about your situation.

It takes too much energy being angry, so you might as well find the little things in life to lift your spirits.

"I bet they're excited for Christmas," I reply, passing her the cups of cider and going toward the display case for the fritters. "I remember how much I loved this time of year when I was little. Everything was so…"

"Magical," Jenna finishes for me with a warm smile.

I return the smile easily before transferring the fritters into the small heating oven to warm.

Leon clears his throat, shifting his cane and looking behind him at the tables. "You wouldn't happen to have a few minutes to sit down, would you?"

Elena is in the back helping Bea, but things are slow enough for a quick break. "That shouldn't be a problem. Is everything okay?"

He nods. "As good as it can be. I just think it'd be great if you and Jen had a chance to sit down and chat a bit while she's in town."

I put their fritters on plates and set them down in front of them. "Grab a table, and I'll meet you over there in a minute. I'm going to get a drink and let them know I'm taking five."

Wiping my hands off on my apron, I untie it and pop my

head into the back. "Lena, can you take over the counter for a few minutes? Leon is here with his daughter, so I'm going to sit with them."

Bea waves her granddaughter off. "Go on. I've got this covered for now."

After pouring myself a glass of water, I head to the back and pull out the chair between Leon and Jenna.

Jenna starts the conversation. "I read the paper that Dad helped you with. It's really good. Reading that stuff about him and Mom brought up a lot of good memories from when I was little." She gives Leon a nostalgic smile that I can see his lips slowly curling to return. "It made me think about how grateful I am to have them as parents."

Hearing her say that makes me happy, knowing that there were rough patches along the way for the three of them. "I wish I could have gotten to know Annemarie. She seems like she would've been the perfect mother."

A fondness warms Leon's face at the sentiment that I know to be true.

Jenna turns to me. "I actually wanted to talk to you about something. I know you know about Mom's fertility issues. He mentioned that you understood on a personal level, and reading that paper made me think about everything my mother would have loved to do before she passed away. Did Dad ever tell you she was into charity work and volunteering?"

I shake my head, racking my brain for a time that might have come up. "We didn't really discuss that, but I'm not surprised to hear it. That seems like something she'd do."

Jenna beams. "Exactly. Which is why I think it'd be a neat idea to do something in her name. Like some sort of charity event or work that helps women somehow."

"Are you thinking a donation in her name, or something bigger?" I question, leaning back in my chair. I've definitely seen people do stuff like that for loved ones, but I've never researched it before.

Leon sets down his cider. "Annemarie was someone who'd want to go big or go home. She had a big heart. The more she could help, the happier she was."

Jenna nods. "I don't know what your experience is with reproductive health. I know you're not in school for anything like that, but you do want to help people. I figured the best way to mesh the best of both worlds was to ask you how to start. Maybe see if you had any ideas."

While I didn't know Annemarie personally, I can guess her personal struggles. I haven't thought about being an advocate for reproductive health, but I'm sure it's something she would have partnered with me on if she were around.

Something she would have started.

Go big or go home.

"I'd have to look into it," I start, looking between the two of them. "But I think somebody like Annemarie would want to help as many people as she could. Educating. Raising money for organizations that would benefit universal reproductive health to reach the audience who needed it most. Something like that."

Leon's eyes lighten the same way Jenna's do. Even if they're not blood related, their expressions are uncanny. A true case of nature versus nurture. Everything Leon and Annemarie did for her is evident in the way she carries herself. If I can see it, so can anybody else.

Annemarie is the perfect spokesperson for the people who need her kind of story.

People like me.

The ones who need hope.

"You could call it the Annemarie Project," I suggest, toying with my water glass.

Maybe if I'd had that kind of resource when I first found out about my diagnosis, I wouldn't have been so scared. So destructive. I'd like to think I would have told my parents and Caleb what was going on instead of thinking worst-case scenario. If there are women out there who can be helped before they make the same choices as me, they'd have a better chance at being happier with themselves in the long run.

Jenna and Leon share a look, silently communicating through their eyes. When they turn back to me, their smiles say it all.

"*We* could call it that," Jenna corrects.

I swallow, knowing I already have a lot on my plate but also feeling something tug in my chest that encourages me to take this opportunity.

Annemarie isn't here to share her story.

But I am.

I have nothing left to lose anymore, so maybe it's time to finally open up.

"I'm in," I tell them, giving them a watery smile at the release of emotion suddenly crashing through the barrier I've kept it behind.

Long after I've said my goodbyes to them and they've left, I feel a warmth take over the emptiness of my body. It lights up the part of my chest that has been anything but for a while now, and I wonder if it's the one thing I've been missing out on.

Hope.

As if the universe knows how badly I need it, another spark of contentment travels through me when I walk up to my house after work and see something sitting on the front step.

A little stuffed polar bear holding a heart that says two words. *Forgive me.*

It reminds me of the others I have stashed in my bedroom closet.

I freeze when I hear "I'm still upset you didn't trust me enough to be honest."

Slowly standing with the bear tight in my hold, I turn to see Caleb with his hands tucked into his jacket pockets.

Throat thickening as I swallow, I try to gather my thoughts and say something. The only thing I can muster is "I understand."

Caleb's eyes move to the ground before heaving out a sigh. "I don't want to do this anymore, Raine."

Those words are a kick to the gut, causing my fingers to clench around the bear. He's officially ending it with me. In person. Right here.

I guess I can't blame him. Isn't this what I was trying to get him to do the whole time? Hate me? Move on from me?

Instead of giving me the final send-off, he says, "I can't keep acting like this is over when we both know it's not. I need you to be honest with me. Do you still love me? Because I never stopped loving you, no matter how damn hard I tried. It killed me. Every day. Every thought of you living a life without me. No matter what you said, I was still in it. And I need to know if you feel the same."

Gaping at him, I loosen my hold on the bear and stand taller. "After everything that happened, you still love me?"

He doesn't answer.

He's waiting for mine.

Shakily, I nod. "I love you."

His dark eyes glisten, as if he's relieved by the response he wasn't sure he'd get. "Okay. Good." He nods, looking away for a second before taking a deep breath. "Good."

My eyes go to the bear again. "Why on earth would I need to forgive you? It's me who needs to earn *your* forgiveness."

Fingertips brushing over the stitched words that look handmade, I peek at him as he walks over to me and stops a few feet away. "I asked your mom to teach me how to sew. It's not very good…" His eyes are on the bear. "But it's legible. She fixed a couple of the letters for me so you could tell what it said."

My mother taught him how to sew? "You did this for me?"

"I bought the bear," he admits. "I didn't have that much time on my hands to go all out. Just did the message. Pretty sure your mom wanted to wring my neck whenever I'd mess up. Remember the bears I used to get you?"

Of course I do. "I remember everything."

My eyes go back down to the bear, wondering when Mom would have had time to teach him anything. I'm surprised she didn't say anything about it either.

Caleb pulls me from the thought. "I was a jackass to you before. That's why I want you to forgive me. It was a lot to take in, and I know I didn't handle it well. I'm not going to lie, Raine. That shit is going to take a long time to get over. Because we could have avoided so much pain if you'd just *told* me what was going on. From the day you got back that summer all those years ago."

I know that now—know that none of this was worth it. "I'm sorry."

His head moves back and forth. "I don't want your

apology. I'm done with apologies. All I want is to fix it. Better it. No more lies from now on. We won't make it if something like this happens again."

He's right. There'd be no trust, no foundation, if we came back to this place.

"I promise," I whisper. "No more lies."

Caleb closes the distance between us, cupping the back of my head and pulling me into his chest. I feel his lips against the top of my head and his shuddering breath release against my hair. He holds me tight, crushing the bear between us like he's afraid to let go.

Against my hair, he muffles, "I fucking missed you."

I manage to wrap an arm around his waist and hug him back for the first time. "I missed you too. Every day."

If it's possible, his grip tightens. "Dad wants to see you. If you're up for it. You can bring Sigmund. You know nobody would mind."

His dad? "Are you sure?"

Caleb nods, his chin brushing the crown of my head. "He doesn't have much time, Raine. It's now or never. My parents never stopped loving you. None of us did."

I clench my eyes closed to fight off the tears. I haven't seen his dad since graduation, but I've heard that isn't the man who exists anymore. I'm not ready for it, but I have no choice but to be. For him.

For Caleb.

For Denise.

For *me*.

"Okay."

Chapter Thirty-Seven

CALEB

I DON'T KNOW WHAT Dad says to Raine, but after nearly forty minutes in a room alone together, talking in mumbled tones, she bends down to give him a peck on the cheek and a hug that he feebly returns.

More words are whispered.

More nodding.

Then, Raine stands up and smiles down at the man who enters another coughing fit until the nurses surround him.

Mom's hand finds my back, brushing it once before walking into the living room to be with Dad.

When Raine approaches me, studying my parents at the doorway of the room, she tucks herself against my front for a hug. "What did he say to you?" I ask curiously.

I hear a soft laugh that gently shakes her body, causing me to look down at her. She pulls back enough to meet my eyes, hers light with humor as she smiles up at me. "He told me if I ever break your heart again, he'd come back and haunt me for the rest of my life."

I blink.

Then blink again.

Then I start laughing until she joins in.

It's only after I shake my head and pull her back into me for another hug that I look over her head to see my parents staring at me with the same peaceful smiles on their faces.

They look happy.

Despite everything, they can still smile.

"Hey, Caleb?" Raine peeks up at me, resting her chin on my chest. "I was wondering…"

I look down and wait.

"Do you want to go get some chicken?"

Snorting, I playfully poke her side. "I'm never going to live that down, am I?"

She shakes her head. "Nope."

I hook an arm around her shoulder and turn to my parents. "We're going to grab dinner. Want us to bring you guys back anything?"

They both shake their heads.

Dad says, "Go be with your girl, kid. I'll see you when you get home."

It's a promise I hope he holds on to.

Chapter Thirty-Eight

CALEB

THAT NIGHT, DAD PASSES away in his sleep.

It's a somber moment.

Silent.

Inevitable.

My mother lets out a choked sob.

She wraps me in her arms as the nurses surround his unmoving body. "He waited to make sure you were going to be okay. And that…that has to be enough."

Chapter Thirty-Nine

CALEB

DAD'S SECOND FAVORITE HOLIDAY was New Year's because it meant fresh beginnings. "It doesn't matter what happened in the past because this is your new chapter of life, son," he'd always say when the countdown began.

Two arms wrap around me from behind, stirring me from the staring contest I'm having with the stars. "I thought I'd find you out here," Raine says quietly. I feel her forehead rest between my shoulder blades before her arms tighten around me briefly in a hug before loosening. Walking to my side, she tugs on her jacket and leans against the railing. "Are you sure you don't want me to go with you this week? I know your mom is busy working with the stone carvers to get the gravestone finished and delivered to the cemetery, so if you need me to come with you to help with the other arrangements, I will."

Dad didn't want a funeral. He said he wanted people to celebrate their lives, not waste them mourning the end of his. Apparently, he and Mom had an in-depth conversation about it a month or so ago. "He knew," Mom told me the night he was taken out of the house. "He knew his time was up, but he wanted to stay just a little bit longer. For you and Raine."

Tears burn the backs of my eyes as I clear my throat and try fighting them off. The bitter air doesn't help any. Between the nip of chill against my face and the way the wind clings to the tears threatening to spill, it makes my vision even blurrier as I attempt to keep it together.

"You hate missing school," I reply, knowing she's mapped out the remainder of her degree. Every course and clinical hour is color-coded in her calendar. I don't want to put her behind.

Raine looks from the sky to me. "I'd rather be there for you right now. I already emailed my professors saying I'll be out for a few days."

My heart clenches. "You don't have to do that for me."

Her brown eyes sadden. "Didn't you once tell me that you'd do anything for me?"

I nod, watching her closely when those lips curl softly upward at the corners.

"Then what makes you think it's any different for me? We're a family, Caleb. I'm going to be there for you because I wasn't when you needed me to be before. I'm going to make that up to you every single day to prove I'm in this."

"What about what you need?" I ask.

Her hand rubs my arm slowly. "This isn't about me, Caleb. Taking a day or two off classes isn't going to kill me."

I'm not surprised that's her answer.

Scrubbing my face, I lean against the railing next to her. "Did you know that my favorite thing to do was feed you?"

Head tilting, her hand stills on my arm before lowering to her side. "No. I didn't know that."

I let loose a breath that eases some of the tightness in my lungs. "It may seem small, but it made me feel good to know I could provide for you in any way possible. My dad was the same way with my mom. I bet your dad felt the same way when he was able to bring something to the table for you and your mother."

Raine glances down at the top of the railing. "I never really thought about it like that, I guess. Mom and I both got used to letting the men in our lives handle that stuff."

"Because we *wanted* to," I tell her. "My dad loved cleaning, doing the laundry, cooking dinner, anything he could for my mom. Because they loved each other, and he knew it made her happy to have someone dote on her once in a while. It's no different from when Mom made Dad a homecooked meal on the days he had long shifts at the store and came home exhausted."

For a while, she doesn't say anything. "I always loved their love."

I look over at her.

"You were right before. A lot could have been solved if we'd only talked about it. I shut too many things down because it's what I'm used to seeing other people do. Mom. Dad. My aunt. Their version of communicating was always fighting until somebody gave up trying."

There are obvious similarities between her and her mother that I won't point out because there's no reason to. She knows where she went wrong, and I'm determined to make sure we don't go back to that place.

"We're not your parents," I remind her.

She nods. "I know." Holding up her hand, she says, "I have something for you. Wait here."

Raine disappears into the apartment. Not even a minute

later, she reappears in the doorway holding a container of something in her hands. "It's not going to be as good as the cake your mom makes, but I tried my best. My mom helped me with it. Don't worry. She didn't spit in it or anything. She's obviously over her tiff with us. I guess asking her for help winning me over got her to realize we're the endgame."

That makes me smile. Knowing her mother approves is the kind of reassurance I need because I know how much her family's approval means to her.

"There's also soup in the fridge that I brought over. Leon helped me make it. It was his wife's recipe."

All I can do is stare at the dessert container that she passes me. She spent the time to make this for me. With her mother. Who may or may not have spit in it for hurting her daughter's feelings when she told me not to. I'd take the chance.

Raine steps closer. "It's officially after midnight. Happy birthday, Caleb. I wish your dad could be here to celebrate with us."

Taking a deep breath, I gently set the container down beside us and pull her in for a frontal hug, resting my chin against the top of her head. "The nurses said he was the strongest patient they'd ever had. Nobody with the same form of cancer as him survives this long. Not even when they get treatment to slow the progression of it."

Her arms go back around my waist. "I'm not surprised. Your father was always one of the strongest people I met."

"One of?" I question, staring at the birthday cake she made me.

I hear her take a soft breath before nuzzling closer to me. I try keeping her as warm as possible when the chilly breeze starts blowing a little harder. Her voice is muffled when she replies, "I always considered you to be the strongest, so it makes sense. He raised you to be."

Closing my eyes, I move my fingers to the back of her head and lightly brush them through her hair. I feel her cheek press against my chest as we stand like this for a while longer.

Moving her hat farther down so it's covering the tops of her reddening ears, I press a light kiss against her head and say, "Friend had a nice ring to it, but I've always preferred calling you mine. Just about ended me when you weren't."

She's quiet for a long time, and I wonder what's on her mind. Eventually, I feel something press against the spot just above my heart.

Her lips.

"I missed the sound of that too," she admits.

That's when Dad's words echo in my head for a second time tonight. *It doesn't matter what happened in the past because this is your new chapter of life, son.*

While I never wanted to live a chapter of my life without my dad, it makes me want to be the best one I possibly can be to my own kid someday, no matter how we have it, so I can give them even a fraction of the things I got when I was growing up.

As if she knows what I'm thinking, Raine places one of her hands over mine. "It's going to be okay eventually. Maybe not right now, but someday."

Someday.

I'd like to think that someday, everything will make sense. "Someday" sounds like a promise from her that I have every intention of holding her to if it means I still get to have her in my life. For now, I'll take the little moments because those will build into much bigger ones.

I find myself smiling in the dark.

Someday.

"I like the sound of that," I tell her, tipping her chin up so she's looking at me.

After watching each other for a few seconds, she closes the distance. The kiss is slow, patient. Tender. So are the little touches—a stroke of her hand against my beating heart, fingernails lazily dancing over my collarbone, and fingers curling over my shoulder and squeezing.

We move inside to the bedroom, taking our time peeling each of our layers off until there's nothing between us at all.

I lay her down carefully, brushing loose hair away from her face. "Are you sure?"

She places her hand on top of the one I have cupping her cheek. Then she says the one word that could have changed our story a long time ago. "Yes."

It fuels the fire that ignites under my skin, coaxing every flick of my finger and hitch of breath until Raine's back arches. Webbing her fingers through my hair as I kiss down her body, she tugs the moment my mouth meets the spot between her legs.

Every sound I draw from her gets me harder until she's pawing at my shoulders to pull me up. Climbing up her body, I look down from where I hover over her and say, "From now on, no matter what, it's *us*. We're in this together. Hear me?"

She nods. "I hear you."

I press a kiss against the crook of her neck and ease myself inside her. "Do you *feel* me?"

Her fingernails dig into my shoulders as her legs wrap around my waist to welcome me deeper. "Y-yes, I feel you."

Another kiss against her throat as I start moving. She

meets my hips every time I slide inside, causing me to swallow a groan.

When I meet her eyes again, I say, "Us."

She stares, her hand cupping the back of my neck as we bring each other closer to the edge, and repeats, "Us."

That's all it takes before I let go, knowing we're finally on the same page. Together. Us against the world, as it always should have been.

From the other side of the closed door, we hear a loud bark that breaks up the moment.

Snorting, I drop my forehead against Raine's. "And Sigmund, apparently."

She cracks a smile. "We're sort of a package deal."

~

In the following days, it seems like things are starting to go back to normal. Or whatever my new version of normal is without Dad. I miss him every day but remember he's looking after me and everything I do still. Even if he's not here.

Which makes today frustrating, because even though he's reminded me it's okay not to have it together all the time, I still want to make him proud.

Staring at the bill in my hand, I let out a frustrated sigh before dropping it onto the pile of other mail with red lettering on it that nobody wants to see. I try counting my blessings that not all of them are for the store—some are for school. Not that getting anything from the financial aid office is necessarily a good thing. But it makes the choice I've made about taking a break from school that much smarter.

It's time to shift gears, like Dad would have wanted me to.

I'm listening, old man.

When Matt walks into the store with two coffees, I know one of them is for me. He pauses when he gets halfway in, eyebrows raised, when he sees the way I reorganized the shelves. After getting rid of all the old inventory, I decided it was time to clean up the place a bit and do some revamping.

"Hey," Matt greets, passing me the cup and nodding toward the aisles with his chin. "It looks great in here. You've done a lot of work."

We slap hands before I lift the coffee to my mouth and take a much-needed sip. I haven't had any all day, and it's amazing I'm still functioning considering I spent most of the night helping Raine study for one of her upcoming exams.

The space feels a lot more open between the shift in shelving and all the work to clean old grime up. It wasn't that the place was dirty, but it's amazing what some deep cleaning can do.

"What did you want to talk to me about?" Matt asks, leaning against the countertop. "You said something about whatever it is being a good opportunity for me."

I set my coffee down and lean back in the new chair I got for behind the counter. Bea dropped it off, saying it was an old one from the bakery she didn't like anymore because it didn't match the "aesthetic," which I think was bullshit considering nothing matches there and I've never even seen this chair in all my years of getting baked goods and caffeine at her place.

"You know a kid on the football team named Wells? He's one of the new running backs that took over my position." Whenever I see the kid on campus, he always waves a little too excitedly at me until one of his friends smacks him into stopping.

Matt's brow wrinkles. "I don't know. Maybe? I've only

been to a few of the games. One of the new coaches is a fucking snake, so I don't really feel like going and watching him fuck up the team more than Pearce did toward the end."

My lips twitch upward. "I'm actually kind of glad you said that."

Confusion twists his expression.

I grab the paper that I took off the corkboard by the student center out of my bag and slide it over to him, watching as he scans the bolded lettering across the front.

"You thought of me when you saw a job posting for the university?"

I tap the bottom. "It's for coaching. Wells came up to me a while ago saying he thought I should consider it, but I had way too much on my plate to even entertain the idea. Then I started wondering if I should reach out to someone in HR because they're willing to pay for grad school during my employment."

Matt looks up at me. "Why didn't you reach out then? If they could take some of that stress off your shoulders, then it's worth a conversation."

"I'm actually going to be taking a break after this semester to. Right now, I want my attention to go to the store and family stuff. Dad was right. I don't really need this degree. If I change my mind, I'll come back to it, but I have other things to focus on. Adding coaching into my schedule would have been impossible when I've barely had time to even get my schoolwork done as it is now. It's not in the cards for me."

Matt frowns. "That sucks, man. So you're leaving the university in May?" He acts like I won't be minutes away.

"Don't miss me yet. I'll obviously be here, and you know where my apartment is. But yeah. It's time for me to step back and stop trying to do it all, like you guys keep telling me."

It's about damn time I accepted that taking care of myself doesn't mean I'm showing weakness. I know my support system will ensure I don't keep burning both ends of the stick like I was, and I'm good with that. Happy to have people who I can turn to.

Took me long enough.

He huffs out a sigh and nods, eyes going down to the posting again. "So you think *I'd* be good for this? I've never been much for leadership."

That's because he's never had to be. "You know the same things I do, and you said yourself the current coach is a joke. What better way to change that than to *be* the change the team needs? You're in grad school too. You'd be just as well off getting the financial help. Plus if you're on staff, then maybe things with you and Rachel won't seem so damning."

He stands a little taller at the mention of her. "You've really thought this out, huh?"

I lift a shoulder. "I'm looking out for a buddy. You should call them or pop by the office if you're interested. But, Matt?" His brows go up as he meets my eyes. "You'd make a great coach. This is your chance to prove that. I know how you miss that life."

His eyes go back to the paper. "I have to admit, part of the fun with Rach was the chase."

I don't say anything.

His nostrils twitch. "That got old though," he murmurs.

All I do is nod and pat him on the arm. "I bet. But this is your opportunity to do something about that. If you two want to make it work, here's a way to do it."

He grabs the paper and folds it, tucking it into his back

pocket. "Your dad would have done something like that. I ever tell you about the time he got me an interview at the grocery store to be a bag boy when I was fifteen?"

I hadn't known that, but I smile. "Sounds like something he'd do. He wanted to help anyone who needed it. Why didn't they give you the job?"

Matt flinches. "They might have remembered me from an incident a couple of years before then."

"What was the incident?"

He looks sheepish. "Shoplifting. It was *one* pack of gum and a candy bar. I was dared to do it. Turns out the cameras actually worked. The douchebags who dared me to steal that shit said they were dummy cameras to scare people from stealing."

Shaking my head, I ask, "Did my dad ever ask you about the job after the interview?"

Matt snickers. "Yep. When I admitted why they wouldn't hire me, he said, 'You better pull your head out of your ass, son. You've got too much potential to screw yourself over by doing dumb shit.'"

I can practically hear Dad saying that, which makes something in my chest lighten under the pressure that's been sitting on it for a while. "He was right."

"Yeah. He was." I can tell he's thinking about Rachel when he mumbles, "Still is."

We're quiet for a long moment.

"Thanks for this," my friend finally says, patting his back pocket. "I think I'll reach out to them this afternoon. It's probably time I do what your dad says and make something of myself."

Standing with my coffee, I point out what he obviously doesn't see. "You already were. This is just another option to explore. For you and whatever future you decide to have."

He glances at his phone, then at the door, before turning back to me. "You've probably heard this a lot from your mom, but I know your dad would be proud of you. I'll miss bugging the shit out of you on campus, but I think the move you're making is a good one. Selfless."

Even if I have heard it before, it still means a lot to me. My tone is a little gravelly when I offer a thick "Thanks" in response. "Hey. Before you go…"

He waits for me with raised brows. "You okay?"

I swipe a palm down my leg. "You've had a good life, right? Being adopted didn't make any big changes that you regret or anything, did it?"

Matt blinks. "Wow. Uh…"

I haven't told him or DJ about the situation with Raine or what the future holds. That's not necessarily my story to tell. Not yet anyway. So I understand why he's looking at me like I'm insane for asking that question.

"No. All the changes I went through were good ones because of my parents. I doubt I'd say the same if I were with my biological ones, whoever they are. My dad says life has a funny way of putting us where we need to be. We may not always understand it, but we should never fight it."

Yeah, my dad would always say the same thing to me. "Thanks. Again."

He dips his chin in acknowledgment as he backs toward the front door. "Oh, by the way, DJ texted about the celebration party for Shelldon. They're doing RSVPs so they know how much pizza to order. It's *Teenage Mutant Ninja Turtles* themed."

Why am I not surprised that he's throwing a party for his new tortoise? "I still can't believe Skylar agreed to getting him one."

My friend snickers. "The things we do for love. Am I right?"

I find myself smiling, thinking of everything I'll do for Raine to make sure she knows I'm in this no matter what. "Right."

Epilogue

RAINE

THE SOFT KNOCK FROM the doorway has me lifting my smiling face from the sleeping six-month-old in my arms to the old man watching us rock in the chair he made from scratch. "Told you he'd love the rocker," Leon says, walking in slowly with his cane.

I bend down to press a kiss against Bentley's head. "He hasn't been as finicky since we started using it. And those bottles you suggested have been a godsend. He doesn't puke as much as he did. My mom had to come help me with laundry when I was going through all the shirts he was getting sick all over."

Leon stops beside me, carefully reaching down to brush his fingers along Bentley's plump cheek. "Jenna swore by those bottles. Their youngest had the same problem with colic, so I was hoping they'd help."

Bentley coos, making my heart melt. He's had a choke-hold on me ever since Skylar put him into my arms for the first time. I always knew she and DJ would have cute babies, but I never expected them to be *this* perfect.

"You know," I tell Leon quietly, hugging Bentley a little tighter to my chest, "you're basically his honorary grandpa. Sky said so herself when she picked him up last time. She's glad he has a grandparent figure since hers are so far away in Cali."

Leon's lips twitch. "God help the child."

I snort, shaking my head at the man I've grown close to. He likes to bring over food for us even though I'm getting better at cooking these days, but I think it's really an excuse to see the baby since he makes appearances whenever we're babysitting for the new parents. It was a few weeks after the birth that he met little Bentley Lucas for the first time, and he brought over a goody basket of diapers, binkies, and hand-me-down clothes that Jenna wanted to pass along to someone who needed them. Like the rest of us, Leon has been wrapped around Bentley's finger ever since he was born during Sky's junior year.

When DJ and Skylar told us that they were expanding their family beyond their four-legged tortoise son, I was ecstatic. Shocked but ecstatic. Apparently, we weren't the only ones surprised by the news. The parents to the adorable infant were too when they found over the summer how far along Skylar was. And when DJ invited Caleb and me over for dinner shortly before he was born, the last thing we expected was to be asked to be their son's godparents.

What made it even more special was the name they chose. DJ went as far as finding someone with a 1938 Bentley like the one Richard wanted to restore and getting a picture with a custom-made onesie for their future son to frame for Caleb and his mother. They wanted to honor a man so many in Lindon loved.

And they did.

Caleb's mother has the picture in her living room, hanging next to the other images of her, Richard, Caleb, and me over the years.

Even though he was worried about his mother being alone in his childhood house, I can tell Denise is happy to be surrounded by so many good memories. She's even come back to the store, which is good since the website has boosted business for them like Caleb hoped it would.

When I'm not at Bea's or school, I try popping by to help whenever I can too. But it's easy to see the mother-son duo have things handled. And it gives them time together that I know they need now more than ever.

I get it. Every Friday, I see my father for our usual lunch dates, and every Saturday, I see Mom for homecooked meals in. Even though we still burn a third of what we try creating, it's fun. They're both doing better than they ever have, and it makes me happy for them. For all of us.

"Want to hold him?" I ask, standing up and gesturing toward the rocking chair. I wait until Leon's carefully seated before putting the baby in his arms. "How's Jenna and the family?"

His eyes are focused on my godson when he says, "They're doing well. We're celebrating Thanksgiving at my house this year. I was wondering if you and Caleb would like to come."

I smile as he plays with Bentley's tiny hand. "I'll have to see what we've got planned because we might be doing something with our parents, but I'll let you know."

Our families have been talking about doing a group holiday together at Caleb's mom's house since our apartment is too small to have everyone over at once. It'll be our first get-together with both our parents, so I want everything to go smoothly.

Leon smiles when Bentley's fingers wrap around part of

his thumb. "Well, they're all more than welcome too. The more the merrier. Annemarie would invite half the town for the holidays and make enough food for the county."

He still tells me stories about his late wife all the time, especially since Jenna and I formally started the Annemarie Project, which has gone viral in the local news after a 5K walk we planned back in March for endometriosis awareness month.

Our goal is to start small, raising funds to give to other organizations that we can partner with in the future for educational purposes. We'd love to host events for other national awareness months and to find educators to speak to health classes in high schools, so we've been mapping out the best nonprofits to work with while building a name for ours.

I know Leon is proud to have his wife's legacy full of so much love, and it's only going to spread farther and wider the more we share our stories.

Even though I'm focusing on finishing my clinical hours, we still get together so he can teach me new things. For my twenty-fourth birthday, he gave me roses from her rose bushes and told me he'd help me with a garden out front if I wanted. "It could be our next lesson. Annemarie taught me everything I know," he said, studying the front yard of our apartment building. It's bland at best, barely any lawn for Sigmund to go on, but it'll do until we figure out something else.

"Can I ask you something?" I ask, watching the two of them together as he makes little baby noises.

His lips twitch higher at the common question he gets a lot from me. "It's never stopped you before."

I huff out a laugh. "Have you ever thought about life

after Annemarie? Seeing somebody new? Having a companion again?"

"I got a dog, didn't I?"

He knows I'm not referring to the golden retriever he adopted earlier this year. "But what about a human companion who isn't a baby or related to you?"

There's no hesitation. "No."

"Why not?"

He continues to rock my godson. "For the same reason you went back to the Anders boy," he answers easily. His eyes lift to mine. "Because no amount of time or distance could ever make us forget how much we love them. You can never lose that feeling when it's the person you're meant to be with."

His loyalty to his wife is adorable. There's still a light in his eyes whenever he talks about her. She's one of the few people outside of Bentley and his own grandchildren who could soften his features.

Leon's eyes go back down to the little boy in his arms. "Do you want to know the wisest thing Annemarie ever said that still sticks with me to this day?"

Interest has me standing a little straighter.

"She said," he tells me, playing with Bentley's chubby cheeks with his finger, "that you will never know the true value of a moment until it becomes a memory. I'm sure she got it from one of those books she loved reading, but it's true. Looking back, there's not one thing I would change because that was how our story was supposed to go. Hard times and all."

Before I can say anything, I hear Caleb call out as he walks through the front door. Within seconds, he's in the guest room where we keep Bentley during his visits, with a huge smile on his face as soon as he sees his godson.

He presses a kiss against my temple. "I'm sorry I'm late. Ronny brought his little girl by the store, and we got to exchanging war stories."

My eyes roll at his reference to the diaper fiasco we experienced one time when DJ and Skylar had a date night. It was messy and the foulest thing Caleb and I have ever smelled, but it was practice for the future we're determined to build for ourselves someday. Once I finish my certification and get a stable job in an office and Anders Hardware finally quiets from the big business he got from the website remodel.

"We'll have to have them over for dinner sometime. Speaking of"—I turn to Leon, who's in the process of standing up to pass Bentley over to Caleb—"we'd love to have you for dinner tonight if you can stay. I finally put that turkey casserole recipe you gave me to good use."

Leon simply says, "I've got nowhere else to be tonight."

I turn from him to the man holding our godson and feel a warmth in my chest that hasn't gone away since Bentley first looked up at me with those gorgeous blue eyes. Leaning my cheek against Caleb's shoulder, I let out a content breath and soak in what we've made for ourselves despite the obstacles.

And I realize in that moment that I wouldn't change a single thing about my story with Caleb either.

Because we learned from all the pain.

"One day," he whispers, kissing my temple and staring down at the baby, "this will be us. You ready for that?"

And I reply with the same word I hope to tell him when he asks to marry me again. "Yes."

WANT MORE LINDON U? READ ON FOR A PEEK AT **BEG YOU TO TRUST ME**, NOW AVAILABLE FROM BLOOM BOOKS.

Chapter One

SKYLAR

BAD DECISIONS TASTE LIKE rum, coke, and something metallic. A taste that reminds me of the time my older sisters dared me to see how many quarters I could fit into my mouth at once.

With fluttering eyelids and heavy limbs, I come to with a dry mouth and cloudy head, finding it hard to move in the soft sheets covering my chilled body. Sheets that don't feel as soft as the expensive, certified-organic cotton threads covering the twin mattress in my room.

The bed under my leaden limbs feels too lumpy, nothing like the thick, foam pad covering the school-supplied mattress on my raised frame.

One of my sticky eyelids peels open in confusion, vision blurry but able to take in the unfamiliar setup of the room. It's bigger and colder than the double I share with my freshman roommate Rebecca, and the furniture is nothing like the stuff I have.

It takes a few seconds, but I quickly realize the reality of the situation. Bolting upright, I careen to the side when dizziness slams into me. The black sheet falls down my body, exposing the untied, wrinkled purple wrap shirt I borrowed from my friend Aliyah that's exposing the peach bra I'd slipped on underneath. I suck in a sharp breath when my eyes go to the empty spot beside me, then slowly to the side, where I see what's thrown onto the carpet.

Time stops.

Panic seeps into my rib cage.

I lift the sheet and shakily lower it once I see the naked skin it's covering, then glance back at the black leggings and panties in the middle of the floor. They're the only things I'd worn that were mine. The shirt, shoes, and new pushup bra were all from the girls I befriended who insisted I needed to dress up for the party they were dragging me to.

You'll have fun.

We won't let you out of our sight.

My recollection of the events beyond letting them play with my stubborn, black-dyed hair and telling me what makeup would look best on my tan skin is fuzzy.

Too fuzzy to put together how I got in a room I don't recognize with my pants off.

Doing a quick scan to double-check that I'm alone, I toss my legs over the side of the bed and wince at the ache between them. I bolt toward my clothing, worried someone will bust in. Tugging the panties up my legs, I stop when I glance down and see the small smears of blood on the insides of my thighs.

I stare.

Not breathing.

Not blinking.

Thud, thud, thud. The drumming between my head and heart is in sync, demanding my attention as I stare at the red smattering my skin.

A moment or two later, I force myself to finish getting dressed with shaky hands.

Pressing an ear against the wooden door to see if I hear anyone outside it, I quietly turn the knob and creep out of the room with my borrowed black heels tucked in my hands and my heart lodged in the back of my throat.

I cringe at each creak of the floorboards under my bare feet as I tiptoe down the narrow hallway toward the wooden staircase. I don't know what time it is because my phone is dead, but the sun is out and blinding me, making the headache throbbing inside my temples ten times worse.

As I creep down the steps and toward the front door, I notice that there's no remnants of a party left. No plastic cups lying around, no food on the carpet, no weird boozy smells that I vaguely remember from the night before. The bits I do recall consist of a packed house that made me feel claustrophobic, loud music that made it impossible to hear what my friends were saying as I followed them into the mass of bodies, and the scent of cheap beer.

I'm almost to the door when I freeze midstep after hearing, "Who the hell are you?"

My body locks up from the deep voice behind me. I don't recognize it, not that that says much. I'm not familiar with most men around here, since my small circle of peers is made up of my roommate Rebecca and a few other girls—Deanna and Aliyah—I met during orientation a month before.

Footsteps come from somewhere else, stopping close by. A second voice, less deep and more amused, says, "Huh. I thought everyone did their walks of shame already. Sorry, big man."

I make myself look over my shoulder, but I don't know why. I'm met with two different faces. One boyish and clearly amused, if the mischievous glint in his blue eyes is any indication, and the other full of...nothing. No emotion. Nothing readable. The shorter of the two—though not by much—grins at me before scoping out my body in a once-over that makes me want to make a break for it.

If I were smart, I wouldn't let them stare and leer. The shorter one cocks his head until his messy blond hair flops over his forehead and lips kick up. He elbows his friend, who looks massive and far less enthused by my presence in comparison.

Both are built like athletes. Strong. Broad. Like they could take down another person their size or larger if they wanted to. Deanna said the party was at the football house.

We won't let you out of our sight is what Dee promised me.

How did I get separated from them?

"We didn't know anyone else was here," the taller, stoic-looking one tells me. His lips press into a firm line as he watches me, eyes narrowing. Accusatory.

I'm uncomfortable.

Hungover.

Confused.

It doesn't take much to figure out what exactly happened last night, and it makes me feel itchy. Dirty. My mouth feels dry as cotton, and I just want to go back to the dorms and take a long, hot shower.

We won't let you out of our sight.

But where are they now?

ACKNOWLEDGMENTS

Caleb and Raine's story would not be possible without the wonderful Bloom team. I struggled with these characters from day one and went through so many different drafts before finally writing this beautiful romance. If they didn't believe I could do it, I might have thrown in the towel long before now.

And a BIG thank you to all the readers who have patiently waited for this book. I know it's been a long time coming, but I'd like to think it's been worth the wait.

Until the next books

xx B

ABOUT THE AUTHOR

B. Celeste is a new adult and contemporary romance author who gives voices to raw, realistic characters with emotional storylines that tug on the heartstrings. She was born and raised in upstate New York, where she still resides with her four-legged feline sidekick, Oliver "Ollie" Queen. Her love for reading and writing began at an early age and only grew stronger after getting a BA in English and an MFA in English and creative writing. When she's not writing, she's working out, binge-watching reality game shows, and spending time with her friends and family.

Website: authorbceleste.com
Facebook: AuthorBCeleste
Instagram: @authorbceleste
TikTok: @authorbceleste